# Password
# novus orsa

**A novel by**
# Grant Payne

 Grant Payne Sci-Fi Author

Dedicated to three very special friends:

Barbara Spiwak
Catherine Bartke
William David Garland

If it had not been for the three of you, hounding me
for the next chapter, I would probably still be writing.
It's been a fun journey, can't wait for the next one.

# Prologue

Dylon was your typical five year old, full of energy and an endless supply of questions, about how and why things work the way they do. He was always the one disappearing, only to be found completely consumed by whatever curious thing it was that he had recently discovered.

It was the Thursday of a Labor Day weekend, the annual company picnic. Once again, Dylon had found himself away from the crowd. He had wandered off to get the Frisbee, thrown too hard by one of the other kids, and got side-tracked exploring a small stream near the park. By the time he had realized it was starting to get dark, he was standing in an empty field staring up at the impressiveness of the full moon.

"Hey weirdo!" Dylon nearly jumped out of his pants. "I've been talking to you for a minute now, didn't you hear me?" Kevin asked, getting no response. "C'mon kid, everyone is looking for you." At fifteen, Kevin was ready to leave hours ago. He hadn't planned on spending the last part of the party looking for some lost kid, nor was he planning on what happened next.

Still getting no response from Dylon he grabbed

his hand and started walking back towards the rest of the group. He only made it about twenty feet or so, when he felt Dylons hand yank away. When he turned to see why, Dylon was pointing to the other end of the field asking "What's that?"

Kevin looked in the direction Dylon was pointing. There, hovering at the other end of the field, was a vehicle sized craft. His jaw dropped. They both stood there, just staring at the object. With darkness setting in fast, the object glowed with a soft blue-white light. There was a faint humming noise that seemed to hypnotize them both. When the craft started slowly canvassing to the left, it broke Kevin's trance and he remembered that he had a flashlight.

Not wanting to take his eyes off the object, his fingers anxiously searched the flashlight for the on switch. When he finally found it, he pointed the light at the craft and turned it on. The craft darted about twenty yards to the right so quickly it startled both boys. Dylon latched his arms around Kevin causing him to drop the flashlight and almost knocking him down.

When Kevin retrieved the flashlight and shined it to where the object was, there was no sign of it. Hanging on to Dylon, Kevin's eyes searched the sky for any trace of what they had both just seen. He saw nothing.

# Chapter 1

Everything was a fog. Dylon and his parents were standing in a wide open space. It seemed like they were standing on a cloud. They slowly started drifting away from him. He reached out for them and they just stood there, looking at him, as if they were saying goodbye. It became increasingly harder to breathe.

Dylon grabbed his chest. He looked up again and his parents were still getting farther and farther away. He closed his eyes and thought of his sister. Where was she? Was she alright? He tried to call her name, "Kat!" No words came from his lips. The crashing sound of metal against metal and shattering glass all came rushing into his head.

"We've got him!" was the last thing Dylon heard before he slipped into unconsciousness again.

Dylon was startled out of his daydream when he heard the receptionist call his name. "Dylon Rosier," she said, "Mr. Tuttle will see you now." Rosie said as she showed him into the office.

"Hello, Mr. Tuttle." Dylon said as he extended his hand to meet his interviewers.

"Call me Harry," he energetically replied and extended his hand as well, "You're looking more like your father every day. I'm hope you'll do just as good as he did."

"Well, I'm going to give it my best shot, sir." Dylon quickly responded.

"Your father brought me on less than a year after opening the business. He taught me some very valuable lessons." Harry sounded like he was getting ready to tell Dylon the same story he had heard time and again from his own father, Steven.

Dylon politely let Harry finish his story, even though heard it many times before. Steven Rosier could not emphasize enough how important the company was and that he needed to embrace the whole concept of the ideas presented by them and that the Rosier family business was a fourth generation business which had recently opened a new venture. Dylon's father's contribution to the family's small empire was a small architectural and engineering firm. Steven was very hopeful to make it a successful part of Rosier Enterprises. That is, if he could get them to accept the risk.

Just out of school, Steven would have a hard time juggling the task of getting his business going and taking care of Dylon while his wife, Angela, finished her schooling and carried the next addition to their growing family.

The six years since their wedding date had been

an uphill battle all the way with his parents. The acceptance and the backing of Steve's company was the first real sign of a release in the tension and pressure from the family and the family business. Rosier Enterprises was a very stern and reserved company. Always pushing the importance of family and education. In addition to your typical benefits, the company matched any contribution to college funds for your children. If you were lucky enough to be employed by the Rosiers, there was enough information, options, and support to make you and your family's lives a lot better for generations to come.

Dylon had embraced this concept with every ounce of ambition and drive he had. He knew from childhood that he had to figure out how to make it. He didn't know how, but thought that following in his father's footsteps would lead him in the right direction.

"….and so with all the formalities wrapped up." Harry said, "I'm delighted to take you under my wing, as your father did for me. Rosie will help you get settled in and introduce you to everybody."

As Rosie led Dylon down the hall to his office she asked how his sister was doing.

"Kat's doing…. I mean Elizabeth is doing just fine." He quickly corrected himself, knowing he was the only person that could ever get away with calling her Kat. "Starting her third year of school….halfway there."

"Oh, it goes by so quickly. Seems like just yesterday she was graduating high school." Rosie said. "Dylon, I just wanted to say what a wonderful job you've done with her as an older brother. Your father would be so proud of you both."

"Why thank you, that really means a lot." Dylon replied.

Rosie continued singing his praises. "So many younger people, these days, would have just wandered aimlessly trying to figure out what to do after such a loss."

This was very true, Dylon thought to himself. Once again he had to count his blessings and be thankful for his father's accomplishments, and his strict teachings. Truth be known, Dylon and Elizabeth, nor their children or their grandchildren, would ever have to work if they didn't want to.

\* \* \* \* \* \*

Dylon had taken a year off after graduating. He retreated to *the estate* and nearly drove himself crazy being consumed by his little projects.

*The estate* was located on a plateau in the

mountains in Peru, nearly a thousand acres. Accessible only by plane, it was a place to escape from everything.

Once again, Dylon felt himself being dragged back to reality when he heard his name called for a second time.

"I'm sorry, Rosie," he stated. "Yes, this is just fine."

Rosie replied, "I know the offices are kind of small, but the majority of your work will be done out here in the work area." Dylon glanced over at the work area, which was one continuous drafting table backed by another one, with enough stools to sit six on either side.

Several young men were already working and they stopped only to be introduced by Rosie. "This is Bob, Mike, and your project leader Trevor, who will catch you up to speed on what's going on. Well you boys have fun." Rosie jested, as she quickly wound up her tour and headed back to her station.

Trevor picked up two oversize blue binders and headed toward Dylon, who was already getting settled into his office.

Binders under his arm, Trevor entered Dylons office extending his hand and introducing himself. "Trevor Thompson", he said as he laid the binders on Dylon's desk.

Dylon responded promptly with a firm handshake, "Dylon Rosier, nice to meet you."

"Oh, the pleasure is all mine," Trevor commented, "I had a chance to look at your portfolio. Very impressive drawings you have there." Before Dylon had a chance to thank him, Trevor started talking again. " Are you familiar with the Felderson Corporation?" Without pause, Trevor continued, "The aeronautical division located near Knoxville? They customize private and commercial Lear jets. They're building a new hangar and it needs to be big enough to hold eight jets, but not look like a hangar. The first binder is filled with schematics of the current buildings. The second binder has drawings of the existing buildings from several different angles and a blank area where the hangar should be. We would like to present them with three different options, and a rough draft of the floor plan of each. Will three weeks be enough?"

Sensing that Trevor might be nervous with the Rosier family name, Dylon assuredly responded, "I sure hope so. My grandfather would have my head on the chopping block quicker than you could blink your eyes."

Trevor stepped back, "Really?"

" You better believe it. As firm as he is with his employees, he's twice as bad with family. He doesn't want anyone thinking that a Rosier got anywhere by riding the coat tails of the family name. Plus the fact that I took time off after school instead of going straight to work doesn't help either. So if I have any problems with this project I hope I can pick your brain a little."

You could see a sigh of relief wash over Trevor's face. "Sure thing, anytime you need some help, I'm just across the room. By the way, I know these offices are kind of bland, you're allowed to put some personal things on the walls if you want. It kinda lets everybody know a little about yourself. Keep it clean though." Trevor winked jokingly as he left the office.

Dylon sat down at his desk, hoping he covered any problems that might come up in the future. As an heir to his father's ventures, it was true that he was part owner of the company he now worked for, but he really did have to prove his worth, just the same as his father did.

He reached into his briefcase and pulled out a framed picture of Kat and placed it next to the computer monitor he had just turned on. Then he grabbed his cell phone to text his sister "OMG! My first day on the job and I already have homework! I thought I was finished with homework when I finished school. LOL!"

He put down his cell and started flipping through

the pages of the binder to try to get an idea forming. As Dylon was checking all the different angled pictures, he heard a slight tap on his door. It was Rosie, "I just wanted to let you know, so you can mark it on your calendar, the company picnic is Labor Day weekend. Its really important to try to make it, and by the way it's a paid day off if you make it."

Dylon shook his head and thanked Rosie as she moved on to the next office. A text tone came through, he picked it up and read it. "You poor thing….the only good thing about school is summers off. By the way I aced my finals!…..and Greece is nice…LOL!"

He quickly responded, "You are EVIL…..LOL and congrats!"

# Chapter 2

As the days pressed on, Dylon eventually got into the groove of things. Good thing too, otherwise the Felderson Corporation would have Mars-type space pods for their hangars.

Not being one for the happenings of the social scene, Dylon had a lot of time on his hands to do what he chose. Whether it was playing games on his computer, or work, which is what it turned out to be this time.

He was able to get his assignment done with a week to spare. Trevor was impressed when Dylon asked for a meeting to present the finished drawings.

The meeting was set up for Monday morning, so Dylon spent the weekend putting the binders back together and gathering up some things to finally start personalizing his office. He had several of his own drawings framed, three or four bookend-sized models, a universe calendar and a small C.D. player with a handful of C.D.'s.

Mentally going through the items that he was taking to work, Dylon walked over to his movie collection and flipped through them until he came across the movie *Contact*.

He could have picked any movie and it would

have been one he had already seen at least five to ten times. It was really just for background noise anyway.

After cueing the movie to play, Dylon returned to his desk and started flipping through the binders, to make sure everything was in order. The hangars were really pretty easy to draw. From what he gathered, all this guy Kevin wanted was more storage area, so they could upgrade their old hangar. He just wanted the new hangar to look more like a showroom so the clients would get a warm fuzzy feeling when they picked up their toys.

He thought aloud, "These people spend too much time with their hobbies, and who am I to talk, I spent a year on mine and still haven't gotten anywhere." Dylon could hear his sister's words running through his mind, as he reached for his personal project binder. "But yours isn't a hobby, it's an obsession."

Dylon started taking the binder apart, glancing at each drawing and sorting them into two piles. Each page had a duplicate, it was the only way he could discuss them with his chief mechanic, Kat.

Being occasionally distracted by the movie, Dylon made pretty good time with his task, and before he knew it, found himself putting the binders back together and double checking his notes to his sister.

Then came the part of the movie he always found himself drawn to, the second machine. He put down the binder momentarily and allowed himself to be sucked into the part of the movie that always fascinated him. Dylon couldn't help himself, he always compared the machine to a familiar piece of garden art. A sundial-that's what it was called. Dylon had always seen this piece in any setting discussing Da Vinci or Nostradamus, and always thought that it was more than what it appeared to be.

"What did you know, Da Vinci?" Dylon said aloud as he turned to package up the binder he was sending to Kat.

Deciding to call it a night, Dylon put the package next to the box going to work with him in the morning and headed to the fridge for some leftover pizza.

Contemplating on the meeting tomorrow, Dylon popped the pizza in the microwave and decided to go in a little earlier than normal. For tonight, though, he was going to watch another movie.

When morning came, Dylon was actually a little nervous about going in to work. He couldn't really put his finger on why. After thinking about it for a minute he figured out that it wasn't because of his appointment with Trevor, it was actually the fact that he was personalizing his office.

He obsessed about it all the way to work. Then he popped in a C.D., to try to stop himself from worrying about something he couldn't control, and before he knew it he was at the office.

"Thank God, nobody's here yet," he thought to himself. "Hopefully I can get this stuff inside before anyone notices how much of a geek I truly am." Dylon actually spent a little too much time with his thoughts.

He could hear the guys now, "You actually believe in UFO's?" Then after giving it a little more thought he decided, the razzing he would probably receive would pass in no time. After all, he did believe in UFO's. He saw one when he was five. With that final thought all of his anxieties finally subsided.

When Dylon got to his office, he heard a shout coming from the down the hall. "Dylon Rosier, are you trying to wreck my entire week?" It was Rosie. "In all my years of working here, no one has ever arrived at work before me!" Then her head popped around the corner with a wicked little grin on her face. "Would you like any coffee this morning?" she asked.

"No thanks Rosie, I brought some from home." Dylon replied, "and if anyone asks, I will tell them you were here first." as he gave her a quick wink and a smile.

"Thank you dear," she smiled back at him.

A few minutes later, after he had placed his assignment on the drafting table, Dylon found his way to the break room where Rosie was preparing a second pot of coffee. Dylon, trying his best not to interrupt her routine, asked if she might know where he could find a tool kit.

"Storage room at the end of the hall, third drawer on the left is where you will find the picture hanging kit, and the hammer is in the top drawer on the far right." She answered as if she had read his mind.

"How did you…?" Dylon paused, "You're good. Is there anything you don't miss?"

Rosie quickly replied, "I want to see it when you're finished, if that's okay."

"I'll let you know." Dylon shouted back, as he headed to the storage room.

He quickly found what he needed and hurried back down the hall to his office. As he passed the break room he could hear Rosie saying, "You have about thirty minutes before everybody starts showing up."

Dylon really wanted to get everything done before everybody arrived. So he quickly started placing the items in the box around his office and the pictures he sat on the floor just below where they would hang.

Before he knew it, he found himself standing just inside his door, giving everything the once-over, just to make sure it all flowed right and everything was hanging straight.

On his desk was an acrylic paperweight,

pyramid-shaped with the Starship Enterprise encased within. On the bookshelf were bookends in the shape of the *Stargate* on one side and the mother ship from the same movie on the other side, a globe-shaped sundial sat on top of the bookshelf, and an eight by ten standing calendar of the universe stood on a lower shelf.

On his desk, to the left of the monitor, sat a picture of Kat and next to that, a picture he had drawn.

On the wall behind him, there was an eight by ten drawing of the Roswell crash. On the left and right walls in front of his desk were two drawings, one of the craft from the *Rama* series by Arthur C. Clark and one of the *Star Trek* space station thanks to Gene Rodenberry. Dylon was very proud of them both, seeing how he was the producer of the drawings. They were both drawn in a format where you could see half of the craft in blueprint form and the other half as if you were seeing it in space.

As Dylon was looking over the Rama drawing, he heard Rosie say, "Hey, space cadet, here's some fresh coffee for you. I hope you like Amaretto creamer." He turned in time to see the smirk on her face, but also an underlying interest in the drawings.

As he fixed his coffee up with the creamers she had brought he watched her carefully study every piece of the personal items he had brought in. Each one was examined and then with a nod, as if to say I know where this is from, Rosie would move on to the next item. When she arrived to the Rama drawing, she just could not place it.

Then, when she thought she had it, she blurted out. "They never showed the inside of the craft in that movie. Where did you come up with this idea?"

"No they didn't." Dylon said with a touch of excitement in his voice and without giving Rosie a chance to respond he started talking again. "But they describe it in detail in this book." He paused, just to take a breath. "I'm not even sure if it is the same craft, but they do look similar. Do you like to read?"

Surprised to see the amount of passion Dylon had for this topic Rosie stammered, "Well, yeah."

"Sci-Fi? It doesn't matter, it's not just the sci-fi part of it, that's just the icing on the cake. It's the *Rama* series by Arthur C. Clarke and Gentry Lee. I have a copy of the whole series if you want to borrow it." Not giving Rosie a chance to answer he continued. He was so excited he started pacing while he was talking. "The details, the struggles, the triumphs, and the sacrifice. Oh, it's just a great series, and did I mention the minute details of this craft, all the futuristic types of buildings and transportation and….."

Dylon suddenly felt more than Rosie's eyes on

him. He turned to see that his excitement had also caught the attention of Bob and Trevor.

"Well, anyway…" Dylon continued "…why this series was never put to film just baffles me."

Trevor put his bid in: "I get it after Rosie's finished. And good morning to everybody,"
As she was leaving Dylon's office, Rosie said "I'll get the first book when I go to lunch, and thank you for beating me in today, it was certainly a pleasure to see your face light up with so much enthusiasm. You reminded me so much of your father. What a wonderful man."

"Well, thank you Rosie, that really means a lot." Dylon said. As he walked out of the office with Rosie, Dylon noticed that Trevor was already flipping through the binders so he nudged her and whispered, "Well, let me go see how I did with my homework assignment."

When Dylon stepped over to the table where Trevor was standing, he noticed that Trevor was flipping through page by page just shaking his head and mumbling. "I can't do this. Not by myself."

Not understanding his words, Dylon asked. "Do what by yourself?"

"I can't present this." Trevor responded.

Looking despondent, Dylon nervously inquired, "Well, what's wrong with it? I'm sure I can fix it."

"Wrong..." Trevor quickly said, "There's nothing wrong at all. It's brilliant. I would have a hard time choosing which one to go with."

Dylon breathed a huge sigh of relief.

Trevor was beside himself. "You have to present this, there's no way I could possibly cover all of this."

Dylon got nervous all over again. "No, I couldn't, I can't. I don't do well in front of people. I freeze all up. I...."

Trevor cut in, "Are you kidding me with that? You just gave a presentation on a book to somebody that doesn't even like to read and I'm ready to go get a library card! You'll do just fine."

"Oh, please don't make me do this." Dylon started begging.

"I'll be there too, you won't be alone. Besides it's easy. All you have to do is talk about your work. Once you focus on explaining your drawings, the customers kind of disappear. They just turn into people, not customers." Trevor, trying desperately to convince Dylon to go, said "You'll do fine, trust me, just focus on explaining the drawings."

Dylon started heading to his office like a child being sent to his room. "Okay, okay. I just don't think this is a good idea."

Trevor closed the binders and headed off to Harry's office to request expenses for two for the presentation.

Dylon was actually pleased that his work was that good, but dreading the fact that he was going to have to talk in front of a group of people. He started looking through the books on his shelf, trying to redirect his thoughts to something else. He was looking for the first book of the *Rama* series for Rosie.

He found it pretty quick, and in remembering the way this book sucked him in the first time he read it, he sat down at his desk and started reading it again.

Before he knew it, what was left of the morning had slipped by him and Rosie was tapping at his door.

"Is that the book?" she asked

Dylon slightly startled, closed the book and handed it to her. "I really hope you enjoy it as much as I did."

"I'm sure I will." Rosie reached for the book, noticing the picture of Kat, she had to ask. "Was that picture taken at *the estate*, the one in Peru?"

"Sure is."

Rosie's face lit up, "I'm so glad you kept it. Your father was so excited when his bid for that piece of property was accepted. Do you still go down there?"

Dylon had an idea forming, "We sure do. As a matter of fact, we're going after the picnic. Four days of paradise, you should come."

Rosie stood there in thought, as Dylon carried

on. "It will be a nice break. Do you have anything else planned?" Rosie began to object, but Dylon continued talking. When she realized he probably wasn't going to stop talking until she gave in, she finally nodded her head and agreed. "Okay, I'll go. It will be nice to get away from it all. Only if you're sure I'm not intruding."

Dylon just looked at her with that 'Don't be ridiculous look.' which Rosie picked up on right away. "Well, I guess I have some planning to do then." She stuffed the book in her purse and headed off to lunch.

Dylon reached for his phone, opened it to the keypad and quickly typed, "We have a third going to *the estate*." In an instant, he got a response. "Make that four."

Dylon smirked as he was typing. "So, I finally get to meet your boyfriend." Kat's response was all in caps. "HE'S NOT MY BOYFRIEND, DICK!"

"Lol" Dylon sent back, followed by "Still love you Sis."

"Whatever!" Kat replied.

Trevor was the next person to tap on Dylon's door, grinning from ear to ear. "Harry was very impressed. After seeing the drawings, he agrees completely. It's time to get your feet wet, bud."

With no enthusiasm whatsoever and a roll of his eyes, Dylon said "Yea, I'm so happy." Dylon looked at Trevor, "So when do we leave for my public humiliation?"

Trevor rolled his eyes, "We leave Friday morning. You'll do fine, quit sweating it. Oh, and Harry said you could have a couple of paid days off for finishing early…. that is, of course, if you want them. But if all you're going to do is sulk about your presentation, you might as well just stay at work."

Dylon smiled and started getting his things together. "Paid days off…who's sulking, I don't see anybody sulking, do you see anybody sulking?"

# Chapter 3

After spending a couple of days engrossed in his own personal projects, mostly the Agripod project, Dylon had almost completed the base of the pyramid. There were just too many gears to try to figure out. After spending countless hours trying to get them to work simultaneously, he felt he knew what a clockmaker must go through.

Thinking aloud, Dylon brought his hands to his head. "Good God Sis, how does this stuff come to you so easy? You could have done this in a fraction of the time. I just know it."

Sitting down at his computer, Dylon logged in and started navigating the net to see if he could find his sister logged in anywhere. "C'mon sis, where are you?" He had hit every site he knew she visited with no luck.

Deciding to give it a few minutes, he stayed logged on with his instant messenger open. He thought about texting her but didn't want to bother her that badly. Remembering his school days, he thought, "If she's not busy, she'll contact me."

Dylon grabbed the card from his camera and started downloading the pictures of the work he had accomplished on his agripod. He would have to size them, sort them, and put them into jpeg format before emailing them to Kat. This would give him a little more time, while waiting to see if she was going to show up online. About the time Dylon hit send on the finished photos and a short video of the pod opening, he received an I.M. tone.

"Geez brother, have you sent me some more homework? You know classes don't start back up for a couple of weeks. LOL."

It was Kat that messaged him. "I received your package today."

The package, Dylon had forgotten all about it in his hurry to take advantage of his days off. "Thank God for Rosie." he replied.

"So what project have you sent me this time?"

Dylon, realizing Kat hadn't opened the package yet, quickly typed in a response. "I need a pod mover, you'll see my notes on that, nothing fancy. I think I have finally figured out the inner workings of the pod to get it from the collapsed form to the transformed, full size pyramid. But I haven't figured out how to incorporate the corridors to connect them all together."

Kat sent back, "You're sure there isn't anything else? Why don't you go after an easier project like world peace or something like that? Really Dylon, I'm shocked. LOL."

Dylon chuckled as he responded, "Well actually, my next thought was a transformable factory, and a planet seeder, but that will have to wait until you graduate."

Kat's next response floored Dylon, "Well it's a good thing for you I only have two semesters to go."

Dylon did not respond.

"Oops."

Dylon sat there for a minute before he started typing. "Elizabeth, what are you talking about?"

Although Kat preferred to be called Elizabeth, she knew when Dylon did it, he was flustered with her. Dylon asked again, dreading the answer. "You're not dropping out, are you?"

Kat started typing, "Dylon, I'm just so tired of school. I want to get out there and start applying what I know. Every night it's homework, or studying, or cramming for finals."

Before she could finish typing, Dylon's words popped up on the screen. "I know it's hard, but we're not quitters."

"Dylon, please let me finish." Kat typed, "Every year after the summer break, my first semester was a normal class load, just to get back into the routine of studying and homework. Then, with the help of my student counselor, we figured out which courses I could take to help me finish early. She monitored my grades, just to make sure I wasn't taking on too much. I buckled down and buried myself in my studies. Dylon, what I'm trying to say is that I doubled my class load. I've carried a 3.62 GPA. I'm going to graduate with a major in mechanical engineering and a minor in micro-robotics. I was going to surprise you, but I guess I screwed that up."

Dylon just sat there, feeling kind of selfish.

Kat, worried that Dylon had walked away from his computer before hearing her out, nervously typed. "Are you still there?"

"Kat, why on earth would you put that much on yourself? I don't know what to say. Congratulations, seems like such a small word for what you've accomplished." Dylon just sat there with his jaw dropped.

Kat felt as if a huge burden had been lifted from her shoulders. "So I take it you're happy?"

"Astonished, is more like it." Dylon had so many thoughts running through his mind. "I'm so proud of you. Also I'm sorry for sending you all my projects to work on. I won't send you anymore, until you finish school. I had no idea that you were taking that much on. Why didn't you say something sooner?"

"Don't you dare stop sending them," Kat responded. "your projects are the only break I get from my studies. LOL." Kat continued. "So speaking of your projects, did you make any progress on your sphere?"

"Not much, just a small light show and maybe an inch of lift. And that may be wishful thinking." Dylon typed.

Kat had almost as many questions as Dylon had projects. "And how about the R.S. model…what are you up to now, seven?"

"Actually, I'm up to twelve. Or should I say we are up to twelve." Dylon laughed to himself as he typed. "I wrecked two more of them and Reese wrecked the other two. I must say, they are getting easier to build. LOL"

Kat smiled, "LOL… and how is Reese doing?"

"Growing like a weed, that boy is a little sponge when it comes to soaking up knowledge. When I'm not there he is his father's shadow and mine when I'm there." Dylon responded to Kat's question and hit her up with one of his own. "So this fourth person for the Labor Day trip is he….?"

Kat knew what 'he' meant. "I'm not sure, I mean I don't know what he is. We go somewhere on the weekend, whether it's a movie or just dinner. I think we are just friends right now. With our schedules we really don't have time for too much of anything else."

Dylon asked, "And does 'he' have a name?"

Kat grinned, "Of course, Marcus Williamson.

Did I mention he's a rocket scientist, LOL. Seriously though, he is, or that's what he's studying to become."

"Leave it to you sis."

Kat quickly inquired, "And your third person is?"

Dylon smiled thinking of Rosie. "She's great, like a mother figure. Rosie is her name and she's the receptionist where I work. She's awesome, I think her title should be office manager because she doesn't miss anything and she does everything. She's been working there from the start. Dad hired her when he was still alive. She was around when dad bought the place in Peru and was inquiring about it so I asked her to come along and check it out."

"Boy is she going to be in for a shock." Kat was trying to recall all that they had added to *the estate* since the purchase. "What all have we added?"

Dylon thought for a minute before he started typing. "Well, there is the one room school, the two quad-plexes, the new storage/mechanic shop for the equipment, the observatory, the garage, the hangar/shop for my toys, and that doesn't even include the improved and extended runway, the upgrades to the tower/security center. And of course we still need to find some goods that can be produced by automation, to bring some revenue in so it doesn't turn into a complete money pit."

Kat shook her. "Oh my God, where does it all

end?"

Dylon smiled with his next statement. "Oh forgive me father, I have failed you. I tried to teach little sis, that which you passed on to me. Oh where did I go wrong? LOL"

"I know, I know. Where there is self-sufficiency you will find little waste." Kat typed the familiar quote that had been handed down for at least four generations now. "So, getting back to your projects, do you think NASA might actually do something with your Agripod?"

Dylon had asked himself that same question too many times. "Short answer yes, after I'm dead and gone. I mean, they are not even projecting to put an actual research team on Mars until the year 2050. The way I figure it sis, if it's going to happen, it has to be the private sector. Even then, there will still be so much bureaucracy and government bumbling that it's going to be next to impossible. If we can actually accomplish it, there will, more than likely, be some grave risks I fear. I kinda hope we can get it done and then beg for forgiveness, when they discover what we have done. Honestly, I have thought a lot about it and haven't come up with a plausible solution yet. If there is a way, it will show itself in the appropriate time. You know what they say, '*everything happens for a reason.*' Oh, have you checked your email yet? I sent you a video and some pictures of the pod, it's just the base so far. It might make it easier for you to understand the drawings and my notes."

"I'll check it now, it might take a few minutes." Kat switched over to her email and started the download. After a couple of minutes Kat switched back to the instant messenger. "Do you think you have enough gears in there brother? LOL.... Let me work on this a little bit and I will probably be able to lose about two thirds of them for you."

"Thanks a million sis, I knew you would be able to make this half the work I could. But don't let this interfere with your studies. You've worked too hard to finish early. By the way, did I tell you how proud of you I am?" Dylon was still astonished at Kat's determination and accomplishments.

Kat beamed with happiness, "Thank you very much, Dylon. That really means a lot to me."

"Kat what you've done is astounding. It would be pretty selfish of anyone not to commend you for it." Dylon was starting to get tired and tried to finish the conversation on a funny note. "So how much would it cost me to have you do my presentation on Friday?"

"No way brother, I love you, but not that much." Kat had one more question for Dylon before she called it a night. "I have a huge favor to ask of you, Dylon. When you meet Marcus could you make a very strong effort to call me Elizabeth?"

"What's wrong with Kat?" Dylon chided.

"Dylon, please." Kat begged.

"Okay, okay,….I'll give it my best effort." Dylon couldn't understand why she didn't like Kat. "Well sis I have a couple of busy days coming up so I'm going to say goodnight and love ya! It's been a great talk."

"Me too, Dylon, talk again soon. Love you too." Kat smiled as she turned off the computer and headed to get a shower and turn in for the night.

As Kat stripped down and stepped into the shower, there was a series of questions that started forming in her mind. "So what is Marcus? Friend or boyfriend? Did he want more? Why hasn't he asked for more? Was she too much of a tomboy? Was he gay? No, he definitely wasn't gay, she caught him checking out other girls when he thought she wasn't looking. Maybe it *was* her." Finally when she was tired of running through the questions, she spoke aloud. "Damn it, Dylon, you and your stupid questions!"

# Chapter 4

The next couple of days would go by pretty quickly and Dylon knew that. He was actually looking forward to it. He just wanted his presentation to be done and over with. Thank God Trevor gave him a new assignment. This would give him something to keep his mind busy. He kind of felt like Trevor knew that.

It was a small assignment, a college house for the Rosier Enterprise, another project in Knoxville. It would be a five bedroom home, designed with college students in mind. The homes fell under The Steven and Angela Rosier Scholarship Foundation, formed after their untimely death.

As the Rosier Enterprise grew, they would acquire land in the surrounding areas of their different divisions. Then build homes from four to six bedrooms. This would employ a house mother and have enough rooms for three to five students, depending on the size of the division in that area.

If the rooms were not filled by Rosier employee's children, then a scholarship would be awarded to an orphan who was at the age of eighteen.

Dylon basically knew what the layout of the

homes looked like. He lived in one while he was going to college. "Finally," he thought out loud, "a chance to have a say in what I wanted in these homes away from homes."

When Friday finally came Dylon was bouncing off the walls and Trevor was popping Dramamine. Dylon gave him an odd look, "You don't like flying, Trevor?"

"Actually bud, I love flying." Trevor answered. "But my stomach doesn't. I'll be fine once we're in the air."

Rosie came around the corner with two envelopes. "Here is your verification for your flight, and boys…Trevor, I expect to see some legitimate receipts in these envelopes when you come in on Monday. The shuttle bus is waiting for you. Oh, and Dylon, don't let Trevor get you into any trouble."

"What's she talking about?" Dylon again, found himself giving Trevor an odd look. "Rosie, what are you talking about?"

Rosie smirked, "Why don't you ask Cowboy?"

Trevor objected, "Cowboy?" his face reddening, "Rosie, how could you?"

Dylon chuckled, knowing there was an untold story here.

Trevor was quickly searching for anything to change the subject. "You got your notes, Dylon?"

"Sure do, Cowboy." Dylon answered as he climbed into the shuttle behind Trevor.

Trevor cleared his throat. "So I guess I'm going to have to tell you the story, just to clear my name. It's not my fault, really. I was dancing with this girl, she said she was there with some girlfriends. Well, then her boyfriend showed up...."

Dylon just shook his head, smiled, and closed his eyes. He didn't think Trevor even noticed, because he just kept talking. By the time they arrived at the airport Trevor was still talking. "So I ended up with a black eye, and some bruised knuckles, but the worst part is that Rosie had to come bail me out."

"Now that's a woman that seems to have it together." This time it was Dylon that was trying to change the subject. "So I guess I'll have some time to go over my notes while we're in flight. Just to make sure I've got all the right answers." Dylon said as he grabbed his briefcase from the shuttle van.

"Yeah, I should look over mine too." Trevor was starting to feel the effects of the Dramamine as they headed toward the jet. "Man. I'll be glad when we get on board and are finally in the air."

Dylon looked up at the sky as he was boarding. "Me too, looks like a great day to be flying. I'll bet you can see for miles." Dylon was hoping so anyway. Ever since that day in the park, he would frequently find himself looking to the sky in the hopes of seeing something. That's why he loved flying so much. You could not ask for a better view, a better chance to see something you might not see, if you were on the ground. Dylon would end up spending the entire flight, gazing out the window, hoping to see something.

Dylon did go over his notes a little while they were in flight, but not the notes on his meeting. He noticed that Trevor had fallen asleep and decided to pull out the notes he brought on his new spacecraft model. This one he designed after one he had seen on one of his favorite television programs. The craft had been seen by a police officer in Mexico. Thus the name M.S. One, short for Mexico Spacecraft One.

As the plane started descending, Trevor, who had been knocked out by the Dramamine, started to stir. Dylon closed his notebook and binder and started to put them away. Trevor, still a little groggy, looked at Dylon. "Well, at least one of us will be prepared." Dylon smiled nervously as he responded to Trevor. "I sure hope so. Is there anything you can tell me about this Felderson guy?"

Trevor reached for a bottle of water before he started to answer. "Well 'this Felderson guy', his name is Kevin Felderson. His division of the company has done very well for such a young corporation. Your grandfather was quite impressed with their numbers. That's why we're here. Normally the separate divisions have to fund their own expansions. Rosier Enterprises is funding a third of this one. Your grandfather must have a lot of faith in this guy."

As the plane rolled to a stop, Dylon asked Trevor. "So how long before we get there?"

"We're there bud."

"What?" Dylon could feel his stomach knotting up with anxiety.

Trevor just rolled his eyes. "Look around Dylon, does any of this look familiar? C'mon man, you had the drawings for a couple of weeks, you can't tell me you don't recognize any of this? Quit sweating it man, you'll do fine, I'll do fine, and then we'll go have some fun."

Dylon didn't really hear anything Trevor said, he just kept going over everything about the plans and drawings in his head. So much so that he just kept walking when Trevor stopped and greeted Claire Bailey, who was standing just outside the main entrance. She and Trevor stood there a second and watched Dylon. "You'll have to forgive him, he's really nervous about this presentation. Hey, Dylon."

Dylon realizing what just happened, blushed and just hung his head. Trevor tried to break the silence of awkwardness. "Dylon, this is Ms. Claire Bailey. Claire this is…"

Claire interrupted. "I know of Dylon Rosier. Your grandfather has very high expectations of you. According to him you're going to take Rosier Enterprises into the next generation with an unprecedented edge and a vision for a brighter future for the company."

Dylon looked surprised as he reached for Claire's hand. "Is that what he thinks? I thought he was expecting something a little more. Whew, well now that the pressure's off, I guess I can relax a little." Claire laughed at Dylon's humor as she shook his hand.

Claire, not wanting to waste time, got right to the point. "I have some bad news for you. Mr. Felderson, unfortunately, has come down with some virus and could not make it in today. I called as soon as I could, but Rosie said you had already left. Mr. Felderson feels just awful about this. Oh Trevor, Rosie asked me to remind you, no repeats of the last trip. She said that you know what that means?"

Dylon just chuckled and Trevor reached out and gave him a friendly shove. Claire continued, "I've got a company car for you and directions to the company lake house, it's just on the outskirts of town. Your flight back leaves tomorrow at two in the afternoon. If you could be here at one-thirty, that would be great."

Dylon spoke up, "Well I guess you'll need these." He handed the binders to Claire. "There is a link set up in case you, or Mr. Felderson, want to take a virtual walkthrough of any of the plans. You just need to put in the drawing number when cued."

Claire took the binders. "I will get these to Mr. Felderson as soon as I leave today. You will probably be hearing from him on Monday. Is there anything else I should know and is there anything else I can do for you?"

Trevor quickly popped a question with one word. "Nightlife?"

"Try the *Electric Cowboy*, a lot of the guys head there on the weekends." Claire looked at Dylon. "If you're joining him tonight you're gonna have to loosen up a little."

"Got it covered Claire, we're going shopping." Trevor said as he was loading the car that had just been pulled around.

"*Trixie's?*" Claire asked.

Trevor smiled. "Where else?"

Suddenly Dylon was feeling uneasy, "Who's Trixie? Why do I feel like I'm in for a long night?"

After stopping to get a bite to eat the boys headed to *Trixie's*. As soon as they stepped in the door they were greeted by a very attractive brunette, who seemed to be drawn to Dylon. "Hi welcome to

*Trixie's,* my name is Kaylee. Is there anything I can help y'all with?"

Trevor wasted no time in throwing Dylon under the bus. "Well, take a look, do you think he will fit in at *Electric Cowboy's* tonight?"

Dylon shot Trevor a look. "Thanks a lot there bud!"

Kaylee smiled, slid her hand around Dylon's arm and led him off to the dressing rooms. "Let's see if we can get you set up. Do you have any boots?" Dylon just looked at her. She batted her deep green eyes flirtatiously. "C'mon honey, when I'm finished with you every girl in the house will be askin' for yer number." Dylon blushed a little and smiled.

Kaylee kept tossing things over the saloon-type doors and they were piling up quicker than he could try them on. He didn't know if it was the accent or the way she was pampering him, but he sure was enjoying the attention. Dylon was a little winded when she finally handed him the last item- a hat. Then she asked him to step out for inspection.

Kaylee stood there looking at Dylon like she would just eat him up. Dylon not getting it asked, "What's wrong, is it too much?" Kaylee just shook her head. "Honey, there is nothing wrong. You are fine."

Standing 5'10"- almost six feet with the boots- Dylon did look good. It was a shame to cover that wavy brown hair with a cowboy hat. Kaylee almost got lost in those ocean blue eyes as she looked him over. She really did do well by Dylon.

She had set him up with black boots, belt, and hat. A black t-shirt under a fitted white collared shirt and chestnut colored jeans, which were a little tight fitting but Dylon filled them out nicely.

Trevor had finished picking out what he wanted and was walking up to the counter to pay. He noticed a group of girls hanging around some guy in a black hat. When he realized who it was, he took a step back. "Damn dude! Looking good, somebody should get lucky tonight."

Dylon blushed at the attention.

Trevor noticed it. "Sorry bud, not trying to embarrass you, just trying to bring you out of your shell a little."

"No worries man," Dylon replied

Kaylee slipped Dylon a business card with her number on it. "So what time are you boys gonna get to the club?"

Trevor responded with another question. "I'm not sure. When is the best time to get there?"

"Well my girlfriends and I usually show up 'round eleven or so. That's when it really starts getting fun." Kaylee answered Trevor, but smiled and winked at Dylon.

"Eleven? Isn't that a little early?" Trevor was trying not to seem desperate or too eager. "Maybe we'll see you there. Afternoon ladies." He said as he subtly urged Dylon toward the door, whose attention was still captured by Kaylee's beauty.

When they were out the door heading to the car Dylon asked. "So what are we going to do until then?"

Trevor opened the unlocked car and as they were getting in responded. "I don't know about you, but I'm going to get a shower and a nap."

Dylon agreed and they were off to the lake house. When they arrived, they unloaded the car and checked out the place. It was a small house, nothing overdone. After all, it was a lake house. A place where you would rather be outside enjoying your vacation, small business trip, or whatever. Trevor ducked in the first bedroom he came to and threw his bags on the bed. He then went to the kitchen to check the refrigerator. Just as he thought, your typical set up. A six-pack of each, Pepsi, Coke, Bud Light,and some bottled water.

He grabbed a beer, twisted the top off and said aloud "Thank you Rosie.". Noticing that Dylon had already hit the shower Trevor grabbed the remote and plopped down on the couch. This in turn knocked Dylon's bag over, spilling some of the contents. As he was cleaning up his mess, Trevor noticed a binder marked M.S. One. Trevor, always an admirer of

Dylon's work, started flipping through the binder. Once he realized what the drawings were, his curiosity was piqued, but he heard the bathroom door open and quickly started stuffing the binder back in the bag.

Trevor didn't want Dylon to think he was being nosy so he called out to him as he picked up the bag. "Hey bud, I knocked your stuff all over the floor. I crammed it all back in, but you may want to check it just in case anything rolled under the couch. Sorry man."

Dylon reached for the bag. "No problem man, I did just kind of drop everything, didn't I?" Dylon didn't give it a second thought and put it on the floor inside the bedroom. "Alright Trevor, I hope you got the alarm set, because I'm hitting the sack."

Trevor yelled out of the bathroom. "Got it bud." Trevor finished up his shower, set the alarm, and tried to go to sleep. He tossed and turned for a little while. He just couldn't get Dylon's drawings out of his head. Finally he fell asleep.

# Chapter 5

Trevor woke up, feeling like he had been hit by a bus. At first he couldn't figure out why. He had always taken naps before going out and never felt like this. Then it hit him, his mind was preoccupied with Dylon's drawings and the questions it posed. The drawings were pretty detailed, like he had done this before. Trevor didn't realize he was actually this interested in the possibilities of this kind of craft.

Actually he hadn't given it a lot of thought at all. He'd seen a lot of the shows on The History Channel and The Science Channel, but only now that he had seen an actual blueprint drawing could he visualize it.

He had to know more. He thought to himself, "People always open up a little more when they have a drink or two in them. So that's the plan then, I'll just ask him on the way home." Trevor smiled to himself as he was getting ready. "You almost ready, bud?" Trevor called out to Dylon.

Dylon was tucking his shirt in when he half heard what Trevor said. "Yeah, I think so." He was actually looking forward to going out. Not so much the drinking part of it, but the getting to know Kaylee  part of it. She seemed like a sweet girl, genuine. Plus those green eyes, that was probably the kicker.

Trevor popped his head around the corner. "You ready bud?"

Dylon was looking around the room, feeling like he was forgetting something. "Uh, yeah, I guess so. No wait, my hat." As they drove down the road Dylon still felt like he was forgetting something, but just couldn't put his finger on it.

When they pulled in to the parking lot Trevors jaw dropped. "Damn man, now this looks like the place to be."

Dylon was checking out all the cars in the lot and started getting an uneasy feeling. "Man, that's a lot of people." Dylon wasn't real comfortable with big crowds. "Shit! Shit, shit, shit! Stupid ass!"

Trevor stopped quick. "What is it? Don't tell me you forgot your I.D."

Dylon was just shaking his head. "Shit, I can't believe I'm so stupid. I left the card at home. You know, the card, the one with the phone number."

Trevor was sympathetic, but also a little relieved. "Don't worry bud, you'll probably find her."

Dylon looked at Trevor like he was crazy. "With as many cars as there are out here, I hate to even think about how many people are in there. I'll never find her man."

"Think positively bud, and besides if you don't

find her, I'm sure there are plenty of girls here looking to have a good time." Trevor said as he reassured Dylon. "C'mon man, let's go have some fun."

Once inside the club the guys headed to the first bar they could see. Trevor reached for his wallet. "I'll buy the first round, what are you having?"

Dylon could barely hear himself think let alone hear what Trevor was saying. "Vodka and Sprite."

Trevor ordered the drinks and left a heavy tip, in the hopes of being able to catch the same bartender again. As the night carried on, the drinks did too and Dylon was getting a little more loose. He was also getting more frustrated about not being able to fine Kaylee. After an hour and a half of walking around the bar looking for her Trevor was about over it. He was walking back past the mechanical bull with the fourth or fifth round of drinks when he finally noticed her.

Dylon looked at Trevor out of the corner of his eye. "Trevor buddy, tell her, please, help me out here."

Trevor smiled. "Tell her what? You want me to tell her how you cussed yourself for being so stupid when you realized you left the card at home. How you didn't even want to come in, when you realized it. I know, how about the part where you were whining about it being so crowded, and that you'll never find her in here, even when I told you would."

Dylon and Kaylee laughed a little as Dylon

objected. "Well you didn't have to tell her *all of it.*"

They all laughed a little more when Trevor responded. "Hey bud, what are friends for."

Kaylee grabbed Dylon by the hand. "C'mon guys I'll introduce you to my friends." She led the two back towards the mechanical bull. As Trevor followed he noticed that Dylon was already having a hard time walking, but it was so crowded he didn't think anyone else noticed.

When they reached the bull Kaylee was looking around for her friends. "I don't know where they went, they might be on the other side. That's where you line up to ride. C'mon let's go." She grabbed Dylon's hand again, but she was moving too quickly. This in turn put Dylon off balance, causing him to spill half of his drink all over some guy.

Trevor caught what happened and stepped up. Before he got a chance to say anything the guy had already grabbed Dylon by the shoulder and spun him around. "Hey, dumbass!"

Dylon just stood there, not realizing what he had done. Then Trevor jumped in. "C'mon bud, he doesn't drink that much and it was an accident."

The guy started to say something but was grabbed by both arms by the bouncers. They also grabbed Dylon and Trevor. As they were escorting Dylon and Trevor to the exit, Kaylee followed. Dylon caught her eye and mouthed. "Sorry, I'll call you." He felt good when she acknowledged what he'd said.

When the guys got in the car and were headed down the road Dylon kept rambling. "Oh, the girl of my dreams. I met her, lost her, found her, and lost her again." Trevor just laughed at Dylon, while he was thinking to himself about how to change the subject to the drawings.

They pulled into the drive with Dylon still talking about Kaylee. Dylon looked up at the night sky as he was getting out of the car. "Wow, Trevor. Look how clear the sky is. I wish you could see the stars like this in the city."

Trevor looked up as he got out of the car. "Oh yeah, stars, wow." There was a note of sarcasm in Trevor's voice. "Come on bud, let's get inside and get some water or we'll be hating life in the morning."

They made it to the door and Trevor realized the opportunity had just been placed in front of him. He went to the kitchen to get him a bottle of water. When he got back to the porch he found Dylon still looking skyward.

"You know Dylon, if you like the stars so much, why didn't you become an astronomer or an astronaut?" Trevor asked as he handed him the water.

"Too much physics, and besides this is what my father expected to do. What he trained me to do."

Dylon opened the water and took a big drink.

Trevor looked at Dylon and decided to go ahead and pursue the answer to his own questions. "Yeah, but you obviously like everything about this stuff. I mean, look at the drawings in your office. And then there is the bag you brought with you. When I knocked it over, your binder fell out. I saw some of the drawings. You are good man, all your drawings are very detailed."

Dylon cocked his head and looked at Trevor, but before he got a chance to say anything Trevor continued. "So what is it bud, a UFO? Come on man tell me, I got to know. Does it fly?"

Dylon was digesting Trevor's words. He finally came to the conclusion that he was truly interested. Not the kind of interest that he would use to tease or mock him with later, but actually interested. "You really want to know? I mean, you're not going to make fun of me, or think I'm weird?"

"Dude, I already think you're weird." Trevor smiled and laughed as he replied. "And I would never make fun of you, not in a mean spirit anyway."

Dylon could see that Trevor was sincere. "Okay then, let's go inside." When Dylon got inside he headed straight to his room to get his binder. Trevor headed to the fridge to get two more waters. When they both returned to the living room Dylon had a smile on his face like he had just hit the lottery.

"What are you grinning about?" Trevor asked.

Dylon responded. "Well, the only people I talk to about this stuff are either too far away to talk to, or their schedules are too full to talk about it. I just kinda think it's neat that you're interested." Dylon handed the binder to Trevor. Trevor looked over the cover of the binder. "So what does M.S. One mean?"

Dylon taking a drink of water when the first question came. "Oh that's easy, kinda lame, but easy. I named it after the UFO that was seen by a Mexican policeman. It was on *The History Channel, UFO Files* or something like that, thus the name Mexican Spacecraft One."

Trevor interrupted. "So why not the *Roswell* craft?"

Dylon beamed with excitement. "I've already done that. I'm up to R.S. twelve now. They're only made with electric ducted fan jets which kind of limits the capability. I designed that one after the original design, not all these new ones that the model making companies keep coming out with. They keep changing the design. I guess they figure the more they change the way the original one looked, the more people will forget it."

Trevor had more and more questions but could barely get them in. "Does it actually fly? And what do you mean the original?"

Dylon was starting to get more and more animated. "Yes it does fly, not the way it is supposed to though. The original was designed by, well actually who knows, it wasn't us. The replica craft was drawn out by a guy named Bob Lazar. He supposedly worked at Area 51. Well *Testor*, the model company, I think it was them. Anyway, they must have hooked up with him, because they came out with a model of it. There was also a mini-book with the model that explained everything. So I built one based on that design, minus the anti-gravitational devices. I replaced them with the fan ducted engines. That's why it doesn't fly like it should, the A.G. devices."

Trevor was doing his best to keep up. "So if it flies, why build a new one? Why not concentrate your energy on the A.G. device?"

Dylon smiled. "Why do they keep re-designing cars? To make them better or to add newer components or more features. As far as the device, the anti-gravitational device, I have, continuously. It kinda works, I think." Dylon paused. "Do you know what an E.M.P. is?" Trevor shook his head no. "It's an electromagnetic pulse. A lot of people who have had experiences with UFO's say they have lost power in their cars. Of course, that's mostly with the earlier cases. The only thing I can figure is the electromagnetic pulse. If that's the case, that means the anti- gravitational device is some kind of electromagnet. Are you still with me?"

Trevor was trying to digest Dylon's crash course in UFO technology. "I think so.... If you can figure out how to make an anti-gravitational device, you could end up changing the entire dynamics of flight?"

Dylon paused for a second. "I guess so. I hadn't really thought about that aspect of it. I'm just trying to build a better way to get into space. There just seems to be so many things that are ....oh what is the word...." Dylon was trying to find the right word to describe his thoughts.

Trevor thought he could help him out. "So what you're saying is, that the crafts we have today are like a stone wheel, and what *you're* trying to develop, is like the tires of today."

Dylon nodded his head vigorously. "Yes, that's it, that's exactly what I'm talking about. Trevor, technology has come so far, I just can't believe that we haven't tried a different way. Actually we probably have but, in the name of quote *'national security'* , we will probably never know. Anyway, back to the A.G. device. If I can actually get it to work it would almost be a perpetual motion device. Are you familiar with perpetual motion?"

Trevor thought for a minute. "Isn't that where a

machine basically runs on its own energy, or very little energy at all, but has a great deal of output?"

"Yeah, basically." Dylon was excited that Trevor actually had a little bit of a clue as to what was being explained to him. "So with the A.G. device the need for fuel would be almost nothing. Without the need for mass amounts of fuel, space travel would be so much easier."

Trevor still had questions. "So let's just say you can design the device, where you have gravity working against gravity. That would explain the reason that these UFO's can go so much faster than anything we could possibly think of at this point. But how do you explain the fact that the metal, or whatever they are made of, doesn't melt at that velocity?"

"Ah-ha!" Dylon enthusiastically exclaimed. "I have a theory on that! Keep in mind I'm no physicist. Let's just say that the A.G. device actually creates a center of gravity for the UFO and thus it creates a gravitational field for the craft. If that's the case then the heat from the friction would be affecting the field and not the UFO itself. So then, you wouldn't need protective heat shields and all the extras that the shuttles have on them. This only makes sense to me because when you hear anyone describe a UFO they never mention that the craft is two different colors, like the space shuttles with the heat shields on the bottom. It's always one solid color."

Trevor nodded his head as he thought. "That might be possible, but I'm no physicist either. So bud, I have one more question before I have to call it a night. What ever happened to this Lazar guy?"

Dylon shrugged his shoulders. "Not really sure. He had done a couple of interviews, I think in the hopes of keeping himself alive. I mean think about it, how comfortable would you feel if you opened a can of worms on one of the government's secret projects. I don't think he's dead, he just kind of faded out of the picture."

Trevor got up from the sofa. "Well bud, I have to say that was quite enlightening, but I'm wiped out. I'm gonna call it a night."

Dylon was still high on his own enthusiasm. "Thanks a lot for listening. I'm usually going over all this stuff in my own head. It was actually nice being able to talk to somebody besides myself."

"Sure thing, bud." As Trevor walked to his bedroom, he couldn't help but wonder. "What planted this kind of desire and drive in someone? Something must have happened to Dylon to make him want to work on a project that seems to defy known physics."

# Chapter 6

Washington, D.C.

"Good morning General Grant. I have everything set up for your meeting in the board room. Here are the additional files you requested. Looks like you have about twenty-five minutes before everyone else arrives. Good luck with your presentation, Sir." After handing him the files, she quickly turned and went back down the hall.

The General had started to thank her, but she was gone before he had a chance to. "How did I get so lucky to be blessed with such a good assistant?" He thought to himself as he turned to go to his office to review the files he just received.

As the General flipped through the pages and briefly scanned them, he just couldn't help but wonder what had changed. "Why all of a sudden all the interest? What had happened to change everything so much?" He really didn't have a clue as to what he was looking for, he was just hoping to find something. Anything he could find to help him understand, why there was such a high priority put on *The Estate*.

Even the topographical photos didn't show much

more than what simply appeared to be standard upgrades. It really didn't make much sense. Especially with the background information they had on the Rosiers and how their enterprise operated, this all seemed normal to him.

The General felt like he failed. When he left the position, he was on the verge of getting the higher ups to abandon the project altogether. Turning over all the reports to the Peruvian government and washing their hands of it completely. Then he thought of Major Wilburn, the person who took his place. He thought the Major was a very capable person. He was not privy to all that the Major was involved in but overseeing the monitoring of the estate was not that difficult of a job. "Hell, my assistant could do it." The General just shook his head as he gathered up the papers and put them back in their proper files.

He mumbled to himself as he headed toward the board room, where he had heard the faint sound of voices as people were slowly filtering in. "This is not what I had in mind for one of the first operations of this new division."

Truth be known, each of the three department heads had something completely different in mind. All three of them also came to the conclusion that this was simply an order that came down through the ranks designed specifically to let them know that they were not in charge. An order from a bunch of bureaucrats, who had no idea how to run anything, to make themselves feel good about spending the money on this new division.

As General Grant entered the room he noticed Sergeant Mobley from the CIA, Lieutenant Steiger from the FBI, and of course the Head of the Division, Senator Emerson. There were a couple of other people in the room that the General didn't recognize.

"Ah, gentlemen and ladies of course. So glad you could all be here today." As the Senator started speaking everyone took their seats. The General's assistant closed the door and sat down beside him. She situated herself in front of the stenotype. "Most of you are familiar with each other, but we do have a couple of new faces with us today. This is Valerie Walker, my assistant." The Senator said as he started introducing the new faces. "And this is Billy Kolmonski, Senior Foreign Relations Officer, and of course his assistant. Mr. Kolminski has been overseeing *the estate* for the past two years, while Major Wilburn has been overseas. Mr. Kolminski has been in the Foreign Relations division for about ten years now and has proved to be quite successful, in persuading uncooperative officials to see the bigger picture. As a matter of fact he was the one, that brought to our attention the massive build-up of *the estate.*"

Kolminski just sat there with a smug little smile on his face, enjoying the praise he just received, like he just discovered a new planet, or the cure for cancer. The Senator continued talking. "Of course once this was brought to light, we enlisted the help of the CIA and the FBI and discovered that Mr. Dylon Rosier is also shopping for some rather large transport crafts. He has also been inquiring about other types of heavy machinery, possibly to install a factory on said property. All these things point to something that just doesn't look quite right considering the remote location we're dealing with."

The Senator then switched gears a little in his presentation. "Now I just want to personally thank all of you for your cooperation and also let you know how important it is that we succeed in the handling of this operation. We don't need a lot of bickering between the different agencies, because ultimately you all have the same employer. If this division can prove that it has the ability to distinguish which agency is the best suited for the task, assign them that task, and then keep the two agencies and the armed forces, if that should be the case, working hand in hand, then the possibilities of this division flourishing into a permanent agency of the government will be almost a certainty. Now with all of that said, I'll turn it over to

58

General Grant, your first Director of the Division of Special Operations for Foreign Relations."

General Grant stood up. "Thank you Senator Emerson and I would also like to give thanks for the outstanding job my colleagues have done in combining their efforts to accumulate as much information as they have on the situation. I welcome Mr. Kolminski's efforts and initiative in pursuing what he feels as a possible threat. *The Estate* at one time fell under my duties and when I passed it on to Major Wilburn, keeping up with the progress of it just kind of became a pet project of mine. Well with everything that has been going in getting this new division going, I kind of lost communication with the whole thing. I really wish I would have kept up with it. I guess I should have and I am happy to know that Mr. Kolminski and I will reopen the lines of communications on what was really a surprise to me. I guess that is nobody's fault but my own."

Mr. Kolminski squirmed just a little. He wasn't really sure if he was being thrown under the bus or not. He remembered quite clearly the conversation, that the Major had with him about passing the reports on to someone, but at the time didn't really think it was all that important. After the Major had left on special assignment, anything that was important seemed to go out the window. Unless of course it was important to Mr. Kolminski and whoever it was that he was trying to impress. Mr. Kolminski was one of those types of people that just kind of slithered up the ladder of success.

After discussing everything that he had to say, the General proceeded to get right into the specs of the operation. "The operation will be code named 'Watchdog.' In the folders in front of you, you will find all of the information on *the estate* and the Rosiers, specifically Mr. Dylon Rosier. You will also find photos from five years ago and from the present, so you can see the amount of progress that has been made. Our job is to analyze the site, predict the safest possible location for any surveillance equipment, and make sure it's the best we have. As you all know it is a very remote location and we will not find ourselves with very many opportunities to perform any routine maintenance, so let's do this right the first time."

General Grant closed the meeting and slowly made his way around to the Senator, who was talking to Mr. Kolminski. On the way he leaned over to his assistant and asked her to make sure she gave Mr. Kolminski all of the contact information he might need. "And by all means make sure you get his. I wouldn't want this to bite us if you understand what I'm saying." She quietly responded. "Cover your ass." Then she slipped around the group unnoticed and made it to her desk, before anyone had started to leave.

When General Grant got to the Senator, Kolminski was just saying his goodbyes. General Grant quickly reached out his hand. "Mr. Kolminski, before you leave, I just wanted to thank you for being so diligent. I would have never thought anything bad could possibly come out of *the estate.*"

Mr. Kolminski shook his hand. "I would really like to stick around, but I've got an appointment that I can't miss."

"I understand completely. Oh, by the way, my assistant has my contact information for you. If you could give her yours, I'll be happy to call and set up an appointment to talk with you a little more about the operation." General Grant promptly thanked him and immediately turned to the Senator and started a conversation, in order to make sure there were no objections.

"I really don't have time for this." Kolminski mumbled as he turned to leave.

"Mr. Kolminski, General Grant asked me to make sure you get this." The assistant said as she handed him an envelope with all the contact information inside. As soon as he took the envelope, the assistant asked for his card. "Thank you very much, General Grant will be in touch," she said as he fussed about having to dig through his briefcase to find a card.

# Chapter 7

The morning came too quickly, way too quickly. After a night of drinking, and not getting in bed until about four thirty in the morning, the alarm clock was the last thing Dylon or Trevor wanted to hear. Both of the guys were getting their things together, but moving at a snail's pace.

After stopping to get their morning fix, Trevor having a strong cup of coffee and Dylon having a Mountain Dew, they finally made it back to the Felderson Corporation. The thirty-minute trip seemed to take forever in their slightly hung-over state. Trevor did happen to mention how much worse they would feel if they hadn't drank any water before going to bed.

There was a security guard waiting at the front gate to escort them to the hangar. It was an older gentleman who didn't have much to say. "Follow me boys, I'll take you to the hangar." Upon reaching the hangar, they noticed the pilots were boarding. Dylon looked at Trevor. "Looks like we made it, without a minute to spare."

Trevor reached down beside the seat to find the lever that popped the trunk open before responding to Dylon. "Good, now I can go back to sleep. Oh, and

I'm not finished with you, I still have questions."
Trevor and Dylon got out of the car to get the bags and
head to the jet. Dylon just smiled thinking to himself.
"So Trevor is actually interested in UFO's, or at least
the possibility of building one. *And* he doesn't think
I'm a loon."

Upon boarding, Trevor quickly closed the
window blinds by his seat, stretched out, and got
comfortable for the flight. Dylon, remembering the
procedure before the flight down, decided to check
and see if Trevor reminded himself of his Dramamine.
"Are you going to be alright for take off? I mean, I
didn't see you take anything for your motion sickness
and I honestly don't think I could handle seeing
anybody get sick this morning."

Trevor grumbled. "I took it while you were in the
restroom at the gas station."

Dylon decided instead of going over his drawings
on M.S. One project, that he would just sit back, relax
and enjoy the flight. Which meant, he would swivel
the seat around facing the window, in the hopes of
seeing something and probably fall asleep dreaming
about it.

Trevor had fallen asleep before the plane even
started to move. Dylon just sat there looking out the
window, waiting to get in the air. As he was gazing
out the window, his mind started to drift to the first

few days at *the estate* in Peru.

\* \* \* \* \* \*

He thought of his trip with his mother, to one of
the villages near Cusco. There were other little
settlements that they would eventually visit, but on
this trip they were visiting the newly opened clinic
near Cusco. Dylon' s mother, Angela, had trained to
be a doctor. She did *not* want to join the Rosier family
enterprise. She, like Dylon' s father was very
stubborn, but  also carried a little more resentment
than her husband, Steven Rosier. She couldn't forget
the treatment Steven received from *his* father for, as he
put it 'screwing up his future by getting her pregnant.'
These were words she wasn't supposed to hear on
that night, but she did. Angela never let Steven know
that she had heard them. She loved him and she knew
how important his family was to him; how important
his father's approval was, so she decided that she
would bury those words in the very back of her mind,
for future use.
When the time came,  she graduated at the head
of her class. Angela just smiled at her father-in-law
when she rejected his offer of getting her seated on the
board of directors of one of the local hospitals.
"Oh, didn't Steven tell you? I'm surprised, he's

so excited for me. I'm going to Cusco, Peru to do some volunteer work. It always looks good on your resume, and it's kind of expected. Most of your better doctors and nurses volunteer at least once a year. We decided that with the opening of the firm and all, it would be the best time to do it. Dylon' s going with me, it will be a good character building experience for him. Don't you think?"

As Angela turned and left her father-in-law standing there speechless, she smiled inside. She knew that Steven would back her up because she had already primed him with the idea that she wanted to help those that were, not less fortunate, but did not have the advantage of being in the twentieth century as far as medical technologies were concerned. She didn't want to change their cultures or traditions, she just wanted to be able to help where she could.

Dylon, as a ten-year-old, had been to Cusco several times already. This time was different though. Steven sent Dylon with his mother because he was 'too busy living in a fantasy land'. Angela, knew that Dylon was pouting, so she decided to ask him for his help. "Honey, could you help me when we get to the clinic?"

"Sure Mom, whatever you need."

Angela was trying to get him to open up a little. "So, would you like to know what I need you to do?"

"I guess so." Dylon was still sulking.

Angela looked at him, thought for a minute, and then just shook her head. "You know what kiddo, having two stubborn parents doesn't fare well for your future."

"What do you mean mom?"

"Just thinking out loud dear." Angela answered and then continued. "How about we try this? Instead of talking about your dreams all the time with your dad, try drawing them out on paper."

"Well what's wrong with dreaming mom?"

"Honey there is nothing wrong with dreaming at all, but if that's all you talk about then that's all it is, just dreams. Now if you were to draw them out, or write them down, in your own personal book, then you will always have something to go back to. You know, to see if there is any way to change them. Make them better or just change them around a little. Does that make sense?"

"I think." Dylon responded. "Does that mean you and Dad don't want to hear my dreams?"

Angela hugged Dylon. "Of course we do dear. Your father just wants what's best for you, but all he can get out of you is your dreams. This makes him think you're not listening to him. He thinks he is not doing his job in raising you well. I'll tell you what, if you try really hard to put your dreams on paper, writing, drawing, however you want to do it. Then I promise I will make sure that we set aside a day where all we talk about is your dreams. Do we have a deal?"

"I'll try mom, I'll try real hard." Dylon said, then he was silent as he thought hard for a minute. "Mom, what is dad's job?"

Angela wasn't really expecting this question from Dylon, but she did have an answer for him. "Well honey, your dad's job is to teach you as much as he can, in the hopes that you will be able to make good decisions as you grow. He also hopes that by teaching you, you will be able to avoid mistakes that we may have already made. His job is also to protect you from harm. Most importantly though, it is to love you for who you are. You know what honey? That's my job too."

"Really?" Dylon asked.

Angela knew there was another question coming, she could almost see the gears turning in his little mind.

"So what is my job mom?"

"Well Dylon, your job is to learn as much as you possibly can, but right now your job is to enjoy being a child and never forget your dreams. Okay honey?" Dylon nodded his head yes. Angela reached out her arms. "Now give me a hug." Dylon reached out and hugged his mom tight.

* * * * * *

Trevor didn't think he would be able to wake Dylon. "Dylon, Dylon. Buddy wake up, unless of course you want to go to New York. You were sleeping pretty hard there, must have been a good dream."

Dylon was still a little groggy but did manage to catch the last thing Trevor said. "Yeah, it was a good dream." Dylon looked up and just under his breath said. "Nice to see you again mom."

Trevor had stepped to the back of the plane to get the rest of their bags and didn't quite hear what he said. "What are you mumbling?"

Dylon just smiled to himself, "nothing bud," and reached out to help with his bags. When they departed from the plane, Trevor's car was just outside. "Man, I guess I was sleeping pretty hard. How long have we been here?"

Trevor put the bags in the trunk. "Twenty minutes or so. Hop in, I'll take you to your car."

Dylon was a little confused. "How did you get your car here?"

"I had my roommate drop it off." The guys got in the car and Trevor suggested they get a Bloody Mary. Dylon agreed and as they drove off Trevor had to ask,

"So this A.G. device, do you have any ideas on how to build one?"

Dylon just smiled. "Well of course I do, I've already built one. It doesn't work right, but I've built one. I also have drawings on it."

# Chapter 8

When the boys returned to work, Rosie gave them her normal "Good Morning" followed by "I expect to see some receipts by ten sharp, boys." Then she promptly reminded them about the company picnic. "The picnic is just two weeks away boys, and I don't expect to be disappointed with some lame excuse of why you can't make it." They nodded and agreed with Rosie and headed to their offices to get their day started.

The first thing Dylon took care of was his expense report. He put it in an interoffice envelope, and then immediately took it to Rosie's in box. The next thing he did was to get out the maps of the four building sites available for his 'college house project'. Dylon couldn't figure out why there were four different sites to choose from. Out of the corner of his eye, he noticed Trevor walking by with an envelope in his hand. He asked him for some help with his project. Trevor stepped into the office and started explaining what he needed to do with the four different building sites. "It's easy, all you have to do is look at your overlay, see what each site is close to, and put yourself back in college. Where would you want to live, as a college student?"

Dylon shook his head. "Okay I get it now, but what will happen with the other three sites?"

Trevor looked at him in disbelief. "Are you sure you're a Rosier? Think about it, how do you think the house mom earns her salary? She is not just baby-sitting a bunch of college kids. The other sites are rental properties, mostly tri-plexes. It's part of her job, to show the units and rent them out, call a plumber, electrician, whatever is needed."

Trevor paused for a minute, pointing to the picture of the UFO beside Dylon's computer monitor. "So is that it?" Dylon picked up the picture, but before he got a chance to answer, a voice came from behind Trevor, it was Rosie. "Whatever *it* is, I'm sure it's not an expense report." She was tapping her watch as she was giving Trevor that look. He immediately handed her the envelope.

Dylon interrupted. "He was on his way, Rosie. I stopped him for some pointers on my next project."

Rosie just looked at the both of them. "So what is the *it*, that you were talking about? I'm guessing the question was about the UFO picture your'e holding."

Dylon started to question Rosie, but just smiled. Remembering she didn't miss a thing, he handed the picture to her for a closer look. Trevor excited to see the picture chimed in. "It's the R.S. model, the little space cadet built a real live UFO, and it flies too."

Dylon just buried his head in his hands. Rosie looked at Trevor and then at Dylon. "What is he talking about Dylon?"

Dylon looked at her. "Trevor doesn't know what he's talking about. It's not the R.S. model, it's something completely different." Trevor just looked at Dylon but before he could say anything Rosie beat him to it.

"So what is the R.S. model and what is this?" Rosie held the picture up. She was patiently waiting for an answer, and Dylon knew she wouldn't leave without one, so he took a deep breath and started to explain everything. "Well the R.S. model is a radio controlled toy that I designed after the original model that they came out with when I was a kid. Yes, it does fly, but not the way a real UFO does. It flies with electric ducted fan jets." Dylon stopped there, hoping that would satisfy Rosie's curiosity.

Rosie and Trevor still just stood in the same spot, waiting for the rest of it.

"Aw, come on guys." Dylon said, hoping to get a break. He paused as long as he could, before realizing that they were not going to give him one. " Jeez, you guys are impossible. Okay, when I was a kid, five or six, we were at a company picnic and I wandered off. Well, I lost my way back and one of the other kids had found me. He was older than me, but he was still a kid. Well, we saw something. We saw that." Dylon pointed at the picture Rosie was still holding. "I made the drawing, to the best of my recollection. We weren't abducted or anything, not missing any time, and it was only there for a minute. It made a sudden move, which scared the sh-. Sorry, Rosie. It scared the crap out of both of us. Ever since then I've always been interested in…" Dylon was looking for the right words to explain what he wanted to say.

Rosie broke the silence. "So you're interested in the unknown and the unexplained, *and* you've actually had an experience. Now what was so hard about that?" Rosie tried to make nothing, out of what Trevor was trying to make a big deal out of. She was hoping that it made Dylon feel a little easier about admitting to seeing something that most people wouldn't admit to, and it did.

Dylon smiled. "Thank you Rosie."

"You just be careful who you share it with, young man." Rosie said and she started to leave the office, but stopped and turned to Dylon again. "I hope you don't think that story gets you out of going to the picnic." She winked and smiled at him, then left the office. As Rosie left the office Trevor spoke up. "Well, seeing a UFO at five sure explains a lot, but it still doesn't explain why you didn't go into a field where you would be a little closer to your passion. So what gives? Why didn't you try something else?"

Dylon didn't really want to answer this question either, but knew if he didn't Trevor would never stop asking. "Well, I did try. It was half way through the semester and the professor wanted us to write a small essay, on why we chose physics. He said, that with physics, there were so many fields that we could get into and the essay would help him guide us better. He could choose some other electives that might make our transitions into our career choices easier. Well, after reading mine he told me I should drop out of school, take some flying lessons, and possibly become a flight instructor. He really was a dick about it. He also said that I should quit wasting the school's time and my parents' money."

Trevor stood there in disbelief. "Damn man, you're right the guy sounds like a major dick. So did you report him to the dean or anything?"

Dylon's reply kind of took Trevor by surprise. "No, I didn't report him. I just put my dreams away for a while and folded to what my dad was pushing me into before he passed. It was just easier, because my grandfather was pushing for the same thing. It wasn't until Kat's sixteenth birthday that I started playing with my dreams again. I never really knew why she was so interested in UFOs. I guess my dreams just kind of rubbed off on her."

Trevor pointed to the other picture, that was beside Dylon's monitor. "So is that Kat? Dude she's hot."

Dylon chuckled. "That would be Elizabeth to you, if you ever meet her and yeah she is, but she's my sister too, and I think she has a boyfriend. I don't think she knows it yet, but I'm pretty sure that's where it's heading. Actually you might get to meet her at the picnic. I'm not sure what her flight plans are yet, but I'm hoping to see her there."

Dylon thanked Trevor for the pointers on his project and went back to his computer to shoot Kat an e-mail. "Hey sis, hope all is well, just writing to confirm an arrival time and flight information for next weekend. Love ya, Dylon." After sending the e-mail, Dylon thought that he had better reconfirm the fact that Rosie was going to the estate after the picnic.

He didn't find her at the front desk so he decided to wait a few minutes. As he was waiting he noticed a picture sitting on her desk. There were three guys in Hawaiian shirts, standing in a setting that looked like a bar in the Caribbean Islands somewhere. There was a tall black man with a very stern face, most likely the one that kept the group out of trouble. In the center was an average built man, with a shit-eating grin. Dylon figured that this was the guy that always made the best of a bad situation. Then on the right there was a younger guy, he was smiling, but his eyes showed nothing but fear. Dylon thought that he actually looked too young for the group.

"Is there something I can help you with young man?" Rosie was trying not to laugh as she spoke in a stern voice. Dylon almost jumped out of his pants and quickly started apologizing. "Oh my God, Rosie, I was just… I'm sorry, I didn't mean to…" Rosie laughed a little. "Oh dear God child, stop groveling, I'm teasing you. If I can invade your office and thoroughly inspect your personal belongings, then you can surely look at one little picture, that I have placed on my desk."

Dylon breathed a sigh of relief. "I was actually just checking to see if you were still going to the estate. You can bring someone along, if you want." Dylon motioned to the picture, not knowing who the people might be.

Rosie smiled. "Of course I'm still going, I wouldn't miss it for the world." She reached for the picture, as she continued. "As far as bringing someone goes, the person I would bring on a trip like this, has been gone for a while now."

Dylon felt worse now, than he did when she caught him checking out the picture. "I'm sorry Rosie, I didn't know."

"Don't be silly, how could you know? Actually, I

like talking about him every now and then. He was a wonderful man. He died doing what he loved best, serving his country." Rosie was very proud when talking about her dearly departed, but would never give too much detail about his service to his country.

Dylon could see that she loved her husband and was very happy to talk about him. "So which one is he?"

Rosie's face just lit up. "Well thank you for asking Dylon. The one in the middle is my Frank. The guy on the left was his immediate boss, Sgt. Jared Stein, and the young man on the right is Corporal Brian Foster, he's a little green in that picture. Frank died saving that poor boys life. Brian still feels guilty about the way the whole mission turned out, like it was his fault. We've both leaned on each other through the whole healing process. I don't know how I would have made it, if I hadn't been helping him get past the guilt. I guess life has a funny way of helping you through its little difficulties. We still stay in touch, I guess I'm his adopted mother."

Dylon offered an open invitation for him, but Rosie insisted that he was way too busy with work to do much of anything else. As he started to go back to his office, Rosie had a question for him. "By the way, have you thought about naming *the estate*? Honestly, a piece of property that large should have a name other than just '*the estate*'.

Dylon just shook his head no. "Hadn't really given it much thought."

Rosie just gave him a look. "Well dear, you really should think about it."

Dylon was walking back to his office, thinking about what Rosie said. His phone gave off a text tone and when he read it his jaw dropped. The message was from Kat, it read: "Possible life on Mars, methane clouds discovered."

Dylon quickly made it to his computer and started searching the web, for any news blurbs on the information Kat just sent to him.

# Chapter 9

The days leading up to the picnic passed quickly. Dylon was able to finish his college house project and present it to Trevor, which was a normal chain of command procedure. He also set his appointments with the builders, almost a month away, and was able to help Rosie out with some of the arrangements for the company picnic. Then the last email he sent, was to Kaylee. Hoping to spend a little time with her, he sent a copy of his schedule and when he would be available for anything.

In his time away from work, Dylon found himself to be more productive than usual as well. He spent some time doing some research on methane, sparked by the recent discovery of the clouds found on Mars. He altered his design on the Agripod project, just in case there actually was life on Mars, and also set up the flight plans for the trip to *the estate*. The only thing that Dylon found disappointing was the fact that they couldn't just skip the picnic and head straight out.

He reached for the phone and just as he started to dial a number, Rosie interrupted him. "Well kiddo, I'm locking things up, are you ready to go to the picnic?"

Dylon gave Rosie a quick nod. "Yes ma'am, just have to put Jose on standby. Did you want me to put your bags in my car or do you just want to drive to the house and go from there?"

Rosie didn't have any preferences. "Whatever is easiest, it doesn't make a difference to me. So are you excited about going?"

Dylon replied. "Well of course I am, I can't wait for you to see what all we've done to the place. Plus it will be good to see Reese again, he's like a nephew to me."

Rosie just rolled her eyes. "I'm talking about the picnic."

Dylon reluctantly answered this question. "Not really. I mean, I'm anxious to see Kat, she should show up some time there, but the last picnic we attended was the day our parents died. It doesn't really bring back a good feeling. I'm actually looking forward to trying to find... well never mind."

Rosie stopped Dylon for a minute, to unload the bags from her car, to his. "I'm sorry, I had forgotten all about that. Did they ever catch the guy that caused the accident?"

Dylon shook his head no. "You know, it was raining pretty hard that day. I don't think they ever got a clear description on the car, but I'm sure life is giving it back to him ten fold. You reap what you sow,

Rosie."

Rosie just smiled. "You're a firm believer in that, aren't you?"

"I have to be. Otherwise I would go crazy trying to figure out the *why* part of it. Besides just look who you're working for. They take care of their people, push a positive attitude, push learning and higher learning. Tell me, do you know anybody that has been with the company and kept a negative attitude? I bet you can't come up with one that has lasted longer than six months. I'll bet you can't tell me one mean person that works here either."

Rosie was still smiling. "Okay okay, I get your point, but what about the part you're looking forward to. You skipped over that part."

Dylon looked at her and just grinned, being reminded of who he was dealing with. "Do you remember my UFO experience story? Well, this is the park."

Rosie was silent for a moment, then her curiosity got the best of her. "So are you actually expecting to see something?"

Dylon had a typical fact-filled answer. "Well, in a lot of the cases, where there have been eye witness reports, they tend to repeat themselves every two to three years. Although I haven't done the math it doesn't matter if I see something or not. It will at least be neat to revisit the memory, don't you think?"

Rosie shook her head in agreement. "Yeah, I do. It's always nice to revisit fond memories. Oh, just a reminder, Mr. Felderson will be here. So if someone starts thanking you for your work, I thought it might be useful to have a small clue as to who the person might be."

"Well thanks Rosie, that would be nice to know." Dylon said as they drove down the road to the picnic. "So where do we start when we get there?"

Rosie looked at her watch before answering. "Most people check out the activities board, so they can find something for their children to do, then they usually just mingle with old friends. As for myself, I'm heading straight for the food area. I can't believe I thought I could make it to lunch time without some sort of snack. Then of course there's the adult beverage line, which moves fairly quickly for the amount of people that are here."

Dylon noticed the entrance to the park. "I can drop you off at the front and find a spot to park the car, if you want. But you have to get me a hot dog with ketchup." Rosie agreed. "I'll meet you at the fountain." Dylon stopped the car and let her out.

After searching for what seemed like forever for a spot to park Dylon finally was making his way to the fountain. Taking in every site that he could, he noticed that there wasn't much that had changed, that he could remember. He found Rosie waiting at the fountain. She had gotten him a hot dog and a drink.

Dylon thanked her and quickly started gobbling the dog down. Before he got a chance to thank her she noticed an old girlfriend, and got up to meet her. Dylon quickly blurted out. "Meet back here at four." Rosie turned and acknowledged him with a nod, and was off. He looked around trying to see anybody he knew, without much luck. After a minute of sitting there, Dylon decided to walk around and try to find his way back to the field he found so many years ago.

As he walked around and noticed how many people were there, he never could have imagined that there were actually this many people, working for Rosier Enterprises. Dylon finally made it to a field where there were a bunch of kids playing. At one end of the field there was a small group of mostly teenagers playing football, in teams were five each. At the other end there was a younger group of kids playing Frisbee and it looked like there were a couple of soccer balls being kicked around.

As Dylon was walking around the end of the field, looking for any sign of a small trail running off into the woods, a Frisbee whizzed by him, barely missing his nose. "I'll get it." Dylon said as he stepped into the brush to retrieve the Frisbee. When he reached to pick it up, he noticed a small worn trail about fifteen feet to his right. "Could that be it?" he thought to himself as he gave the Frisbee a good toss back to the kids.

Dylon quickly returned to his exploring and was getting more anxious with each step. "There should be a small stream, and there it is." He was talking to himself as he recovered his memories, trying to walk through everything he did back then. "Next there should be an old broken down retention wall with a pipe. After I found that I climbed up the hill and there should be the field." It took Dylon a little longer to find his way than he thought it should. He started to question whether he remembered it correctly or not.

After a good thirty-five minutes of searching he finally found what he thought to be the spot. He figured the stream must have run around the entire park, judging from the time he started. He found his way up the small path near the embankment with the drain pipe. Sure enough this was the field, but there was already somebody else here, standing at the other side of the field. The person started walking toward Dylon.

Dylon brushed himself off and started walking to meet the other person, thinking to himself on the way, "The guy probably thinks I'm some kind of freak, hanging out in the woods. Jeez, I can hear it now. I better think of something to say." As the guy approached him, Dylon extended his hand. "Hi, I'm Dylon Rosier."

"Well, that answers that question. I'm Kevin Felderson." He reached out and shook Dylon's hand. "Well, now that I know who you are, the only question left is, what were you doing down there?"

Dylon stumbled around looking for an answer. "Just trying to find my way back..." He paused for a minute as he looked around the field. "...back to here."

Kevin gave Dylon an odd look. "So were you lost?" He asked, as he watched Dylon check out the field like he just found the end of a rainbow.

"Not exactly," Dylon said as he was processing his memories. Then Dylon had a chance to turn the tables on Kevin. "So tell me Kevin, what are you doing so far away from the group?"

It was Kevin that was now in the hot seat. "Oh, just always thought this part of the park was such a wasted area. I found it when I was a kid, just kept coming back after that night. Wondering if....well, just wondering I guess."

Dylon gave him a funny look, then it hit him. "You! You're the one that called me a weirdo."

"That was you?" Kevin laughed as he felt a big wave of relief come over himself.

"So did you ever see it again?"

"No, I thought I did once but it was too foggy to really tell. So,...Dylon Rosier? You did some good work on those drawings. It's nice to actually thank you in person."

Dylon accepted the compliments and went straight back to the UFO conversation. "So did that night change all your perceptions about everything or what? I know it did mine. I'm always looking to see something. I've built one, you know." Dylon felt like he found a long lost friend and Kevin felt the same.

"You've built one? Does it fly? And yes, it did change everything. How big is it, airplane sized?"

The two hit it off really well and spent almost an hour talking about everything. Kevin had question after question about the UFO Dylon had built and even though he found out it was just an oversize toy he was still interested. "So where is it, can I see it?"

"Sure, you can see it. It's in Peru, at *the estate*."

Kevin looked at Dylon. "You mean as in the Peru in South America?"

Dylon shook his head. "Yeah, you should come, unless you already have plans. Do you have plans for the weekend?"

Kevin stuttered. "Well, no, I don't have plans, but..."

"But what? I'll have the driver pick up your

things. There's a small group of us going, you should come along."

Kevin thought for a minute. "What the hell, why not? I'm just going back to the hotel room and then back home to an empty house. Sure, count me in."

"Great, let me just get in touch with Jose." As Dylon pulled out his phone he noticed the time. "Oh shit. We have to get to the fountain." They started to make their way back to the center of the park. Before he could dial Jose, Dylon's phone rang. It was Kat. "Hey Dylon, Jose just picked us up from the airport. Our flight was delayed a little. We are heading straight to the house."

"Hey sis, glad you made it. Can I have you make a quick stop?"

"Sure thing, what's up?"

"Oh, I just recruited another person for the trip. I just need Jose to pick up his things from his hotel room." Dylon said as he looked to Kevin to make sure it was okay. Kevin nodded and took out his phone to make the arrangements with the hotel.

When they reached the fountain they had all the arrangements in place. Rosie hadn't made it back yet. Dylon was anxious to get on his way and started searching the crowd for her, but she slipped up unnoticed.

"Well Mr. Felderson, how have you been?" Rosie

greeted Kevin with a big hug.

"Rosie, now how many times do I have to tell you to call me Kevin? I'm doing great, and how about you?" Kevin released the hug and held Rosie's arms out. "Wow, you look just as good as the last time I saw you."

She slapped him on the arm. "And you're just as big a flirt as ever."

Dylon just watched the two of them, enjoying their friendship. Kevin turned Rosie to Dylon. "I just want to thank you for turning this young man on to my latest project."

Rosie gave Kevin a friendly nudge. "You need to stop."

"What? Rosie, everyone knows you're actually the one that keeps that place running. Dylon, tell her I'm right."

"He's got you on that one, Rosie. We all know it."

"Okay, whatever. Kevin, did Dylon tell you we were going to South America."

"Of course he did, but he never said what we were going to do for four days in the middle of nowhere," Kevin said, then he and Rosie just looked at Dylon.

"Oops, I'm sorry guys. Well, it's *the estate,* it's a mini vacation. It's not in the city, and it's some place different, some place you haven't been before. Shall we get on our way?" Dylon led the way to the parking lot.

When they reached Dylon's car, Kevin opened the door for Rosie. "I'm right over there, so I'll be behind you in a second."

It didn't take long to get to the house, where Kat and Marcus were already waiting. As they pulled up behind the van, Dylon noticed Kat was nowhere to be seen. "She must be out back in the garden," he thought to himself, as he stopped the car and reached for the button to pop the trunk. Jose was at the trunk transferring luggage before anyone even opened their doors.

"Jose, do you know where Kat is?" Dylon said as he exited the car.

"Ms. Elizabeth went inside for a moment, Mr. Dylon."

"Oh God, thanks for the reminder Jose. I just have to keep remembering that. Elizabeth, Elizabeth...." Dylon repeated her name at least four or five times trying to break himself from her nickname. As he made his way up the steps, Elizabeth and Marcus came out the front door. They heard Dylon repeating Elizabeth's name and she couldn't help herself giving Dylon a hard time. "That's very good brother, now can you say M-a-r-c-u-s?" She sounded it out nice and slow for him.

They both laughed and gave each other a big hug, before Dylon turned to shake Marcus' hand. "Come on I'll introduce you to everybody." Dylon said as he led them down the steps. "Everyone, I would like you to meet my sister, Ka.. I mean Elizabeth." Kat stepped forward to shake Rosie's hand first, making sure that when she did that she stepped squarely on Dylon's foot. Of course, she didn't even give him a second glance, and continued shaking hands with the rest of the group, as they each introduced themselves. Dylon knew that it would be best for him to just take his medicine and not say a word.

After everybody introduced themselves, they loaded into the van and were off to the airstrip. It was a small privately owned strip, mostly for private crafts and just a handful of corporate jets. On there way to meet the jet, Dylon found an opportunity while the others were talking to grab Kat's attention. He mouthed to her. "Did you bring it?"

She just looked at him like she couldn't understand what he was saying. Before Dylon got a chance to repeat it, the opportunity slipped away, and Kat was dragged back into the group's conversation.

# Chapter 10

When they got to the jet, the pilot met them at the bottom of the steps. "So how many are we short on this trip, Mr. Rosier?"

This question was not out of the ordinary for Dylon, for any time he scheduled a group flight, the number of guests was always ten. Even though there were normally no more than six, ten was the magic number, just in case there was a last minute invite.

"Oh, I think we're only missing five this time, Captain Todd." Dylon said, as he walked up the steps behind Rosie, just for safety's sake. Kat stayed at the back of the group and let everyone else board the jet. When it came to her turn, she stopped to chat with the Captain. "Hi Todd, it's nice to see you."

"Well, Elizabeth, it has been too long. And how is school?"

"School is great, thank you for asking. By the way, did Jose send his brother over with a package for me?"

Captain Todd motioned to a closed door, just inside the jet. "Gave me strict instructions, not to let anyone see it until you arrived. I'll make sure I unlock the door when we board."

"Those boys are good. I don't know what we'd do without them." Kat smiled and took the hand Todd offered to help her up the steps. When she stepped into the cabin, she noticed Marcus and Dylon were scoping out the slim line refrigerator. Kevin was checking out the woodwork on the jet, he refurbished this one about four or five years ago. Rosie was looking for the most comfortable window seat she could find, seeing how they were going to be in the air for close to eight hours.

Within a couple of minutes, the captain stepped into the cabin to make sure everybody was comfortable and found everything they needed to be satisfactory. He gave them a brief rundown of the two small weather fronts, they might be flying through, but was fairly confident that they would break up before the plane even reached them. When he covered all the small stuff, he aimed a remote at the TV to turn it on. He let the group know after a five minute safety clip, it would automatically switch to the normal satellite stations. The captain then returned to the cockpit to ready the plane for takeoff.

Once the plane was in the air and they got the okay to move around, Dylon was up and heading to the fridge. "Anyone for a sandwich? We have turkey, ham, and roast beef." Kevin and Marcus weren't far behind him.

As a matter of fact, Marcus had already found the bread and Kevin was scrounging for some plates and napkins. Dylon was becoming more relaxed with the group and had forgotten his promise to his sister. "Hey Kat, you and Rosie want a sandwich?" No sooner than the words came out of his mouth, did Dylon realize what he just said. "Did she catch it?" He looked at Kat and realized she was deep in conversation with Rosie.

Marcus was watching what just unfolded and figured it would be better to stay out of this sibling matter. Kevin was oblivious to the whole thing, so he asked in a little louder voice, thinking they just didn't hear Dylon. "Would you girls like a sandwich?"

"Why Kevin, I haven't been called a girl in ages. Are you flirting again?" Rosie said and she gave him a nudge. As they stepped up to the table Elizabeth had to get a dig in, just to let Dylon know that she did hear him. "Thank you, Kevin. It's so nice of you to offer, too bad my brother doesn't have a little better manners." She shot him a look, and he knew very well, he wouldn't get another chance, or warning.

Rosie did step in for Dylon's defense. "I'm sure he was just wrapped up in making the best sandwich he could for his guests." Elizabeth agreed. "You're right Rosie, I probably shouldn't be so hard on him, but after all, isn't that what big brothers are for?" She walked around behind him and gave him a monkey bite.

Dylon stood there and only flinched a little, as Kat took two fingers and gave him a small pinch on the inside of his triceps. He was very lucky that was all he got. She usually picked up the closest thing she could and threw it at him.

After they finished their sandwiches, the boys settled in front of the TV, and were surfing the channels looking for something interesting to watch. The girls cleaned up the small kitchen area and talked a little more. "That brother of yours is something very special and talented." Rosie said. "And I hear your quite the talented young lady yourself."

"Oh Rosie, I'm not all that. I'm basically Dylon's mechanic. He sends me his projects/ideas, and I make them work better."

"I've heard about your schooling feat, and that my dear, is something to be very proud of." Rosie quickly commented to Kat. "Elizabeth, have you ever seen anything like what Dylon saw?"

"Rosie, I wish I could be that lucky. All I've ever seen is the projects Dylon sends me, but it must have been a profound experience. I mean look at him, he questions everything and does not accept conventional physics. Do you know he failed physics? How does someone continue to have that kind of drive, when he is told that what he wants to do is impossible?"

"I don't know?" Rosie replied. "But you're right, it must have been quite an experience."

"Would you help me set something up Rosie? It's a surprise for Dylon. Just head to the front of the plane, like you're going to the bathroom and I'll be behind you in a minute." Rosie followed her instructions and Kat was behind her in no time. As the girls passed by the boys looked up, and as they watched the two heading towards the bathroom they all exchanged glances. "Why do girls have to go to the bathroom with each other?" Marcus was the first one to ask the question out loud. He got his answer from the other two in unison. "Because they do." Kevin and Dylon replied.

A few minutes later, Kat peeked around the corner to see how preoccupied the boys were. She motioned the all clear for Rosie to head to the kitchen, which she did unnoticed. A moment later Kat did the same, but she caught the boys attention. She did not reveal what she was carrying under the colorful piece of fabric, but did pique their curiosity, which Rosie noticed. When the boys started to ask what they were doing, Rosie's mind had already been working up a plan to discourage their interest. She quickly grabbed a magazine, folded it open, and started walking toward Kat. "Here it is Elizabeth, I told you that color would match up with this perfectly." Sure enough, the boys all turned back to the TV.

Kat looked at Rosie in disbelief, who simply stated. "What? It worked." Kat just smiled and shook her head. "You're right, it did." When they finished setting everything out, Kat placed a binder next to everything and placed a remote on top of the binder.

Kat wanted to get Dylon to the kitchen without telling him why, so she quickly thought of a way to accomplish this. She nudged Rosie and gave her a quick wink. Then as she was opening the pint of ice cream she just pulled from the freezer. In an angry voice she started giving Dylon a reprimand. "Dylon Rosier, I cannot believe you didn't have any ice cream stocked for such a long flight. That's strike two, mister. One more and you better start ducking."

Knowing that there was a good possibility that Kat would actually throw something at him, Dylon jumped up from his seat. "Oh my God sis, I did get ice cream, all you have to do…." He stopped in mid-sentence, when he realized what Kat had set up. Then he also noticed the pint of ice cream in her hand. "Why you little witch, I thought you didn't bring it. This is just awesome, thank you thank you thank you!"

Kat and Rosie were both just standing there smiling. By this time, Kevin and Marcus had gotten up to see what was going on. Dylon looked at everything she had set out and noticed there were a few items that he hadn't sent her plans for. Kat noticed the look of curiosity on Dylon's face and urged him to use the remote first and ask questions later. Dylon did as he was told and pressed the green button on the remote. When he did, Kevin and Rosie just stared in amazement. Marcus, on the other hand, had already seen it, while Kat was building it, or rather rebuilding it.

What looked like a child's attempt at building a pyramid with only half of the parts needed slowly started to open up. The two opposing corners started extending away from the center. After a slight delay, the other two corners did the same. When they were about two thirds of the way to being completely extended, the center started to rise up. After the center which was basically the top half of the pyramid, reached full extension, the four corners of the base simultaneously started retracting. Once the base of the pyramid was completely formed, with all the edges closed to make a smooth surface, the top started its descent. When the top came to rest on the base and Dylon thought everything was complete, he started to say something. Kat, knowing that he would, stopped him before he got a word out. "It's not finished."

She pointed at the acrylic pyramid, and as they all

looked, they could see the inner workings of it moving. The hydroponics pans slowly lowered into place, and what appeared to be gutters lined up to empty into the pans. This time Dylon didn't speak until the last sign of movement was made, from the transformable agripod. "Elizabeth, you have completely outdone yourself this time. This is just incredible, and what are all these other things?"

Kat smiled and placed her arm around Marcus. "Well thank you, but I can't take all of the credit. I did have Marcus help me out with some of this." She started out explaining the object closest to her. "This little eight-wheeled flatbed is your pod mover. The one next to it, the one with the dual mirrors, is your solar reflector. It has one function, but two purposes. You can use it to direct sunlight for either a heat source, or to boost your energy source." Kat stopped for a minute while Dylon inspected each vehicle. When he was finished and placed them back, she continued. "Now the next one is kind of familiar, your excavator. The only reason I put that one in there is to unload the corridor transport, which is that one over there. It's the one that looks like an underground storage tank with wheels. Of course I'm sure you will be able to find some other uses for the excavator, but that's the only reason I need it. Now all of this stuff can be made as big as you want, but I have in the binder the minimum specs for them. Everything is solar powered to start off, but you will also find in your binder some speculative plans for a collapsible wind-powered device."

Dylon could hardly contain his excitement, but before he got a chance to say anything, Rosie spoke. "Good grief, I thought this whole space-Mars obsession was all Dylons." The two of them laughed, "It's not an obsession, well not really, okay it's an obsession." Dylon responded. "But it is a very good possibility, and seeing how it's a private sector operation, we could do it in less time and the cost would be cut in half, if not more than any government agency could do it."

Kevin, being the only one who didn't have even the slightest bit of information, that the others were privy to, had a multitude of questions. "So what exactly is all this? Are you seriously planning on putting a complex on Mars?"

That's all that had to be asked to get Dylon started. "Well yes, and to start out this is the Agripod, and obviously it's collapsible, for easier transport. It could, in theory, also be used as a basis for any early habitat structure to be built on Mars. I designed it to start an array of tests and studies on the development of agriculture on Mars. And of course, if we're going to be up there we'll also need to produce our own food supply. Then there is also the prospect of seeding the planet, to begin the whole terraforming and atmosphere building process."

Kevin's interest was starting to pique. "But I thought it was too cold to do anything on Mars. And besides, I thought they had some kind of balloon type structure they were testing in the arctic or some other remote area."

Dylon was always very careful not to put down someone's ideas, so he carefully chose his words. "Well, they do have a structure that is in the trial stages. I would just feel safer in my structure. As far as how cold it is on Mars, did you know the surface temperature is actually about eighty degrees in the summer? So if you were to put a greenhouse-type structure up there, you could create an environment where plant life might survive."

Kevin did not want to sound disapproving with his next question. "Don't get me wrong, I think what you want to do is great, but you're planning to do all this on a *might work* plan?"

Dylon smiled and looked Kevin square in the eyes. "Why not? Columbus discovered the New World on the premises that the world *might* not be flat."

Kevin searched Dylon's eyes for any doubt in what he was talking about, and found none. "Okay man, I just wanted to make sure I was on the same page."

Kevin wasn't the only one with questions. Marcus was ready to hit him up with one. "So what about the lack of water? How are you going to get water to Mars? Isn't that a lot of weight to carry?"

"I've got this one." Kat interjected. "We don't have to take water, we'll take hydrogen. If we release the correct amount of hydrogen into the pyramid, the agri-pod, then nature should run its course, and we should end up with condensation. You with me so far, hon?" Kat asked Marcus. "Okay, remember when I told you Dylon should go with a ridged panel, at least on the inside? Well, once the condensation forms it should, in theory, ride the ridge until gravity takes over and it falls into the hydroponic trays below. The trays, which will start out being filled with the gelatin crystals, will soak up the moisture and turn into the gel we need to grow plants. Now there will only be two pods producing plants/food, and the other two will be strictly for water production, which of course means we will need a little more hydrogen for those two."

Rosie had to say something. "Dylon, is there anything a little harder to drink on this bird? This is a little too much information to digest all at once. I really need to slow down the thinking process a little." As the night carried on so did the questions. One by one the group each found their own spot and drifted off to sleep.

Sometime during the last leg of the flight, the plane hit a little turbulance. Rosie was immediately awakened. As she looked around, everyone else just stirred a little, readjusted, and resumed sleeping. She looked out the window and couldn't believe her eyes. She even held up the magazine, to block any light, that might be reflecting from the inside of the plane, onto the window. She leaned closer to the window to get a closer look, but in the instant she took her eyes away from the window, it was gone. "Shit, now I'm seeing things." she muttered before going back to sleep.

# Chapter 11
## Special Ops Watchdog
### S.O.W.

The commander was really pushing the schedule tonight. "Damn it, I can't believe this. We've never run a mission so close. I would really like to know who was asleep on this one. Jones, the occupants we're setting up for should be about forty five minutes behind us. How are we doing on time?"

"Drop zone E.T.A. twelve minutes sir."

"S.O.W. zero four breaking left, S.O.W. zero three breaking right." The last two CH-53E helicopters in the formation called in their maneuvers as they broke formation. Inside one of the remaining two helicopters the commanding officer began speaking.

"Alright men, listen up. We are not here to engage anyone. Set your monitoring devices as close as possible and meet at your rendezvous points. This is a very remote area and the occupants seem to stay within the perimeter of the estate, so you shouldn't have any problems along the way. There is the possibility of running into local villagers that trade with the estate, so by all means do not traverse anything that looks like it might be a regular path. Our objective here is to get in and get out without being seen. So lay low during the day and hustle to the pick-up point during the night. Alright ladies let's get ready."

The men all started double checking their gear, to make sure everything was in order. Each of the four groups of three would be dropped with a small crate. The crate contained several surveillance cameras with remote capabilities and high zoom lenses, rechargeable batteries, wire, and a small solar panel for each camera. The cameras were to be aimed at specific areas carefully selected from the satellite survey of the estate.

Truth be known, the U.S. government had been periodically monitoring the estate. The estate had been seized in a joint drug operation between the U.S. government and Peruvian government. After numerous failed attempts by the Peruvian Government to sell it, they turned it over to the U.S. to sell it. The only stipulation the United States made, was that it was to be continuously monitored, just to make sure both countries were not letting it fall back into the wrong hands.

With all of the building and upgrades that had been going on over the past five years or so, both governments were kind of leery. When the new hangar was built and the runway and tower were upgraded, their curiosity was piqued a bit more. The straw that broke the camel's back were the reports that the owners of the estate purchased a retired cargo plane and were rebuilding it. This is what brought about 'Operation Watchdog'.

\* \* \* \* \* \*

"Seven minutes till drop zone sir. What the hell… Sir did you see that?" Jones watched the object fly past them with an incredible speed. Then off in the distance it appeared to stop, jut around a little, then just as fast as it stopped, it shot off to the west and was gone.

The next thing that happened surprised them as much as the object that just flew past them. The sound of an incoming text message alerted. 'Warning of unidentified aircraft in your airspace. Do not engage. Tactical maneuvers in place. Do not respond, do not break radio silence. Report immediately to debriefing upon completing first leg of mission.'

After reading the message the commander spoke. "I didn't see anything soldier. I see that we are on a special operation and that we have a deadline to meet. I also see that if we spend too much time stargazing that we won't meet that deadline. So tell me Jones, what is it that you wanted me to see?"

Jones had been serving for two terms now and had a little experience under his belt and understood completely what was being said. He also knew that there would probably be other traffic in pursuit. "Altitude, Sir. We could probably lose a few hundred feet and not jeopardize anything. That is, just in case we're in a flight path of….um…. anything else, that we might not want to be in the flight path of….Sir."

"Good thinking, Jones, two hundred feet should be enough." The commander quickly turned his attention back to the special ops drop teams. "Alright men, you're gonna have a little less time to deploy your chutes, so do some quick recalculations, and let's get ready to go."

At just about the time they finished their descent two jets flew over them and banked hard to the right. Apparently the unidentified craft changed course. Within seconds another text alert came across. 'Craft should be out of your area. Remain alert. Maintain radio silence.'

"E.T.A. five minutes sir."

"Alright men you heard him, let's get your supply crate ready. Has the timer been reset for the chute deployment?"

"Yes sir." The men shuffled themselves around to drop position. Two of the men would drop out of the left side of the chopper and the other man would drop out of the right side after dropping the supply crate. The co-pilot would signal the other crew when the first team had dropped via green laser light.

"What are your orders, soldier?" The commander barked.

"Drop and place equipment, sir, move to meet west team and then move to meet east and south teams at rendezvous point, sir, all done at approximately forty eight hours from now, sir."

"And what is your code for pick up soldier?"

"Good boy, stay." the team leader responded, "in text format only, sir, only sent once, sir."

"And what do you do then soldier?"

The team leader looked at his team and looked back at the commander. A bead of sweat started to form on the soldier's forehead. His mind was racing 'Shit, what did I miss', he thought as he was going over everything in his head. He glanced at the commander again, who was fighting back a smile.

Finally the commander chuckled a little, letting the soldier off the hook.

"You do just what your message said. You *stay*, you be a *good boy* and *stay*."

The soldier smiled and acknowledged. "Yes, sir"

"Alright, we've wasted enough time, let's do this." The commander reached for a corner of the crate. The team leader quickly hit the timer for the chute and they gave it a quick shove. He turned back to face the commander and gave him a quick salute and was out the door himself.

The next teams to drop would be the east and west teams, simultaneously, then the south team. The time it would take to set up the surveillance equipment would be the shortest part of the mission. Most of the mission time would be spent on reaching the rendezvous point without being noticed. The mission planners wanted the pick-up point to be as far away from the estate as possible, without putting the teams or the mission, in any danger of being picked up by the extensive surveillance system that was in place there.

After the last team was dropped the commander spoke to Jones. "Let's get these birds to the nest so we can get this debriefing crap over with." The debriefing part was the worst thing to deal with when confronted with an anomaly. Otherwise, it was actually kind of like end of day paperwork.

* * * * * *

"Lieutenant Vasquez, I've been expecting your call. I just got word that the first part of the mission is under way. I know you're not quite up to our technological capabilities, but I thought I would let you know, our escort jets picked up an unidentified craft that seemed to hover over the target site momentarily. Just thought that might be of interest to you, in case you need to come up with an explanation for whoever might report something like that. Oh wait, I just remembered, all those little villages don't have phones do they?"

Lt. Vasquez despised the fact that he had to deal with the caliber of person that Mr. Kolminski turned out to be. "Thank you, for the update."

"So, do you have that file on Pasco, or whatever his name is? You know, your…um…agent….um that you plan on using to infiltrate the estate."

Lt. Vasquez had just about enough of this little weasel's condescending manner. "Yes, Senor Knobbobski"

"That's Kolminski!" He interjected very defensively.

"Oh, exscuz me. Forgive me, my engles, it's not so good. So why for you need this, eh, file on Paschel? I no completely understand." Lt. Vasquez could speak perfect English, this was the best way he could verbally insult Kolminski's intelligence.

Kolminski, played right into Lt. Vasquez' hand. "Listen closely Lieutenant, all you need to understand is this, if I don't get that file General Grant will be giving you a call."

"Oh, that would be great. Could I talk to him now?" Lt. Vasquez was anxious to talk to someone who actually had a little more experience under his belt.

"No! You can't talk to him. He has been in meetings all day, and with this unidentified craft popping into the picture, I don't know when he will be available. Just send me the file….comprende."

"I no intend to offend you. I will send the file, okay. Could you have Gen. Grant call me when he become available?" Lt. Vasquez, just shook his head. He knew he would probably not hear from Gen. Grant.

"Sure, as soon as I get the file, I'll pass the message along." Kolminski quickly responded.

"Is this line….how do you say….secure? I keep hearing a clicking noise, do you have a safe connection?" The Lt. said, basically just to annoy Kolminski.

"Well it is on my end….I don't know what you have going on down there on your end," Kolminski snidely responded.

Lt. Vasquez glanced over at Paschel, who just happened to be sitting in on the call. "Okay senor, I send it now." Paschel waited to hear the phone click before he spoke.

"What a dick."

Lt. Vasquez gave him a look. "We must be

respectful, Paschel. They have shared some technology with us. This is all for the advancement of our country. We can learn a lot from the Americans, whether they realize it or not. You just be careful and keep a watchful eye, I don't trust this Kolminski fellow."

"And what about the Rosiers, sir?"

"Oh, I don't think the Rosiers are doing anything more than building their own village. I will be surprised if you find that they are doing anything wrong. Did I ever tell you Mrs. Rosier saved my nephew's life? There was a Cholera outbreak in several of the villages near Cusco, not long after they bought *the estate*. Mr. and Mrs. Rosier set up a small clinic in the village. If it wasn't for them and that clinic, my nephew would have died. They have done many good things for our people. I do not agree with the American government that they need to be continuously watched, but it was part of the arrangement which was made. My hands are tied. I just thought it might be useful for you to know that, Paschel. Be mindful of who you are actually watching. I will have complete instructions of your mission in a few days. Now go enjoy your family before you go undercover."

# Chapter 12

"Dylon, Dylon, did you see it? Wake up Dylon, come on, wake up! Dylon, hurry, we have to go see." Reese was happy to see Dylon, but that feeling was abated by the fact that he saw something in the sky the night before. Reese started rushing around the room, gathering Dylon's clothes. He piled them on the bed, and grabbed Dylon by the hand. "Come on, hurry. Let's go check the film."

It was not out of the ordinary for Reese to wake Dylon, when he was at *the estate.* Dylon actually welcomed the energy and the excitement that Reese displayed. Being reminded of the vigor and curiosity of a child was refreshing. It seemed, though, this day was earlier than normal. As Dylon slipped on his day old jeans, he listened to hear if anyone else was stirring.

As he watched Reese scurrying around the room, gathering up Dylon's things, he was thinking to himself. "I wonder what time it is?" He found his watch in the next pile of items that Reese placed on the foot of the bed. "Oh my God, it's not even five yet. How late were you up, buddy?" He noticed that the boy didn't hear a word he said. "It's good to see you

Reese." Still no response from the child, who was halfway under the bed, digging out a shoe. This really got Dylon's mind turning.

"So, what did you see last night, Reese?" That was all it took. Reese was so excited, he could hardly form a full sentence. "I was waiting for you in the tower with daddy, and we waited forever, until daddy got tired and went to bed, and I stayed with Humberto, and then I saw your lights, but they weren't your lights cause they were going really really fast, and they went all the way to the end of the runway, even past it, and they stopped and came back and flew really fast past the house and stopped again, and then they went over to where we fly the saucer and stopped, and Humberto shined the spotlight on it and it went straight up and then it was gone, and I was really happy and I wanted to go look at it last night, on the film. Humberto told me to wait for you, and I tried real hard to stay awake, waiting for you so we could go see it. But I couldn't, and I fell asleep. So can we please go see it now? Can we go see the film? I got you a Mountain Dew and a muffin. Please, can we go see?"

Dylon's curiosity was starting to pique, he looked at Reese, and it was as if the boy read his mind. "I'll be downstairs," Reese said with excitement and ran out of the room. Dylon finished up his morning routine and was downstairs in no time. When he stepped out the front door, Reese was sitting in the *Mule,* waiting patiently.

Dylon hopped in the driver's seat, grabbed the *Mountain Dew* and as he was opening it, noticed Reese had one sitting in front of him. It wasn't opened yet, but he knew why it was there. "Does your mom know you have that? Never mind that, do you really think you need that this morning, as wired as you are?" Reese just hung his head and reached for the bottle of water, he had also brought out, just in case.

"I'll tell you what bud, you can have it if you promise to just drink half of it." Reese immediately grabbed the soda. Anything he could do to be like Dylon, he would. He looked to Dylon like an older brother and Dylon knew this and welcomed it. It was a nice feeling, to know he was helping this child grow up in a positive environment. The thought of helping him learn all he could, without pushing him to get into a set path of training was a wonderful feeling.

It wasn't long before they were pulling up to the observatory, which was broken into four separate areas. The main part of the building housed the telescope. The other three buildings, connected by a simple breezeway, consisted of the Mars complex room, which was basically an ever changing model room. Next came the studies room, which was one-half classroom and the one-half work room with larger tables. Then the computer room, where they were headed. This room consisted of several larger computers that processed all the incoming data from the *Vision Scope* program.

As Dylon opened the door, Reese bolted inside. "I told you, see I told you," he exclaimed, pointing to the flashing light on the wall, which signaled significant movement in the skies the night before. Dylon sat down at the computer and typed in his password for the program which he had custom built. It was designed to monitor any moving objects in the night skies and differentiate the regular objects, planes and helicopters, from the unknowns, based on speed, flight patterns, altitudes, and trajectories. When it pegged an object as unknown, it would automatically direct any or all of the fifteen cameras linked to the program, to focus on the object.

Dylon looked at Reese, who was doing everything he could to get the best vantage point for his size. "Hey buddy, why don't you take my seat."

"Really?"

"Really, after all you saw it. Show me what you've learned while I've been gone. You have been checking the film, haven't you?"

Reese was ecstatic. He was very proud that Dylon entrusted him with the task of checking for sighted objects. "Yes sir. We've had seven small

meteors and three unknowns, all logged and filed."
Reese looked at the clock just below the flashing light,
which was showing the time the light started flashing.
He turned his attention back to the computer and
started searching for the time designated. "I've got it,
but I don't know how to do all that stuff you do. You
know, the stopping it and saving it and all that."

Dylon was very impressed with Reese's progress.
"Just stay right there and I'll walk you through it. You
will want to pause it when you see a shot you really
want to get a better look at. Once you pause it, record
your running number. You with me so far?"

Reese nodded. "I've watched you do that part,
but I don't know what to do with all the numbers
when you're done. You know, how do you bring them
up, when you get all of them you want?"

Dylon found himself wondering how much
information this kid's mind could hold. "So you have
been paying attention. When you get all the numbers
you want written down, you hit control 'Q'."

"Why 'Q'? I mean, what does it stand for?"

"Well Reese, it stands for query, which basically
means question."

Reese gave him a puzzled look. "So, why don't
they just say question?"

"It has a little more meaning than just the word
question. I guess that's why they use it." Dylon said as

he focused on the screen, trying to figure out what Reese saw last night. As he was watching the screen the phone rang. He looked at Reese and said, "I think the others must be awake." he stepped over to the next desk and picked up the receiver.

"Good morning sis, we're at the observatory. Okay, we'll be there in a few minutes." Reese paused the program and Dylon noticed what Reese had seen. Wanting to get a better look he asked Kat to meet them at the observatory. "On second thought could you bring some to us? Sausage on toast will be fine, thanks, sis. Yeah, apparently we had a visitor last night. You have to see it, we're working on it now."

\* \* \* \* \* \*

Elizabeth and the rest of the group finished up breakfast and started getting ready to head to the observatory. As they all met at the front door, Elizabeth was making sure all the ATV's had helmets with them and checking to see if everyone was comfortable driving them. "They are all automatic, so you won't have to worry about changing gears or anything. Your throttle is on the right handle and your brakes are…" Kat's words were cut off by Kevin and Marcus who were revving their engines for all they were worth. Caught up in being boys again they just couldn't help themselves. Kat raised her voice.

"Apparently we're starting our tour at the observatory."

"So, how do we get there?" Kevin shouted.

"Take the first fork to the right." The boys were off as soon as the last word crossed her lips. Kat leaned towards Rosie and slyly said, "We'll take the second fork. The first one leads straight through a mud bog. The way they're driving they won't be able to miss it." Rosie just laughed out loud. "I'm beginning to like you more and more." They put their helmets on and raced off to beat the boys to the observatory.

When the boys finally made it, they were covered head to toe in muck. They were greeted by Rosie and Elizabeth, holding towels and grinning from ear to ear. They could hardly contain their laughter.

"Ha, ha, ha….that was a real good one, Elizabeth." Marcus said with a sarcastic tone as he was walking up to get his towel. When he got within a couple of steps from her, he lunged toward her, grabbing her around the waist he picked her up, trying to get her as dirty as he was. He didn't have to try to hard, just her trying to release his hold was enough to get her as dirty as he was. As Kevin was walking up to get his towel from Rosie, she just looked at him. Trying to read his eyes, she wasn't sure what he was going to do. "Don't you even think about it mister. I was an innocent bystander." She threw the towel at him and ducked into the first door she came to.

Dylon heard the ruckus the others were making as they arrived and tried to hurry Reese. "You almost done there kiddo?"

"Almost." He said as he was writing down his last set of numbers.

Dylon leaned over Reese's shoulder and noticed two red dots on the monitor, but he couldn't see much more than that. Before he could really get sucked into focusing all of his attention on this, his train of thought was interrupted by Kat's voice.

"Hey, space boy! Are you going to help explain this stuff to our guests, or are you going to make me stumble all the way through it by myself? This is your sales pitch, you know."

"Give me just a second, K…. I mean Elizabeth." Dylon turned to Reese, "What do you want to do? Do you want to work on these pictures or do you want to hang with us?"

Reese looked at Dylon like he had lost his mind, who read the look with exact precision. "Who am I kidding? I don't want to go either, let me give you a crash course." Dylon jotted down the next steps for Reese to finish working on the pictures. In addition to that he wrote down one last set of numbers for the frame containing the red dots. "There you go, that should help you get finished with your pictures. This last one, you might be able to do something with, but I will probably have to use the infrared filter on it."

# Chapter 13

When Dylon entered the Mars Complex room, Kat had already started explaining how everything was laid out. The complex was quite extensive, but she had already finished explaining the Agripods and the water filtration system. She had also explained that the first two sectors of the complex would be finished within six months to a year, leaning closer to the six month period and the importance of the equal distancing between all of the complexes for future building plans.

"All together there will be four sectors in this complex, and for the first year the living quarters will be kind of cramped. With the addition of the next two sectors, which will contain four pods each, we will be able to move the labs and make the living quarters more accommodating. Any longer than that and cabin fever will start setting in, and we all know what that will do to a group of people that cannot escape from each other."

As she finished explaining the complex, Dylon couldn't help but be proud of his sister. "Very good, Elizabeth, I couldn't have explained it better myself. Thank you for all your hard work in helping me out with all of this." Dylon said as he stepped up next to her. "Truth be known, guys and girls, this originally started out as a dream. But in all actuality, with the way things are in the world today, we're running out of room and time. The way the current space program is heading, well, it just seems like we're going backwards. If someone in the private sector doesn't step up and take a swing,….Well it just doesn't look like we're going to have a lot of room to move. We'll eventually destroy the planet and die out in the process."

Dylon continued. "NASA has scaled back all of their 'publicly known' plans for space exploration and taking a very cautious approach for future plans in this area. It doesn't seem like they want to even try some of the new propulsion systems that are being developed now. With the shuttle disasters they've had in the past, it seems like they don't want to put themselves out there for any more failures. What they don't seem to understand is that there are everyday ordinary people that are willing to put their lives on the line, for the advancement of our society and for the advancement of our understanding of our place in the universe. Columbus did not accept the conventional thoughts that the world was flat, he refused to accept it. Thank God he did, otherwise who knows where we would be."

The more Dylon talked, the more you could see the passion he had about his belief in the success of his ventures. "We are all natural born explorers and we are becoming stagnant by not pushing ourselves to do that simple thing. Guys, that is one of the reasons why we need to take these steps. It is also the driving force behind all of my dreams and expectations. It is the reason I've worked so hard on building up this estate the way I have." Dylon reached under the lip of the domed oval table and found the button to switch the hologram to the overlay of the future plans of *the estate*. "This is the future look of Rosier Enterprises' newest division. Rosier Enterprises Space Exploration-R.E.S.E. We'll build our foundation on the basis of launching satellites for third world countries, bringing them into the twenty first century. Out of all the telecommunications and defense satellites we launch, we can piggyback on these satellites the pods and any other supplies we may need for the Mars Complex. Of course all of this is speculative on how many customers we can acquire, but with the rate that technology is moving…. I don't think this will be a problem."

Kevin and Rosie both started to speak at the same time.

"How…"

"I'm sorry Kevin..go ahead…. but I think we

have the same question."

Kevin thanked Rosie and continued. "How are you going to convince your grandfather to go along with this?"

"Well, Kevin, I did think about that, and honestly I have enough, or we, Elizabeth and I have enough to do this without the backing of my grandfather. It will leave us completely broke if it doesn't work, but we have enough to get us there, to get it started. If that's all we accomplish, at least it's a start, and look at what we will have accomplished. I don't know how land claims would work for another planet. I don't know anything about where we're heading with this plan. What I do know is that we are heading somewhere. And I also know that we will take every measure we can to not disrupt another life form, if we find one, but according to all known records, Mars is a lifeless planet. It has a lot of possibilities, but lifeless. I just think with all the resources and information we have that we need to do something. If we don't someone else will, maybe not today, but soon."

Dylon paused for a moment, and watched everyone digest this information. "So what do you say, do you want to see the progress?" They all looked around at each other. Rosie spoke first. "Well, I didn't come down here to be stuck in a room all day. I could have stayed home and done that."

"Okay then, I need a minute and someone is going to have to give up a ride and we'll go check it all out." Dylon stepped out of the room to go check on Reese. He popped his head in the door and saw Reese working away on the computer. "You doing okay in here?"

"Yeah, I think I'm getting the hang of it."

"Okay, I have to show everybody around. I'm leaving you the Mule. Call me when you're done and I'll tell you where we are. Oh, and if you want you can bring the two crafts and remotes." Dylon knew he would see the toys later. Reese never passed on a chance to play with the saucers.

\* \* \* \* \* \*

Rosie and Kevin were the ones sharing the ATV, and were hanging back just a little.

"So what do you think of all of this?" Rosie asked, a little louder than normal, simply because she wasn't sure if they would have a chance to be alone again. Kevin just shrugged his shoulders. "He talks a good talk."

"Yeah he does, but is it feasible?"

"Columbus found America in a flat world, Rosie, anything is possible. It's the government interference that I'm worried about. Do you know how ruthless

126

they can be when it involves something that they might lose a little 'power' on?"

* * * * * *

Rosie was instantly taken back to her meeting with Colonel Maxwell Grant.

"Don't give me that shit you son of a bitch, this is my husband you're talking about. He would never put anyone in danger before himself. No! This all falls back on you and that fucking kid that you put in this mission to make yourself look better. If it wasn't for my husband that child would be dead too. You had no business putting him in there and you know it. You know what, so did my husband. No, he wasn't stupid. I have more information, placed in just the right hands, than you would care to know about. And if you think you can use your 'power and position' to do anything about it just try me, mister. You just fucking try me! You know what, I loved my husband and *I know the truth.* You do whatever you need to do. If you need my husband to be a scapegoat, God rest his soul, then you do it. Maybe it will at least ease the burden of guilt for that young man, but let me tell you something right now. There may come a day, God forbid, and when that day comes. If you do not come through.....well, may he have mercy on your soul…..because I won't!"

\* \* \* \* \* \*

"Yes Kevin, I know how the government can be." She responded as she thought to herself. "All to well."

"We better catch up with them before they start thinking the wrong thing." Kevin said as he pushed down a little more on the throttle. Rosie wrapped her arms around him tight and as she felt the speed pick up.

When they pulled up beside the rest of the group, they were at the foundation for the factory. Not your ordinary factory, though, this was where the components for the rockets/satellites would be assembled. It would be a completely sterile environment. Standing next to it, it looked to be a rather large area. As Kevin stepped over to Dylon he had to say something. "So, do you think you'll have enough space to work with?"

He smiled, knowing Kevin was being a little sarcastic, he responded. "There are three different parts to this structure. The building area, the sterilization area, and the staging area."

Kevin, being the owner of his own facility, really wanted to figure out how prepared Dylon was. This was as much of an interview process for him as it was for Dylon. "So where are you planning on receiving your supplies? And what about storage? Do you have a good security system? I mean, other than just the remoteness of *the estate* itself."

Dylon was relieved that Kevin was asking as many questions as he was. To him, it showed more interest on Kevins part than he was expecting. "Behind you there will be a duplicate building, as far as layout goes. This will be the receiving, storage, and an available section for whatever may come up. Security system is updated every three months, and the remoteness will not only help with the security factor, but also will give us a prime location for launching. It's not close to anything."

Kevin nodded his head as he looked everything over. "And what about your launch pad? Are going to be set up with everything you need for that?"

Dylon was really impressed with the questions that were being thrown out. "Actually there are two new reservoirs that have just been completed near the launch pad site. Would you like to go check it out?"

\* \* \* \* \* \*

Reese started gathering up the two saucers, the R.S. 12 and the M.S. 1, and was loading them on the Mule while the pictures were printing. "I don't need to call them, I know exactly where there heading." he said to himself. "I'll sneak up just close enough and buzz them with the R.S. 12. This is going to be so much fun."

When he got the last one tied down, he ran back inside to get the pictures that he left printing. He scrambled around checking drawers for an envelope. After finally finding one he went back to the printer. As he was pulling the pictures off he glanced at each one. They turned out pretty good-even the one of the two red dots. Reese, who had been exposed to the UFO phenomenon his whole life, was a little desensitized to all of the excitement that most people had for it. He was more excited about flying the saucers with his Uncle Dylon.

He stuffed the pictures in the envelope and rushed out the door. "Man this is going to be great. I'll catch one of them, off from the rest of the group, and then.....it will scare them so much they will just scream." Reese laughed a little as he played his plan out in his mind.

He hopped into the Mule and headed off towards the hangar. He figured with the amount of time they had been gone they should at least be that far. With the run of *the estate,* he and a few of the other kids had created their own paths. This gave him a few shortcuts from the main road and he made it to the hangar in no time. As he was coming over the hill he saw the others heading out. It looked like they were heading to the launch pad site. He turned around and followed the short cut he knew would put him ahead of them. It looked like they were trying to talk while they were riding, so he knew he would have enough time to get himself set up and hidden.

Reese had just made it. He had unloaded the R.S. and made it up the small embankment when he heard the others. He found a flat, rocky area where he could take off from and was cleaning it of any small debris. Occasionally he would peek up to see where they all were and then finally he saw his opportunity. Elizabeth, Marcus, and Dylon were talking and Kevin and Rosie had stepped away from the group.

"He seems to have everything in order, Rosie. So why do you think we're here? What could he possibly need us for?" Kevin asked Rosie.

"What I think he's looking for is experience." Rosie said. "Seriously Kevin, look at them. They're just a bunch of kids."

Kevin gave them a look and agreed with her. "Well Rosie, you work with him. Is he that good? Do you think he will be able to pull all of this off?"

Rosie thought for a moment. "Yeah, I think he could….maybe not as quick as he wants to, but I still think he could do it."

"Still sounds like there is a 'but' in that statement." Kevin said as he was trying to get Rosie's true thoughts on the scenario.

"Kevin, now why do you want to ask a question you already know the answer to? Have you ever been on the wrong side of what *they* want to happen? It's not pretty and it's definitely not easy."

Kevin responded. "If by *they* you mean the government, no Rosie, I haven't."

"Well let me tell you. It's no picnic."

Kevin just looked at her. "Rosie, I've known you for a long time. It still sounds like you're not completely over what happened and I wouldn't expect you to be. Whatever you decide I'm with you."

Rosie heard what Kevin said but chose not to respond to it, even though she knew he was probably right. She took a deep breath and fought back the memories that tried to come through. "In any case Kevin, there are no coincidences. They need us, our age and our wisdom.

"Sounds like there's a but in there somewhere, Rosie," Kevin said.

"There is, Kevin....I just don't think I have enough cards to pull us all the way through this. We just need to know more, I need to know who else we might be dealing with. We just need a few more cards than what I have," Rosie said in response.

# Chapter 14

Kevin and Rosie started walking back to the rest of the group, when they nitoced something not quite right. Before they could say anything Dylon, also noticed it. Then he recognized what it was and started to look around for Reese.

The R.S. model swooped down on Rosie and Kevin. They both ducked down in the fear that it was going to hit them. Then they heard a faint laughing sound off in the distance. Dylon had heard it, too, and was closing in on the location. He hunkered down trying not to be seen. Kevin saw what was going on and figured to play along. He grabbed Rosie's hand and told her to act like she was scared. She did so by letting out a quick scream. They both started running away from the craft, and could hear the laughter getting louder.

Reese was having so much fun he didn't realize that Dylon had made it all the way behind him and was standing there with his arms folded in a disapproving manner. When Reese finally felt the presence of someone watching him, he slowly turned around.

Dylon could see the fun he was having just drain

from his body like a balloon deflating. Then he realized the craft was doing the same thing. "Buddy, you're gonna crash!"

"Oh crap!" Reese quickly turned and focused his attention back on the R.S. model.

"Nice save, Reese. Why don't you go ahead and land it near the others so they can get a closer look at it." Dylon started looking around to see where the Mule was. As soon as he found it, he walked down the path to get it and bring it around to the rest of the group.

Reese was halfway across the field when Kat noticed him with this mischievous little grin on his face. She just smiled to herself. "You've been hanging around Dylon too long." She said as he got a little closer. "I missed you this morning. A little bird told me you were up at the crack of dawn."

Reese reached out to give her a hug. "I missed you, Kat. When are you going to be finished with school?"

"Not soon enough kiddo, and I missed you too, sweetie. Why don't you go over and show the others how to fly your saucer, while I go talk to Uncle Dylon for a minute."

"Sure, I hope they like it." Reese said as he hurried off to the others.

Kat immediately turned around and went to meet

Dylon, who had just pulled up with the Mule and was readying the other saucer. As soon as she reached him she gave him a quick slug on the arm.

"Owww! Damn sis, that really hurt."

"Yeah? Well it was supposed to. Damn it Dylon, it's bad enough you can't call me by my own name. Now you're teaching Reese to call me by your stupid little nickname. I swear, I hate that name. It just sounds like I should be on the prowl or something. I can hear it now. 'Hi this is my sister Kat if you're nice to her she'll purr for you.' I don't like it, Dylon, and it's a habit you need to break. As far as Reese is concerned, well you need to fix that, too." She grabbed the remote for the saucer and huffed off.

"Hey Reese." Kat said as she walked up next to him. "Do you think you can show me how to operate this one?"

"I'll try. This is a new one, but it should work about the same." Reese took the remote and looked it over, trying to see if there was anything different. "This lever is the one that makes it go up and down. And this one over here makes it go side to side. And this one in the center gives you your speed, it clicks as you move it, that way you can move your engine speed up in small amounts. I'm not sure what this one does so I probably wouldn't touch it until Dylon tells us what it's for."

Dylon finished placing the M.S. model and gave Reese a thumbs-up signal. "Okay, Kat, he's ready, just push that button to catch a signal, it should flash green pretty quick then you can push your speed lever and it should start going up."

"Ahhh, it's moving." Kat squealed with excitement. "Ohh, what do I do now Reese? What do I do, what do I do?" She was a kid all over again.

Reese was getting wrapped up in her excitement. "Just fly it, play with it really slow till you figure it out. Go higher so you can have some recover time. Move your speed up, it will make you go higher." Reese was actually repeating, almost verbatim, what Dylon had taught him, when he first tried flying the saucers.

After a little over an hour of playing with the saucers, the batteries had given them about as much as they could. Kevin and Rosie were quite impressed with the toys, which were nothing more than prototypes for the real thing. As they were playing with them, Dylon had a chance to go over all that with them, while they took turns flying the saucers.

As they were loading everything onto the Mule, Dylon let everyone know that Senorita Juanita was bringing some sandwiches to the old hangar, which would be their last stop before they hit the pool.

"Well I can't imagine how much more there

could be to see." Rosie said as she climbed onto the ATV with Kevin.

They all headed off with Dylon in the lead. It didn't take long before they were pulling up behind the old hangar that Dylon had turned into his workshop. As they were pulling up, Kat noticed a structure she had never seen before. She just shook her head and once they got off the ATVs she walked over to Dylon.

"Now what in the world is that?"

Dylon just kind of smiled. "Sis, I needed more power."

"But, what is it?"

"It's hydro-power." The structure was about thirty feet tall and made of concrete. It looked like two differently-sized storage tanks molded together with a very steep waterslide-type feature connecting the larger and the smaller one. There were pipes running out the side of it. Two were running to a generator and two ran to the top of the taller structure.

Kat just shook her head and Dylon questioned her with a rather shocked response. "What? Sis what was I supposed to do? It's not like I can call the local power company and say. 'Hey, I'm working on an anti-gravitational sphere up here and could use an extra thousand kilowatts or so.' C'mon sis, give me a break here."

"So does it actually work?"

"Of course it does. It almost doubled my power output." Dylon said in defense of himself.

"And what about the other….the sphere, does it work?" Kat said with one eyebrow raised.

"It's close. It's so close." Dylon said with a hopeful tone in his voice.

At this point Kevin had really been thrown for a loop. "Anti-gravitational sphere? Mars complex, Agripod, roving solar-deflectors. Man I thought this was just going to be a trip to a mountain estate. It feels like I've been teleported into the future."

"Oh you have. And once we go inside we're going to strap you to a machine, extract all your DNA, and create a clone army of you so we can take over the world. Isn't that right, sis?" Dylon said trying his best not to crack a smile. He quickly turned away from Kevin and headed for the door, to hide his face. Rosie couldn't help herself and let out a loud laugh. She nudged Kevin as she passed him and quickly said. "Come on in guinea pig, I wouldn't miss this one for the world." She snickered again as she finished chiding him. Marcus also laughed a little as he heard what Rosie had said and Kat just rolled her eyes.

"You guys are truly twisted." She said as she followed everyone in.

When they stepped inside the hangar you could

almost hear the jaws hit the floor. The hangar was sort of divided into three sections. On the left was a work area, with a vehicle size craft. The Avrocar was parked in this section. It was one of the crafts that Dylon, with Reese's help, had built. It was a replicated version of some of the early crafts that were built when UFO's were first coming into the public curiosity. The right side of the hangar also had a replicated version of one of the early crafts. This one was a German version of a flying disc. Both were fully functional, and flew a little better than their original versions.

The center of the hangar is what really baffled the Rosiers' guests. This was something they hadn't seen before, well, not in person anyway. In the center of the middle section of the hangar was what looked like an armillary sundial. It also looked similar to the transportation device used in the movie *Contact*, except this one was attached to two lubricated suspension rods. They were attached to the ceiling, but there was a large piece of metal about four feet from the top, which connected the two rods together and also acted as a containment device. That is, if Dylon could get the sphere to raise more than just a few inches.

Kevin, Rosie , and Marcus were checking everything out like kids in a candy store, and Reese was explaining how everything worked. He was very proud of the fact that he had a hand in helping build them, and had a very profound knowledge in explaining how each worked. He captivated the threesome with his ability to put the technological workings of these crafts in simple and understandable language, basically in layman's terms.

Kat stepped over to see what Dylon was fidgeting with. He was standing in front of a large control panel. It looked like a tall commercial desk from the back. The top of it had several gauges, a couple of levers, and several power switches on it.

Noticing all the buttons there were to turn the thing on Kat couldn't help but wonder. "Dylon, do you really need all these buttons? I mean, why are there so many power on buttons?"

"Well, there's the button that turns on the gauges here, there is one for the computer to record all the data coming from the sphere, there is on for the speed control for the rotation of it, and this one is for the amount of electricity I want to use for the electromagnet and that's what these two levers are for."

"Tell me again, what exactly happens when you turn this thing on?"

Dylon looked at his sister, trying to figure out what he was sensing. "Are you afraid, sis?"

"Who me? You're kidding right? What would I have to be afraid about?" There was a long uncomfortable pause. "Well Dylon, I just…. Sometimes you're stuff doesn't quite work the way it should….and I just want…"

Dylon laughed out loud. "You are afraid. Look, if you're that uncomfortable you can stand next to the door with Reese. Sis, that's why I have everything hooked up the way I do. That way if anything were to go wrong, it's all recorded. Every piece of data you would need is in that computer over there, behind the firewall. I've got all the precautions in place that I can just in case."

"Oh, I see. So I guess that's why Reese has to stand by the door."

"Really, sis, nothing is going to happen. I haven't even been able to get up to the halfway point on my speed and electromagnet controls, because of the power issue. I've even stood beside it while it was running, it's perfectly safe."

"Okay, if you say so." Kat said, still not sounding all that convinced. She stepped over to the sphere and really took her first good look at it. She didn't notice the others walking up. Kevin asked her a question and she nearly jumped out of her skin. "I'm sorry Kevin, I didn't catch the question."

"I was just curious about the gyroscope you're

playing with."

"Oh, the sphere. This is the final piece of Dylon's UFO obsession." Kat laughed a little as she responded to Kevin.

Dylon heard the comment and objected. "Come on now sis. Give me a little more credit than that. Kevin it's the anti-gravitational device I mentioned earlier."

"How does it work? Does it work?"

"Well, it's still in the development stage, but progressing along nicely. As for how it works, well I took the most nonmagnetic metal I could find, Bismuth, and made an electromagnet out of it. Each ring is its own magnet. This little ball in the center houses a small electric rotary motor which operates the bands, and once I get it going at a steady pace then I flip the switch to turn on the magnetic part of it. Honestly it would probably be easier to show you."

"Well, what are we waiting for?" Kevin said, anxious to see the thing work.

Dylon called out to Reese. "Could you open the hangar door please?" He did so promptly and looked around for something to climb up on to get a better view. Rosie noticed him and asked why. Dylon looked at her and explained what he was doing. "It's kind of a procedure that we started when I first tried this. I would die if anything happened to him on my watch."

She gave him a stern look. "So should we be standing over there."

"No, it's just me and my paranoid self." Dylon called out for Reese again. "Hey buddy, you can come a little closer if you want to."

"Cool, thanks D." Reese said as he was making a mad dash to get a closer spot to watch.

Everybody else had gathered behind the control panel and passed a box of sunglasses around that Dylon handed out. He started flipping buttons on for the gauges, the computer, and the sensors first. Then he flipped the button for the motor and the sphere slowly started spinning. Once it reached a steady pace, he turned up the speed to the mark he made beside the lever indicating the last speed he was able to get it up to before it shut down the last time, which was not even half of the speed it was capable of going. The speed of the sphere lifted it about an inch just from the rotation itself.

The next button to be turned on was the electromagnet. As soon as he flipped the switch you could hear a faint humming noise coming from the sphere. Rosie turned her head a little, unsure of where the noise was coming from. Once she figured it out, she unconsciously took a couple of steps back.

As Dylon slowly increased the power for the electromagnet, something peculiar started happening.

A light started to form. At first it was soft colors of the entire spectrum, shimmering as if it were a reflection. As Dylon increased the power for the magnet they started to get more intense and changing into a soft blue color. Dylon had seen this show before, but it was still amazing to him. As for the others, they were completely in awe of the show that was taking place. The light increased in intensity and was now a brilliant white with just a subtle hint of blue. The sphere had also raised at least another six inches.

Dylon was now to the mark on the magnet lever where it shut down before, so anything past this was all new to him. The light was now changing to a steady stream and as he increased the lever it seemed to become a lot more intense. The amount the sphere raised though was only minimal, so he pulled out a marker and marked the new position of the magnet lever and started to increase the rotation speed lever.

As he started increasing that speed, in an instant, everything went dark. Well not dark, the power had kicked off.

"Damn it! The breaker switched off. I didn't change the power grid, the breaker box, I didn't put in a larger breaker. Man, I'm so stupid sometimes. I upgraded my power source and everything else, but I didn't upgrade the breakers."

# Chapter 15

Dylon flipped off all the power switches and went to turn the breakers back on. At about the same time Juanita pulled up with the lunches she had fixed for everyone. She tried to make it simple, seeing how she had to transport it such a long distance from the kitchen. So lunch turned out to be an assortment of fajitas, tacos, and burritos. She was setting everything out, in a build your own kind of setup. Kevin and Marcus had stepped over to the sphere and were checking it out more closely, when they caught the scent of lunch wafting throughout the hangar. Kat and Rosie had seen her come in and went over to help her out. It wasn't long and Kevin and Marcus had fallen in right behind the girls.

When Dylon got the power switched back on, he too caught the scent of the food Juanita had prepared. He quickly made his way back to the group, who were already in line fixing their plates. All of them were discussing the fact that with all of the excitement of the day, they hadn't realized how hungry they were. Dylon caught Reese's attention and asked if there were still charger packs in the hangar. He acknowledged that they were and promptly ran off to get them. While the others were still getting their plates fixed, Dylon stepped out to the *Mule* to get the batteries from the saucers. He reached to open the glove box to get the tool kit, which was very simple, consisting of a screwdriver, a set of pliers, and a set of Allen wrenches.

When he opened the glove box a white envelope fell out. He picked up the envelope and looked inside. The photos from this morning he had forgotten all about. He quickly retrieved the batteries from the saucers, grabbed the envelope and went back inside the hangar. When he got inside he spotted Reese plugging the chargers and handed the batteries to him. With both hands free now, he really started looking at the photos. He continued to walk towards the group and the lunch table, but was engrossed in the photos.

"What do you have there, Dylon?" Kat said trying to break his train of thought so he wouldn't run into the pole.

Realizing she had broken his concentration just in the nick of time, he answered her by handing the photos to her. "Thanks for looking out, sis. This is what Reese woke me up, so early for. We had a visitor sometime last night. Right before we got here it looks like. Reese actually saw it."

"Well, lucky you!" She said giving Reese a quick rub on the head, who had walked up when Dylon was talking. "Wow, these are pretty good." Kat passed the photos around one by one as she flipped through them. She winked at Rosie before her next comment. "So Dylon, now are we on the *intergalactic tourist must see locations* list?"

Dylon chuckled a little. "Well I've never heard it put like that before, but I guess so, according to Reese. Apparently, it made a couple of passes, before it darted off to the west. Then it was followed up by that last picture. A couple of red dots which are probably military aircraft in pursuit. I'll have to see what the infrared picked up, because the regular cam didn't pick up that much at all."

"Wow, not just one but two visitors. Do you think you might be playing with something that would be catching the interest of more than just who you want?" Kat said with a raised eyebrow.

"Possibly, but out of the two choices, I think I would rather deal with the unknown." Dylon replied.

"I'm with Dylon." Rosie interjected rather quickly.

"So what do you think, Rosie? Do you think this is a craft the government might be interested in?" Rosie was shuffling through the photos looking at each one carefully. "I'm sure if the craft is more advanced than what we have, then the government wants it. This craft doesn't look like anything I've ever seen."

"Me either, and I have seen a lot of different aircraft in my career." Kevin said as he took the last of the photos Rosie was passing on.

"Well the big question is, do you think we can build one? We know it can be done. Right there is your proof, along with all the sightings that have ever been explained away as 'weather balloons' or whatever excuse could be believed." The group all looked around at each other. Each was waiting for the others to respond. Finally, it was Kevin that spoke first.

"Dylon, it looks like you have a pretty good start at trying. Do you think you can figure out that anti-gravitational gizmo over there? I mean it is an impressive piece of machinery but...."

Dylon interrupted Kevin before he could finish. "But it's not impressive enough. If it can't even lift its own weight it will never be able to lift...." Dylon stopped himself before he revealed the third craft, which was hidden away in a cellar. Hoping he had corrected himself in time he turned and pointed to the avrocar. "...to lift something like that. The sphere should automatically jump up at least to fifteen feet, just in idle mode, according to my calculations. Once it is installed in something with some weight to it, the weight of the avrocar, then it will bring the craft to a slight hover."

Dylon looked at Kat and Marcus. "That's where these two come in. Do you guys think you can get this working better than I can?"

Kat let out a laugh. "I'm sorry, Dylon. Of course we would give it our best shot." Marcus continued where Kat left off. "Of course, there are all kinds of new techniques being experimented with. There's the magneto plasma rocket, the laser-powered flight experiments. I would actually like to try my hand at making this work better."

Kevin spoke up again. "Speaking of making it work, how exactly is this going to work? I mean in a craft. Haven't they tried working with magnets before and had horrible results? What was it?" Kevin said as he was searching his memories. "The Philadelphia Experiment, that's what it was. Where they found the men melted into the deck of the ship, or something like that. "

Dylon responded. "Yes they did, and they weren't melted into the metal. The metal was basically liquefied and when they finally figured out how to turn the machine off, well it went back to its normal state, regardless of where the men were in relevance to that normal state. Anyway, I have drawings that will show you and reports of all my experiments with the metal bismuth. In addition to research information on where bismuth has been found."

Dylon grabbed an empty plate and put it on the floor. Then he grabbed some olives and placed in a triangle formation on the plate before continuing.

"Basically there will be three of the spheres in the craft that will create your center of gravity. When they are powered up they will, in theory, create a gravitational field for the craft. The hull of the craft is built in three layers: A layer of carbon fiber metal on the inside, a layer of the special recipe of the bismuth metal compound, and an outer layer of a carbon fiber and metal compound. I used carbon fiber, because it is one of the better deflectors of any space radiation plus it is super strong and lightweight. The bismuth, being non-magnetic, isn't affected by the magnetic field therefore the craft won't 'melt'."

Kevin was digesting everything Dylon just explained. "Okay, but I still have one more question. Why do you need us?" He motioned to himself and Rosie. "I mean you have all the ideas, you've got your mechanic, and you've got your rocket scientist. What is it that we bring to this gang of future technological pioneers?"

Dylon paused before answering. "Well first and foremost, experience. Experience in getting what you want or need when dealing with other people. Second, you bring a couple of extra hands to the crew. Not just that though, it's the extra hands of people that I can trust. Reliability, commitment, shall I go on? Guys, I feel like you two are the best for the team. I think you would tell me if I'm completely out of my mind or if I'm on the right track. Basically I think you would help in keeping me grounded."

Rosie was the one who spoke up this time. "and what about the governments? Both of them, ours and the Peruvian government."

"Well Rosie, I'm hoping to have the Peruvian government on our side by bringing them into it. By proposing to bring them into the twenty-first century, with the testing of all these future technologies happening in their own backyard, I think it would be the best and most upfront thing to do. We don't have to let them know everything, but if we are recording everything and reporting it to them on a voluntary basis, I think that would be the best persuasive measure we can take. Plus I do have funds set aside to put at least two satellites up for them, free of charge, just to make it a little more enticing. But I'll hold that back for the last option."

"Good Lord, child, why are you even working for your father's firm?" Rosie jokingly asked before continuing. "You do know it's still the government you're dealing with right?"

"Yes Rosie, that's why I really hope you will join

the team. Like I said, it's the experience and knowledge of both of you that I'm counting on." Dylon paused for a minute, to see if anyone was going to come up with anything else.

"Well, if there are no more questions I say we all go relax by the pool or where ever, and take some time to enjoy ourselves. After all, it is a holiday weekend. Plus that will give us all some time to digest everything we've found out this weekend. You guys can go ahead, I'm going to put the saucers away, and I'll meet you there."

Marcus followed Dylon out and called back to Kat. "I'm going to give him a hand, I'll see you at the pool, okay Elizabeth?" He waited for a response and he finally saw her hand motion to him while she and Rosie were talking.

\* \* \* \* \* \*

Dylon and Marcus got in the *Mule* and headed off to the observatory. Dylon started off the conversation. "So are you and Kat....dating, just good friends, what?"

"Oh God, I wish I knew. I was going to ask you. We've been hanging out about a year and a half now, and we've only made out a couple of times. With our schedules being so screwy, it's kind of hard to really plan any real alone time. Has she talked to you about me? I really like her but I haven't really figured out what she wants." Marcus really didn't have any idea where he and Kat were headed.

Dylon just smiled. "That's almost the same thing she said. I think you guys complement each other very well. But you both have no idea what you want, except to focus on getting out of school, with somewhat of a decent grade. It's obvious that you care for each other, but you're both focused on something else. I think you should continue with what you've been doing and everything else will come in its own sweet time."

"Thanks man, that's kind of what I figured, but it's nice to have another person's point of view. Hey, I've got another question." Marcus said as they pulled up to the observatory. "Why do you call her Kat? If you know it pisses her off so much why do you still call her that?"

"Well her name is Kathryn Elizabeth, so it's short for Kathryn. Has she ever talked to you about mom and dad and what happened?" Dylon asked.

"No, she always steers away from that topic. I just figured it was something she wanted to keep private." Marcus said as he shrugged his shoulders.

"Yeah, she's kind of like that, but the truth is she's the one that bounced back first. I had a harder time dealing with it than she appeared to. I was the older brother. I was the one that was supposed to be there for her. But she landed on her feet quicker than me. In everything that life has thrown at her, she always ends up landing on her feet. Even what she's done with her school schedule, I can't believe she would put that much on herself. But once again, she will land on her feet and come out of this exactly how she wants to. Thus the nickname Kat, but don't you dare get into the habit of calling her that, because it will come back on me."

# Chapter 16

At the poolside Kevin and Rosie were doing their usual flirting. "Damn Rosie, you still look good. How long have we known each other and we still haven't hooked up yet?"

"Kevin, if I've told you once I've told you a thousand times, you simply could not handle me. I'm way too demanding. Besides, I'm not into one night stands, but if I were, you would be the first man I would call."

Kevin just grabbed his heart and fell backwards into the pool. Rosie looked at Kat and rolled her eyes. "Men, I swear, you can't live with them, can't live without them. So, Elizabeth, tell me a little more about Marcus, he seems like a nice guy. Are you two....well what are you exactly? Are you dating, just friends, what's up?"

Kat paused for a moment, trying to grasp the right words. "I'm not really sure Rosie. He's a really good friend, he's always around, and I do enjoy his company. If the timing were a little better things might be different. Why do you ask? Has Dylon been talking to you about us?"

Rosie glanced over at Kat. "Elizabeth honey, Dylon hasn't said anything. A blind man could see that Marcus is taken with you. He just seems to be confused about what you want. Do you know what you want? Because if you do, you need to let it show a little more, before you lose a good one."

"You really think he is taken with me?"

"Elizabeth dear, I may be a little older and completely out of the dating scene, but I still can see when somebody is smitten. The only shame of it all is that you may let one of the good ones slip right through your hands, and you're not even aware of it. Goals are great and all that, but if you lose the most important thing in the world trying to achieve them, who will you have left to share them with? He would follow you to the moon and back, you just better make sure he knows you want him there. That boy is in love with you and I know love when I see it."

Kat glanced over to the other side of the pool at Kevin. "Oh you do?" Rosie noticed the glance and the raised eyebrow. "That? Girl, you don't understand. We are just really good friends. If it wasn't for Kevin, I would probably be in a clinic somewhere or homeless."

"Oh, I can hardly believe that, Rosie. You? The person that has it all together. Dylon has told me how you run that office. He also told me how much trouble he got into that day he showed up at work before you. I couldn't stop laughing, he was so afraid he had gotten on your bad side. He was walking on eggshells for the next two weeks."

Rosie laughed. "Good Lord, I wasn't that harsh. Seriously, though, when I lost my husband, the Rosiers nearly lost me. Kevin was the one that pulled me out of it. He was just as persistent then, as he is now. This whole flirting thing is just our way of letting each other know how grateful we are to have each other as friends."

The two girls were so wrapped up in the conversation they didn't realize that Kevin had swum across the pool and was at their side. Close enough to catch the last part of the conversation.

"Don't believe a word she said, Elizabeth. She's been trying to get into my pants for years." The girls jumped a little when they heard Kevin speak up. Then when Rosie realized what he actually said she got to her feet in a hurry. Kevin kicked off the side of the pool in retreat. Rosie called out to him. "You better behave yourself, I'd hate to have to explain why you didn't come back from this trip." She turned and looked at Kat, who was trying to keep from laughing. "Well dear it's getting kind of warm out here. I'm getting in to cool off a little." She slid herself into the pool and started swimming toward Kevin.

Kat got up, walked over to the pool box where Reese kept his toys, and dug out a small *Nerf* football.

She joined the others in the pool. She tossed the ball to Rosie and a game of catch ensued.

As Kevin passed the ball to Kat he started quizzing her. "Elizabeth, do you think your brother can do all this stuff he is proposing?"

"Well I sure hope so." She laughed as she answered. "With me being the chief mechanic and all, it wouldn't look all that good on me if he doesn't."

Rosie caught the ball and passed it to Kevin, before she asked her question. "Where does he come up with all of these ideas, have you ever asked him?"

Kat rolled her eyes and laughed a little. "Daydreams, who knows? He gives me his ideas and then after I tweak them a little they become our ideas. Soon, I hope, you two will be a part of them too. Marcus and I will be able to help out with the propulsion systems. I hope the both of you will be able to point us in the right direction if there is something we missed."

Rosie raised an eyebrow. "I'm glad you brought that up. What exactly are your plans for getting a foot in the door with the Peruvian government?" She asked, knowing she had a little more experience in dealing with the government than the others.

Kat quickly replied. "Well, thanks to my mom we kind of already have a foot in the door, so to speak. My mother, when she established the clinic, saved the lives of a few family members of some influential people in the government. We still finance the clinic and keep in touch with the children we've helped.

We've actually built a pretty good working relationship with them. There is one gentleman in particular, Sergeant Vasquez, actually I think he's a Lieutenant now, who has already been to *the estate* several times. I've only briefly met him, but Dylon has helped pass along some information on the new technologies and designs for the new wind-power devices.

If I remember correctly, he even donated several of them to him for a few of the villages, just to help bring them a little more into modern era. Seems they don't want to lose their heritage and values. It took a lot of convincing between the Sergeant or Lieutenant and Dylon to get them to actually accept them. Thus, our foot in the door."

Rosie was in awe and Kevin looked like he was still having a hard time believing all of it.

Elizabeth continued. "Speaking of Dylon, where the heck is he? Once again he's left me to do the explaining, while he's running around playing with his dreams and toys."

* * * * * *

As they were pulling up to the observatory, Marcus hit Dylon with a question that caught him off guard. "So where are you hiding the back-up crafts?"

Dylon was taken by surprise with Marcus's question. "I don't know what you're talking about."

Marcus just rolled his eyes. "You don't honestly expect me to believe that you're going to completely disassemble the two crafts in the hangar just to put the propulsion devices in them, do you? Come on man, you seem to be a guy that's a little more prepared than that. I would bet that you already have one built. From what Elizabeth has told me about you, it wouldn't surprise me if you already have two or three of them built. Besides, I don't believe that you would have the patience to wait to install these devices into a craft that you have to tear down. I think you would want to install them the second you have them working."

Dylon still denied that there were other crafts and Marcus kept his plea up. "Dylon, if we're going to work together we have to be able to trust each other."

Dylon responded, "You're right. Can I trust that you can get the sphere working?"

"Well, I haven't had the chance to play with it, or read the reports and schematics on it, but I'm pretty sure I can. Elizabeth and I should be able to get it working in no time. Come on man, you got to let me see it."

Dylon was trying his best to remember if he told Kat about the other crafts. He searched his memories and couldn't think of a single mention of it to her. "You can't tell her I have them and you can't see where they are."

"Okay, exactly how is that going to work?" Marcus was really beginning to wonder what kind of weirdo he was going to be working with. "Besides that, why wouldn't you want her to know? You're really starting to get a little….'mad scientist' on me here bud."

"For protection, for both of you." Dylon was rummaging for something to make a blindfold out of, while he was answering Marcus' questions. "If you don't know where they are then you can't show anybody. If you can't show anybody, well then you'll be the one who looks crazy. Make sense?"

"Kind of, but if you're that paranoid about it, why even show me?"

Dylon gave Marcus a quick spin around, and started tying the cloth he found around his head. "Well number one, because you're right, you do need to see them. Number two, I really don't think you would tell Kat anyway."

"Yeah, and what makes you so sure about that?"

"Because, Marcus, I think you have just as much interest in her protection as I do. Can you see anything?" Dylon asked as he made sure the knot was good and tight.

"Just a little light around the edges."

Dylon quickly wrapped the rest of the cloth around his head. "And how about now?"

"Geez bud, are you sure you don't want to tie my hands up? Check me for weapons?" Marcus joked as Dylon led him to the *Mule*.

As they drove around to the back of the observatory, which was built on a small hill, Dylon reached into the glove box and pulled out an old universal remote. They were headed for the garage, which was just big enough to hold three golf carts. When they came around the corner, the door was already open. Dylon aimed the remote in that direction and pressed the VCR button. The back wall started to separate and revealed a dimly lit tunnel.

As the boys headed in, they passed by a sensor, which triggered the wall to close behind them. The entire trip took about fifteen minutes and ended in a room about the size of the hangar. While the tunnel entrance at this end was closing, Dylon did a few circles just to kill some time and make sure the door was closed.

When they finally came to a stop, Dylon started to warn Marcus. "You're probably going to be a little surprised. Let me just get the lights, I'll be right back.

You just got to make sure you don't tell Kat or anyone. Once we bring the government in….. well, I just want to make sure we have something to bargain with if we need to."

By the time Dylon had all the lights turned on, Marcus already had the blindfold off. He found himself standing in a pretty decent sized room. There were no visible doors, but there were windows around the top, or what appeared to be windows. As the lights filled the room and slowly hummed to their full brightness Marcus' jaw dropped.

There in front of him, he counted a total of nine crafts. There were two different models, the R.S. and the M.S., just the same as the radio controlled ones. These looked big enough to hold a crew of at least four. There were six bays on either side and all the crafts were raised to about six feet. As Marcus walked under one of the crafts, his emotions were mixed. He reached up and touched it, and let out a barely audible gasp of awe.

"I wonder if this is how Columbus felt as he discovered the 'New World', or how Neil Armstrong felt as he looked back on Earth ." Marcus thought to himself. As he was standing there in disbelief he ran his hands across the vehicle. Dylon just watched as Marcus was discovering his own emotions, and the actual possibility that exploring other worlds may actually happen in his lifetime. Plus the fact that he, would be a big part, in making this happen.

With every hair on his body standing at attention, Marcus suddenly felt a sense of unknowing. Just the pure adrenaline of completely walking through a universe with no idea of what was going to happen next began to overpower him. The only words that could come out of his mouth was a very simple but profound. "Wow."

He turned to look at Dylon, and all words escaped him. As he stood there almost gaping, Dylon tried to bring him back down to earth a little. "Did you notice the one at the end? There are a few things I would like your input on."
Dylon was having a hard time getting Marcus back, and kind of snickered to himself. "Marcus, this one down here at the end is a little different."

"Yeah, okay." These were the only words that formed from Marcus' mouth as Dylon practically had to push him toward the craft at the far end of the room. Dylon was trying his best to redirect Marcus' thoughts. "So this one down here, will be set up as a probe. I was just wondering if there is anything different that we may need to do as far as protecting any data that it might pick up. I mean, should we house the computer in lead or something? Because this will be the one we send to Mars, that's why it's a little bigger, with all the computers and sensors, I had to make it a little bigger." Dylon already new the answers to these questions, yet he was grasping at straws.

Finally, Marcus started to come out of his overwhelmed state. "Um, yeah, maybe. We really have to know what affect the device has on its surroundings before we can say for certain. It might be possible to run it without anything substantial protecting it." Marcus was looking at Dylon kind of funny. "Hey, you're not some kind of alien yourself are you? I mean you're not going to get everything up and running and like crack open our heads and eat our brains or anything like that are you?"

Dylon let out a laugh. "Dude, you need serious psychiatric help. Are you sure you're up for this? I mean if you're not, after showing you all of the goodies I have hidden here...." With a shrug he said "Well if you're not, then I guess I just going to have to kill you. I mean, I can't just let you walk out of here knowing everything you know now."

"That's not funny, man. Yeah, I'm up to it. It's just a little bit overwhelming." Marcus replied.

"Well come on then, let's go join the others at the pool."

# Chapter 17

By the time they made it back to the main house, Kevin and Rosie were the only ones left at the pool. They were sitting at the table in what looked like a pretty involved conversation.

"Well I'm not getting into the middle of that. I'm going to get changed." Dylon said before he disappeared into the house. With that said, Marcus was left standing there by himself, wondering where Kat was. He looked to the table where Kevin and Rosie were, trying to decide whether he wanted to interrupt them or not. About that time he noticed Rosie pointing to the end of the house. He waved his thanks and ventured around to the side of the house.

As Marcus came around the corner, he noticed a small path that forked off into two separate garden areas. He made a guess and took the path to the right. It was a very nice garden, full of all kinds of small areas with various items of garden art. As he made his way down the path, he came across a birdbath, a gazing ball that had been turned into a water feature, two separate seating areas, and finally a granite obelisk that had something written on it. Before he got a chance to finish reading it, he heard Kat talking.

He started heading in her direction, but stopped quickly when he heard her say 'Mom'. He wasn't sure if he heard it right, so he listened a bit longer, then he heard it again. This time he was sure he heard it right and then started cursing to himself. "Shit…. I shouldn't be here. This is not what I need to be a part of. Damnit, this is her private time, I can't believe I'm here….leave now Marcus, before you get caught." He thought to himself as he quickly made a retreat back the way he came.

When he made it back to the pool Rosie, Kevin, and Dylon were having a drink. He breathed a sigh of relief. That is until Rosie blurted out. "Did you find her?" Marcus quickly waved his hands back and forth and then put his finger to his lips, signaling her to shush. When she realized something wasn't right she stopped and Marcus quickly disappeared inside.

Dylon, who was kind of baffled at what was happening, just smiled when Rosie explained what was going on. "That's a smart man." He said. Now it was Rosie and Kevin that were confused, until Dylon started explaining. "Kat only goes into the garden alone if she wants to spend some time with Mom. That was her favorite place, and now it's a place of solitude. If you want to be alone, with your thoughts or with passed loved ones that's the place to go. You should take some time to check it out. Alone or with somebody, either way is nice."

The trio continued talking. Not long after Marcus disappeared into the house, Kat came around the corner. She noticed the three of them standing at the table and waved. Right before she went in the house, she stopped and called out to Dylon. "Do we have supplies ready to go to the clinic?"

" Yeah sis, but they aren't expecting them until Monday."

"Do you think they would mind getting them early? I would really like to go to the clinic tomorrow."

"Sure thing, I'll let Juan know to ready the helicopter. What time…..never mind, it will be ready by nine, okay." Dylon turned back to Rosie and Kevin, who were working up to telling him their decision about everything. Rosie started first. "Let me start with saying, I am….we are truly honored that you would choose us as partners in this venture. You have a brilliant mind and no offense intended, but…." Rosie was trying to find the right words to put it as softly as she could. "….you're a little naïve. Before you object, let me say that I think that's why you chose us. If I'm wrong, I apologize."

Dylon did interrupt with a statement that kind of floored them. "You're absolutely right in both the observation and the assumption. Anyway, continue."

"Well…." Again Rosie found herself carefully choosing her words. "…..there needs to be some….ground rules sounds too controlling….let's just say stipulations. We have to agree on an 'abort plan' for lack of a better word. The biggest hurdle we have to face is the involvement of the governments. Now I have had a little experience in dealing with our government. I may even have a few connections. My best advice to you would be to keep our government out of it as long as possible. Also I would like to play a major part in dealing with the Peruvian government. I would be sort of an advisor/lawyer type person. We really have to be careful in exactly how much information we divulge."

"Oh, I'm in complete agreement with you on that one, Rosie. The last thing I want is someone else telling me how to play out my dream." Dylon whole-heartedly agreed. "So we should make sure you and Kat get together and share some notes, because she has had more contact than I have. Seems there is a Sergeant that has a niece who is one of the heads at the clinic. We're hoping that's our foot in the door."

Rosie nodded her head letting Dylon know that Kat had already given her that information. "Now, there is one more thing, and at this point I'll let Kevin talk."

"Thank you, Rosie. The thought that I had was to

bring in some investors. I know, that's probably something you might not want to do, but the people I'm talking about, are the kind of people that trust my judgment. They are also the kind of people that will throw money at an investment and sit on it for three years minimum before they even ask a question about it. I know, it's a touchy situation, but it is something you might want to consider. These people would trust me when I say nothing more than 'I know an up and coming company that could use some investors.' They have more money than five generations of their families could ever spend. So this is not something I need an answer on right away."

Dylon was impressed with the two of them and their proposals. "You know, I had a good feeling about both of you. I know there are a lot of things that we'll have to work out as we go along, but as far as I'm concerned, sounds like we have a team." With that said, he raised his glass to give cheers with the others.

* * * * * *

Marcus had just finished his shower and was heading down to join the others. He almost knocked Kat down when he came around the corner. "Oh crap, are you alright, honey?"

"Yeah, I'm alright. So where have you been

hiding all afternoon?"

Marcus suddenly found himself at a loss for words. He had never kept anything from Kat, and with everything he saw, he was dying to tell her. "Well um, we took the saucers back, and ah, we ...."

"Marcus, has anyone ever told you that you're a horrible liar? Let me help you out here, babe. I'll play you okay. 'Hey Elizabeth, you wouldn't believe what I saw. Oh my God, your brother is a genius, or really obsessed about this whole UFO thing. Would you believe me if I told you he already has three of these things built?' How was that Marcus? Did that cover everything you saw this afternoon?"

Marcus just held up his hands, showing a count of nine. "He said you didn't know, he made me swear not to tell you."

"First of all he's my brother and I know how his mind works. Second of all, he has nine?" Kat said with a touch of disbelief. "So he showed you where they are?"

"No, he didn't, he made me wear a blindfold."

"That shit. I've been looking for his little secret room for a couple of years now. He was really messed up one night and let me know that he had started building them." Kat paused for a minute then looked at Marcus again. "Nine? Really? Oh and by the way, we did not have this conversation. I'm going to shower, I'll be down in a few." Marcus started to leave, but Kat stopped him. She put her hand around the nape of his neck, pulled him towards her, and gave him a good long kiss, then turned and headed for the shower. Marcus just stood there, not really sure what just happened or what he was supposed to do next. When he heard the bathroom door close, he figured he wasn't supposed to do anything, except enjoy the moment.

* * * * * *

"Reese, buddy, are you going to wake up?" Dylon said as he gently shook him. "Come on buddy, you've slept long enough. If you don't wake up now you'll be up all night." Dylon knew he was going to be awake half the night anyway. It was his normal routine. "Come on, kiddo. You need to get up and go wash up. Supper is almost ready."

Finally Reese had worked himself into a sitting position, and with a little more prodding, he was off to get washed up. In no time he was back downstairs bouncing around like he had just started a new day. He found everybody outside around the pool. Dylon, Kevin, and Marcus were hanging out by the grill. They were comparing their recipes for grilling, all of them swearing they made the best burgers. Of course no one could beat their ribs. Reese came running up to Rosie. "Do you want me to teach you how to fly the saucers tomorrow?"

"Why, that would be absolutely wonderful, but I have to go somewhere with Elizabeth first. Then after that, I'm all yours. Sound like a deal?"

"Cool, you'll have a lot of fun. I bet I can teach you how in an hour."

"You think so? Now is that because you can tell I'm a quick learner, or are you just that good?"

"Well if you're a quick learner, then I could teach you how to fly it in a half an hour."

Rosie and Elizabeth both laughed.

"Well I guess that question is answered for you." Elizabeth said as she reached out and tousled Reese's hair. Rosie reached out to Reese to give him a hug as Kat left them to go inform Marcus of their plans for tomorrow.

"Excuse me boys, do you mind if I steal Marcus for a moment?"

"Go ahead sis, his recipes suck anyway." Dylon said, and they all had a good laugh, as Marcus walked off with Kat.

"I just thought I should let you know, I have planned to go to the clinic tomorrow. I would just like to go and visit with some of the people there. You don't have to go, but Kevin and Rosie are going too."

"Dylon's not going?"

"No, he's going to spend some time with Reese, he's kind of a big brother to him and usually sets aside a day for him."

"Okay, whatever you want to do is cool with me," Marcus said then he leaned in and whispered in Kat's ear. "So you never told Dylon that you know, about the crafts?"

"No, dear, and I never will. Why should I ruin what he thinks will be a surprise. Don't worry, I also won't tell him you don't know how to keep a secret either." Kat said as she pinched him on his belly.

"That's not fair, you caught me off guard."

"Whatever, I just hope the government doesn't interrogate you first if this all goes awry." She said as she walked over to pour herself another glass of wine.

"Oh man, you're brutal." Marcus teased.

The evening carried on and they all enjoyed a wonderful meal and good company, as they shared stories about their personal *faux pas*. Nightfall crept up fast and the newcomers to *the estate* could not help but notice how many stars they could actually see. There were billions upon billions, so many that they could hardly pick out the constellations.

Rosie posed a question to the group in general. "So how many do you think are out there?"

Kevin answered first, with another question.

"How many new stars are born each year?"

His question was followed up by Dylon. "Who really knows, but I think the question was about intelligent life forms. There has to be something out there. I mean other than us. I just think we have to be pretty vain to think that *we are it.* Seriously, think about it."

"I agree, Dylon." Rosie said. "I couldn't have put it better myself. Out of all those stars and all the planets they may have, I can't imagine that we are the only intelligent life forms. We are probably preschoolers compared to some of the advanced civilizations out there." They all seemed to agree on that point and were silent for a moment as the gazed at the wonder of it all.

"One more thing, Dylon," Rosie was still gathering information on her decision to partner up with the group, mainly for her own piece of mind. "What are your plans, if you get to Mars and it turns out that everything you try fails? You can't create an atmosphere, you can't get anything to grow, nothing, works out the way you want it to."

"Well, we got to Mars. We tried everything we could. We would have all the recorded attempts of everything we did try. Even if we fail at terraforming Mars, look at everything we will have accomplished, just by simply trying."

"Okay, just wanted to see where you stand on that possibility. But there is one more thing I have to say. Completely different subject, when are you going to give this place an actual name? Really Dylon. You have such a magnificent estate here and the best you two can do is call it *The Estate.* You really need to put your heads together and come up with something better than that."

Kat and Dylon had an expression on their faces that they hadn't had since they were kids, as Rosie scolded them in a friendly manner. "Now I know, you're young and probably haven't given it that much thought, but this is something that your father was very proud of and I think you would do him justice if it had a name. Not just any name, but one that means something to both of you, as well as honoring your parents' memory. I don't mean to be harsh about it but I hope you get my point."

# Chapter 18

The next morning came and everybody was eager to visit the village near Cuzco, and see the clinic that was not a part of the Rosier Enterprises family, but solely owned by Kat and Dylon. As the helicopter lifted off, Kevin and Rosie were checking out the view of *The Estate* in the daytime. It was a pretty expansive layout. Kat was pointing out to Marcus and the others, all of the parts of that they did not see on their little tour. There were several reservoirs, another solar collector field, several water towers, and another small grouping of the new wind power devices. There were also living quarters for resident workers and also visiting workers.

The trip to the village didn't take that long at all, just under an hour. When they landed, Kevin mentioned the fact that there were children running to the landing pad. Kat pointed out to him that he was going to be helping unload and to grab the boxes marked children first. She also explained to the rest of them that they always brought some small toys for the children. That would be the best way to get them on their way so the crew can finish unloading the helicopter.

"Most everybody here is friendly and some of the children may adopt you for a little bit. I'm going to visit with some friends at the clinic for a bit and just see how things are going. Joe is the guy at the back of the crowd of children. He is pretty good with giving tours of the village and speaks a good amount of English. If there is anything specific you want to see just ask him." Kat said as she grabbed a cooler marked with a medical symbol. She then turned to Marcus. "This is really going to be kind of boring. It won't bother me if you want to go with the others." He didn't have to say a word Kat read the answer on his face. She leaned in and gave him a peck on the cheek and headed off to the clinic.

As the children cleared out to go play with their new toys, Joe finally made it to the others and greeted them all with a firm handshake. He took control of the group very quickly, and soon they were off walking through the village, with Joe pointing out the different areas of the village. He discussed how they try to keep the heritage and culture of the old ways, while trying to accept some of the modern things the Rosiers had to offer.

* * * * * *

As Kat entered the clinic, she was greeted with

screams and hugs. Carmen, who was now the head of the clinic, (saw her first). Carmen was taken under Angela's wings when she was just a teenager. Kat's mother guided and encouraged Carmen to pursue a medical career, and she let Kat know how grateful she was every time she came to the clinic.

"Oh, what a pleasant surprise, Elizabeth, it is so good to see you." They shared a few good laughs, and caught up on happenings with the village. Kat didn't really want to talk about business too much, seeing how this was an unofficial visit. Carmen mentioned that she had another visitor coming that day. It was her uncle and she would like to introduce Kat to him.

After going through the cooler and putting the cold supplies away the two girls started unpacking the dry goods. There were gauze pads, syringes, and an assortment of other items for the dry storage area. It was getting close to lunch time and Kat started wondering where the others were. The village wasn't that big and she and Carmen had put everything away by now. As the two were closing up the storage area, a tall handsome man entered the back room where they were.

When Carmen turned around she noticed him, and let out a joyous scream. "Ricardo, you should come out to see us a little more."

"Carmen, my dear niece, it's so good to see you.

And who is this vision of loveliness you have with you today?" Before she got a chance to formally introduce the two of them, her assistant came in and quickly blurted out something in Spanish. It was so quick that Kat didn't get a chance to hear what she said.

"You'll have to excuse me, a little boy cut himself pretty bad, and you Ricardo, better be on your best behavior. I would hate to have to tell Alita you were flirting with someone young enough to be your granddaughter. Elizabeth, let me know if he bothers you." Carmen left the room to go check on the child.

"I have no idea what she is talking about," he said, as he offered his hand to Elizabeth, he couldn't help but take a second look. "You look very familiar, my name is Ricardo Vasquez."

"Vasquez? Sgt. Vasquez?" Kat said as she put her hand out.

"It's actually Lt. Vasquez, it's been many years since I was a Sergeant. So where do I know you from?"

"Oh I'm sorry, Elizabeth Rosier."

"Angela's daughter, no wonder you look so familiar. Your mother's eyes, and her beautiful head of hair. Such a tragedy, what happened."

"Thank you. My mother mentioned you several times throughout her diary. Talked about how much of a flirt you were." Ricardo just blushed.

"Well, she was a very beautiful woman. Your father was a lucky man."

"She also mentioned some special word you had for her. Something about if she was ever in trouble, she could send a message to you with this single word."

Ricardo recalled the time of that conversation. "Yes, Amistad, it means friendship. I had received word of the former owners of *The Estate* were trying to retaliate. Seems they wanted their land back. I just wanted to make sure she was safe."

As their conversation continued Kats brain was in high gear, trying to put her thoughts together in presenting a small sample of a meeting soon to come. She wasn't supposed to meet Lt. Vasquez for a few more weeks. Before she got a chance to get them completely together he had asked the question she was hoping he wouldn't.

"So how are things at *The Estate*? Do you have everything you need up there? It is quite a remote location."

"Oh, well it is remote." Kat agreed trying to avoid the subject completely. Just in time, the others came through the doors and a wave of relief came across Kat. Finally, a distraction to gather her thoughts.

"Oh Lieutenant, these are some friends of mine,

you should really meet them." The group was quite loud, as their last stop on their tour of the village was with the local medicine man who had shared a special friendship and welcome concoction with them He had also adorned Rosie with a special handmade necklace and the two guys had received pipes with some local herbs for when they needed, with very special instructions not to be used until they truly felt they had exhausted every possible attempt for success in their task.

"I see you have been to see the doctor. You will have some good dreams tonight. Make sure you write them down so he can translate them for you later." The group all looked at each other. And Rosie popped off with a quick response.

"Oh my God, we've been drugged." Ricardo just laughed at her response.

"I assure you, it's simply a tea of local herbs that enhance your dreams. You would probably have the dream anyway, this just gives it a little more.... eh...well, it just makes them a little better."

This little distraction gave Kat just enough time to complete her thoughts.

"Rosie, I would like you to meet Lieutenant Ricardo Vasquez. Lieutenant, this is Rosie Patterson. Now this is all unofficial as of right now. I really wasn't expecting to talk to you just yet, but I figured seeing how we're all here, I might as well take advantage of the opportunity. Rosie is our chief liaison you two will have plenty of time to get to know each other." As the group figured out what was going on, they tried to give their best first impressions to the Lieutenant. Kat continued on to Marcus. "This is Marcus Williamson, our chief engineer of propulsions, and last but not least, this Kevin Felderson. He is our chief of construction operations." Lt. Vasquez shook everyone's hand as he met them.

Kat continued on with her conversation. "Now like I said before, this is all unofficial, your visit kind of threw me off. We have done a lot of construction to *The Estate*, and are hoping to get together with you to open a satellite launching operations from *The Estate.*"

"That's quite a venture you're trying to start up there. I will be glad to get more information, when this is all official." Lt. Vasquez said as he winked at Kat. Rosie noticed out the window that the helicopter pilots were going through their preflight checklist, or that's what she assumed anyway, and had to say something. "Elizabeth dear, I hate to cut this visit short, but it looks like we need to head outside so we don't miss our ride."

"Oh my God, I didn't realize what time it was. Well Lieutenant, it was a pleasure meeting you and

we'll be in touch soon, with a few more details." As
they were leaving, the Lieutenant reached out and
grabbed Elizabeth's hand. "The pleasure was all
mine," She thanked him and started to leave, but he
still had her hand. When she looked up at him, he gave
her a firm look and simply said, "Amistad." She
clasped her hand over his and replied. "I understand."
With that said, the Lieutenant let go of her hand and
she was off.

As they were loading into the helicopter, Kat
noticed someone running to the helicopter pad. He
was shouting and waving a piece of paper. She tried to
make out what he was saying but couldn't quite catch
it. With the helicopter already running and ready to
take off, it was just too noisy. She leaned up to the
pilot and asked for a moment.

It looked like the medicine man's apprentice. Kat
left the pad to meet the man. He handed the note to
Joe, and said. "El constructor de escalera a las
estrellas."

Kat who was a little rusty with her Spanish asked
Joe what he had said, and he repeated it for her in
Spanish first then in English. "The builder of stairs to
the stars. Do you know what this means?"

Kat shrugged her shoulders. "I've heard it before,
but I don't remember where from." She started to hand
the note back to Joe but the apprentice wouldn't allow

it. She opened the note and made Joe read it to her. "Un viaje largo le espera. A long journey awaits you."

Kat just looked at Joe and didn't have a clue of what to do with the note. He recommended she take the note with her and thank the apprentice for it, and she did so, very appreciatively. When she got back in the helicopter, the others had asked her what that was all about. "I'm not sure, but a long journey awaits one of us."

\* \* \* \* \* \*

When the others left, Dylon and Reese made their way to the observatory to get the saucers. They ended up playing with them until the batteries ran down. Then they loaded them up, took them to the hangar, and put them on chargers. While they were recharging, the two of them worked on the breaker box, putting a bigger breaker in, so it wouldn't trip when it reached more amps than it could carry. All the while Reese was happy to be right there at his side. He didn't complain a bit.

When they were finished with the breaker box, they went back to the saucers. It was basically a day of two brothers, hanging out together. Dylon had to take a break. He knew the others would be getting back soon and wanted to get some burgers going on the grill.

"Hey bud, don't forget to make sure you put enough batteries on charge, so you can show the others how to fly the saucers."

"Okay, Uncle D."

"Do you want me to stay and help?"

"No, I got it."

With that said Dylon headed off to the house.

Reese had the batteries hooked up in no time. He also installed the fully charged ones into the saucers. He was so focused on what he was doing he didn't hear the helicopter fly over and land. When he got everything prepared to give the others some flying lessons, he wandered over to the anti-gravitational device. He gave it a good look over, since he hadn't really had much chance to look at it up close. Dylon always made sure everything was locked up when he left *the estate* for any length of time.

Reese walked over to the control console and looked everything over. Everything was in exactly the same position it was when the breaker tripped. Dylon had flipped all the switches to the off position, but he didn't return the power control levers to the start-up position. Reese didn't notice either.

"Cool, everything looks good."

He walked back over to the device and picked up the two connecting wires, one red and one black.

\* \* \* \* \* \*

The helicopter ride back seemed to be a quicker trip, probably because everyone was sharing with Kat their adventures for the day. After they landed everyone was in a hurry to get to the house. Dylon was able to reach them by radio and let them know lunch was on the grill. As Kevin and Rosie headed out Kat heard Dylon's voice come across her radio, asking her to hurry Reese along and letting her know where she would probably find him.

"You can go ahead Marcus, I'm sure he has a buggy over there." Kat said as she started walking toward the hangar.

\* \* \* \* \* \*

Reese finished hooking up the wires, which looked the same as a car battery connection. He walked over to the console, and started recalling every step Dylon made when he fired up the device. He started flipping the switches, first was the sensors. He heard the very faint hum of them as they warmed up.

He then switched on the printer which put out the reports of everything the computer recorded. The next thing was the computer, and he stepped over to make sure that all the lights lit up and everything seemed to be running properly. He had to jump a little to see them, where all Dylon had to do was look over his shoulder. The boy didn't miss a thing, it was like he could recall even the slightest detail. Even if it was as small as a wisp of wind blowing a dust ball across the floor, he caught it and could repeat it to you.

Once he made sure all the lights were on, he stepped back to the console and reached for the final two switches. He flipped the first one, starting the rotation of the device. It jerked into motion, kind of like dropping a car from neutral to drive while you have your foot on the gas pedal. Reese didn't make the connection. Instead, he figured it was the upgrade to the breaker panel. The printer started up slowly printing out what the computer and sensors were recording. "Well, where's the lights?" Reese asked himself as he looked at the panel making sure he followed every step. Then he noticed it: the magnet switch wasn't turned on.

He reached for the switch, the tip of his finger was right at it as Kat walked in the door. Once she saw the device spinning and realized what he was doing she yelled out to him. "Reese! Stop!" It was too late. Reese's hand was already in motion, and the yell from Kat, just pushed the action further, finishing the move. The switch for the electro-magnets was thrown and a brilliant flash of light filled the room. The device fired up and shot through the roof like a cannonball. Reese just stood there looking up at it and a single sound came out of his mouth. "whoa!" It was long and drawn out, in a disbelieving and yet astonished tone.

Then he was hit with a thud that knocked him down. The next thing he knew, he was under a table with Kat. After it seemed like all of the debris from the hole in the roof had stopped falling, Kat removed herself from her protective position over Reese. She sat him up and frantically started checking him out. She was in a state of panic, she was running her hands all over him.

"Oh my God, are you alright? Are you hurt?"

Reese, not realizing just how panicked Kat was, just stared up at the hole in the roof. "Did you see it? It works, I made it work. Did you see it Kat, I mean Elizabeth?"

"Oh my God! You scared the shit out of me! Yes, I saw it."

"So where is it now?"

"I don't know, honey," she said as she crawled out from under the table and helped Reese to his feet. "Are you sure you're not hurt?"

"I'm fine." He said as he brushed himself off. "I made it work....I can't believe it, I made it work."

# Chapter 19

Kevin and Rosie brought their *Mule* to an abrupt stop when they saw the object flying toward the house. They had already made it far enough away from the hangar that they couldn't hear the noise of the object crashing through the roof. Marcus, on the other hand, did hear the ruckus and had already turned around. He started booking it to the hangar, fearing the worst. He had no idea what had happened- he was just following the sound of the noise. The device had shot through the roof so quickly he didn't even get a chance to see it.

Dylon had his music cranked up and was enjoying the small amount of private time he would have for the weekend. He had already pulled the burgers and dogs off the grill and had just finished setting the tomatoes on the tray with the other dressings for lunch. He was carrying it over to the table when all of a sudden he was covered with a wave of water from the pool. It startled him and almost knocked him over.

The tray he had been carrying was no longer in his hands, but all over the pool deck. When he got past the initial shock of having the crap scared out of him, he looked at the pool. There, lying at the bottom of the pool, he saw it. At first, he couldn't believe his eyes, and then the realization of what was down there hit him. "Oh my God, Reese!" were the next thoughts that ran through his mind.

He grabbed his radio and in an instant he was running around the side of the house, to get to the hangar as quick as he could. "Kat! Kat, do you copy?" There was no answer. A thousand thoughts ran through Dylon's mind. A burst of adrenaline shot through his veins. His speed increased and he ran right past Kevin and Rosie. He didn't even see them.

"Hang on, Rosie!" Kevin yelled as he whipped the *Mule* around. They pulled beside Dylon and finally got his attention. He jumped in the back and Kevin floored it. When they finally reached the hangar, Kat and Reese were with Marcus. Reese was holding a cloth on his knee, which had been scraped when he hit the floor. Marcus was cleaning a cut on Kat's shoulder. She had no idea how she received it. All she could remember was that when she came in the door, she screamed at Reese and then they were on the floor.

A wave of relief came over Dylon, then a little anger. "Reese! How many times bud…." Reese just hung his head, he knew he was in big trouble. "Buddy, I just don't want you to get hurt. Do you understand that?" Dylon didn't wait for an answer, he just walked away. He headed into the hangar to check everything out. It was quite a mess. There was debris from the hole in the roof all over the floor. Closer to the console, he saw Kat's broken radio on the floor. "Well I guess that explains why she didn't answer." He thought aloud, still shaken a little.

Dylon was having a hard time bringing himself down. He wasn't sure if it was the thought of losing the last people in his life he loved, or remnants of the adrenaline rush. "Probably a little of both," he told himself as he started walking over to where the device used to sit.

That's when he noticed it. He went over everything in his head, every report, every test, every stupid little thing that he tried to get the damn thing working. "figures, that it would be something that simple." He shook his head and walked over to the console. He looked everything over and started flipping switches off. He was also walking himself through the steps he made yesterday, when the device tripped the breaker. As he flipped the last switch to the off position, he remembered it. He had left the console and headed for the breaker box, he didn't return the control throttles to the start-up position. He didn't return them to the idle position. "Well, this one is completely my fault. I guess I'll need to install a lock, or put in an ignition switch or something that requires a key." Dylon said to himself as he stepped away from the console and started walking back to the device pad.

"I still can't believe it would be that simple…. actually I can." He just shook his head as he looked at the terminal wires, the red one and the black one.

"Uncle Dylon, I'm sorry I broke your machine…" Reese said as he was looking at the floor. He couldn't even look Dylon in the eyes. He had never been yelled at like that before and wasn't sure what to expect. Dylon turned and looked at Reese, or tried to anyway.

"Reese, look up here, look at my eyes." When he lifted his head his eyes were full. He wasn't crying, but the tears were welled up in his eyes. Dylon spoke again: "Reese, I just don't want to see you get hurt and a lot of the stuff we play with can hurt you really bad if you're not paying attention. Okay?"

Reese nodded his head in acknowledgement.

"I want you to take a look at something with me." Dylon said as he guided the boy a little closer to the terminal.

"Do you see the two wires, the red one and the black one? Well the red one is a positive wire, which is usually marked by a plus sign. The black one is a negative wire, usually marked by a minus sign. Can you tell me what you did wrong here, without touching anything?"

Reese leaned in and studied everything over again. Though it took him a minute, he finally figured it out. "I hooked the wires up backwards." he said, " I guess that was a bad thing huh?"

"Normally, I would say yes, but I think you figured out what I haven't been able to."

"So I made it work?"

"Yeah bud, you made it work, I think. We'll have to see what we can do with what you put in the pool."

"It made it to the pool? He he," Reese covered his mouth as soon as the little laugh slipped out. Dylon just gave him a look and a little shove. "Go on laughing boy! Let's get back to the house, so we can get you and Elizabeth fixed up."

\* \* \* \* \* \*

Lt. Vasquez couldn't help but play the events of the visit over and over in his mind. "There's something not right here. If they were doing something wrong, why would they invite me to look at it? Why would they want to include me in on it? And besides, I like the Rosiers, they've been very good to me and my people. If I could only talk to General Grant, I would find out what is really going on." As Vasquez drove on, he came to the conclusion to pull his man out of the mission. He didn't feel good about the whole operation, and with Kolminski seeming to be pulling all the strings, he really didn't want anything to do with it. Vasquez hadn't liked this guy when they were introduced a couple of years ago. With General Grant's promotion, he had to let go some of his former responsibilities, one of which was the liaison for the handling of reports on *The Estate.*

Vasquez had exhausted every avenue he could to break the U.S. contract concerning that plot of land. They insisted that it was too risky. There were still too many of the drug cartels in the Peruvian politician's pockets. General Grant had even put in a word for Vasquez, but to no avail.

\* \* \* \* \* \*

The next morning, Vasquez sat down at his computer to type a letter.

*Mr. Kolminski,*

*I am sorry to inform you that special agent Paschel has had an unfortunate family emergency. At the present time I have no other agents available to assist in your special operation concerning the surveillance of the Rosier Estate. Please accept my sincerest apologies for any inconvenience this may cause to the mission. I will continue to search my ranks to find a willing and suitable person to help with the mission if it is still needed. I understand this is a very delicate operation, so I will only select the best possible candidates and send the files on them to help in your selection process. Again, my deepest apologies and I will send him and his family your best wishes.*

*Awaiting your response,*
*Lt. Ricardo Vasquez.*

\* \* \* \* \* \*

When Kolminski read the e-mail he lost it. "Why does this not surprise me? Fucking third world countries. Why do we even bother messing with them? Whoever it was, probably has malaria or something stupid like that. It wouldn't surprise me if they were drunk and wandered off a cliff somewhere. My job would be so much easier if I didn't have to deal with such imbeciles."

Kolminski sat down to type his response.

*'Dear Mr. Vasquez,*

*If your country would concentrate a little more on modernizing yourselves, instead of producing so many drugs, stupid little 'emergencies' like this wouldn't arise.'*

Kolminski stopped himself. "No, I can't say that. Somebody might actually read this, which I highly doubt, but just in case somebody is actually doing their job, I better reword this. Delete, delete, delete," He said aloud as he was trying to figure out how to respond. He wrote:

*Dear Lt. Vasquez,*

*Sorry for your loss. Send me the files, if you should find somebody suitable. Our man is highly capable, and shouldn't need any assistance. Thank you for the update.*

*Senior Foreign Relations Officer,*
*Mr. Billy Kolminski*

Kolminski hit the send button. "I seriously doubt you will find anybody suitable for the job. I read the file on Paschel, and if he was one of your best....Well, I would say I feel sorry for you, but I don't."

Kolminski turned off his computer, picked up his

drink, and walked back to his party. As he stepped out the back door Nicole put her arm around his and asked if everything was all right. "Oh, somebody thought they had something important to say, but it wasn't anything at all. You know if people would just think for themselves, before getting into a panic and relying on somebody else to fix their problems. Well, I guess I would be out of a job." They both laughed and walked out to join the rest of the partygoers.

# Chapter 20

Being a weekend, the majority of the staff that worked at *The Estate* had gone home. The handful that remained, about seven or eight, were also caught off guard by the events that had just unfolded. By the time the group had returned to the main house, the staff had already retrieved the device from the pool and were checking it out. There was a lot of chatter amongst them discussing not only what it was and how it worked, but also how it ended up in the pool.

Dylon asked Juan if he and a couple of his guys could take it to the hangar. He also apologized for interrupting any plans that they might have had. Juan just shrugged it off and replied, "No worries, Senor Dylon." Juan leaned closer to Dylon and lowered his voice. "Enrique was cheating anyway, good thing this happened or I would have been breaking up a fight." He patted Dylon on the shoulder and hustled his guys off with the device.

Rosalie, who had given Juanita a break from her daily duties, had already cleaned up and remade the lunch Dylon had prepared before all of the excitement took place. Once again, Dylon apologized and thanked her for her hard work in making sure everything was taken care of and once again he got the response that it wasn't a problem. Dylon was thankful for the people he had working for him and always made sure to treat them in a manner that he would like to be treated. This practice earned him the respect and the friendship of all of his employees, and was something he tried very hard to honor.

* * * * * *

The day's events proved to open a lot of doors that no one expected. As they were eating lunch they, discussed what all they needed to do before they left *The Estate*, which only gave them a day and a half. The boys and Kat would spend the majority of the next day getting the device hooked back up and trying to get it running again. Rosie would spend most of her day taking a look at all of the things that had been donated to the surrounding villages. Just a basic knowledge of what had been done by the Rosiers, so that when she started building a more business-type relationship with Lt. Vasquez, she would know everything she needed to.

Kat found her mind wandering, even though, the majority of the talk was geared towards the projects that needed to be done, the conversation still ended up returning to the incident with the device and the profound effect it had on everything else. Kat's thoughts kept going back to their departure from the village, and the note the medicine man's apprentice had brought.

It wasn't so much the message about the long journey but who the message was for. She avoided bringing up the message, until she could be sure of whom it was meant for. *The builder of the stairs to the stars,* she knew she heard those words before but just couldn't place where. When the subject did come up, she just brushed it off. "Now you know I don't believe in all that fortune telling stuff," she said and quickly tried to change the subject, but it didn't work. She was asked again and gave in. "It was something about a long journey, honestly I don't know why it's such a big deal. We can go back if you want and all have our fortunes read, if you believe in that sort of stuff." Kat said and laughed hoping that it would pass the conversation on to the next topic.

The conversation did pass on and Kat's fears were at least halfway put to rest. The truth of the matter is, she did sort of believe in it. Not necessarily that it was set in stone, but that the predictions marked a major decision. A point where, once the decision was made, your path would be altered. She felt that once you passed that point, if you followed that stuff, another reading would be required, because as your paths changed so did your choices in the future. It just seemed to be a lot of faith to put into one person, instead of just following what your gut told you.

That's when she figured out where she had seen the message before. "The diary," she said to herself. She remembered the conversation with her grandmother, as she handed Kat her mother's diary. "The best person to trust in is you. You may not want to accept what you know to be true, but eventually you will. Then you will see you put yourself through a lot of needless pain and suffering. You will also see that this is needed to help you learn and grow, to help you figure out who you want to become and who you want to share that with. It may hurt now dear, but trust me, it will pass." These are the words Angela passed on to her daughter, the same words her grandmother told her. They were also in Angela's diary. Kat's mom never got a chance to actually say these words, but wanted her to know them and wrote them in the diary under the section titled "A Mothers Advice".

Kat mentally shrugged off the memory and came back to reality when she heard her name again. "Are you still with us, Elizabeth?" Dylon asked.

"I'm sorry, I was just lost in thought, I guess it's just been a busy few days." She responded, but was still preoccupied by thoughts of the meaning of the medicine man's words. Rosie, who was becoming a little overwhelmed with all of the excitement, also wanted to get lost from all of it. Still not completely sure about her decision to join the group she just wanted to take a minute to be alone with her thoughts. She gathered up her glass, topped it off with the Pinot Grigio, and excused herself. "If you guys don't mind, I think I'm going to walk off some of this lunch."

"The garden?" Dylon asked.

"Yes, I think I'm going to take you up on checking it out," she said as she headed in that direction.

\* \* \* \* \* \*

Rosie had been gone about half an hour. Kevin had helped clean everything off the table and grabbed himself a beer and the bottle of Pinot. "Well, I think I'm going to see if Rosie's lost." Kevin made his way around the house and through the garden.

Rosie heard someone calling her name and quickly got up from the sitting rock and turned facing the opposite direction, quickly doing everything she could to regain her composure. When Kevin came around the corner, she turned to greet him. "And just what are you doing sneaking around in the bushes?" She said trying to make a joke.

"Just thought I'd bring you a refill," he said as he

held up the half empty bottle. Then he noticed a tear on her cheek. "Are you alright?"

"Oh, just out of wine." She answered with a half-hearted laugh.

"Well, let me help you out, ma'am." Kevin said, realizing she wasn't going to talk about whatever had brought her to this point.

"This place is just magical, it has a sense of being in another world. I can certainly see why Elizabeth's mom spent a lot of her time out here."

"It is pretty impressive. Are you sure you're going to be okay?"

"Yes, I'll be fine. I was just questioning myself. Wondering if I, if we were getting into something we shouldn't…."

"And?" Kevin said as she paused.

"Well, then I saw this." She turned Kevin around, to face the obelisque. He started to read it.

*Often*
*times*
*the answers*
*you seek may*
*not come from*
*any one person,*
*but will be revealed*
*when you allow*

*yourself to become*
*more open to the signs*
*of your*
*surroundings*

*Angela Rosier*

"Wow, that's pretty good. So what do the signs tell you?" Kevin asked.

"Well, getting here, all just seemed to fall into place. Like we were meant to be here. That doesn't mean it's all going to be that easy, but there have been too many things that have pointed us in this direction, led us to this place. So I guess, from this point forward there will be no looking back." Rosie held her glass up to Kevin's bottle of beer and they made a quick 'cheers'.

"Come walk with me. This place is really beautiful."

\* \* \* \* \* \*

**Special ops:**

Two and a half days had passed since they had dropped. The teams had made it to the rendezvous point a half a day ahead of schedule. The two senior members of the group were debating on calling in now or giving it a couple of hours. If they called in too early, future missions would surely be on a more constrictive time restraint. However, if they did call in now it would reflect well on the team, and both men agreed that they had finally built a good team. They finally decided to split the difference, giving the men a couple of hours to wind down a little. This would still put them calling in a couple hours ahead of schedule.

One of the younger members of the team asked why this place had been chosen. After a long discussion on why he shouldn't be asking such questions, the team leader had explained all he knew about the arrangement between the two governments. The mission of the past few days was just a long-awaited update to the surveillance process. This of course, was not the whole story, but was what the team was told.

* * * * * *

At the command center, the captain of the mission had just finished writing his report. Cautiously, he had made a very brief mention of the occurrence that put them in the position where slight course deviations were needed.

It was something he knew Kolminski would not approve of. He also knew General Grant would appreciate the opportunity to present the report to his special interest group *The Five*. *The Five* was a group that had formed long before the Majestic Twelve, and it was a secret that was very well kept. There was a time when a member of *The Five* held a seat in the twelve, but when they started getting more publicity *The Five* vacated that seat for fear of being exposed themselves.

*The Five* was never mentioned by name, and typically, unfortunate coincidences would arise if they felt you were getting too close. The only rumor that was ever spoken about the group was, if you ever joined up with them you would basically be in a completely different world, because it would seem that you disappeared off the face of the earth. It was almost like you joined the witness protection program.

* * * * * *

Not long after Kevin went to look for Rosie, Kat decided she was going to soak in the tub, just so she wouldn't feel so sore from the stresses she put her body through that day. Dylon and Marcus were left alone sitting at the table with their drinks. It didn't take long for them to decide to head to the hangar and see what they could do with the device. By the time supper rolled around, they had the device reattached to the test supports and had rigged up a temporary but workable breaking system.

During the process, they had discussed all the conspiracy theories they could about the whole UFO cover-up and the possibilities of the 'why factor'. Marcus thought he had read and researched all of them until they came to the subject of the Majestic Twelve.

"Well, there was allegedly a group that was formed before the Majestic Twelve." Dylon said, which really piqued Marcus' interest.

"Really? I've never come across that one," he said in response to Dylon.

"Yeah, I only ran across it once. I was seventeen and visiting my normal sites and came across it completely by accident. It was called *The Five.* It was just a group of college kids that met at some world science and technologies competition. They immediately befriended each other and grew to be very influential scientists. There was one from each of the major countries- the U.S., China, Japan, the U.K., and Russia." Dylon stopped there and kind of left Marcus hanging.

"Okay, I never heard of them." Marcus said

waiting for more of the story. Dylon didn't respond.

"Well, don't stop there, dude. You've kind of walked me to the edge of the cliff and left me standing there."

"I pretty much have to stop there." Dylon said. "As I was reading on how they bonded and made a pact to do research on UFO's and their technology my computer lost its connection and shut down. When I brought it up and went back to the web address, all that came up was 'You should forget you were here.' Then the computer crashed in a really odd sort of way. Not only that, I had to get new phone lines throughout the entire house, and replace all the computers. They all crashed in that same weird way. I never could find the path back to that site."

# Chapter 21

Later that evening, long after the sun had disappeared from the sky, the group found themselves at the hangar. Marcus and Dylon were all animated and excited about the progress they had made. They hadn't told anyone, but they already did a test run on the device, and it worked exactly the way they wanted, once the polarity was reversed. Dylon was going to re-mark the terminals where the power source was hooked up, but thought better of it. What he explained to Marcus was that if someone were trying to steal the technology they would hook it up normally, unless it was marked otherwise. If they didn't mark it nobody would think it worked.

They were leaving *the estate* tomorrow, so the rest of the evening was spent discussing their game plan in a more relaxed mode. They were basically reviewing things they already covered. The whole time the device was floating about twenty feet or so in the air. Every now and then each one would put a different probe a little closer, just so the computer could read the reactions.

Dylon mentioned that with Reese's discovery of how to make the device work, he would go ahead and order enough parts to make some additional devices.

Marcus mentioned that he could check into finishing his last semester off-campus. Labs only counted for a third of his grade, so he figured he could take the hit on his grade point average. "Being able to be at the estate, would be the best way to get a good feel for how this device is actually going to work. Plus I really would like some hands-on experience in building one of them, especially if I am going to have to install it in…" He quickly pointed to one of the two crafts in the hangar, hoping to cover his near blunder. "… one of those things."

Rosie was the next to speak up. "Well, Dylon, you were not supposed to know this for a few months, but I had planned on retiring from the firm. I will still go through with that, but no one there can know you know. I will announce my retirement plans when the time is right. I should have some extra time on my hands while training my replacement to go over everything I need to know about anything we might want to know. I would also like to suggest going on a few sales calls with Elizabeth, just so I know what exactly our sales pitch is. If that's not a problem."

Kat responded to Rosie. "I would love to have you along, and I think it's a great idea. Everyone knows sales are done better with a team instead of just one individual. As for myself, you all know that I've piled my plate about as full as I can get it. I will be available to answer questions via e-mail but you'll have to be patient. You may not get your answers as quick as you would like."

Kevin was the last to lay his plan out. "I could check and see about doing one of my refurbishments at *the estate*. There are a couple of clients that have vacation homes in Peru and it might be better for them. I'm sure there wouldn't be a problem with me bringing some of my work down here. This would give me a little time to help oversee the upcoming construction process. If I heard correctly, that would give you two of us down here during that time. Marcus and I could split the responsibility of making sure things are done to spec." Marcus shook his head in agreement to Kevin's last statement.

* * * * * *

The helicopter landed quickly. The men boarded, and it was off as quickly as it landed. The captain informed them that the mission was a success. "We came online within a few minutes after you called in. As far as your debriefing goes, what you saw was a weather balloon and some training maneuvers that we interrupted. We should have been a little more careful in researching our flight plans for the mission. Luckily for you guys I was able to convince command to

forego your debriefing on that subject. You still have
to go through the normal debriefing on the mission,
though."

\* \* \* \* \* \*

5

*Information sketchy, Special operations
Watchdog. Upgraded surveillance approved on former
Vanderitos Estate. I.P. address for Watchdog
infiltration 512.87.154.659 passcode not required.
Possible UFO production in process. Sensitive
handling required. Construction permits applied for
and approved. Launch pad capabilities have also been
approved. Other persons of interest include Lt.
Ricardo Vasquez and special agent Humberto
Paschel.*
*Updated list of persons of interest to follow.*
 *Special note: Dylon Rosier happened on one of
the Clean Sweep websites ten years ago. Devastation
Virus was employed and successful. Only one future
attempt to revisit site, led to porn site.*
 *Dylon Rosier current owner of former Vanderitos
Estate. Files have been accumulated on this person
since Clean Sweep.*

*5 End.*

\* \* \* \* \* \*

After spending a long weekend of partying and removing the people from his guest list that were not overly grateful for being invited to such an event, Kolminski found himself in his office, preparing for Captain Atkinson's report. He was going through e-mails, mumbling to himself the entire time.

When Mrs. Hall showed the Captain in, all Kolminski had to say to her was a complaint about not having fresh sugar cubes for his coffee. "How do you expect me to use something that's been laying in the office of such an old building all weekend. Just the thought of how many bugs could have been crawling all over these makes me ill." The poor woman was apologizing all over herself as she removed the tray. The Captain couldn't help but feel sorry for her as he held the door open.

"That's really not necessary, Captain. She's at least half capable of doing her job without your help."

"My apologies sir, just good raising and good manners."

"Well isn't that nice. If we all got paid for being a good boy.....well I guess the world would be a nicer place to live in, wouldn't it?" Kolminski gave the

Captain a really fake smile. "So, if we can get back to reality for a moment. Do you have a report for me, or did you just come in here to make me feel all warm and fuzzy with your good manners?"

The Captain dropped the envelope containing his report on the mission on Kolminski's desk, stood back at attention, and mumbled. "I really don't think that would be possible."

Kolminski didn't even hear it. He quickly opened the envelope and started to read the report. He pulled out a red pen and started marking what he considered to be grammatical errors. He marked and mumbled as he read and finally what he was mumbling was audible enough for the Captain to understand. As he was correcting more mistakes than the Captain thought he had made, he distinctly heard Kolminski mumble. "For a Captain I would have expected better." Atkinson had to defend himself.

"With all due respect, sir."

Kolminski slammed the pen down and blasted him. "With all due respect? Is that what you said, Captain?" Kolminski didn't wait for a response. "With all due respect, Captain. I am the one that has to answer to General Grant, not you, me. I can't believe an officer of your credentials can't even write a decent report. You know this will have to be rewritten and of course I'll be the one that does it. You should be grateful that I have your back on this one. Oh, and one more thing, this bit about the UFO….it will be deleted. I bet you still believe in the tooth fairy too, don't you?"

The Captain was about to explode. "So I guess we're finished here, sir?"

"I should say so." Kolminski snapped. "I hope you know this is going to throw my schedule off for the entire day. You should be grateful."

As the captain left the office, he stopped at the assistant's desk and asked for a pen and pad. He jotted down a name and number and as he handed it back to her he asked if she had a pencil. She said yes in a quizzical manner. Just then time Kolminski stirred from his office, blabbering about how much work his assistant had to do and didn't need any distractions from the Captain. The Captain hurriedly told her. "If you're as smart as I think you are you'll know what to do with the pencil. When I wrote that information down, I was pressing a little harder than I should." He winked at her and turned to leave.

When Kolminski got to her desk he found the pad with a name and number. He picked it up and tore off the page. As he walked back into his office he mumbled, "Nice try, Captain." When Kolminski returned to his office, the assistant picked up her pencil and brushed it across the pad that remained.

The indentations gave her with the information the Captain had left her. She smiled, took the sheet of paper, folded it, and put it in her purse.

\* \* \* \* \* \*

The next morning was a pretty laid back morning for the group. The flight out would be leaving pretty soon, and then it would be back to the regular grind. Except the regular grind had all been changed by the events, that unfolded this weekend. The mission now was basically to build a habitat on another planet, sweet-talk two different governments into allowing them to do it, sell no less than five multimillion dollar satellites in order to piggy back your payload into space, and build the rest of the build/launch complex, all in just under a year's time.

They were all kind of quiet as they digested how they were going to handle their normal lives and take on the duties of the new challenge that lay ahead. There was some small talk, but mainly making sure they had contact numbers and addresses. There were some best wishes passed along for the two college students and a congrats for the retirement plan, which was promptly followed by a witty statement. "Thanks, I think."

While all the bags were being packed into the

jet, Reese was running across the field for one more goodbye hug. It wasn't long and the small Lear was ready to be boarded. Before everyone boarded Reese handed Rosie a small package about the size of a compact disc. "It will help you fly better, for when you come back." He said and smiled. She laughed a little and thanked him with a big hug. "See you soon. Now run along and don't play with anything you shouldn't." She winked at him, and he knew she was referring to the device.

# Chapter 22

The next few months would prove to be a little trying for everyone. Rosie had already gone through one assistant and was almost ready to get rid of the next when she finally had a realization. She and her new assistant went to lunch to hopefully come to an understanding of how to do her job.

"Lexie, it's really very simple." Rosie said, trying to find a comparison that Alexandria could relate to. "You said you raised three children, correct?"

Lexie nodded as she took a drink of her tea.

"Well then, there you have it. Think of the office as your house, and the others as your children. Would you want your children to be embarrassed by not doing something they were supposed to? Of course you wouldn't, so you would remind them. That's all you have to do here. Now I don't expect you to be all friendly and personable at the start. It would probably be easier if you just left notes on their door, and just slowly slide into the 'mother' position. Trust me, you'll see, they will start coming to you and depending on you for that. Before you know it you will be one of the guys, and whatever you do, stand your ground. Don't let them walk on you, not that they would. Dear you've got all the computer knowledge you need. You know some operating systems I didn't even know existed, so I think you're good on that end. Just keep it in mind that these are your children and you'll do fine."

"Thank you Rosie, I've just been trying to do the best job possible while trying to remember everyone's name."

Rosie stopped her. "Lexie, forget their names. There are too many, you'll get their names in time. All they have to remember is one name, yours."

\* \* \* \* \* \*

Marcus and Kat had decided to move in together for the last year of school as Marcus only had one semester left and would be leaving for *the estate* after he was finished. His plans to take that last semester off-campus were squashed, so the two of them figured it would be in the best interest of the work that had to be done.

With Kat's persistence in getting out of school as quick as she could, the previous hard work she had put in was starting to pay off. Most of her classes were becoming a little easier. She did try, though, to cram it into just two semesters, but course scheduling just didn't allow it. This actually worked in her favor, as it helped free up some time for her. She had already set up two different meetings for presenting some possible new clients who were looking to launch satellites. One was a telecommunications company that was preparing to start offering satellite internet for colleges in South America. The other company already had an aging satellite and was taking proposals for replacing it.

* * * * * *

Kevin was able to transfer two of his refurbishing projects to *the estate*, and had also come up with six different investors. Combined, the total amount of outsider money that was interested in investing came in at over just two hundred sixty million dollars. When Kevin passed this information along to Dylon via text message, Dylon almost fell down the stairs. The text that followed floored him even more.

> *They actually hope you fail. They*
> *need a tax write off. LOL*

Dylon and Kevin ended up having several more conversations about how they wanted to proceed with bringing in investors and the ins and outs of how they would repay the money, or if they even would. Ultimately they decided on the founding of a nonprofit organization. It would be called B.A.B.F.O.C.

Building A Better Future for Our Children.
The organization would make small donations of
money to groups of the same mindset. The majority of
the money would be used for the research and
development of future technological advancements,
and all the equipment for the Mars mission.

\* \* \* \* \* \*

Dylon was able to convince Mr. Tuttle to allow
him to do one project at a time, instead of three or four
like the others in the office. If he wasn't as good as he
was at his job, this task might have proved to be a
little tougher.

The one thing Dylon had a hard time doing was
convincing his grandfather to take his new venture
under the wings of Rosier Enterprises.

"There are just too many unknown variables
involved when dealing with putting things into orbit.
If you really want to see how to waste a bunch of
money, we'll just put a briefcase full of it up there.
Then we'll wait and see how long it is before one of
those marble-sized meteors rips through it," were his
exact words.

Dylon thought he had all the information needed
to at least convince him to give it a small amount of
consideration, but more words of wisdom befell him.

"Dylon, we did not take four generations to build this company by taking radical risks. At the bare minimum we need a seventy five percent factor of success, and all you've shown me is a fifty percent possibility of success. I'm sorry, boy, we just can't do it. Besides, I thought you were going to take over your father's engineering firm."

"Oh I still intend on doing that, this is just a different field and I want to explore the possibilities. Not just for myself, but for the future of the company." Dylon responded in the hopes that 'the future of the company' statement might hit a soft spot somewhere, but it didn't.

"Are you sure this isn't just you wanting to fulfill a childhood dream? You always have had a special fascination with outer space," his grandfather replied.

Dylon knew he was fighting a losing battle and gave in to his Grandfather's words. "Yeah, you're probably right." Dylon packed up his reports and was getting ready to leave. When his grandfather asked why he was rushing off. Dylon simply told him that he had an appointment, something to do with some new cooling units for the college dorms in Tennessee.

As soon as he got out of the building, he texted Kat.

> *We are on our own. No*
> *Granddad's help.*

223

She responded with a simple statement, that meant a lot to the both of them.

*We've always been on our own, big brother, we'll be just fine.*

Dylon just smiled as he read her response and remembered where it came from. When they were children, after they lost their parents, this is the little saying they came up with when they didn't understand the answers their nannies gave them. As they grew into their teen years and had to deal with the normal growing pains of any child, all they had to lean on was each other and the saying got more use as they grew.

Dylon's phone rang, and broke his recollection of the memory. It was the ring producer for the anti-gravitational device. He rushed to the shelter of a nearby building entrance to get out of the winter wind. When he answered the phone he was delighted to hear that the first shipment of rings was on the way. What he heard next caught him off guard. Apparently, there was a man touring the plant in the hopes of hiring them to produce an item for his company. He had been very interested in the rings that were being produced, and even offered a lot of money to use the same metal that was being used in Dylon's project. It seemed that the gentleman really liked the look of the metal. Dylon was already putting his thoughts together on what he needed to say as he was digesting the information he was receiving.

"Not to worry, though, Mr. Rosier. I convinced the gentleman we could produce the same look at a lot cheaper cost. By the way, what exactly is it that you're building again?"

"Well, first off, Mr. Norton, thank you very much for your honesty and your loyalty in protecting my patented metal formula. What I'm building is merely art. Do you know what an armillary sundial looks like?"

"Yeah, isn't that one of those globe-looking things with an arrow through it?" He responded to Dylon's question.

"Yeah, that's exactly what it is. Well, I've found a market for them in South America, pretty close to the Equator. Damn the humidity down there, every one of them I've built so far has already begun to rust, thus the special formula for the metal. I really appreciate your confidentiality in protecting my secret formula. I also hope you understand the importance of keeping this formula a secret, because I'm really not in the metallurgy business and don't have a desire to pick up that field of trade. I'll be sure to have my assistant send out a payment to you right away, and please keep me informed on any further inquiries into my formula. You know how companies can be when it comes to finding out the trade secrets of their competitors. If they are really that persistent and come back, you could always replace the Bismuth with Aluminum. It gives you the same look but not the same durability. "

"Yes sir, I understand. I'll be sure to keep you posted." Mr. Norton said as he hung up the phone.

As soon as Dylon hung up with Mr. Norton, he began typing a text to the four others of the team.

Let the games begin. Details at seven.

* * * * * *

It was only a fifty minute flight, but that sure beat a three, maybe four-hour drive, with rush hour traffic. Dylon made it home in time to shower and fix himself something to eat before the conference call.

Communications between the team members over the three months that had passed since their visit to *the estate* had evolved. Any talk about the anti-gravitational device was now referred to as the parts for the sundial. This was brought into play by Rosie, who trusted the government a lot less than the others.

She thought it would be best if certain things they talked about over the phone were mentioned in code.

When the phone rang, Dylon had just taken a bite of his sandwich. His greeting was kind of mumbled. There were a total of three of the other team members on the phone. Rosie, Kat, and Marcus, Kevin had responded earlier that he would be a little late, only fifteen minutes or so. Knowing that, Dylon started the conversation.

"Well first of all, congratulations on your graduation Marcus." Rosie seconded the sentiment. Of course Kat had already passed that message along.

"For the second order of business, the first shipment of parts for the, ah… sun dial, left today and on a more serious note, we're possibly starting to attract some attention. The manufacturer of the parts mentioned that someone was ….how do I put it…a little *too* interested in our product. So I just wanted to give you a heads-up. Just be a little more aware of what's happening around you."

About that time Kevin dialed in to join the call. Dylon repeated everything he had just gone over to Kevin. As far as Kevin's reports on the construction process at *the estate*, everything was running at about a day ahead of schedule. He was dying to know when Marcus was going to make it down to help out with overseeing some of the construction sites.

"Hey Kevin, I'm scheduled to leave this weekend. I should be there around two in the afternoon on Saturday. Hopefully we'll have some time for you to give me a rundown of what's been going on and what I'll be overseeing," Marcus said with some excitement in his voice. Everyone could tell he was anxious to get started.

\* \* \* \* \* \*

After about an hour on the conference call, they all decided they were happy with the progress reports they each had to present. Dylon gathered up his dinner plate and put it in the sink. After organizing all his notes on the call, he put them in the briefcase, locked it, and put it beside his coat.

He sat down on the couch, turned on the TV, and started flipping through the channels. He was hoping to catch a rerun of the *UFO Hunters*, which he knew he would end up falling asleep while watching. Sure enough he did, and he awoke at about three in the morning. He shut everything off and headed to the bedroom. On his way, he noticed a small dark brown envelope lying on the floor, just inside the front door. He reached down, picked it up, and threw it in a stack of unopened mail.

# Chapter 23

It seemed incredibly dark the next morning when Rosie was driving in to the office. It didn't really surprise her, since weathermen were predicting another four inches of snow today. From the look of the sky, they were going to get that and then some. She mumbled under her breath as she pulled into the parking lot and noticed that Lexie's car was not there yet. "That girl is going to be the death of me before this is all done. I thought I had made some progress yesterday at lunch with her I guess not." She shook her head as she parked the car and hurried up to the front door.

When she made it to the door she already had the key she needed in hand, but before she could open the door to get out of the cold, she noticed a small dark brown envelope lying inside on the floor. She hurried up and got herself in, and then noticed that the alarm wasn't beeping, which instantly put her on guard.

She looked around the lobby and nothing seemed out of place. Rosie stepped over to her desk, quickly unlocked the drawers, and reached into the back of the bottom drawer, where she retrieved a small billy club. She dropped her purse on the desk, quickly shed her coat and anything else that would bind her or hinder her abilities. This also included her shoes, which were just pumps, but she wanted the best advantage she could have.

As she looked around all that she could see on were just the night lights, which consisted of a light about every twenty feet or so. Then she thought she heard an unrecognizable noise. She jumped slightly and then focused on the direction it came from. She stepped lightly down the hall, peering into each office ever so carefully. As she came to the bathrooms at the corner of the hall, she noticed a more light coming from down the hall near the break room. She tightened her grip on the club, raised her arms a little and cautiously stepped around the corner.

"Well, good morning, Rosie." Lexie noticed her going around the corner, but she didn't see the club in her hand.

"Die sucker!" Rosie yelled as she turned and swung the club.

"Aaahhhh!" Lexie ducked. "You crazy bitch!" She yelled as the club hit the wall and put a hole in it.

"Oh my God, Lexie? Where's your car?" Rosie said as she realized who was in the office with her.

"Oh my God! I can't believe you tried to hit me with that. Where did you get that and who else would you think was here?" She was moving quickly down the hall away from Rosie.

"Oh dear, I'm so sorry. Why didn't you turn on the lights when you come in? I didn't have any idea who was in here. Anyway, where is your car?" She said as she followed Lexie down the hall.

"My car is in the shop! My son dropped me off. I've been here for two hours now. I knew I should have taken a cab."

"So where is your stuff, I mean your purse and everything? I didn't see anything on the desk."

"Well, there was a car that followed us in. It made me kind of nervous, so I've been hanging out in the break room, and I didn't want to leave all my stuff sitting at the front desk for anyone that made me feel that uneasy to see. I didn't think anyone got here that early, I figured if it was anybody that worked here I would hear them come in. When I didn't, well, I went back and checked and I just saw the brake lights of the car leaving, so I went back to the break room and waited for you to show up. I didn't think you were going to try and take my head off."

After listening to Lexie explain her morning, something finally clicked in Rosie's mind. She reached for the brown envelope she picked up on her way in. "I found this on the way in, is it yours?"

Lexie looked at the envelope. "I've never seen that before. Where did you find it?"

"Just inside the door, it's probably just an advertisement for somebody wanting to sell us something. I'll look at it later, let's go get some coffee," Rosie said as she laid the envelope down.

\* \* \* \* \* \*

A couple of hours had passed and after Rosie finished observing Lexie's morning routine, she sat down at the desk. She only had to give Lexie a couple of pointers. Yesterday's lunch meeting really seemed to sink in. She reached for the brown envelope and as she was beginning to open it, Lexie passed the phone to her.

"Hey Elizabeth, how are you?"

"I just got some news about our first sales call and I just wanted to let you know, they need to move the meeting back an hour."

Rosie was listening to Kat but continued opening the envelope. Her jaw dropped when she read the message on the card inside.

"Thank you Elizabeth. I hate to cut this short but I have to go. I'll call you later." She quickly hung up the phone.

"Well that was odd she didn't even wait for me to respond." Kat thought as she hung up the phone.

Rosie got up and headed to Dylon's office with the envelope and card in hand. When she reached his office she went in and closed the door behind her. She dropped the card and envelope on his desk. He looked at the envelope, remembering the one he picked up at his house, and then read the note.

> *"On a more serious note, we're possibly*
> *starting to attract some attention."*
> 5

"Do you recall this part of our conference call?" Rosie asked without giving him time to respond. "Well, I would also like to let you know that Lexie was followed in to work this morning. It made her kind of nervous. Apparently we have to take some better steps at protecting ourselves and the innocent ones around us. I've got some friends that I can talk to about some new hardware that's allegedly capable of disabling any listening devices. Dylon you watch yourself, okay?" Rosie left his office about as quickly as she came in. She stopped by the desk and made sure Lexie was going to be okay by herself. When she covered all her bases she was off to call on an old friend.

* * * * * *

By the week's end, Rosie had passed along the information she needed and was supposed to hear something back by early next week. She and Kat were on their way to their first sales call with a little time to kill. They laughed and shared information about the odd things they were starting to notice, and found that they were becoming a bit more resourceful in there ways of eluding a possible tail. As they passed an electronics store, Rosie stopped Kat and headed inside the store.

"What are you looking for in here?" Kat asked.

"Oh, just need to get us a few more cards to play with." Rosie said vaguely.

"Memory cards? I didn't realize you brought a camera with you," Kat said, questioningly.

"Not those kind of cards, dear. We need to start filming what we're doing. You know, kind of like a documentary."

Kat was still a little confused, her answer still came out as a question. "Okay?"

"Honey, where is the best place to hide something?" Rosie didn't give her a chance to answer. "In plain sight. We need to record what's going on at *the estate*. Not everything, but enough to let Lt. Vasquez feel that everything is on the up and up. In addition to that, you need to record what is not on the up and up."

"I'm sorry Rosie, I'm having a hard time keeping up with you on this one. Why would we record what we don't want them to know anything about?"

"You're not a card player, are you?" Rosie smiled as she looked at Kat. "If you're going to play cards with the big boys, you have to learn how the game is played. You need 'an ace in the hole,' a 'card up your sleeve'. Do you understand now?"

"Yeah, I got it."

"So we're going to start to record our actions. What we want people to know and what we don't want people to know. Lt. Vasquez is going to help bring his country into the twenty-first century, and we are going to help him. Of course he will have to take all the credit, so we need to invite him to *the estate* and make him part of this documentary. That will be another play to help in boosting his confidence in us." Rosie picked up the little hand held recorder, a couple of extra batteries, and headed to the checkout counter.

* * * * * *

*Special ops*

"Send Mr. Kolminski in." General Grant's voice came over his assistant's phone. Before she could even get up, Kolminski had already made it to the door and was letting himself in. She followed him in, just to make sure the General didn't need anything else, and to make a point to Kolminski that her job was to *escort guests in*, not for them to just barge in. She handed Gen. Grant a fresh notepad and asked him if he needed any more coffee. When he declined she just looked at Mr. Kolminski with a pleasant but condescending smile, as if to say, 'I really wouldn't ask me for anything if I were you'. "Well if you need anything, you know where to find me." She closed the door behind her.

"Is our man ready, Kolminski?" Gen. Grant asked.

Kolminski handed Grant the file. "His name is Strickland. He has been with the agency for a while now. He's one of the best we have. His specialties are in I.E.D.'s, computer viruses, and he has an extensive knowledge of almost anything mechanical. The boy is a genius, literally."

"And what is our plan for getting him in?"

"Well sir, you've seen the surveillance tapes. We plan on slipping him into the construction crew. They have three different crews that work four on and four off. That way they can have a continuous construction process. They really are in a hurry to get this complex up and running. What exactly do you think they're up to, and why would they do it without our permission?"

General Grant just shuddered at Kolminski's last comment. "God help us if this man ever gets complete control of anything." He thought to himself. "Well Kolminski, they don't have to ask our permission for anything. They are their own country. It does surprise me that Lt. Vasquez hasn't contacted me about his plans. He has always been very interested in making sure that things are done in a proper way. A way that would not cause a lot of controversy between the two governments."

Kolminski cringed a little. "Well sir, he did try to contact you. You were in a meeting though and well he did say that it wasn't that important and would try again later." Kolminski recalled the conversation with Vasquez and knew he could never let the two talk to each other again. "Oh he also said that he knew you were a busy man and just wanted to catch up with an old friend before he went out on mission himself."

"Out on mission? Did he say for how long?"

"No sir, but he did send me a file on a guy named Paschel, that I would be conferring with. He said he was probably going to be the next one in line to take his office. I could bring it by if you would like to see it."

"Maybe at a later time, Kolminski. Well it sounds like we're finally going to get someone in the inside. You know there's only so much you can see with these surveillance cameras."

"I understand, sir, I'll make sure to keep you posted." Kolminski said and turned to leave the office. "This is going to work out better than I thought. I'll just have to make sure Paschel really isn't going to be at *the estate.*" He smiled as he left the meeting with General Grant, knowing it wouldn't be long before the old man retired and then he would be the one in charge of all of it.

\* \* \* \* \* \*

Rosie smiled as she watched Dylon rushing the day to an end. "So how many weekends are you going to spend in Tennessee trying to snag this girl?"

"What? I'm not trying to *snag* anyone. Honestly Rosie, it's for the business. I've…we've got these other three plots of land to develop and I'm just trying to see what would be the best possible business to…."

Rosie cut him short. "Well Dylon, if that were actually the case, then I would have to assume that your aren't doing your job properly. I haven't seen a single business report cross my desk."

Dylon looked at her like a deer caught in the

headlights, but Rosie continued before he started stuttering out some lame excuse. "You know, if you ask me, maybe you should spend some time showing her your world, instead of getting all wrapped up in hers. Just an observation, you have a good weekend now."

Dylon just gave Rosie that look, the one where he was trying to figure out how she knew the things she knew. He thanked her and wished her a good weekend too, then, he was off to catch his plane to Tennessee.

After boarding, he couldn't help but replay Rosie's words in his head. He thought maybe she was on to something, so he pulled out his laptop and started searching activities for the weekend in Tennessee. He had already sent Kaylee an email of what he thought they could do for the weekend, but now he was rethinking his plans.

He finally found something that piqued his interest. One of the local museums was hosting an air show this weekend to introduce the NASA exhibit that would be on display for the next month.

"That would be great to see." He thought to himself. "I hope it would be something she would be interested in. She should be, everyone loves a good air show." Before he got too involved in beating himself up trying to make sure she had a good time, he recalled Rosie's words of advice. *Show her my world.*

"Okay Rosie, this one's on you." Dylon said out loud as he jotted down the information and closed his laptop.

* * * * * *

Kaylee was having a blast watching Dylon in his element. She enjoyed the fact that he was actually coming out of his shell and not so wrapped up in impressing her. "Dylon, I had no idea that you were this excited about this stuff."

"Stuff! Oh my God, Kaylee, do you realize that all this stuff is what dreams are made of? To find yourself in the same position that Columbus may have found himself in, to be able to prove to all of those that look down on you with questioning, disapproving, and almost hoping you would fall flat on your face glances" He responded in an excited tone. "To be able to do all the things that you only see in movies, because in reality, that's the only place that they're possible. Kaylee, you really need to take a trip with me. You would be amazed at what you can actually do when you set your mind to it."

"This stuff really turns you on. Out of all the times you've come down here to visit with me, I've never seen you this excited." Kaylee said as she was watched how animated he was getting.

240

"Oh God, yes it does. Hey, we're planning a trip in the spring. Would you like to go?" Dylon said with high hopes.

"Well, that all depends on who the 'we' is." Kaylee responded.

"Oh, I'm sorry. That would be my sister and her boyfriend, and a couple of other business colleagues of mine. It will be a blast. You should consider it. If you really want to know who I am and what I'm all about, it would be a real eye opener for you." Dylon said with enthusiasm.

"Well, with an offer like that, how could I refuse?" Kaylee responded as she smiled and took Dylon's hand in her own. They wandered down a path that connected the park to the small airstrip where the air show was taking place. They found a spot on a small hill and laid out the blanket. Dylon had picked up a picnic basket and filled it with some snacks so they could eat after the show.

They spent the next couple of hours talking and laughing at stories Kaylee told about her childhood. With nightfall creeping up, the fireworks show was about to begin. Dylon reached in the picnic basket and pulled out the bottle of wine. It couldn't have been a more perfect day and the two of them enjoyed the rest of the night with the same enthusiasm as they had throughout the day.

# Chapter 24

With another three months past, winter's chill was almost gone. The girls had sold a total of three satellites, and for the record keeping process two probes had been donated to the Peruvian Government, by a foundation that wished to remain anonymous. The two probes were part of a science donation for the colleges in the country. The first probe would be going to Mars and the second would be a deep space probe that would send pictures back as long as there was a signal.

The complex at *the estate* was nearly two-thirds of the way done. And there was beginning to be a lot more excitement in the air amongst the members of the group. As their excitement grew, so did the odd happenings. Rosie's best advice was to make sure that everything appeared to be linked to the business Rosier Aerospace Solutions. 'The best way to hide something is in plain sight', became the motto amongst the group.

The group had all planned to meet at *the estate*, during Kat's spring break. It seemed that Kevin and Marcus had a surprise for them. Dylon thought he knew what it was, but kept quiet so as not to take anything away from both of their time in the spotlight, seeing how they were the ones who actually installed them.

\* \* \* \* \* \*

They got off the ground a little later than they had hoped. Kat's flight was delayed in takeoff and when they finally got in the air they ran into some bad visibility. Although the weather radar showed no storms, there was a small system that popped up after takeoff. It was a pretty bumpy ride for her.

"Looks like it's going to be another late landing Rosie." Dylon said as he kept checking his watch.

Rosie kept fidgeting with something. Dylon tried not to pay any attention to it but it was really starting to get the better of his curiosity. At first he thought she was just texting somebody, but now it looked like whatever she was playing with, she couldn't get it to work.

"Do you need a hand with that, Rosie?" He asked, stepping a little closer to her.

"What? Huh? Were you talking to me?" She said, revealing how consumed she was with her new toy.

"Yeah, I was talking to you. I asked if you needed a hand. What do you have there anyway?" He asked as he reached for it.

"Apparently, it's just another piece of electronic

crap that's going to take me a couple of years to figure out how to work." She said, all flustered as she handed it over to Dylon. He took it and gave it a good look. It seemed like a pretty simple device, like a cross between an ultrathin cell phone and a remote control. There were only three buttons on it, one marked with a plus and one with a minus, then a larger button in the center.

"So what exactly is this supposed to be, Rosie?"

"Well it's something my friend gave to me. It's some kind of electro-magnetic pulse interrupter. It's supposed to interrupt or stop anything with a computer chip in it."

"Okay...and why would you need something like this?"

"Well, just in case...." She stopped and Dylon got the message.

"So what all is it supposed to work on and did your friend tell you how it worked?"

"Of course he did, you just aim it at what you want affected and press the button. I don't understand why it's not working, it worked fine yesterday."

"Oh really, and you know this how?"

"Well, that's kind of a silly question I tested it."

"What did you test it on Rosie?"

She snickered a little when she answered. "I just wanted to see if it worked." She responded, much like a child about to be busted.

Dylon raised an eyebrow. "Rosie?"

"Oh, a couple of ATM's and a couple of vending machines." She quickly blurted.

"Rosie, who were you harassing with your new toy?" Dylon asked accusingly.

"Why, Dylon Rosier, I can't believe you would ask such a question. I did not make it to my age by causing other people discomfort."

"Mmm-humm." He just looked at the device a little more.

"Well, you know Mr. Fussbucket?" She confessed.

"You mean the man at The Lunch Place, that guy that never has anything nice to say about anything, no matter how nice you try to be to him?"

"That would be the one."

"And….." Dylon said, waiting for the rest of the story.

"Well, the day I got the device, we were both headed to the ATM and I smiled and stopped to let him go first, you know just trying to be nice. Well, he popped off with 'What the hell are you smiling at?' and I guess the rest is kind of self-explanatory. I sure was hungry when I got back from lunch, but you know what? So was he."

Dylon laughed out loud. "So how do you turn it

on?"

"It's on. The button is right there if it's not." She said and pointed to the button on the back.

Dylon turned the button on. The activate button lit up and immediately went back off. "I think you ran the battery down, Rosie."

"Oh well, I guess we'll have to charge it on the plane." She said and snickered a little more as she thought about the stranger at The Lunch Place that they had nicknamed Fussbucket.

\* \* \* \* \* \*

After waiting for what seemed like forever, the trio had finally boarded the Lear jet for the long flight to meet the others at *the estate*. Rosie and Kat performed an exaggerated greeting, much like two old high school girlfriends that hadn't seen each other in years. Just as they suspected, Dylon rolled his eyes and found a seat on the plane near a table. "Thank God I brought some work to do." He said as he sat down.

The girls just giggled and laughed as they headed to the back of the plane. Once they found a spot they started talking in an almost inaudible tone. They really didn't want Dylon to know what they were talking about. Kat leaned a little closer to Rosie. "I see what you mean. So has he been that snippy since he got the letter?"

Rosie shook her head no. "He eases up every now and then. He gets worse when he's getting ready to try and contact her, then when she returns the letter it's like he's sulking, almost depressed. He did start getting worse in the days working up to this flight. You know he asked her to come along and she was going to."

"Oh God, I didn't realize she was supposed to come along on this trip." Kat hung her head, feeling bad for her brother.

"Well there's something else." Rosie reached into her purse and pulled out an envelope that had been marked return to sender. "This came at the beginning of the week. I just didn't have the heart to give it to him. It's the third one he's written."

Kat took the envelope and stuffed it in her bag. Before she had a chance to say anything, Rosie handed her a folded up piece of paper. "I would probably read this in the bathroom if I were you. It's a little tough to swallow." Kat took the letter and stuffed it in her pocket. On her way, she reached over and grabbed a throw pillow. As she passed Dylon she tossed it in his direction and when it hit him in the head, she called out. "Bulls eye!"

"Oh c'mon sis, I'm trying to get some work done here." He fussed.

"Yeah, and I'm just trying to lighten the mood a little D. Jeez man, why do you have to be such a sour puss? She huffed off to the bathroom. Dylon turned to look at Rosie, who already had her nose buried in a magazine.

When Kat got to the bathroom, she opened the folded piece of paper. It actually looked like it had been crumpled into a ball at one point. She wondered how many times the note had been read and reread, before she started reading it.

*Dear Dylon,*

*It breaks my heart to have to write you this letter. I just want you to know that I have had the most wonderful time with you. You are a very interesting, sweet, and caring guy. I really like you a lot. These past few of months have been great, and this past weekend. It was one of the best times we've spent together. I was waiting to see when you were going to come out of your shell. I can see that you're a very special person and you're going to make some woman very happy someday.*

*After you left, I was approached by two*

*guys who told me they were with the FBI.*
*They scared me to death. I was*
*interrogated for eighteen hours. They told*
*me that I would be under constant*
*surveillance as long as I kept seeing you.*
*They told me that even if I broke it off now,*
*that I would still be watched for quite some*
*time. I don't know   exactly what you're into*
*and I don't want to. I don't think that it is*
*anything bad I just  don't see that coming*
*from a person of your character. You have*
*to understand, I'm  just a country girl and I*
*lead a simple life. I really can't see myself*
*living a life where I have to watch*
*everything I say and do, for the simple fear*
*that two government men are going to do*
*bad things to me if I slip up.*

*I really hope you can forgive me,*
*because I really do like you. I just can't live*
*that kind of life.*

*Love always,*
*Kaylee Yates*

*P.S.*

*Please Dylon, don't try to contact me.*
*This is already hard enough.*

Kat wiped the tears from her eyes and fixed her makeup before leaving the bathroom. She folded the letter up and put it back in her pocket. When she left the bathroom, she sat down in front of Dylon. "So what is your little mind concocting up this time?"

"Huh?"

Kat didn't want to see a repeat of the recluse she saw in Dylon when they lost their parents. So she prodded. "What are you working on, what are you playing with? Is there anything I can help you with?" She reached for one of the drawings he wasn't working on. "This almost looks like the M.S. model, what is it?"

"Don't placate me, Kat. I know you're not actually interested, you're just trying to figure out what's eating me."

"I'll let that one slide. I didn't realize there was something eating you. So Mr. Dick, would you like to tell me what this is or do you want me to psychoanalyze you?" Kat said in a very disciplinary manner.

Dylon thought for a minute. Knowing that she could tear him down in a matter of seconds, he chose the easier of the two options to deal with. "Well sis, it is similar to the M.S. model. You probably won't remember this, but I mentioned that one of the things that I wanted to work on in the future was a planet seeder."

Kat nodded her head. "You're right, I only vaguely remember it."

"Well the planet seeder is not really the problem. I'm trying to figure out how to develop an expandable terrarium. You know, something that will kind of grow with whatever plant I put in it, or will be big enough at the start."

Kat just looked at him kind of funny. "Forgive me if I'm missing something here, but what about the agripods?"

"Well if it's a true planet seeder, the areas I'm looking for might not hold an agripod. Some of the area may be on the side of a mountain, in the worst case scenario, but a lot of them will be in areas where it looks like there may have been some evidence of water runoff." Dylon explained as he grabbed a couple of other drawings.

"I don't expect this to be done any time soon. We probably won't even be ready for this stage of the mission for at least a year, if not two."

Rosie was going to join in on the conversation, but figured she would just let the two of them alone. Kat seemed like she was actually getting Dylon's mind off of things and that was the best thing that could happen. Instead she headed for the fridge. As she was pulling out some items to make a sandwich, Dylon and Kat got up and walked over to join her.

They were still discussing the different options for a terrarium, but quickly got wrapped up into helping make something to eat. The trio enjoyed some small talk about arriving at *the estate*. They were all anxious to see the progress that had been made with the new construction that had been going on. Kat, of course, was anxious to see Marcus, who was already there.

After finishing their sandwiches in front of the television, Kat gathered up Dylon's notes and drawings and put them away. Rosie had already gathered up the plates and was getting a blanket to throw over Dylon who had fallen asleep. The two girls left the television on and returned back to the original seats.

"Wow, he's really taking this one hard." Kat said. "He must have really liked her."

Rosie shook her head. "I don't know about any of the other girls in his past, but he sure has thrown himself into his work. That's a sure sign that any man is having a hard time dealing with, whatever."

Kat almost laughed out loud. "I'm sorry, I'm not making light of the situation, but that is so true. I don't understand why they just can't talk about it and save themselves all the hard work." Kat said. "The only thing that really bothers me is that it comes from the people that we feared the most interference from. I really didn't expect it to affect our personal lives."

Rosie looked at Kat with disbelief. "Don't you fool yourself, young lady. They will interfere with anything they want to and not even bat an eye. So what about the girl, I mean, it really sounds like she liked him?"

"Yeah, it does, but until we know what she knows or what Dylon has told her, we really can't do anything. She must have really been special. I've never seen Dylon this bad. I guess the only thing we can really do is keep him as busy as we can until he's willing to actually talk about it." Kat said. The two of them continued talking a little longer before drifting off to sleep themselves.

# Chapter 25

The storm had moved in rather quickly, which gave a perfect cover for the events that were unfolding that night. As the staff were preparing for the arrival of the remainder of the group, the probe had started moving along its designated path.

There was only a slight concern about the probe being out in these conditions. The storm that was moving through did not contain a lot of electrical activity, and the probe was able to be shut down if that activity were to increase.

The soft glow from the craft was not visible to anyone at *the estate*. It slowly moved through the woods. The craft stopped only four times as it made its journey. The targets were located at four points around *the estate:* due north, south, east, and west of the center. When it stopped, it was only momentarily and then it hurried on to the next target. The probe was gone as soon as it had finished without anybody noticing it… well not yet anyway.

\* \* \* \* \* \*

The next morning Dylon found Kevin and Marcus at the launch pad surveying the damage from the storm that blew through night before. There were a lot of things blown around but not any real harm had been done.

With all that was happening on this particular weekend, most of the workers at the estate had been given some time off. The only people that remained were essential staff. Even Reese, against his wishes, went to spend some time with his grandparents. Kat and Rosie would be delivering medical supplies to the clinic and picking up the Lieutenant from the village. He was visiting with Carmen before coming to *the estate*, something about a surprise for her.

As the guys made their tour of *the estate*, making sure everything looked its best the girls left for the clinic. When the guys got to the hangar, Dylon asked if he was going to get a sneak peak. Marcus replied to his question, "Of course, as soon as you let me know where the others are." Marcus had actually discovered where the other crafts were stored. He just needed Dylon to tell him, so he didn't feel like he was sneaking around to get to them.

Marcus continued to plead his case, and finally after about fifteen minutes of continuous talking, Dylon finally caved. "Oh my God, alright already, I'll tell you. Just show me what you've done with the one I left out for you."

"Thanks bud. I'll do better than show you, I'll even let you drive it." Marcus said with a big smile on his face. "It's really easy, easier than those toys you built."

"You're kidding, right?" Dylon asked.

Kevin interrupted. "He's right. They really are pretty easy to fly."

Marcus was as excited as a father teaching his son to ride a bike. "When you get in and turn it on it's going to lift about ten feet off the ground. I had to rework your steering mechanism to a joystick instead of the regular yoke type that you had in there. It was the easiest thing to use. You barely have to move it to get a reaction, and I put an emergency stop in it so if you're heading for something you think you're going to hit, just hit this button. Don't try to correct it with the joystick because you'll overcorrect yourself. It's just human nature, trust me. Use the button, it works. Oh yeah, I also added a throttle, it's on the left there. There's just one more thing, if you want to go up or down, you have to pull the trigger on the joystick."

Dylon didn't think Marcus was going to stop talking. He reassured him that he understood what he was saying. "The button, use the button if I get too excited. Okay, I'll make sure I keep my finger on the button. Can I try it now?"

Marcus realized he was getting a little carried away and stepped down from the craft, but still couldn't help himself. "Just bump it. Just bump the joystick until you get the hang of it."

Dylon waved his hand as he closed the top of the craft and turned it on. It automatically lifted about ten feet, just like Marcus told him it would. Marcus was a little excited and waved to Kevin to open the hangar doors. He rushed over himself to help get them open.

Dylon was very cautious with the joystick, as he recalled how many of the radio controlled saucers he had crashed.

Once the craft made it past the doors, Dylon hit the button. He couldn't resist it, before he knew, his anticipation got the better of him. He pressed the trigger down and gave the joystick a good bump. The craft shot up in the air about a hundred and fifty feet. As he was watching the monitor he couldn't believe his eyes. He didn't even feel any G-forces. "Cool." He said out loud.

He bumped the joystick again, this time just a little in each direction and was surprised at how much it moved with the slightest touch. He found a small globe to his right, he put one finger on the very top of it and did a very small circle. The craft acted appropriately. As he was playing with his new but old toy, he came to the realization that the controls were way too sensitive. Before he got too caught up in the excitement of it all, he decided to bring the craft back down. This proved to be a little more difficult than he thought. The sensitivity of the joystick made him overshoot his target every time, until he remembered the stop button.

When he finally got the craft to a position where he started from and climbed out of it, he was smiling from ear to ear. "I love it man, it's great. I was afraid to push it too hard though."

Marcus complied. "I know, the joystick is too sensitive. I have some new parts coming in that will make it a little tighter. Other than that though, what do you think?"

"Oh, man it's awesome. I can't believe that you don't feel any force of movement. It's like you're floating around in your own personal bubble that you are controlling." Dylon said and turned to Kevin to see if he had flown it. From the look on his face, he could already tell that he had. Dylon looked back to Kevin and asked how much flying time he had in it. His response was exactly what he wanted to hear.

"Enough to make us look good for the Lieutenant's visit?" Marcus asked. Dylon nodded and the guys helped get the craft back in the hangar. When they were finished preparing everything in the hangar for the visit, Dylon looked at the both of them. "You guys have done a great job down here. I just want you to understand everything that is involved with what we're doing, my reasoning behind being so careful with the location of everything."

They both shook their heads in agreement and started heading towards the *Mule*. Dylon headed towards an old set of lockers, and it didn't take long for Marcus and Kevin to figure out they were headed in the wrong direction. They immediately switched directions and caught up with Dylon. When he made it to the lockers he knelt down and slipped off a lock.

Dylon opened the locker and pulled out a duffel bag that had so much dust on it a small cloud of dust rose from it when he plopped it on the floor. He reached to the back of the locker and pulled up the bottom of it, which revealed a small control panel. Kevin and Marcus just looked at each other and then at Dylon. He felt them looking at him and simply said, "The best place to hide something is in plain sight." He pointed out the fact that the saying did not belong to Rosie, it was something that his father also believed.

Dylon proceeded to give them the code and tell them the steps they needed to take in order to reveal the craft elevator. As he punched in the code and worked through the steps, the control panel area of the test device began to lift and rotate to the right to reveal a large hole in the floor. Marcus was kind of dumbfounded. He had learned of the codes and the tunnel from Reese. The fact that the boy had given him this information was not something he was ready to reveal to Dylon.

All this time he had been going under the observatory, to get to the hidden storage area and it was right beneath his feet. As they rode the elevator down, Kevin was astonished to see a storage area just as big as the hangar above. He couldn't believe his eyes. He was in awe as he saw a number of crafts in storage bays, but could not get a count. When the elevator finished its descent Marcus and Dylon just watched Kevin. There in front of him were nine craft. Kevin felt the same emotions that Marcus had already gone through the first time he saw the area. He also went through almost the same steps and emotions as Marcus, when he was first shown the crafts. Kevin felt like a kid again, but amazed at the amount of work Dylon had accomplished.

# Chapter 26

When they landed, Rosie and Kat both were surprised to see a medical helicopter already at the clinic. They departed from the pad and headed for the clinic. Waiting for them were Carmen and Lieutenant Vasquez.

"Oh the beautiful ladies, please allow me to help you." The Lieutenant said as he reached to take the bags the ladies were carrying.

"Oh, well thank you very much Lieutenant, and how was your trip." Rosie asked. She was growing to like the way he was always flirted with the ladies.

"It's always a good trip when I know you'll be waiting for me at the end." He said in his usual adoring way. The girls just smiled, as they had become accustomed to it by now.

"Why did you bring the medical helicopter, Lieutenant? Is everything alright here, Carmen? Are we transporting someone out today?" Kat questioned.

"No, everything is fine, but I will let my uncle explain all the details to you. After all, it is his gift." Carmen responded.

"Gift?" Kat turned to the Lieutenant.

"But of course," he said and started talking, using

his hands to help animate his words. "After all that you have done for our people you have inspired me to contribute as well. When I came across this deal I just couldn't let it pass by. I thought what a better way to show my appreciation than to offer this gift. There is just one small detail to go over though." He said and paused for a moment to try to read Kats face. "I would like you to meet Carlos Arrellez, he is the pilot. He recently left the service due to medical reasons and cannot return. He was such a good man to serve our country. My amigos and I agreed to cover his expenses to compensate for his reduced income if he agreed to give his time as a pilot and help with some of the other villages in the area. He is very well trained in the medical field. I think you Americans would call him an E.M.T. We thought it would be good to follow in your footsteps and help out some of our people too."

"Well Lieutenant, I don't know what to say. What a noble thing you're doing for your friend and the villages too. You are a very good man." Kat said, sensing that there was a little more to come.

"Well, thank you, Elizabeth." He said as he guided her outside. He looked back at the others and let them know with a small hand gesture that they were going to look at the helicopter to make sure it was satisfactory. Once they made it away from the clinic and out of earshot of the others, the Lieutenant continued. "Senorita Elizabeth, I have a small problem. I have had many conversations with Carmen before we did this, and the best we can come up with is only three days of work a week. Poor Carlos will drive Carmen crazy, and not only that, he would go stir crazy himself. There just isn't enough work for him to do here. I was hoping to see if you needed an extra hand. He is a good worker, he repairs his own helicopter and knows how to work on other military planes. You would not have to pay him, as I said before my amigos and I have taken care of that. We just need to make sure he has enough work to do, to keep him busy and his mind off other things. He is a good man and knows nothing else but work. He lost his buddies in an accident and the doctor said to try and keep him busy to keep his mind focused on other things instead of focusing on the trauma. In time with Carmen's help he will be able to move past all of it, but he will always have a childlike mindset."

"Lieutenant, I'm sure we could find a little work for him." Kat said, feeling like she knew why her mother had befriended the Lieutenant. "You're just a big softy, Lieutenant," she said as they walked back to the clinic.

"Senorita Elizabeth, it would be okay for Carlos to fly us to *the estate*? He has to start earning his keep some time." Kat nodded in agreement with the Lieutenant and let the other pilots know so they could head back without them. The two of them went back inside the clinic and Kat passed on her congratulations to Carmen. "It seems not only have you acquired a new helicopter, but a pilot and courier as well." Carmen agreed and mumbled something about hoping to be able to find enough for him to do.

* * * * * *

The flight back to *the estate* was rather nice. The helicopter was a newer model than the one the Rosiers used to transport back and forth to the clinic. When they arrived at *the estate*, the Lieutenant was quite surprised at the size of the operation. Getting any information from Kolminski was next to impossible. He had been trying for a couple of years now, to get some of the satellite photos of the area, without any success. Carlos was a bit overwhelmed at the size of *the estate* as well. He kept repeating over and over. "Where do I land, where do you want me to land?"

Kat caught the urgency in his voice and answered quickly. "Over there Carlos, by the new hangar, the one with the three guys outside of it." She wondered what kind of accident he had been through, to cause him to be so anxious.

When they landed and everyone was out of the helicopter, Rosie slipped her arm into the Lieutenant's. "Elizabeth dear, you wouldn't mind if I give the Lieutenant a small tour of the new hangar myself, would you?" Kat was expecting this little diversion, so that Rosie could explain the documentary type recordings that they wanted to do.

"By all means Rosie, go ahead. I'll just show Carlos where he will be staying while he's here," Kat said just before she led Carlos away to introduce him to the boys. He seemed kind of timid, almost childlike. Again Kat found herself wondering what kind of trauma the young man had been through. After introducing him to the guys, she took him to the housing complexes for the staff. All the way there he would ask what each building was, and after Kat explained it he would respond with a simple statement. "I would like to go see it someday." By the time she got Carlos to the housing area, Kat felt that she had made the right decision.

\* \* \* \* \* \*

Rosie led the Lieutenant into the new hangar and was showing him all the different areas where the different stages of the rockets and satellites would be built. When they came into the central office area, she closed the door behind them.

"Lieutenant Vasquez, may I call you Ricardo?"

The Lieutenant was actually caught off guard, just a little. "It would be an honor to have such an eloquent lady as yourself call me by the name my father gave me."

"You know Lieutenant, I admire your way with words, but I have some really serious questions to ask you. I was going to try and be all sweet and nice about this but you just have too much of a way about yourself. Instead, I'm going to just get right to the heart of the matter." Rosie's tone changed a little and the Lieutenant took notice of it, but before he could respond Rosie continued.

"I know the U.S. government has been keeping a close eye on the activities here and I just want to make sure we're both on the same page. I also know that you want this little arrangement between the two governments to end. Yes, Lieutenant I have a few connections myself, and I can help you get what you want, but not without your complete honesty." Rosie had a commanding manner about herself that the Lieutenant really admired and respected.

"Now I'm going to tell you what we're planning and you're going to tell me what you know. Do we understand each other?"

"Yes ma'am." The Lieutenant said as he did complain a little about the arrangement with the U.S. government. After Rosie got all the information she needed from him, and a little more than she was expecting, she explained about the video that they would be making and how her beliefs on keeping the majority of everything they were doing, in the public eye would work out to their benefit. When the meeting was over, the two of them came out of the hangar the same way they went in, arm in arm. When the others noticed the two of them, the Lieutenant seemed to have an air about himself. One that showed a little more confidence, in the newfound friends and partners he was able to align himself with.

\* \* \* \* \* \*

After showing Carlos where he was going to be staying while at *the estate*, Kat just didn't feel right leaving him there all by himself with nothing to do. So she decided to bring him along for the tour. What could it hurt? He seemed to have the mentality of a child.  It didn't take long for Kat to arrive back at the hangar with Carlos and join up with the others. When she spotted Rosie out of the corner of her eye, she realized Rosie had gotten her point across to the Lieutenant, and he seemed to be up for whatever.

Kat quickly grabbed the video camera Rosie had bought earlier and handed it to Carlos. She tried to make sure he understood how to use it and exactly what they wanted to record.

The Lieutenant got an abbreviated tour of the majority of *the estate*, but most of their time was spent at two different areas. First, they went to the completed new hangar, which already housed some of the parts for the first two satellites and probes. Next, they ended up at the observatory, where they explained everything that they were planning on doing and how. Dylon also pointed out that the Peruvian government would be the first to put an actual complex on Mars, if everything went as planned. Dylon also explained how the U.S. and a lot of the other countries had redirected their focus on going back to the moon and building a base there. He explained how he felt that they were taking an overly cautious approach because there would be human lives at stake. He understood this approach, but thought with the technological advances in robotics that the majority of the complex could be built before the first human was ever sent.

"Lieutenant, this is really simple and it is going to happen. I would just like it to happen here, and I would like you to be part of it. Now if you want this not to happen here it won't, but that doesn't mean it's not going to happen. I'll just move the entire operation to another country. I'm sure you know I have the finances to do it and I will if need be." When Dylon finished his presentation, the four others in the group almost believed him. However, they knew if the Lieutenant didn't go along with Dylon's plan, it would take another fifteen years, at the least, to accomplish it.

As for Carlos, it was like watching a kid playing with a new toy. He was recording everything that he could. At one point his face was pressed up against the display cover for the Mars complex, with the camera in hand. Kat stepped over to see how the battery and card were holding up. When she tried to take it from him to replace both of the items that were spent, he seemed really disappointed. It was almost like he felt that he let her down in the task she gave him to do.

Kat immediately reassured him that he was doing a good job, she just had to give him another memory card and new battery. When she handed the camera back to him, a big smile came across his face. He instantly took the camera and started filming her. She had to redirect him to film the Lieutenant, which he obediently did.

Rosie stepped over to Kat, while Dylon was still

answering the Lieutenant's questions, and struck up a conversation with her. "So what's his story?" She asked and pointed to Carlos.

"Apparently it's some kind of post-traumatic stress caused by an accident where he lost all of his buddies. He was the only survivor out of his squad." Kat just shook her head. "It's just awful, I can't imagine how he feels. The Lieutenant said he might be in this childlike state for the rest of his life. He's retained all of his training, but his social skills are like a ten year old."

After Dylon had finished with the Lieutenant, they all headed to the main house. The meal was already prepped all they had to do was cook it. Dylon was actually looking forward to this part of the whole presentation. He thought the best way to really get to know someone was to get them to help with fixing dinner. It was the most relaxed part of any meeting. People just opened up a little more when everything wasn't so preplanned.

When everybody had gathered poolside, you could just feel the difference in the air. All of the business proposals were mostly put aside and everybody was a little more relaxed. Dylon was teaching the Lieutenant his recipe for baby back ribs, who were both taking mental notes of every step.

Rosie and Kat were discussing how the

relationship with Marcus had evolved, and Marcus was showing Carlos how to check the memory and battery time on the camera. Everyone seemed to take to Carlos. He was actually pretty smart, once he got over the hump of meeting a new person and trying to figure out what they expected of him.

The rest of the evening went off without a hitch, and everybody was anxious for tomorrow to hurry up and arrive, when the R.S. craft display would take place. Towards the end of the evening Marcus whispered something in Kat's ear and then tried to quietly duck around the house. Apparently Carlos had taken quite a liking to Marcus, because as soon as he ducked around the corner of the house, Carlos was quick to follow. Kat noticed it too and slipped away from the group as well. When she got to Marcus, who was trying desperately to convince Carlos that he couldn't go, Kat assured him it would be alright. "Who knows, he might even be able to help you. The Lieutenant says he's a pretty good mechanic. Plus we need the footage so let him go, just make sure he films all he wants to."

When the two of them made it to the old hangar, Marcus told Carlos he could be his helper if he didn't touch anything he wasn't supposed to. Carlos agreed and they went inside. There wasn't much light when they first got inside and Marcus asked Carlos to wait at the door until he got all the lights turned on. When he came back around the corner Carlos was nowhere to be seen. He scanned the hangar and sure enough, Carlos was walking over to one of the Avrocars with the camera held up.

"Do you want to help me out?" He asked Carlos, who was mesmerized by the crafts. Carlos nodded his head vigorously and walked over to where Marcus was. "I need to make sure they have enough fuel in them for tomorrow. I'll open the cap and you can top them off. The fuel….now where did he go?" Marcus glanced around and noticed that Carlos had already started dragging the fuel line over. "Well okay then, maybe he does know his mechanical stuff." Marcus said to himself. Carlos put the nozzle in the hole and pulled the trigger. "Now, it will shut off automatically, Carlos." Marcus noticed that Carlos had given him a thumbs-up before he even finished the statement.

After prepping the two different Avrocars, they headed over to the R.S. model. Marcus was trying to figure out how to make the joystick a little tighter. Even though he had new joysticks on the way, he wanted tomorrow's presentation to go off without any incidents. As Carlos watched him for a minute, he was able to figure out what he was trying to do. Marcus, who was so focused on completing the task, he didn't even notice that Carlos had stepped away. When he did finally notice and started to scan the area for him, he spotted Carlos over at a table working on something. "Well, at least he's keeping himself busy." Marcus muttered to himself and then continued with what he was doing, while trying to keep an eye on Carlos at the same time.

Marcus looked up again to check on Carlos to find he was not at the table anymore. He started to climb down to look for him but was startled when he turned and found Carlos was right behind him. Carlos handed Marcus something. He took the object in his hand, eyeballed it, and gave Carlos a funny look. Carlos had crafted a rubber washer out of what looked like a part of an old boot. Marcus held the washer in his hand for a minute, trying to figure out how smart this guy that acted like a child really was. When Marcus then gave him a thumbs-up, Carlos just smiled and pointed at the joystick. He then held up the camera and motioned to the anti-gravitational device at the center of the hangar. Marcus nodded his head and Carlos climbed down to go film what he could.

After about thirty minutes of tinkering with the joystick, Marcus had reassembled it with Carlos' homemade rubber washer. He turned to call out to Carlos, who was still engrossed in filming every detail of the device. He tried to get Carlos' attention, when that failed, he decided he would just turn the craft on to get Carlos to stop filming and check out the craft.

When Marcus hit the switch to turn the R.S. on, the craft automatically jumped about five feet off the ground and put out a low humming noise. Carlos heard the humming and turned around. When he saw the craft flying he almost dropped the camera. Marcus motioned for Carlos to come over and he turned the craft off so Carlos could climb up in the craft also. Even though it was a tight fit, you could get two people in the craft.

Marcus turned the craft on and bumped the joystick in the direction of the open hangar door. It barely moved. "Looks like Carlos' washer worked." Marcus thought to himself. He put a steady amount of pressure on the joystick and it started moving. "Gracias, Carlos." Marcus said and pushed a little harder on the joystick. When they made it outside Marcus motioned for Carlos to push the throttle forward just a little. Then Marcus put his finger on the button and pushed the joystick forward. They both watched the monitor as the hangar got smaller. Carlos looked at the monitor in disbelief. Marcus played around with the craft a little just to get the hang of the joystick and then headed back to put the craft away in the hangar.

Carlos was on a natural high. He wasn't saying anything, but his body language and the smile on his face showed everything he was feeling. He reached out and took Marcus's hand and shook it. Marcus didn't think he was ever going to let go. Fixing and testing the craft took a little longer than he wanted but it was done and ready to go. The two of them hurried back to the main house, both knowing that everybody else had probably called it a night.

# Chapter 27

The next morning everyone met at the hangar as planned. The first two crafts that were introduced were the two Avrocar models. Dylon of course flew one of them and Kevin was in the other. Carlos could hardly contain himself. He was pacing outside the hangar door, waiting to open it for the star of the presentation to perform. He had a radio in one hand and the camcorder in the other, waiting for the signal.

When he finally got his cue, Carlos moved into action and pushed the door open. He jumped up in the air when the R.S. craft silently swooshed by him and circled around into position. The Lieutenant almost dropped his coffee. He had seen the Avrocars before on one of *The History Channel* shows, but this was completely unexpected. He watched with great fascination as Marcus maneuvered the craft through some incredibly difficult exercises. No craft that the Lieutenant had ever seen moved like this one.

Marcus brought the craft over in front of the group and landed. He got out of the craft and walked over to the Lieutenant. "So would you like to try it?"

The Lieutenant was speechless. He nodded his head and Marcus led him toward the craft. As they got closer to the craft, the Lieutenant finally got his

276

thoughts together. Marcus had already explained to him that the craft was almost crash-proof when it came to landing. The Lieutenant climbed up into the craft and Marcus explained what each control did. He also explained about the emergency button, which instantly stopped the craft in case of an emergency. He also explained that Vasquez would not be able to see where he was going unless he watched the monitors.

Marcus stepped down from the craft and watched as the top closed. He walked over to join the others and reached out to shake Dylon's hand. "If he's not convinced after this, then you should start looking for a new base." Dylon agreed and asked him about the joystick. He was a little worried when Marcus offered the Lieutenant to try it out.

"Not to worry Dylon, our new little friend is quite the mechanic." Marcus said and pointed to Carlos. "You might even feel a little better about flying it now."

"I'll have to take you up on that after our guest leaves." Dylon said as they watched the Lieutenant buzz around in the craft. He looked like he was having a lot of fun.

\* \* \* \* \* \*

Special Ops

Agent Paschel, as he was come to be known, finally found an internet café that was out of the main drag and had plenty of open seats. He pulled out his laptop and waited to get a connection. There were several hoops he had to jump through to make sure he had a secure line. When he was through all the firewalls, he started typing.

> *Special surveillance utilities required, mandatory time off enforced, was not able to stay at required location. Special visitors arriving. Possible equipment demonstration suspected. Crucial staff only, cover almost blown in attempt to remain. Repeat special surveillance utilities required.*
>
> *Paschel out.*

\* \* \* \* \* \*

The next morning when Kolminski got out of bed to start his day of glorifying himself for his friends, if that's what you want to call them, he headed for the bathroom. As he passed by the hall, he noticed an urgent message notice flashing on his computer. He instantly started mumbling to himself. "Don't these people understand I have a life? I have things that I plan on doing for the weekend. Somebody's going to lose their job if this is not important, which I'm sure it's not. Once again I'm sure I'll be in a position to make a decision for them that they should already have made. This is *my* weekend and once again some moron is trying to wreck it."

Kolminski finished up in the bathroom and headed to the kitchen to get some breakfast started. The computer was still flashing the urgent message notice. He checked the time the message came in eleven thirty-four p.m. "Maybe they figured out what to do by now. I'm sure they didn't. No, they're probably waiting for me to figure it out for them."

About an hour after he got out of bed, Kolminski finally sat down at the computer to read the message. Next, he tried to log in to the Watchdog program. After multiple attempts, he realized the system had stopped working. He gathered all the information he could from every resource he had available to him and started to compose a letter to General Grant.

*General Grant*

    *Catastrophic system failure has occurred*

*with Watchdog program. Have been up all night
trying to get it to reboot itself. Checked weather
radar to see paths of current storm systems for
the region. A severe thunderstorm moved
through area at the time of failure. Could have
been electrical in nature, but to knock out all four
cameras seems unlikely. Have contacted agent
and advised him to check systems. To our
knowledge there is not anything significant
happening this weekend. Will keep you posted.*

*Senior Foreign Relations Officer,
Billy Kolminski*

"That should take care of any problems at that
end of this mess. I swear I don't know why we don't
just drop a bomb on the whole mess. We could always
say they were experimenting with unstable
chemicals." Kolminski mumbled as he got up from the
computer to find something to listen to while he
gathered his thoughts for the second letter. He shuffled
through his CD collection and finally found

something. He put it in the player and chose his favorite song on the C.D. When it started playing, it sounded like a C.D. would sound if it were all scratched up. Then when the singers kicked in it was the most awful bunch of screaming and shouting you ever heard. How some people could actually listen to this stuff and consider it to be music was just unbelievable. He sat back down at the computer and started typing the second letter.

*Agent Paschel*

*I wish I could congratulate you on not blowing your cover, but by almost getting caught, you've screwed up part of the reason you're down there in the first place, the surveillance of significant meetings. I could send a more capable agent down to help with the mission, if you think it is needed. Unfortunately, I will have to wait for your response to see if you need assistance. As for the Watchdog program, there is a major malfunction with it. If you had been successful in your attempt to remain at the estate, we would probably be up and running about right now. Nevertheless, your mission now is to see if the cameras have been sabotaged or if it was just a freak coincidence that they would all be struck by lightning. Try not to get caught. The General did say to pass along to you that there would be other opportunities to get any and all accomplices on the surveillance tapes. Any person involved in this operation is to be treated as crucial witness. Any evidence of their involvement needs to be captured on video. So as I said earlier, if you need a more capable agent to assist you, I'm sure I can find one.*

*Thoroughly disappointed*
*Senior Foreign Relations Officer*
*Billy Kolminski*

Kolminski closed the secure programs and decided to wait around the house a little bit, just in case the General were to call with any further instructions. He was fussed the entire time while getting his gear ready for his planned boating trip. "I hope he doesn't call. I've been looking forward to this trip all week. I can't believe that stupid ass almost got caught. What a moron. I went through the same training. It's not that hard to slip into the background and disappear. I just don't understand why these people can't do what they were trained to do."

The truth of the matter is that Kolminski did go through the mandatory field training. Career choices kept him out of the field and in a comfortable office, but everybody in the division knew that all the training in the world could not compare to actual mission time. There was always an element that was not planned for. The ability to know what choices to make and when to make them is what the actual mission time taught you. Kolminski never had to make those decisions and probably couldn't.

* * * * * *

When the Lieutenant landed the craft, he was beside himself. He smiled, walked up to Dylon, and gave him a healthy pat on the back. "It's good, I'm impressed. So have you taken it into space yet?" Dylon put his arm at the Lieutenants back and guided him to the hangar. Inside was another craft, with the top open. "No, sir I haven't. You know as well as I do that the U.S. government isn't just going to hand over any information that might help somebody out with that endeavor. Especially to somebody that is going to be in direct competition with them. So we've built this craft as a radio controlled version. It's equipped with every measuring device we could think of, atmospheric pressure, temperature, magnetic interference when we go through the gravitational field, you name it and we're measuring and recording it. I've put together a small file of reports for you to read. It contains some of the tests we've done with the device and the results of those tests. I think you'll find it pretty impressive. You must make sure that it is either destroyed or put in a very safe place when you're finished with it." Dylon watched as the Lieutenant walked around the craft. "Of course, after we analyze all the data from a few more test flights, we will try a test subject. If those tests results come back positive then we will try a person, probably me."

The Lieutenant looked at Dylon, surprised. Then he noticed the device in the center of the hangar. He glanced at Dylon in a questioning manner. Dylon nodded and motioned him to go check it out.

When the Lieutenant was finished checking the device out and stepped away from it, Dylon turned it on for a demonstration. Afterwards, Dylon turned to the Lieutenant. "Well sir, I wasn't really planning on playing all my cards but it appears that I have. Maybe I should have let Elizabeth do this. She's a lot better at playing cards than I am."

The Lieutenant shook Dylon's hand as he replied,

"Young man, I can assure you, if I came up here to beat you in a game of cards, I would have brought more booze. I think between the two of us, we can take out the big player." He winked and laughed. The two of them ended the meeting by exchanging contact information.

Kat and Marcus were talking to Carlos about his schedule for the clinic, to get an idea of how many days a week they could count on him being at *the estate*. They narrowed it down to the weekend, which would be non-working days for most everybody. The only work that would be done then was by choice and dedication, of course, nothing that was mandatory, then Monday thru Wednesday. The rest of his time would be dedicated to the clinic and their needs, unless of course an emergency came up. After discussing it with the others, Kat made herself very clear on the fact that Carlos' main priority was the clinic. With most of the details wrapped up everybody left the estate. The weekend's events left a smile on their faces and secure feelings about the future of *the estate* and their relations with Lt. Vasquez and his government.

# Chapter 28

With spring break and the most recent visit to *the estate* two months behind them, everybody was back into their normal routines. The finishing touches of the construction at *the estate* were clicking along at an impressive pace. The majority of the work left to be completed was electrical, painting, and furnishing. The most crucial of these projects, and probably the last to be performed, would be making sure the command center and the launch pad were connected.

The scheduling for the launch month was being set. It was a joint effort, mainly between Kat, Marcus, and Lieutenant Vasquez. Marcus was checking everything from the best weather conditions of the month, to the activity of solar flares and storms. Kat was checking times of availability for each client. She wanted to make sure that if somebody was sinking that much money into their business, that they had the opportunity to watch the launch of their investment.

Lieutenant Vasquez had proved to be very successful in keeping only the most trusted officials in the loop of the joint operation between the Peruvian government and the Rosiers. Two months had passed since he started organizing his part of the operation, and there were no signs of any leaks of information to

286

anyone. Anyone except this group called *The Five.*

Dylon and Kat had discussed it in detail, but still couldn't figure who they were, why they kept sending 'the stupid brown envelopes', and whether or not they were good or bad. Sometimes the messages seemed to help them and sometimes they seemed to almost be a threat.

\* \* \* \* \* \*

Kat was pleased to get the report from the Lieutenant that everything on his end was a go. It couldn't have come at a better time. She had just received the disk back from Rosie with her seal of approval.

The disk was a compilation of all of the footage that had been taken of the operations that were occurring at *the estate.* The documentary style video pointed out that the Mars Habitation Project was a joint effort between the U.S. Government, the Peruvian Government, and the Rosier Enterprises.

Kat pulled out the note that Rosie sent and read it once more before packing up the disk to send it off.

*Dear Elizabeth,*

*I'm just thought I would let you know*

*that you should add 'Director/Producer' to your list of credentials. My dear, you have done a wonderful job with the creation of this disk. I'm so glad that you were able to get the Lieutenant to reveal a name of an operative in the U.S. Government. I have some connections in the U.S. Government, but none that could reveal anyone that had any involvement with The Estate.*

*The thing that I thought was the most ingenious was your ability to disguise the disk as an actual movie. Anyway, I'm carrying on way too much. Great job.*

> *See you soon,*
> *Rosie*

Kat smiled as she placed the note on the table. She wrapped the movie up in simple brown paper. The package was addressed to Lieutenant Vasquez, but the return address was from her last semester's physics teacher. Kat, in her tenure as a teaching assistant had acquired a few of her professor's address labels. With everything that had been going on, her creativity in evading watchful eyes had stepped up to the plate, and before she knew it, she had what she needed to help her in this task.

* * * * * *

At the begging and pleading of both Reese and Marcus, Dylon had planned to use a week of his vacation time at *the estate.* This time, of course fell immediately after one of his last visits to Tennessee. The final construction stages of the last piece of property in Tennessee were taking place and Dylon wanted to be there. He spent an extra day there, which resulted in numerous failed attempts of contacting Kaylee. The trip to *the estate* would be a welcome retreat.

Once he arrived at *the estate,* Dylon started rethinking his trip. The first hitch he was hit with was a tantrum from Reese. This pouting fit came as the result of Dylon's response to attaching a camera to the backside of one of the crafts. Apparently, there was a huge difference between downloading a picture from the internet and capturing your own image from your own craft. No matter how much Dylon tried to convince him, it just wasn't the same thing. He left the boy to pout and headed off to see Marcus and Kevin, hoping that their reunion would go a little better.

As Marcus was going through his list of things he

had accomplished and the 'to do list', Dylon's mind started to drift. He was beginning to wonder if this was what he really wanted. None of it seemed to be as fun as it was in the beginning, when it was all just a dream. He tried hard to shake these thoughts, blaming it on the flight down, the amount of work he was doing. Anything but what the cause really was.

Marcus continued talking. Knowing that Dylon wasn't hearing a word he was saying, he switched up his conversation a little.

"So I thought we could put a camel in one of the last crafts we send to Mars. Once the camel is on Mars, we could set it loose and let it lead us to any water source. After all, camels can go days without water and if there is a water source on Mars the camel will surely lead us to it."

"Huh, what? Camel?" Dylon said, as his brain finally processed part of what Marcus just said.

Marcus scoffed. "So, at least you were half listening to what I was saying. C'mon dude, we're down here busting our asses, the least you could do is give us the decency of listening. I mean after all we *are* a team. Honestly Dylon, I don't know where you're at, but it's not here man."

"Aw, c'mon Marcus, I'm listening. I'm right here it was just a long flight." Dylon said in his own defense.

"Long flight my ass, dude. We all know what you did. You went to Tennessee, you finished what you *had* to do, and then you probably spent the next day looking for that girl. Buddy 'a team' is the same thing as a family. We all know everything about everyone, that's the only way it works. Give it up bud, it's not that she doesn't want you....She doesn't want this. She doesn't want anything to do with any of this. So why don't you do us all a favor and go get laid or something. At this point, I really don't care. Dylon, this is your dream. You have put together a team that is willing to do anything it takes.....You know what, man? If you don't care, why should I?" Marcus threw down the rag in his hand and walked out of the hangar.

Dylon just sat there in silence for a minute. He looked at Kevin, who was also silent. He was brooding over everything Marcus said, which kind of set the tone for his next set of questions. "So Kevin, I guess it's your turn, is there anything you want to say? Anything I've done to piss you off?"

Kevin responded, quite calmly. "Sounds like you have some personal things going on. That aside, there's a lot of things that I need to go over with you. It's all business stuff and we can do it however you want. We can be all business-like or we can grab a drink and just talk about it like we don't have any deadlines to meet. The choice is yours but keep in mind the further we push it back the more we have to rearrange schedules." When Dylon didn't answer, Kevin walked over to the fridge and got himself a beer.

Dylon sat there for a minute and digested what Kevin had told him. After contemplating everything that had been said he got up, made himself a drink, and joined him. Dylon finally broke the silence.

"Tell me Kevin, is there anything that you get excited about? I guess what I'm asking is....well, you were in the field with me. Did you ever dream about anything like that? Seriously, is there anything that you've thought about doing that consumes your every thought?"

Kevin had a simple reply to Dylon's questions. "Dylon, I'm a business man. I create businesses. What I dream about is a better way to run a business or creating a new business. Yeah, I have other dreams; some of them I have accomplished and some of them I haven't. There is one dream though that I did not even consider pursuing. That is, until somebody showed me it was a dream that could possibly be accomplished." Kevin took another drink before he continued. "So in response to your question, I guess the answer is another question....Do we close the business, or do we accomplish the dream?"

As the two of them walked around the hangar,

discussing the progress of the construction and the importance of the completion date, Dylon actually got a first-hand look at the work Marcus had accomplished. Knowing that the majority of Kevin's work was making sure that everything ran smoothly, Dylon really started feeling bad about the way he had been behaving. Marcus's words were finally starting to sink in.

Kevin handed Dylon a sheet of paper, on it were the launch dates. After he looked it over, he looked at Kevin. "Kevin, according to this, we have just over two weeks to be up and running….that only gives us a week to perform any test runs."

"Exactly Dylon, so we need to get a lot of things done before we start to run out of wiggle room." Kevin prodded.

"Wow, this is all coming together a lot quicker than I expected." Dylon ran his hands through his hair, as he realized the magnitude of everything they were trying to do.

"There's something else." Kevin said and turned to go get his notebook. When he retrieved it, he started flipping through the pages. "Got it, take a look at this."

As Dylon read down the page of dates with odd little notes after them, he really wasn't sure what he was supposed to be looking for. Kevin recognized the look on Dylon's face, and started to explain what he was reading. "Marcus and I have begun to notice weird little things. Nothing, that would seem all that important if we weren't building UFOs. Stupid stuff, like our notes not being in the order we left them in. Doors unlocked when we know without a doubt we locked them. Reese's toys, the models you built, in completely different buildings. Nothing has come up missing, just not the way we left it. It's like somebody is taking notes on what we're doing."

Dylon asked Kevin. "Should we bring a couple more security guards?"

"No, I think we'll be fine. I talked to the guards and let them know that Marcus and I would limit our research work to two buildings. They said they would patrol them a little more and redirect a few of the security cameras. There is one thing that might help. Some infrared cameras would prove to be useful. There are a lot of things we could do, but most all of the workers will be gone in a couple of weeks anyway."

"You're probably right. If they did steal anything, where are they going to go? I guess we should probably start putting the crafts in the storage vault when we're done with them."

Kevin nodded in agreement. "Yeah, we usually do, Marcus just wanted you to see what he's accomplished."

"Ouch, I guess I really screwed that up for him, huh? Well, I should probably go try to find him." As Dylon turned to go look for Marcus, he noticed some kind of camera contraption laying on the workbench. He turned and looked at Kevin, who responded. "It's something Marcus is working on, I have no idea what is it for."

\* \* \* \* \* \*

By the week's end Marcus and Dylon had smoothed over their disagreement. They had discussed the camera contraption and the fact that as far as Reese was concerned, it wouldn't be happening. It would be something they could use as a surprise birthday present for him.

The next pressing item they discussed was how to fit the Mars Craft, which was wider in diameter, into one of the piggy back stages of the standard rocket. Their solution was to give it, for lack of a better phrase, retractable wings.

In essence, they would basically cut approximately four feet off of each side and set it up with a hydraulics system. Once the casing of that stage of the rocket was ejected, they would simply send the command to have the craft extend to a full operational position. Then, they would send it on its way.

The main mission for this craft was to explore the surface of Mars at a higher rate of speed and capabilities than a rover could. On the outer shell, they had installed solar panels to the craft to gather all the energy the storage units could possibly hold. The inner part of the craft was equipped with all the computers, probes, and small tanks for air quality samples. They had come close to the maximum weight limit, without jeopardizing the abilities of the craft.

After getting a better handle on things and an updated game plan, Dylon felt a lot better. When he boarded the plane home, the majority of his thoughts were on how close they were actually getting. Something that he always thought would just be a dream was close to becoming a reality all thanks to the people helping him get there.

# Chapter 29

Training Lexie had taken a lot more out of Rosie than she thought it was going to. She had completed the training process with Lexie and finally felt like they were at a point where she was ready to take over. The more Lexie took on the less Rosie was needed.

This led to Rosie being consumed with thoughts of her first days on the job. This kind of made her sad. After all, she had helped Dylon's father and Mr. Tuttle build the company. She was a crucial element in making sure everything ran like a well-oiled machine. She felt like she was losing a child. She also felt like she was losing control of her emotions. She would just die if she let that happen here. Rosie quickly came up with an excuse to leave before she completely lost it. With the others involved in getting her retirement party planned, she really didn't want to stick around. She went to find Dylon to let him know she was leaving.

When she found him, he and the others were having a little more fun, planning her retirement party, than she could take. "Dylon I have a hair appointment that I completely forgot about. Would you mind if I left for the day?"

"You're asking me, Rosie?" Dylon looked at her

for a minute. "The operations master is asking me if she can duck out for the day."

"Oh, don't make such a big deal out of it, Dylon. I'll be back later." She fussed as she got her things together and quickly left the building. Not long after Rosie left, a courier dropped off two large envelopes. One was addressed to Rosie and the other was addressed to Dylon. It took Lexie a few minutes to find Dylon. When she did find him he was busy putting together the final details of the retirement party for Rosie. He asked her to put it on his desk, letting her know he would get it as soon as he could.

\* \* \* \* \* \*

About a mile or two down the road Rosie had to pull off. She was having a complete breakdown. Her eyes had welled up with tears so bad she couldn't even see to drive. As she wiped her tears and checked her makeup, she started talking to herself. "Rosie Patterson, I can't believe you. Pull yourself together girl. This is what you've worked for your entire life. You've helped this company in ways you can't even count. You've watched it grow and flourish into a reputable company. So why are you behaving like this?" All the talking helped get herself to a somewhat semi-controllable emotional wreck. She reached for her phone and searched for Desiree's number, her best girlfriend, who everybody knew as Izzy. She was probably the only one that would be able to help snap her out of her current state.

Rosie cued up Izzy's phone number and hit the dial button. Then she noticed that a car had pulled up behind her. She thought to herself, "You know, if I really needed somebody's help no one would ever stop." She looked at herself in the mirror. "Oh God I'm a mess." She quickly picked up a tissue and tried to fix herself up. She rolled down the window and motioned the person to go on, to no avail.

The phone was still ringing. "Come on Izzy, pick up." When the person got to her door he leaned in and asked, "Are you all right ma'am?"

"I'm just making a phone call I'll be fine, thank you." Rosie said, which seemed to redirect the stranger's attention. He turned and started to walk away. Rosie looked in her rear view again and applied the tissue to her face. "Where are you, Izzy? Why aren't you answering?"

Suddenly, her car door flung open. A hand reached in and grabbed her around the mouth. She felt the pressure of a hard object against her ribs. Her phone fell to the floor. She heard Izzy finally answering. "Hey Rosie, how are you? I was just thinking about you. Rosie?"

Izzy could hear some shuffling around and she thought she heard someone yell for help, then the phone went dead. Rosie grabbed her purse as she was being dragged out of the car. She could hear her phone ringing in the background as she was led to the car that had pulled up behind her.

\* \* \* \* \* \*

Not long after Lexie had put the delivery on Dylon's desk, he had made his way to see what it was. When he pulled the tab on the envelope and peered inside, his heart sank. His stomach knotted up and dread started to set in. He pulled out a small brown envelope.

He opened up the envelope. It was a very simple warning.

*Get out now.*
*Leave while you still can. Pay special attention to Rosie, she is being targeted. Information received later than we prefer. May already be too late.*

*The Five.*

He left his office and went to the front desk.

"Lexie, did Rosie say where her hair appointment was?"

Seeing that Dylon looked like there was a dire need to know where she was. Lexie grabbed Rosie's appointment book and started flipping through the pages. "I'm sure it's in her book."

Dylon noticed the envelope on the desk. "Lexie, what is this?"

"I have no idea, but it came the same time yours did." Lexie said as she answered the phone.

Dylon quickly tore the envelope open. Just as he thought, the same brown envelope.

* * * * * *

Izzy quickly dialed Rosie's work number. When Lexie answered the phone, Izzy's fears heightened. "Where is Rosie?" She frantically asked.

Lexie immediately picked up on the tone in her voice and responded. "She went to get her hair done. I don't know where. She just left, not more than fifteen minutes ago." Then the phone went silent. "Ma'am, are you there ma'am?" Lexie got no response.

Izzy scrolled through her phone and found Dylon's phone number. A number that she thought she would never need to use. Rosie gave her the number almost a year ago now. Actually, Rosie had put the number in the phone herself and said if she ever came up missing mysteriously to call it. Izzy had never paid any attention to it. She thought it was just Rosie's way of covering things that didn't need to be covered.

When she found the number she hit the dial key. "This guy is going to think I'm a lunatic." She thought to herself. Her mind was racing, trying to figure out exactly what to say, to convince this total stranger, that her best friend was in trouble.

Dylon looked at his phone. He didn't recognize the number and even though he normally let these calls go to voice mail, for some reason he felt compelled to answer this one. When he answered all he heard was the frantic voice of a woman. After letting her know where Rosie was going, Izzy blurted out. "If you value your friendship with Rosie and if she was going to get her hair done, she was headed to the *Tranquility Day Spa.*

It's located on seven-ninety-one Bethel Road. It's in the Olentangy Plaza, I'm headed there now. I'll keep an eye out for her car when I'm on the freeway. I know you don't know me, but I know you. More importantly, I know Rosie. She's my best friend and I know she wouldn't have put your phone number in my phone unless she thought she could count on you. I'm not crazy and I'm usually a level headed person, but I just got a really strange call from her and now she's not answering her phone so please don't write me off as a kook. Dylon, whoever you are, she's counting on us, please." Dylon had already left the lobby, heading to the parking lot. Then he heard the line go dead.

Dylon got in his car and sped out of the parking lot. Thoughts raced through his mind about what he would do if anyone were to ever hurt Rosie. She had come to be a mother figure in his life, something he hadn't had in a really long time. He raced down the freeway, taking the route that he thought Rosie herself would take. As he passed an off-ramp, he spotted her car. He slammed on his brakes, almost causing a pileup. He jammed the car in reverse and quickly got into the shoulder lane, doing at least seventy in reverse to get to a point where he could begin his pursuit.

\* \* \* \* \* \*

Rosie was thrown in the back of the limo. As she righted herself and looked out the back window, she saw the stranger getting into her car. The limo sped off and her car was soon falling in behind. Her mind automatically kicked in gear. Thank God her husband went through this stuff with her when he was still alive. She recalled his words as she was still trying to gather her wits. "Whatever you can use Rose, whatever you can use. I don't care if you use the excuse that you're bleeding uncontrollably due to an overactive menstrual syndrome. There is nothing, and I mean nothing, that is too embarrassing to save your life."

The man in the back of the limo with her was kind of a wiry man. The kind of man that looked like he had not put in one hard day's worth of work in his life. That wasn't the only thing she noticed. The limo was fully stocked. She wouldn't have been surprised if the trunk popped open to reveal a hot tub. She mentally thanked her husband as she scanned every loose item in the limo.

Her mind still looking for that 'out', she finally settled on her plan. She put on the craziest expression she could muster up and boldly said. "And just who in the Hell are you supposed to be?" Then she acted like she didn't have the slightest idea where those words came from and started apologizing. "Oh excuse me sir, I'm so sorry. I just haven't quite been myself lately." Before Kolminski got a chance to respond, Rosie started talking again. "Is it hot in here?" She reached over and pressed the button to roll down the window.

Kolminski quickly grabbed her hand. "I assure you Ms. Patterson, it's not hot in here." He quickly rolled the window back up and scolded the driver for not having the limo completely secure.

Rosie yanked her hand away and slapped

Kolminski across the face. She quickly brought her hands back to her own face. It appeared to Kolminski that she was in shock about what she had just done. Rosie immediately started apologizing all over herself again. "You'll have to forgive my instability, sir. I've never even thought of raising a hand to hurt anyone. My doctor thinks I may be….well it's kind of embarrassing to talk about."

Kolminski quickly finished the statement for her. "Psychotic?"

Rosie completely ignored what he had said, like she hadn't even heard it. "Well he thinks I might be menopausal. Are you sure it's not hot in here?" She said as she tried to roll the window down again. With no luck this time she quickly changed modes. "I'm sorry, what did you say your name was again?"

"I didn't!" Kolminski snapped and quickly reached to move Rosie's hand from the door. This time she was ready for him. She grabbed his skinny little wrist, twisted it around behind him and had him on the floor of the limo before he knew what hit him. She grabbed the corkscrew from the wine rack with one hand and took her other hand and clasped it around his neck, slowly turning her fingernails inward a little. With her knee in his back, she pulled on his neck until his head was in a position where she could press the corkscrew against his temple. "One wrong move you fucking little weasel, and you'll know what a cork feels like. Driver!" Rosie shouted. "If you don't want to explain to your superiors how you managed to let a sixty-something-year old woman kill your boss, I suggest you lose your piece. Preferably to me." The dividing window slid open and the gun fell in the seat next to her. Rosie quickly dropped the corkscrew and replaced it with the gun. "And the other one. You heard me. Toss it out the window, along with your cell phone and your radio." The driver didn't respond. Rosie tightened her grip and pulled back a little more on Kolminski's neck.

"Oh my God, just do it already." Kolminski's words were almost inaudible. The driver complied and Rosie searched Kolminski's pockets for phones and guns. All she found was a phone, and she chucked it out the window. She reached over and grabbed the limo phone hanging next to the wine rack and yanked the receiver from its connection and tossed it too.

"Now driver, I know you are a highly trained professional." She said as she raised her hand that held the gun and quickly brought it down on the back of Kolminski's head. "What I need you to do now is stop the car. No spinning or rolling, just a dead stop, or you stop dead." She said as she brought the gun around to his temple. "And you can go ahead and unlock the doors now."

\* \* \* \* \* \*

After causing what would probably take an hour to clear, as far as traffic flow was concerned. Dylon was in a forward motion again. He sped down the off ramp and quickly found the car he was pursuing. Whoever was driving Rosie's car was definitely a professional. Dylon was doing everything he could to keep up, but was slowly losing ground.

\* \* \* \* \* \*

Izzy was barreling down the freeway when she noticed it. Ahead of her in the opposite lanes traffic had stopped. There was someone with a gun shooting at a car that appeared to be the reason for the stopped traffic. Then she saw who it was. "Oh my God. What have you got yourself into now Rosie?"

Izzy quickly worked her way over to the center emergency lane. By the time Izzy got the car stopped and yelled out for Rosie, she had already shot out two tires, put two rounds in the dash, shot the driver in the foot, and emptied the rest of the rounds into the engine block. When Rosie noticed Desiree across the divider, she quickly headed to get in her car.

Kolminski, who had finally come around, was

307

climbing out of the back of the limo when he noticed Rosie making her escape. He barked at the driver. "Well don't just stand there you fucking idiot, go get her."

In an instant Kolminski was on the ground, out cold again. "I hate that prick." The driver said as he rubbed his knuckles and limped back to the front of the car.

# Chapter 30

Rosie slammed the car door shut. "Thank God, hit it Izzy." Rosie was looking for Izzy's cell phone as she sang her praises. "I knew I could count on you, Izzy. So I take it you got in touch with somebody at the office?" While Izzy kept looking in her rear view to see if anyone was following them, she couldn't help but wonder what Rosie was into now. "Girl, I knew you were into something. The last time you stopped calling me was right before you told that Grant guy off. You know, that government guy."

"Yes Izzy, I know. I was the one that told him off, remember?"

"Yeah, well you were out of your mind then. I just thought I would remind you. Just in case you forgot, and this whole thing today kind of makes me think you forgot."

"Oh please, Izzy. This is probably something way worse than that."

Izzy looked at Rosie like she had lost her mind. "You knew that and you still got involved? Please make sure you don't tell me a word, I've got enough problems just keeping up with my boyfriends, I don't need anything else on my plate."

Rosie finally got Dylon to answer his cell. "Dylon dear, I hate to tell you this but…."

"Yeah Rosie I know. I've already arranged for a pick up. I can't, I won't do it myself because I'm probably being followed. So this is where your expertise comes in. This is why you're here, tell me what to do." Dylon said in an anxious and questioning voice.

"That's a very smart move on your part. So as long as you keep up that line of thinking you'll do just fine." Rosie said in a more authoritative tone. "Now the first thing you need to do is get a hold of your sister and both of you lose yourself in a very public place, and by all means don't use your phone. Go pick up one of those throw away phones and use nothing but cash. The next thing we need to do is get a car and a flight out of the country, so you're pick up person needs to know that in advance." Izzy was doing everything she could not to listen to Rosie's plans. She did not want to be in the position where she might have to give any important information.

As soon as Dylon hung up the phone with Rosie, he called Jose. "Yes, the parking garage at the mall. She's an older lady and she will be calling you in forty-five minutes. Don't do it yourself, I don't know if anyone is watching the house. Have a friend do it." After hanging up with Jose, Dylon called Kat.

"I've been waiting for your call and before you ask, yes I got one too." Kat said when she answered the phone.

Dylon had already forgotten about the envelope, and it kind of threw him off. "Oh the envelope, so where are you now?"

"Well, let's just say that I'm lost in the crowd. There just happens to be a battle of the bands concert going on all day on campus. So I'm just waiting for my girlfriend to show up and we're going to swap out clothes. She's going to take my car and I'm going to take hers to the airport. We've already bought a ticket in her name. It just so happens I have a layover in Columbus. I should be arriving at three fifteen."

"Very good sis, I'll have one of Jose's friends meet you there." Dylon started to say good bye but Kat stopped him.

"Hey, how is Rosie, they haven't gotten to her yet, have they?"

Dylon replied. "Almost, but you know Rosie, she's pretty resourceful. Sis, be careful please. This is starting to get a little scary." He hung up the phone and made one more call to his pilot, Captain Todd. "Yes Captain, I was just wondering you had anything going to *the estate?* Great I was hoping to get three more packages on board if I could. Oh you're taking the cargo plane. Do you have room for a small van, something we could use to transport stuff from the storage building to the main house? Yeah, I'll have one of my guys drop it off. Oh yeah it will probably be loaded already. Will that affect your weight? Plenty to spare, okay then, seven o'clock sharp." Dylon hung up the phone.

\* \* \* \* \* \*

Kat arrived at the Columbus airport and started to head to the next gate. She turned on her phone, and saw there were two received messages. Upon listening to her messages she started to become a little more nervous. The first one was instructions from Dylon. The second one though, was from Amber, her best friend and accomplice.

*I lost the goons and then campus security kept them busy while I got out of there. I think they took your car though and I also think they know that we pulled a switcharoo, so watch your back. By the way do they know about your place in Greece? Anyway, you be careful out there and please find a way to let me know you're alright, if it is safe to. Thanks for the trip, even though you didn't have to do it. Oh please, be careful. I would really hate to lose you, you're my best friend ever.*

Kat hung up the phone and followed the instructions Dylon had left for her. She ducked inside the *Barnes and Noble* and started looking through the astronomy section. When she found the book on the Universe she started flipping through it. Inside she found a parking pass which she quickly hid away. On her way out she bought a magazine.

Once she found a bank of pay phones she dropped a couple of coins in one and called her room to leave herself a message. While the phone was ringing, she pulled out her cell phone and placed it on top of the payphone. Before the answering machine picked up, she pressed the lever on the payphone ending the call. Kat kept the phone to her ear and pretended to be talking to someone, while she turned and scanned the crowd for anyone acting suspiciously.

When she felt it was safe, she hung up the phone and headed in the opposite direction of her continuing flight gate. As she made her way towards the parking garage, there was only one person she saw that could possibly be following her. She ducked into the bathroom and quickly shed her jacket. She put the wig back on and the hat and sweater that she had used to lose her pursuers at the concert. She left the bathroom and continued down the corridor. She didn't see her potential pursuer anymore. She made it to the parking garage. She looked around and the only van she saw had the hood up on it. She cautiously walked over to the van. A man peered out from under the hood.

Kat recalled the words that would get her where she needed to be. "Excuse me sir, I need to pay for my parking but all I have is a twenty and the machine won't accept it. Would you happen to have anything smaller?" She handed him the twenty and the parking pass. Just then, she heard the door to the parking garage shut. The closing of the door echoed ominously throughout the garage. The man standing there urged Kat to get inside the van before the pursuer noticed she was there.

When the government agent approached the van, Ric started speaking in Spanish and held up some jumper cables. The government agent brushed him off, only asking if he had seen anyone come out. Ric shook his head no and once again held up the cables and reached for the government agent's elbow, to guide him over to the van for help. The agent just shrugged him off again and exited the garage.

Ric waited about five minutes, just to make sure he wasn't coming back then closed the hood. He told Kat to stay down until he gave her the okay. They made it away from the airport without any tails. Kat climbed into the front seat and started digging through her purse for her address book.

* * * * * *

The van pulled up to the garage. The neighborhood didn't look like someplace they would normally hang out, but Kat didn't feel any danger. If they were friends of Jose's, she knew they would be fine. As they walked through the mechanic shop, everyone continued working, only looking up briefly if they looked up at all. When they got to the back of the shop they exited through the back door.

When they came through the door, the first person she saw was Rosie. "Oh thank God, are you okay?" Kat said as she reached out to hug Rosie.

Rosie just shrugged it off. "You know me, I may be an old girl, but I still know how to take care of myself. How about you, did you have anyone following you?"

"Yeah, I think so, but Ric was pretty quick and was able to get rid of him." Kat paused only for a moment. "So I guess this means that we're going to have to step everything up a bit now."

"Well once we get out of the country and to *the estate*, we should be fine. Dylon's just finishing up some last minute details. I think that I'm the one that they really wanted though." Rosie said as she handed

Kat the card that came in her brown envelope.

*Delay in receiving crucial information.*
*You are being targeted, Rosie.*
*They think you're the ring leader.*
*Protect yourself at all costs.*
*Would be wise if you left the country.*

## The Five

She raised her head and when her eyes met Rosie's, Kat had a really confused look on her face. "You know, I really don't understand who these people are. Where are they getting their information from? Most importantly though, are they on our side or not? Really, Rosie, one minute they seem like they're stalking us and the next, they seem like they're trying to help us."

Rosie nodded her head in agreement. "Well, thank goodness they seem like they're helping us this time." Dylon walked out on to the patio area behind the garage and breathed a sigh of relief when he saw Kat. "It's good to see you're alright, sis," he said as he gave her a big hug. "Well, I'm sure you all probably guessed that we're going to *the estate* tonight." Everybody shook their heads in agreement, then

Dylon continued. "The thing is, we're going as cargo. The van you got picked up in Kat, is being loaded right now. After we finish with dinner, we'll load ourselves into the van and be hidden by some cases of oil and any other supplies we can find to disguise the hidden panel. Needless to say, it's going to be a cramped ride until we get off the ground. That will probably take an hour, because I'm sure everything that is being loaded is going to be inspected by our wonderful friends with homeland security."

Kat interjected. "You don't think they would shoot us down or anything do you?"

Dylon took a deep breath. "Yeah, the thought did cross my mind, but I'm not real sure what to do about it."

"What about Lieutenant Vasquez? Do you think he could round us up a couple of escorts? Some F-14's or something like that." Kat said as she grabbed her bag and pulled out her address book. "He gave me a direct number to contact him."

"It's worth a shot all we can do is try." Dylon said and looked at Rosie for approval.

# Chapter 31

The van pulled up to the back of the cargo plane. "Captain Todd?" Joe said as he was walking towards him, flipping through the cargo list. "What's this? It's not on my list." Joe motioned the K-9 units to move in on the van. They were trained specifically to sniff out drugs or bomb components.

Captain Todd walked over to Joe with his list. The two of them had gone through this procedure numerous times before and he had built as much of a professional relationship as he could. Especially when dealing with a government agent. Todd reached for the list that Joe was holding. He looked it over real good and then pointed out to Joe that he didn't have the updated list. "Here Joe, look at the date and time. Apparently somebody dropped the ball. Here's my list, it was printed out the next morning. I apologize about that, I'll have to make sure I talk to Nancy about it."

Joe motioned for the unit to continue the search of the van as he and Captain Todd walked over to it. "So what is all this stuff?" Joe asked as they peered in the van. "Well I'm guessing that all the oil is for regular maintenance and the food is probably part of their regular supplies." Todd said in response.

"But, why the van?"

Todd just laughed. "Well I guess they're tired of making seven and eight trips with a golf cart to get this stuff where they want it. I don't know why these people spend their money the way they do. Why does it take five city workers to do the job that one can do?"

Joe kind of snickered. "I see your point. That's good boys, close it up." The two of them started walking back towards the front of the plane and Joe started talking again. "You know Todd, I'm just doing my job. I will let the cargo list slip this time, only because you always have your stuff together. Just make sure you talk to this Nancy girl, okay."

"Sure thing Joe, I'll leave her a voice message right now and talk to her as soon as I get back to the states."

"You know I could ground your flight for this?" Joe said, reiterating the importance of having everything together.

"Yes sir, I'm fully aware of that. It won't happen again, you have my word."

* * * * * *

As soon as the plane was cleared for take-off and taxiing down the runway, one of the crew members headed back to the van. He was quickly unloading the wall of cases that had Rosie, Kat, and Dylon hidden.

"I sure hope we don't have to do that again anytime soon." Rosie said as she rubbed her rear.

"You're not kidding. I think my leg is asleep." Kat said as she was lifted it up and down trying to get the circulation flowing again. Dylon also stretched his body once he climbed out of the van, but was more concerned in how the flight was going to go. As he headed to the cockpit he noticed the parachutes stacked beside one of the side doors. He only requested that they have them for safety's sake.

"Well hello Dylon, glad to see you made it with all of the excitement you had today." Captain Todd said when Dylon opened the door.

"Thank you sir, good to see you again too. Are we alone up here? I mean, do you see anything on the radar?" Dylon asked as he glanced over at the radar screen.

"One small blip when we first took off, but going in the opposite direction. Probably going in for a landing."

"Good. I wanted to let you know we might get a couple of escorts, the closer we get to our destination. I mentioned it to the Lieutenant that we might need some assistance. He said he could have a couple of planes ready to scramble if we felt we were in any kind of danger. Hopefully we won't need it."

"Glad to hear it Dylon, I don't think this old bird could out maneuver a military jet. I'll keep my eyes open and let you know if I see anything. You should get some rest while you can." Captain Todd suggested.

\* \* \* \* \* \*

"Mr. Rosier, sir, wake up. The Captain needs to see you." One of the crew members had awakened Dylon. Still a little groggy from sleepingand the trials of the day, he stumbled his way to the cockpit. The door to the cockpit was open and Dylon stepped in. "You wanted to see me, Captain?"

"Ah Dylon, grab a seat." The Captain motioned to the navigator's seat which was directly in front of the radar screen. "You'll notice two blips on the bottom of the screen. About fifteen minutes ago they were located on either side of the screen, heading in the opposite direction from us. I think they might be looking for something, like maybe us."

Dylon caught sight of the two blips on the radar screen. "So what makes you think they might be looking for us?"

The Captain answered. "Well I haven't heard of any lost ships or boats, no chatter from the Coast Guard. That only leaves two options training exercises or search parties. Judging from the flight pattern, it's a search party. Upon your request, once we were out of radar range I altered our flight path, just in case. The only question now is, which government are they from, if that's even the case?"

"Are they close enough to contact yet?" Dylon asked.

"Well, that's why I wanted you up here. If they're close enough to contact, they're close enough to engage us, and if you haven't noticed this is not the best plane to dogfight with."

Dylon started to analyze the information, feeling uneasy about all of it. "Well you said they were coming from the south when you first spotted them right?"

"That's affirmative."

Dylon thought for a minute. "I couldn't give the Lieutenant a flight heading, because I knew we would be changing it. I'm going to go out on a limb here and pray that it's his guys, but I'm still going to have everyone suit up, just to be safe. Do you want me to put a couple of chutes up here?"

"Well I sure don't want to have to go look for them, Dylon."

"Okay then, two chutes it is." Dylon said as he was exiting the cockpit.

\* \* \* \* \* \*

"Kolminski! I can't believe you screwed this up this bad. I told you not to underestimate this woman!" General Grant blasted.

"With all due respect sir, you didn't tell me that she was trained." Kolminski said in his normal 'this is not my fault tone'.

"Mr. Kolminski! Do you not have the file on Rosie Patterson?" The General didn't even give him a chance to answer. "Did you even bother to read that file?"

"Well of course I did, sir." He stammered.

"Well if you don't mind, why don't you share with me some of the information you discovered while reading the file on Ms. Patterson."

"Sir, are you questioning my…"

The General cut him off before he could even finish. "You're damn right I'm questioning it! I'm questioning everything, about everything you know! Now, was there something you wanted to add, before you start refreshing my memory, about what is in that file?"

"Yes sir, Ms. Rosie Patterson, widow of Frank Patterson, killed in action. He also held a classified security clearance of level four and a former agent for department of special classified operations, Unit Two.

Soon to be promoted to Unit One."

The General stopped Kolminski. "Just in case you don't understand where these agents come from, Mr. Kolminski, let me enlighten you. The agents that are chosen for these Special Units are hand-picked Navy Seals. Seals, that have been in the field for a while. Did it cross your mind, that if one of these agents was lucky enough to have a wife that endured the relationship with all the strains the unit would put on it, that the agent might actually be interested in teaching his wife what he knows? Did it cross your mind at all?"

"Well no sir, actually it didn't. That's against policy, to teach a civilian the techniques you were taught as a special agent," Kolminski said very matter of factly.

"Kolminski, do you have someone that you care about very deeply?" The General asked.

"Well, no sir. With the field that I'm in, I don't allow myself to."

"Well I do, and policies aside, I sleep better when I'm out on mission, knowing that I've passed a few helpful hints on to my wife. These helpful hints come in very handy in life, just like the one I passed on to you. So for future reference, if I let you know that a person is very resourceful, I'm giving you a hint. It's a hint that might prove to be a little more helpful in a successful mission. That will be all for now, Kolminski. I expect to see you here at noon tomorrow, so we can regroup and restructure our next move."

"But sir…." Kolminski started to add yet another excuse why the mission was unsuccessful.

"I said that will be all, Kolminski, unless you actually want me to put you on report." The General looked at Kolminski with grave disappointment.

"No Sir, I guess I'm finished." Kolminski left the General's office, dissatisfied. The fact that he did not get to defend himself at all, really pissed him off.

\* \* \* \* \* \*

The next morning, General Grant researched as much as he could find on Kolminski. Most everything he found was that Kolminski was good at his job. His record was just about flawless. He had moved up quickly through the ranks and came with more letters of recommendation than you could shake a stick at. With all of the information he found in his research, there was nothing concrete to back up what he felt about Kolminski. So for now, he had to treat him as a viable resource. Not necessarily one he agreed with and trusted even less, but one he had to use. That is, until he could find a suitable replacement.

When everybody showed up to the meeting for

the restructuring of the mission objectives, General Grant was a little more direct in his approach. He was very careful not to place blame in order to accomplish his goal of restructuring the mission objectives. "It appears that all of the targets of the mission have now absconded to *the estate,* which means that our surveillance there will have to be watched a little more closely. Mr. Kolminski, I have a list of qualified candidates compiled. You all have the same list and if there are any names on the list you recognize or have worked with, maybe we can all put our heads together and come up with a team of four to assist Mr. Kolminski's department. That is, if there are no objections from Mr. Kolminski in receiving our assistance."

Kolminski felt a difference of attitude in the air coming from the General, and did not wish to confront it at this time. Still, he couldn't help but to work a jab in. "Of course General, why on earth would I object to receiving helpful information?"

General Grant overlooked the jab and continued. "According to the reports filed by Mr. Kolminski, his agent at *the estate* has reported that launching will begin within one week. Also according to his reports, what is being launched is nothing more than telecommunications satellites and a couple of probes. One of the probes is to fall into orbit around Mars and the other one is supposedly a deep space probe. There is one report though that disturbs me the most. Allegedly they are working on a new type of aircraft, one that can out-perform anything that we have. Whether or not it is armed has not been confirmed yet."

The General put down the papers he was reading from. "Gentlemen, our best hope is to get an invite to what appears to be the launch of a new space program for the Peruvian government. Mr. Kolminski, do you think that is something you could arrange? I mean, who are we conferring with now that Lt. Vasquez is out on mission?"

"Of course General, I'll get right on that. All of that information is locked in a secure folder on my computer, but if I recall correctly his name is Sergeant Paschel." Kolminski new that agent Paschel was out of the field and would be for a long time, so he took the opportunity to use his name. In the end Kolminski's inside man would turn Paschel into a scapegoat.

"Well then gentlemen, now that all departments are on the same page, I just want to remind everyone of the objective of this newly developed division. It is important for us to pool our knowledge, so that one department isn't in conflict with another's investigations." Everyone sitting around the table nodded their heads in agreement as General Grant was closed out the meeting.

# Chapter 32

When Kolminski made it back to his office he wasn't in the best of moods. His receptionist, on the other hand, was in an exceptional mood. She was back and forth straightening and cleaning up her work area, happily humming to herself the entire time. She had recently received starting date information from her future employer, Rosier Enterprises. The job she would be taking was an executive assistant position located near her hometown. She was so thrilled with the upcoming opportunity that she didn't even notice Kolminski standing there until he spoke.

"And just who are we today, Mary Freaking Poppins?" he said as he tried to squash her jovial mood.

The assistant just sighed, then smiled and answered. "No, Mr. Kolminski, just the same old doormat you're used to having around."

"Well Miss Doormat, do you have the files ready for the three appointments I have today? Plus, these notes and the tape of this morning's meeting need to be typed out. After you're finished with that, I need you to book me a flight to Cuzco, Peru. The first flight available."

"Whatever you need, Mr. Kolminski." She said, undaunted by his disgusted demeanor.

"And stop that incessant humming. It's really beginning to annoy me." He said as he huffed into his office, even more pissed off that anything he said to her didn't phase her. After sitting down at his desk he was surprised to hear his assistant still humming. He got up, walked over to his door, and slammed it shut. The assistant didn't even flinch. She had positioned the picture of her boyfriend just so that the light caught the reflection of Kolminski's office. She could see him coming and he didn't even realize it. She went ahead and booked the flight he requested. Then she wrote a little message on a sticky note.

*Your ticket information is ready and you will find it on the printer. I know that was the most important thing that needed to be done and probably involved a national security issue. That is something I would not want to screw with. You have the first flight out that is heading to Cuzco, Peru. As for the rest of your requests, do them yourself. I quit. I would wish you a nice life, but I don't.*

She picked up the picture of her boyfriend, put it in her purse, and stuck the note to her computer screen.

\* \* \* \* \* \*

Kolminski sat down at his desk to compose the letter to Lieutenant Vasquez.

*Dear Lieutenant Vasquez,*

*Over the past ten months our surveillance operations, both from the satellite photos and from our operative at the estate, have revealed what appears to be the startup of a space program.*

*First and foremost, let me say congratulations in bringing your country into the twenty first century. General Grant also sends his congratulations. I must say though that I'm quite surprised that you didn't ask for any guidance or advice through such a difficult task.*

*With the amount of experience we have in space exploration we could have been an immense help in keeping you from stumbling through this process. The fact that you have kept such an important stepping stone in your country's history a secret is a little unnerving. It would really put a strain on the relationship between our two countries if someone were to*

331

*point out the lengths you took to keep the rest of the world in the dark about this endeavor.*

*The possibilities that you have created with your new facility are endless. You could upgrade the telecommunications industry, of course, there's your space program, and then there will also be opportunities abound to upgrade your military capabilities, not to mention your weapons systems.*

*Yes, your weaponry capabilities.....I hope you fully grasp the underlying implications that you have created by not being forthright about the activities at the estate. Trust me, I understand about national security and I also understand that you might want to keep it on the down low in case of failure. But to deny the U.S. government crucial information about the activities on a piece of property that we have helped you keep a close eye on for years, is ....Well, it's just a bit suspicious.*

*Senior Foreign Relations Officer*
*Billy Kolminski*

\* \* \* \* \* \*

After making it to the estate unscathed, everyone had settled into bed and most of them had fallen right to sleep, exhausted from the stress of the chase and the cramped conditions at the beginning of the flight out of the United States. The two blips on the radar screen, turned out to be some of the Lieutenant's men, keeping barely out of radar range. The truth of the matter was that they were patrolling the skies for any possibilities of trouble, but if there had been any problems, the story would be that they were simply performing training maneuvers.

It was about 4:30 a.m. when Dylon ventured to the storage hangar for the rockets, after an unsuccessful attempt at sleeping. There were a total of four rockets set up and ready to go. Each rocket contained what the crew had come to call a piggy-back, which was actually just another stage of the rocket.

The first one contained a satellite for Mars, with the piggy-back part of the rocket containing two of the agri-pods. The second rocket actually carried the most as far as payload, and as far as anybody else was concerned it only carried a deep space probe. What it really contained was the other two Agri-pods, the corridors that connected the Agri-pods together, and the pod mover.

The second rocket was programmed so that it

would appear to be malfunctioning. Once everyone was convinced of this, the command would be sent to set the rocket on a crash course with Mars, and if everything went as planned it would just slip out of everyone's memory.

The third rocket would contain a small telecommunications satellite to replace one that was deteriorating, and the craft. The craft had gone through a couple of different changes: the retractable wings, for lack of a better word, and the camera package for Reese, which would prove to be useful to Dylon when the craft arrived on Mars. Then the last thing that was added was a hook and winch. This was Kat's idea. She thought it would make the task of placing the corridors in position a little easier.

The fourth rocket contained the actual deep space probe, the one they were going to tell everyone they lost due to a malfunction. The piggy-back stage of this rocket contained a small excavator, four solar reflector vehicles, and the corridor transporter.

After deciding to use the craft to place the corridors, the corridor transporter had been reworked to carry some storage tanks for water. With all of the components packed tightly in the four rockets, they would have everything they needed to set up a small complex on Mars. Dylon's dream was very close to becoming a reality. As he sat there, deep in thought about how much time it would take for everything to get to Mars, he started thinking about the craft.

With the amount of time Marcus had spent on getting everything ready to go, he hadn't had a lot of time to research the new technologies for propulsion. This meant everything would take about six months to get there. The only craft that had any kind of new propulsion was the craft. "Unless…" He said out loud, as his mind furiously processed the idea. He quickly went outside and hopped on the *Mule*. He sped off to the shop at the old hangar. The entire way, the idea was evolving into a precise plan on how to fix the lengthy time problem.

\* \* \* \* \* \*

The others finally woke up at 7:30 a.m. In reality, they didn't have a choice in the matter. Reese had been knocking on every door in the house, trying to find out where Uncle Dylon was. Kat finally convinced him to get dressed and be a little more patient. Then everyone would go look for him after they ate some breakfast. "Don't you think it would be a nice idea to bring him some breakfast?" She asked him as he was standing there defiantly. "Well, he'll also needs a *Mountain Dew*, he always has a *Mountain Dew* in the morning."

"Why yes he does. That's very observant of you, not to mention considerate, and you can take it to him once you get dressed and get something in that belly of yours, young man." She reached out and tickled his belly. Reese laughed and pulled away, then ran upstairs to get dressed.

It took about an hour for everyone to finish eating breakfast and get ready to start the day. Even though there was a lot that needed to be done, just being at *the estate* brought a sense of well-being. Everything would fall into place and if it didn't get finished, then there must be some higher power keeping it from happening. The only thing that ran at hyper-speed at *the estate* was Reese, and well, that was a completely different set of circumstances.

Reese sat as patiently as he possibly could on the front steps. When the door opened and the others came out, Reese jumped up and ran down the steps to get into one of the *Mules*. In his haste to go see Uncle Dylon, he had already brought them around. "Well, I guess we should get going." Kat turned and said to the others as she wondered how far this child would go, to make sure he didn't disappoint his uncle. His ultimate big brother, that he obviously loved very much.

It only took them about fifteen minutes to get to the old hangar. They didn't even attempt to call Dylon on the radio. They just guessed that would be the most likely place to find him. When they got to the hangar they could hear all kinds of noise. It sounded like someone rummaging through a garbage can, with all kinds of clanking and pinging noises coming from inside.

Kat turned to Marcus and rolled her eyes before saying. "I'm not sure if I even want to know this time. We've built just about everything that we can possibly build. What on earth could he possibly be thinking of now? If I didn't know better, I would swear he has A.D.D."

Marcus opened the door and they saw five pieces of steel cable stretched out on the floor, all measuring about twenty feet in length and attached together at one end with a closed loop clamp. Lying at the other end of the cable were five pieces of half-inch sheet metal. Each measured about a foot and a half by two feet.

So intent on his project, Dylon didn't hear the group enter. They were standing there with their mouths half open in surprise at the mess Dylon had created. When he did finally notice the rest of the group staring at him, in his half-crazed state, he almost jumped out of his skin.

# Chapter 33

Startled, Dylon said, "What are you guys doing?" He had a look on his face like a child that had been caught with his hand in the cookie jar.

"The question is Dylon, what are <u>you</u> doing, or rather what are you working on now?" Marcus replied.

"Um, well, it's just a last minute idea that I came up with. It really won't be that difficult to build, and it's the only way to get all this stuff there faster." Dylon stuttered and stammered all around the subject, but couldn't get the others to see what he was talking about. His mind was on a completely different track than theirs.

"What stuff where?" Marcus asked.

"Well you know how in the beginning, we were talking about using all these new types of propulsion techniques to get to Mars faster?" Dylon said, trying to bring the others up to the speed of his thought process.

Marcus and the others nodded as Dylon continued. "Well, we haven't. Not one single rocket has any new propulsion technique in it." He said in a highly excited state.

Marcus got a little offended by this statement and started to say something about it. "Hey Dylon, what did you expect? I've been working on all of this other…"

Dylon stopped him quick. "Marcus, I know, and you've done a great job. You just haven't had the time to do anything with any of the propulsion techniques that you've wanted to try. It's not your fault, there was just too much to do. Trust me, Marcus, you have all done a wonderful job and I'm not saying that you haven't, so please don't take it that way."

Marcus thought for a minute. "So what exactly is it that you're trying to say, Dylon?"

"Without any new propulsion systems in any of the rockets, it's still going to take us six months to get to Mars. I was looking at the rockets this morning when I realized that they all have the old style propulsion system." Dylon stopped for a minute.

Then Marcus got it and before he even realized that he was saying it out loud, he finished Dylon's statement. "Everything, except for the craft."

"Exactly!" Dylon shouted out in excitement then continued. "Marcus, how much have you played with the R.S. One, not the toy, the prototype full scale model?"

"Well, I've had some fun with it, probably about forty five hours in all." Marcus said and smiled as he looked at Kevin.

"And what about you, Kevin?"

"I would probably guess about thirty, Marcus

wouldn't let me fly it after....well it doesn't really matter, about thirty." Kevin said.

"I've probably had about twenty." Dylon said and continued asking questions. "So what's the fastest you've gone? I only got it up to two bars."

"Yeah, I think that's probably as high as I've gone too." Marcus said as he recalled the times he flew it.

"Well, I got it up to three bars. Lucky for you I was able to hit the emergency stop before I passed out." Kevin said.

"You passed out?" Dylon asked "Did you feel any G-forces?"

Kevin shook his head no. "The doctor said that it was from the monitor. She said that what I was seeing on the monitor was coming in too quick for my brain to process, so my body kind of went into shock and shut everything down. But anyway, I know where you're going with this."

Rosie piped in. "Well I sure don't, and if somebody would care to put all of this jibberish into layman's terms for me I might be able to keep up."

Kat had already walked over to look at what Dylon was putting together. As she held the end of one of the cables she answered Rosie's question. "I think what he's trying to say, Rosie, is they don't have a clue how fast the craft goes. They can only figure that out once it's in space then they are going to play with the speed to see just how fast they can get to Mars. Once they figure that out, we're going to try to tow whatever type of storage container we decide to use, whether it's a rocket or something else, to transport the supplies to Mars. Ultimately, using this tow cable he's trying to construct. Does that pretty much cover it, Dylon?"

"Well yeah sis, it does, but when you say it like that, it kind of takes all of the excitement out of it." Dylon said.

"Well D, I'm sorry to burst your bubble of revelation, but if that's what you want to do, we've got a lot of work ahead of us." Kat said as she was examining what Dylon had put together so far. "You've done a pretty good job here, Dylon. You might actually become a mechanic someday." She looked up at him with a smile of approval. Just about that time she heard the helicopter starting up. "Shit! Is that Carlos? I wanted to catch him before he left. I'll be back later." She called out as she ran out the door trying to get Carlos's attention.

Dylon looked at Marcus. "Yeah, she mentioned at breakfast that she wanted to go see Carmen today." Marcus said as he stepped over to look at Dylon's tow cable. He knelt down to look at the sheet metal lying on the floor. "I'm guessing these are going to be magnetized somehow?"

"Well, that was my thought. Do you have another suggestion?" Dylon asked as Kevin walked over to join them.

Rosie looked down at Reese. "So what do you want to do, kiddo? Do you want to stay here or do you want to give me some more flying lessons?" Reese looked over at Dylon and the others. Normally, he would have been right at Dylon's side, but he would really rather be flying the model crafts instead. He only thought about it for a minute. "Let's go play." The two of them got into one of the *Mules* and headed to the observatory where the model crafts were stored.

A couple of minutes later, Kat came walking back into the hangar. Marcus saw her first. "So I guess you're stuck with us all day, huh?"

"I could think of worse places to be stuck, like in class." She laughed a little, trying to hide her disappointment. Marcus read the underlying statement and gave her a hug. He whispered in her ear. "You'll always be able to go back and finish once this is all up and running. Trust me, you'll see."

"Thanks babe, I needed that." They walked over to the desk to look at some of Dylon's drawings on the tow cable. She picked up a pencil and started making some notes on how to store it for travel purposes.

After working on the tow cable all day, the

foursome had abandoned the steel cable all together and decided to go with steel rods instead. The attaching device would be able to open and close like an umbrella. The electromagnetic capturing clamps were attached to the end of each rod. They decided that this style of equipment would be more stable and easier to secure than a bunch of steel cables. The only thing left to do was to write and install an operating program into the crafts computer system.

They all decided to call it a day and headed back to the main house. Rosie and Reese had just got into their swimsuits and were getting ready to get into the pool when the others came around the house.

When Kevin noticed her, he couldn't help but to give her some razzing. "Oh, the hardship! Rosie, you must be just exhausted. I mean the travesty of having to get your own towel or make your own drinks. How did you cope all day?"

Rosie just batted her eyes and responded. "Well, you know Kevin, it's pretty rough for a lady of my age and stature to teach a ten-year-old how to enjoy life. Seriously, all the laughing and doing only what you want to do, it really takes a toll on the body. Especially one as tender as mine." Kevin just rolled his eyes and laughed.

Rosie smiled. "By the way, there's a pitcher of tea right over there. I just brought it out." She pointed to the table with the umbrella up.

"I gotta hit the shower first." Dylon said. Kevin and Marcus, on the other hand, were already heading for the tea.

* * * * * *

When everyone had finished de-grunging themselves, they gathered at the poolside. Juanita had marinated some steaks for Dylon to cook on the grill. She had also prepared the sides and placed them in the warmer for them. Dylon was worn out, from his sleepless night, and after putting in a full day's worth of work, he was happy to oblige Kevin when he stepped up to the grill.

The group all sat near the outdoor kitchen area discussing everything that needed to happen in the next couple of days and weeks. This included rearranging the launching schedule and setting up a meeting with Lieutenant Vasquez. As the night drifted away from them, so did Dylon. He actually fell asleep before dinner was even ready. The rigors of the prior day of chasing and evading combined with the days efforts of rethinking and rebuilding had taken quite a bit of energy out of him.

With everything cleared from the table except Dylon's plate, everyone was calling it a night. Kat and

Marcus stayed behind to make sure Dylon ate something before going to bed. "Come on bud, you've got to eat at least a few bites, it's really good. You've been at it since 4:30 this morning and no one has seen you eat anything." Marcus was feeling the anxiety of Kat's prodding and finally asked, "Elizabeth how often does he do this?"

"Marcus, I haven't seen him do this since mom and dad died. He used to get himself so with making sure I was ok in addition to being consumed with his projects he wouldn't eat anything for days. He put himself in the hospital once. He was doing everything he could do, just so he wouldn't have to deal with what he needed to. He's spent his entire life making sure the people he loves are getting what they need. I just wish he would try to focus a little more of that energy on himself, instead of his projects." Kat said to Marcus, who was still trying to get Dylon to come around and eat a little.

"Well, do you think that's the case this time?"

"No honey, I just think he just got wrapped up in this, for lack of a better description, New Toy/Idea that he didn't even think about it. Here, let me try." She sat down across from Dylon. "Big brother, I'm getting ready to pour a big glass of ice water over your head. If you don't believe me tell me what you feel." She dipped her fingers in the glass of water sitting on the table and flicked it in his face.

"Damn, sis! Alright I'm getting up."

"No, you're not. You need to eat at least a couple of bites of something before you go to bed. Here, drink some water. Its ice cold, so it will help you wake up enough to eat a little before you go to bed."

"Fine, whatever."

"Whatever my ass, Dylon Rosier. If you can honestly tell me that you've eaten anything since yesterday, then I'll leave you alone." She waited for a minute as he thought. "Well, I don't have all night."

"Okay fine, you're right. I haven't eaten since dinner yesterday and that wasn't but a few bites." There was no response from Kat, but Dylon could feel her eyes glaring at him. He honestly felt if she could, there would have been a laser beam burning right through him. "Fine, I'll eat." He sat up and fumbled around for the fork. After he was finished with about half of the food on his plate, Kat was satisfied. She told Marcus she would meet him upstairs and leaned over to give Dylon goodnight peck on the forehead. "Dylon, I wasn't trying to be mean. We just need all of you tomorrow, not just half of you, all of you. Love you D, goodnight."

"Yeah, yeah, you're just jealous that I was asleep and you weren't." Dylon said in a jokingly as he continued to finish the food on his plate.

\* \* \* \* \* \*

Lieutenant Vasquez sat down at his computer to retrieve the message that had arrived from Kolminski. He was not looking forward to it. He poured himself a shot of tequila. After swigging it down, he poured another two fingers in the glass and sat down in front of the computer.

As he read the letter, Vasquez was not surprised with the tone in which it was written. Yes, it was a little milder than most of the communications he had received from Kolminski, but it still carried that condescending manner. What actually concerned the Lieutenant the most was the fact that Kolminski was actually interested in an invitation to *the estate.* This is something that would take a lot discussion and approval of the entire team.

As he was digesting the information he got from the letter, the Lieutenant thought to himself, "Maybe, I might be able to get General Grant down here. He put a lot of energy in trying to break the constrictive contract concerning the surveillance of this piece of property. I must share this with the Rosiers and work on some type of agreement. They should be able to help with this."

The Lieutenant started retyping the document. He

knew he would not be able to print it, because it was sent in a format that would not allow duplication of the document.

# Chapter 34

The next morning Kat realized that Carlos wouldn't be back to *the estate* for two days. So, she joined the guys at the hangar, trying to get the towing apparatus programmed properly. Rosie spent her time looking over the launch schedule. She was trying to confirm which of their clients wanted to be present for the launch of their satellites and which ones didn't.

When she finally put together a list, she had come to the realization that the order of the launches all hinged on whether or not Lieutenant Vazquez needed to have any of his people present. With the launch of the two donated probes scheduled to be first, moving the launch dates up might prove to be quite a task. The importance of contacting Lieutenant Vasquez was steadily increasing.

Rosie just sighed and looked up at the others. Dylon was calling out commands for the towing apparatus and Kevin typed them in the computer. Kat and Marcus were inspecting each movement and making any last minute adjustments. Reese was the designated video guy. He had gotten pretty good at filming everything and was quickly adapting his actions to staying out of the way while doing so.

Watching Reese gave her an idea on what she could work on next.

She flipped a couple of pages to get to a fresh page on the legal pad. She wrote down some information in a column format. There were three columns: People for interview, Questions to be asked, and Footage needed. As Rosie compiled her lists, she thought about how she wanted to do the interviews for the documentary. She wasn't sure if she wanted it to be a sit down type interview, or one with the group walking around the different buildings that made up the complex of the Rosier Aerospace Solutions operations complex.

"Ha, it's done, it's ready to go." Dylon said as the last adjustment was made. His outburst had startled Rosie, breaking her train of thought and she got up to go see the final working piece of equipment.

"Not so fast Dylon," Kat said. "We still have to figure out how to connect it to the craft electronically."

"That's easy." He said with the utmost confidence in his thoughts on the solution for that task. "We can tie it in to the ca....." Dylon stopped himself quick, before he spoiled somebody's birthday surprise. "I mean the power source, the one that Marcus put on for the ...." Dylon was still stumbling for the right words to use. "For the cable and winch system."

Kat had already been told about the surprise photo of the dark side of the moon for Reese's birthday. Nevertheless she was thoroughly enjoying watching Dylon try to cover the near blunder. "Nice save Dylon. Not to mention that you're probably right, about what we could patch into that is." They started to try and load the towing apparatus on one of the flatbed carts and Rosie just shook her head.

"I was just wondering, Kevin," Rosie said, trying to get his attention. When he finally got into a position where he could hold what they were lifting, he glanced up at her. "Yes, Rosie?"

"Well, wouldn't it be easier to use the van? You know the one we stowed away in to get us safely here." She said with a half-crooked smile on her face.

"Yeah Rosie, it probably would. Thanks for letting us know sooner. This thing really isn't all that heavy anyway." Kevin said as they struggled to get the towing apparatus back on the floor.

Rosie caught Reese's attention and motioned him to come over to her. "Let's ride together. I want to pick your brain a little."

"What's wrong with my brain?" He said and gave her a funny look.

"Oh honey, there's nothing wrong with your brain. It's just an expression. It means I want to ask you some questions, spend some time with you, get to know you a little better." She said and tussled his hair.

"What do you want to know, Ms. Rosie?"

"I just want to see all the footage that you have taken. I'm working on a project. I'm putting together a movie." Rosie said.

"Oh, well then you will probably want to see Dylon's movie. He put it together the last time he was here. I helped him too." Reese said. "It's really good, you should watch it. I got to fly the models in it, and he flew the craft and I filmed that. He said I did a real good job."

"Did he now? Well, I will have to ask him about it." Rosie said. "I would still like to see yours too. I might be able to use some of it as well, but let's help them finish this up first. I'm sure they will want you to film it all." Rosie said as she was driving the *Mule* and missed the turn.

"No, Rosie. It's that way." Reese said as they passed their turn.

"Oh good Lord, how do you keep up with all of these turns? You should make me a road map, so I don't get lost." She said and laughed as she made a bumpy U-turn to get back to the right path.

"Don't worry, Ms. Rosie. I would never let you get lost." Reese said as he held on tight while she turned around. When they got to the turn they waited to let the van go through first.

By the time the crew got the towing arm in place, the day was winding down. Reese had already left to go eat at least an hour beforehand and Rosie had taken over the filming process. They closed everything down and locked it all up. Dylon received word from Juanita that dinner was ready and in the warmer at the pool. She let him know that Reese had to go with his father in the morning so she was putting him to bed early.

\* \* \* \* \* \*

When everyone had finished with their dinner, they all retired around the fire pit at the far end of the pool. It was a really nice place to sit and relax, located about ten feet off the pool deck. Kat leaned over to Rosie and asked what she had been working so intently on today. When she started explaining, Rosie made sure to drag Dylon into the conversation. "Well, I was putting together some notes on a documentary video. Something we could use kind of as a press release presentation. Well, I got a lot of ideas written down. I would really like to get everyone's approval on it before I start." Everybody nodded in agreement and Rosie continued. "Well, Reese was telling me that Dylon had put together a 'movie' that I should really check out. He said it was pretty good and that I might be able to capture some footage from there."

Dylon just shook his head. "Oh you know that Reese, he's always playing tricks on people. Do you remember that day in the field, Rosie? When he was playing with one of the crafts and diving at you and Kevin."

Marcus raised his eyebrow, but it was Kat that said something. "Oh my God Dylon, that has got to be one of the worst lies I've ever heard you tell."

"It's not a lie sis, really." Dylon said, trying to hide the truth.

Rosie said something this time. "Dylon, I've only known you a little over a year and I can tell you're not being completely honest."

Dylon just shook his head. "I'm really going to have to teach that child how to keep a secret."

"So what have you recorded that you're trying so desperately to hide?" Kat asked.

"It's just some footage about everything we've done, really."

"Okay, then in that case, I guess it won't hurt if we see it. Really, Dylon, you're being kind of weird if that's all it is." Kat said.

Dylon hung his head. "Well it's not just a video about what we've done. There's more….I put together a couple of things. You know, just in case….well, just in case."

"Oh." Rosie looked at the others. "That kind of video, I must say you're not the first person I expected to put something like that together, Dylon."

"Well, it is kind of separated into two different parts. I was going to show you...after we got most of what we wanted launched. You know, when we've done as much as we can do before the U.S. government tries to step in," Dylon said, trying to explain his actions. "Actually, I was just going to show Rosie. No offense intended Rosie, but really, at your age, what are they going to do to you? They wouldn't expect what you're capable of."

Rosie nodded her head. "None taken, Dylon. Now that the cat is out of the bag, can we at least see the first part of it? Really, I don't want to see a goodbye message from you. I can't believe you would even think we would need it." Rosie was only trying to lighten the mood a little with her next comments. "Seriously child, all we're doing is trying to cut the apron strings from the U.S. You act as if we're trying to take over the world. We've done everything upfront and covered our asses every step of the way. So you just need to stop all of this nonsense. Anyway, Kat put together a very good video for Lieutenant Vasquez. I would love the opportunity to critique at least part of yours."

When Rosie finished, the mood did seem to

lighten just a little and they all headed inside. Once they got inside the house, Dylon headed towards the movie room. The others paused for just a minute, thinking they would be going to the office. He turned and told them to wait there for a minute. He retrieved the movie disc Titan A.E. and joined back up with the others.

When they got into the office, he sat down at the computer and put the disc in the drive. They all gathered around the computer to see what he was doing. Kevin picked up the movie case. "Hide it in plain sight, huh? This was a pretty good movie. Have you seen it, Rosie?" She shushed him and pointed to the monitor. The movie had already started playing. Just through the opening credits, the movie stopped playing and asked for a password.

Dylon spun his chair around. "Now guys, this is very important. If anything were to happen, not that I think it will, but if it did the password for this disc is something you need to remember. All you have to do is think about what will happen if we succeed in our mission to Mars. It will be a new beginning, a new start. The password is 'Novus Orsa'. It's Latin.

He typed in the password and the video resumed playing. It was a very extensive video. It covered almost every process of everything that had happened at *the estate.* It even had some things in it that

happened before Dylon even started work at his
father's firm. Everybody was engrossed in the
production and remembered most of everything. They
poked fun at each other and got lost in their own
thoughts of everything that they'd accomplished, and
what it meant to them. They were brought back to
reality when Dylon stopped the video. "Now, this is
the point where I'm going to stop the disc. You really
don't need to watch any further, unless something
goes bad."

# Chapter 35

"Pssst, over here," Kat whispered when she saw Rosie sneaking out of the house. As Rosie crept over to where Kat was, she asked her. "So where's the *Mule*?"

"I put it a little further away from the house. I didn't want to take any chance of waking anybody." Kat said and pointed to the small cluster of trees about fifty yards away from the house. "Did you notice if anybody was stirring?" Rosie shook her head.

The two girls made it to the *Mule* and started heading to the hangar. They hadn't gone more than twenty feet and the tarp that was in the back lifted and Reese started talking. "So where are we going?"

Not noticing what was going on behind them, both of the girls let out a scream. "Reese, what are you doing? How did you? Oh, it doesn't matter. You need to go back to the house." Kat said as she brought the *Mule* to a stop.

Reese argued with them. "No, I want to go with you. You need me."

"How do you know if we need you, when you don't even know what we're doing?" Kat asked.

"I heard you last night, outside my door. You and Rosie said you were going to go fly the craft in the morning. So I figured you would need me."

Kat just looked at him. "How did you hear us? We weren't talking that loud. Damn." Kat cursed herself for confirming what Reese said. "Reese, honey, you can't go. This is just us girls."

"Okay then. I guess I'll just go back to the house. I sure hope I don't wake anybody when I go inside. I will probably have to explain what I was doing outside this early in the morning." Reese said as he started to turn and go to the house.

Rosie raised her eyebrow and looked at Kat. "The boy's good. I think he's been hanging around all of us just a little too long, not to have picked up a little bit of our skills of persuasion. " She said and let out a little laugh.

Kat just shook her head. "Oh my God, I'm being hustled by a child. Fine, you can go. You better not say a word about what we're doing."

"Yes ma'am." Reese said as he sat back and smiled.

Rosie leaned over to Kat and whispered to her. "You know, he may actually be able to help us."

Kat nodded her head. "I'm kind of counting on that, but don't tell him that."

When they made it to the hangar, Reese hopped out and opened the hangar door. Kat drove the *Mule* into the hangar. Rosie and Kat just stood there while

Reese scurried around gathering up a handful of wrenches. The girls weren't paying attention to what he was doing, instead they were battling with their own anxieties. "Do you want to go first?" Kat asked Rosie, who was looking at the craft nervously.

"Oh, I couldn't do that. After all, you helped design it, right?"

Kat just hem and hawed around. "Well, not really. I just helped make the mechanics a little simpler. So if you wanted to go first, you could."

Reese had finished placing the wrenches on the floor, marking exactly where the craft was sitting. By the time the girls had slowly made their way to the craft, Reese was opening the hatch. He turned around to see who was going first and saw that they still had not decided. Trying to hurry the decision along, Reese finally said something. "It will be daylight soon. If you don't want to get caught you need to hurry."

The two women looked at him, and the realization came to both of them at the same time. Kat looked at Rosie. "No, he couldn't have." Then they both looked at Reese. Kat started to climb up the ladder. "Reese, have you ever flown this thing before?" Reese started messing with the harness on the seat, preparing it for the first passenger of the day. "Uncle Dylon told me I was not supposed to." He said without looking at either of the two women. He continued to fidget with some of the other pre-flight preparations and Kat asked him again. "Reese?" She said with a long pause. "If you have never flown it before, how do you know about all the things that need to be done?"

"I don't know?" Reese said and hung his head even further and started pointing out what all the gadgets were and what she needed to do, once she got in the air.

"Mm-hum" She said. As she watched him ready everything she realized that he wasn't going to answer her question. "You know, there's room enough in here for a co-pilot. Especially one that knows so much about all of these instruments, that is, if you would want to try and help me figure out how to fly this thing."

Before he realized what he was saying the words had already come out of his mouth. "It's really pretty easy once you get the hang of it." Reese stopped for a brief second, before Kat interjected. "That's what I thought. Now I know I can count on you to keep quiet about this little field trip." She said. "So how many times have you flown it, Reese?"

"Fifteen, maybe more."

Kat, Rosie, and Reese spent the next couple of hours flying the craft. The two women walked away with a better understanding of what it was actually capable of doing. After that the trio gathered up the model crafts and headed off to the empty field where Reese usually played with the models.

\* \* \* \* \* \*

The Lieutenant was putting together some things for a couple of days away at *the estate*. It would not be the normal laid-back kind of visit, not at first anyway. The letter he had received from Kolminski, combined with the fact that the rest of the group had to sneak out of the country, bothered him. It just didn't sit well with him, and he didn't want this operation to put his country in an unwelcome position with the rest of the world. He already knew the program would produce an awkward situation with the U.S. and he expected nothing less.

His main concern was to make sure that the original plan was still in place. He wanted to feel at ease. He wanted to know that the group he had signed on with wasn't going to tuck their tails and run at the first sign of real trouble. He wasn't scheduled to be there until tomorrow, but considering the circumstances, Lieutenant Vasquez didn't think it would be out of place if he arrived early. He would be arriving at the clinic right about the time Carlos was finishing his day there.

As he was walking out to meet the car, Lieutenant Vasquez thought to himself. "It would be nice to get there early enough to visit. I haven't seen Carmen in a while."

\* \* \* \* \* \*

It was about ten o'clock when the boys finally found Reese, Kat, and Rosie. Kevin, Dylon, and Marcus had already eaten but decided to pack a cooler with some sandwiches and drinks, just in case the girls hadn't.

Dylon grabbed some drinks for Kat, Rosie, and Reese and started walking over to them. Apparently Kat was getting pretty good at flying the model and didn't want to give it up. "You guys were up pretty early."

"Yeah, we wanted to get some flying lessons from Reese before all the activities started today. You know, he's a pretty good teacher." Kat said as she looked down at Reese and winked.

"Well, that's probably because he's such a good listener. He's like a little sponge, there's not much you have to tell him twice." Dylon said and gave him a friendly nudge. "So I take it you got Carmen's e-mail."

Kat nodded and passed the controls off to Reese, who was more than happy to take them. "Yeah, I guess that's why I'm out here. I just had a lot of energy built up. You know anxiousness, nervousness, just too many emotions swirling around. I'm not really sure what to be anymore. I just want to get going in some direction."

"I know what you mean, sis. We're there. We could launch all of the rockets today, if there was enough time." Dylon said with the same nervous tension that Kat was feeling.

The group spent the rest of the day going over last minute details. Kevin and Marcus finished installing the towing arm to the craft and closed the rocket back up. Rosie, Kat, and Dylon went over the launch schedule a couple more times. Plus, they discussed all the possible scenarios of what would unfold when the second rocket supposedly malfunctions. What their plans would be on how to destroy it, or at least what they would tell the media. The final part of the day would be spent on reviewing the release footage. That would be something that would be gone over when the Lieutenant showed up, in the hopes that a lot of his questions and concerns would be laid to rest.

* * * * * *

At the end of the day the helicopter arrived right on schedule. The group was waiting anxiously. Trying to contain their eagerness to overpower the Lieutenant with too much information at one time, they decided to give him a tour of the new buildings. They would have almost two hours before their dinner of appetizers and finger foods was ready.

They showed him the storage hangar and the four rockets that were ready to launched, the construction hangar for new rockets being built, and ended up at the command center. The Lieutenant had already seen the launch pad from the helicopter on his way in. There were several small questions here and there, but the Lieutenant also seemed like he was trying to keep his emotions subdued. The entire tour felt like they were vying for the Lieutenant's approval all over again.

They had finally made it to the main house where dinner had been put out. It was all set up around the pool which seemed to be turning into the gathering spot where the best ideas came from. Dylon and the others attributed it to the more relaxed atmosphere, and usually, by the time they all got there they were ready to relax. There was only one more thing to go over the documentary type video that would inform the country, and the rest of the international community, of the Peruvian government's intentions. It showed the plan for the exploration and development of a habitation complex on Mars, and the intention of a more aggressive research process for new propulsion technologies.

When everybody had made themselves a plate, they gathered around the television. Rosie and Kat stepped up in front of the group to start the presentation. "Let me start off with a special thank you to Lieutenant Vasquez for taking a chance on us and allowing us to put our best foot forward in starting a space program for the Peruvian government. It would not have been possible to get as far as we have without your help and guidance." Rosie said and then moved a little closer to Kat before continuing. "We have compiled quite a bit of footage on this whole process and, with Elizabeth's expertise, we have put together a video. One that I believe you will be quite impressed with." Kat pressed the play button on the DVD player and the two took their seats.

As the video played each person reflected on what the project meant to them. They laughed at themselves when they saw how excited they got when things happened the way they were meant to. At the end of the presentation, there was a burst of applause and congratulations. Everyone was amazed at the profound implications of what was turning out to be only a few steps away from reality.

When everyone had finished commenting on what a great job Kat and Rosie had done in putting together the production, the Lieutenant stepped up in front of the group and tinged his glass with his fork. "I would like to congratulate all of you for an outstanding job that I must honestly say I didn't think was going to happen." They paused as everyone raised their glasses. "I also have to admit that when I arrived today, I had some reservations. With everything that has been going on with your group and your government, I thought you might want to back down. I had to see for myself where each of you stood. So, forgive me if I seemed a little....distant."

The Lieutenant reached into his pocket to retrieve the letter from Kolminski before continuing. "But I too, have had some difficulties in conversing with your government. There is an officer that I have had several...." He searched for the right words to describe his discomfort. "...let's just say he is a man that I would rather not talk to, and would rather not ever meet in person. However, it appears that he's almost demanding a visit to *the estate* to make sure everything is on the up and up. I don't know if this man is a powerful man or not, but he is the only man that I am forced to have contact with regarding the Surveillance Treaty of the estate." The Lieutenant handed the letter to Rosie.

As she read over it, her mind worked on a solution to this letter. The words did appear to insinuate that this person could start quite a bit of trouble for the program if he did not get his way. What she did read out of it though, was that this person did not seem to be of a military caliber. Sure, his title may say officer, but she interpreted it as to have the same meaning as a manager.

Rosie passed the letter around and started talking to the Lieutenant. "This is just political talk. The man is merely flexing his muscles, trying to bully his way into getting what he wants. You and I, Lieutenant, will take care of this in the morning. I'm assuming that if you brought the letter with you, that you haven't responded yet?"

The Lieutenant smiled really big and assumed his normal character. "That's what I like about you, Rosie. You are always thinking. You capture my heart with your intellect." Rosie just smiled, took the Lieutenant by the arm, and headed toward the bar. "Come on you big flirt, let's fix another drink."

# Chapter 36

Washington, D.C.

Kolminski had finally found everything he needed. A side project he had been working for a couple of weeks. He had gathered all the information he wanted, and compiled it into one file. Using his manipulative skills, Kolminski organized the information from each incident related to the estate, to make it appear that General Grant may not have the Division's best interests at heart.

Kolminski didn't lie or fabricate any of the reports, but only gave enough information to plant a seed of doubt. A seed that would spread out its roots faster than dollar weed invades a lawn. He sat back in awe of himself, enjoying the moment before he started typing his letter.

*Dear Senator Emerson,*

*I have struggled with this information since before I joined your division. I have been very careful in my career to know who I am working for and with, through extensive research on prospective employers. I must say, you have quite an impressive  record. One I can only aspire to mirror. There is one person though, that my research made me pause and question, General Grant. I thought that maybe the information I gathered would prove to      be incorrect. It appears, though, that I can only go by the actions of a person.*

*I am concerned that the information I found gives the impression the General might not be so willing to pursue our current objective. In the files that I'm sending with this letter, you will find occurrences where the General seems to be looking the other way, including several attempts to release the target from the current surveillance agreement.*

*I fear that the General doesn't have the division's best interest at heart in this particular case. I understand how important the success of the first mission is to this new division.*

*I am also sending the latest information on the activities at the estate. I admire the General's position and understand how many years it took to get there. I hope you can appreciate my desire for discretion in handling this situation.*
*Deeply concerned,*
*Senior Foreign Relations Officer*

*Billy Kolminski*

Kolminski put the letter in the envelope with the files and personally carried it to the Senator's office.

\* \* \* \* \* \*

After an evening that lasted too long, most everyone in the group woke up the next morning feeling a little leftover (not hung-over, but definitely feeling the results of the activities of the previous night). They gathered around the breakfast table and started making plans for the day. The Lieutenant was going to be the busiest. He would be shuffled from one person to the next to get him up to speed on all that was going on. Rosie and Kat would be the last to get him.

The launch schedule would be covered by Dylon and Marcus when he went back to the command center. Kevin would show him the process of receiving and storing parts for the rockets. Kat would go over the public relations topics that needed to be covered and get additional names of the people the Lieutenant wanted to be present for the launches. Then Rosie would go over how to handle the political weasels of the U.S. government, not that they were all weasels, but the ones that were, she knew and made sure that the Lieutenant did too.

After breakfast, they all headed out front where they ran into Carlos. Dylon and Marcus headed to the *Mule*, while Lieutenant Vasquez exchanged some small talk with Carlos. When he was finished, he headed off with Marcus and Dylon for the first part of his training and debriefing. Carlos continued up the stairs, carrying a small box which contained the mail from the clinic.

Anything that was to be delivered to *the estate* always went to the clinic. Kat thanked him and shuffled through the mail to see if anything was in there for her. She gathered what was hers and laid the rest of it down. Only then did she notice the larger envelope addressed to Dylon. The reason it caught her eye was because it had no return address. About that time Reese came running up to her and was anxious to go play again. This little action completely sidetracked her train of thought and the envelope was soon to be forgotten. "Oh honey, I wish I could, but we have a very important visitor today and I have a lot of work to do before I get to see him."

Reese nodded his head. "I understand." He said and rushed off to find something else to do.

* * * * * *

The stranger walked through the hall like he was supposed to be there. When he made it to Lieutenant Vasquez's office there were two janitors in the hall. He walked right by them and headed down the hall towards the bathroom. He stopped momentarily at the drinking fountain. As he took a drink of water he noticed that they were just getting started. He knelt down to tie his shoe. When he felt sure they weren't looking he slipped a small spy cam out of his pocket and attached it to the bottom of the fountain. Then he stood up and headed to the bathroom and found himself a spot to sit for a while. He pulled out his receiving device, which was no larger than a cell phone, and watched the hall.

Twenty minutes or so had passed and the janitors had moved on around the corner to the next set of offices. The stranger left the bathroom and continued on with his mission. He quickly picked the lock to the Lieutenant's office. Once inside he closed the door and locked it behind him. He started going through the drawers. He knew exactly what he was looking for and wasn't trying to make a mess in finding it. Everything he moved was returned to its original position. When he finished with the desk he moved over to the filing cabinet, located next to a small bookshelf.

While reaching to open the first drawer he

spotted what he was looking for on the bookshelf. The DVD of Amestad. He quickly opened the case and pulled out a Walkman-sized player. He inserted the disc and confirmed the disc was what he was looking for. He put the disc and the player away and pulled out the receiver again. Once he found a clear path, he exited the office.

* * * * * *

The Lieutenant had spent the first half of the day absorbing everything the boys were showing and teaching him. He was very relieved to know that there was no backing down from their original plans. He also felt very privileged when Marcus and Dylon revealed the plans about their intentions with the second rocket. It really made him feel like he was a part of the group, not to mention it bolstered his trust in his partners.

They arrived at the main house just in time for lunch. Rosie and Kat would be the next to spend time with the Lieutenant, after lunch of course. When lunch was over the women and the Lieutenant retired to the den, where there was an office set up for communicating with clients. It had all the bells and whistles, including a small area set up for video conferencing, several computers, and of course a small bank of security monitors to keep a watchful eye on any would-be intruders. A private bathroom, a kitchenette, and also a comfortable seating/resting area were just a few more of the amenities of this very functional den.

The ladies partially closed the door after entering the room. This was mainly to remind anyone wishing to enter to knock first. This practice was also to let anyone know, there was always an open door to discuss anything that you might need to.

The guys were happy to be finished with the Lieutenant. The biggest part of their day was finished, and now it was time to relax a little. Marcus had some research items with a new propulsion device he wanted to look at, and Kevin just wanted to sit by the pool for a little bit.

Dylon, on the other hand, would be spending some time with Reese, who was waiting patiently at the observatory. He had spent the past hour hanging out, making sure all the batteries for the models were charged. He ended up in the display room, curiously checking out the plans for the Mars complex. He turned out all of the lights and turned on the lights for the planetarium. As he was daydreaming and walking back towards the display he tripped over the backpack he had laid on the floor. He landed halfway under the display case. When he looked up, he noticed the glow of a button. One he had never noticed before.

Reese stood up in front of the display where the button was. He reached under the panel and pressed the button. The landscape in the display started to transform. He watched as water started to appear and new buildings formed. When it was finished what had been four buildings had grown into a small metropolis. The crater that was next to the small city had become quite an impressive lake. Stretching to the north of the city, an aqueduct had been constructed and was supplying a steady stream of water to the lowest elevation of the region, which looked similar to a dried up riverbed. Mentally comparing the landscape to the maps of Mars he had seen, Reese judged that the aqueduct was emptying into a riverbed that led to what had now become an ocean.

Dylon had searched every room looking for Reese. The only one left was the display room. When he opened the door, Reese was just standing there, gazing into the Mars complex display. "Earth to Reese," Dylon said, trying to get his attention.

"Uncle Dylon, this is cool. Is this what it's all going to look like when we get there?"

Dylon just laughed. "Oh, I wish bud. No, this is what you call a hundred-year plan. It's a very optimistic guess of what things will look like if everything goes right. Guess what, though?" He said and leaned down to Reese.

"What, Uncle Dylon?"

"If everything goes really good, it could look like this in fifty years. You could probably move there and raise a family of your own on Mars."

"That would be cool, and I could look at the Earth through a telescope like I look at Mars right now."

"Yes, you sure could, bud. Now do you want to go play a little? I got the crafts all loaded up."

"You bet." Reese said and ran out the door.

# Chapter 37

Washington, D.C.

Senator Emerson sat down at the table with the others and handed each one a folder. After giving them a moment to look over the information in the file, he began to speak. "Gentleman, through sources I can't divulge, it has come to my attention that there may be…" The Senator paused to try to grasp the right words to describe the situation. "Well, um, it appears that General Grant, due to past relationships with one of the subjects, may be a little reluctant to give an objective analysis of the situation regarding our operations in the 'Watchdog' mission."

The Senator flipped through a couple pages of the report as he continued. "After an extensive review of the reports, I have come to the conclusion that we should have a few safety precautions in place. Number one, I have given Mr. Kolminski authorization to take command of operations. There are of course stipulations to this authority. All three of you have to agree it is in the best interest of the mission in order for this to happen. Number two, we will be taking the proper and necessary political steps to ensure an official visit to the location currently under our surveillance. I would be sure to keep your personal schedules open. I couldn't even guess when this visit might happen and you will need to be ready to leave at a moment's notice, all of you. Number three, and the last detail to go over, back up forces. There will be several teams and a couple of Harriers, just in case anybody decides they might want to leave. I'm hoping these precautions will not need to be implemented, but I feel better having them there." When the Senator finished speaking and everyone was in agreement with the steps put in place, the four of them left the meeting room, located in the back of the club. They all headed to the bar to get a drink before being seated for dinner.

\* \* \* \* \* \*

The next morning, Rosie and Lieutenant Vasquez grabbed a quick breakfast and headed to the study. Rosie wanted to compose a few letters for the Lieutenant, just to give him an idea of some of the techniques he could use to stall the impending visit from the U.S. Government.

Kat had planned on sleeping in with Marcus. Kevin, on the other hand, had to get up early. It seems that he had promised to take Reese on a tour of the finished launch pad and the command center, which only had finishing touches that needed to be done. Only enough work that a tour would not interfere with.

Dylon actually went for a short swim before eating his breakfast. He had let everyone know that he needed to take some personal time, just to get things into perspective and prepare himself for the upcoming tasks.

Upon getting out of the pool Dylon decided he would spend some time in the display room, just to look over everything again. He changed clothes, went to the kitchen and loaded up a sealable dish with some breakfast. On his way out the door, he stopped momentarily to grab the few pieces of mail that arrived for him yesterday.

Getting to the observatory turned out to be a more leisurely drive than Dylon had intended. Turned out the *Mule* he was left with was one of the older ones and this particular one had a problem with the steering, it wasn't anywhere near as tight as the others. This proved to make eating his breakfast while driving a bit more of a task than usual. By the time he made it to the observatory, Dylon had managed to eat a little over half of his breakfast. The rest of it, he seemed to be wearing.

Dylon put the dish down, brushed himself off, gathered up the mail he brought with him, and walked into the display room of the observatory. Once inside, he placed the mail on a small table just inside the door. Still not noticing the envelope, that looked a little odd, he walked over and turned on the display case.

When the hologram came up, it was a view of the original base. After walking around the display case looking at the small complex from every angle, he pressed the button that revealed the hundred-year plan. Dylon pulled up a stool and sat down to watch the base slowly grow into a small metropolis.

The original pyramid-shaped agri-pods slowly transformed into larger ones about the size of the Great Pyramid in Egypt. They would end up becoming the major water producing facilities for the growing metropolis while also keeping Crater Lake at the proper level. Crater Lake was the name chosen for the crater that sat just at the edge of the original complex.

As Dylon watched the buildings of the metropolis begin to emerge, he found himself fantasizing once again. There were no square buildings in this city. Everything was designed to withstand the winds of a developing atmosphere. An atmosphere that would help a growing planet, build and sustain life.

Dylon closed his eyes and pictured himself flying one of his crafts through the city. He marveled at all of the pyramid, dome, and capsule-shaped buildings, all of which were connected by either tubes or the angled-type corridors of the original complex. All of the buildings glowed from the reflective glass that was the prominently used façade. Each building had a slight tint of color, a design feature which seemed to bring a little more life to a planet that seemed to only have one hue.

Dylon was brought back to reality with a burst of light that filled the room when Kat and Marcus entered. Kat and Marcus were also taking their day at a leisurely pace, trying to make up for time apart. Their mood was jovial and mischievous, which was apparent when Kat spoke. "Hey space cadet, whatcha dreaming about? You think you might be able to find an alien girlfriend when you get to Mars?"

Dylon popped one right back at her. "Anything would be better than the last earth girl I was trying to court." When the words came out of his mouth, all three of them were shocked, none more than Dylon himself. Wanting to change the subject quickly, Kat looked around the room, trying to find something to comment on. Then she saw the stack of mail, it was not just the stack of mail, but the plain envelope. The envelope that lacked a return address and had no postal markings on it. She reached for it and started to question Dylon about it. "I can't believe you haven't opened this yet."

Dylon glanced slightly in her direction as he was turning off the display case. "Sis, I haven't even looked at that stuff. I just brought it with me because it was laying on the buffet. I figured I would get around to it today at some point."

Kat held up the envelope she was curious about. "Well, this one looked odd, that's the only reason I brought it up."

Dylon started to walk towards Kat. "So if it bothers you that much why don't you just open it?"

"Well, because it has your name on it." She said and handed it to him. As Dylon looked the envelope over, a slight feeling of dread started to set in. He looked at Kat and rolled his eyes. "I'm not even sure if I want to see what's in here," he said as he tore the flap open.

Sure enough, what he found inside was a familiar dark brown envelope. "Oh gee, I wonder who this is from?" Dylon said as he started to open the envelope. "I wonder what kind of friendly threat they're sending us this time? And I thought I was going to have a nice relaxing day of just me, lost in my thoughts. How do they even accomplish something like this? Seriously, no post marks or anything that traces these letters back to their origin. I bet you twenty bucks that Carmen couldn't even tell you what the person who delivered it looked like, if she even saw them."

Dylon was a little surprised when he started reading the message. He even relayed his surprise to

Kat and Marcus. "Oh wow, it looks like they're changing their format for their messages."

Kat's interest was piqued. "Oh really, how's that?" Dylon handed the message to Kat and Marcus.

> *This message is for you and your sister, between the two of you, you should be able to figure out how to use it. Each address can only be used once.*
> *Address number one:*     *657.95.165.9*
> *Address number two:*     *872.25.568.0*

> *One will give you a test run and the other will give you a delivery run. After that, you can use your own address.*

> *Five Out*

Marcus and Kat looked at the letter and the way the addresses were written seemed a little familiar to them, they just couldn't place why. Dylon was silent in thought for a minute, trying to digest the letter's contents. "It almost seems like they're trying to help us, but why?"

Kat now had the letter in her hand pacing around the room, trying to remember why the way these were written numbers seemed so familiar. Then it hit her.

"They're I.P. addresses, the numbers are I.P. addresses."

Dylon looked at her with a confused expression on his face. "Why would they...."

Marcus jumped into the conversation before Kat had a chance to answer. "It's a beacon! A lighthouse, so to speak."

"I still don't understand," Dylon said to Marcus, and then directed his attention to Kat. Knowing her brother, she had already gone over an explanation in her head while Marcus was talking, and when her brother looked at her she started trying to explain it in a manner he could understand.

"Dylon, I.P. addresses are linked to computers. Any computer that has the capability of getting on line, will end up receiving an I.P. address once it is actually on line. Any computer." She paused for a minute to gauge whether Dylon was grasping what she was saying. "This simply means that if we had the I.P. address of a computer we can talk to it. We can send it commands, viruses, or we can find a physical address. A location of where the computer is, like a beacon, better yet a tracking device. We could have a direct line of communications with the International Space Station, if we wanted."

A light bulb went off and you could tell that Dylon figured it out. "You mean like a homing device, right?" Kat and Marcus both nodded and Dylon continued talking. "So we could program the craft to use this address like a laser or line of sight and test how quick we can get to Mars. Then what will we use to get it back here, to transport the other rocket stages that carry the supplies?"

Marcus started to explain the process he could use to Dylon. "Well, that's the beauty of building your own craft bud. You can put all the bells and whistles in it that you want. There's a program already in the craft that allows me to set a distance of how close to an object I want to get. If you want to get close enough to the satellite to dust it, I could program the craft to do that. I wouldn't suggest it, but I could. The closest I would suggest getting is between five hundred and a thousand miles. That's close, but I don't think it will be close enough to draw any attention to the craft. As far as getting back here, there are several options we could use. We could bring it to the orbit of the moon, or we could calculate the distance the rockets will be by the time the craft gets to Mars and back. That one is a little more risky, or we could just affix an actual tracking device on to each stage of the rockets that are supply stages, and if we're lucky they will stay on."

Dylon looked at Kat and Marcus, waiting to see if they had any suggestions on which method to use.

After a brief moment of silence he said something. "Well they all sound like good methods but we don't even know how fast the craft flies. Do you have any ideas Marcus? You've read the printouts haven't you?"

"Yes I have, but they're not that helpful. They all are influenced by the Earth's own gravity, so everything that is there only shows how the craft works in an atmosphere with its own gravitational field. The only way we will really know is to test it in space, a true vacuum." Marcus said with a matter of fact tone in his voice.

"Dylon, the calculations and numbers I came up with seemed so unreal that I just figured I had done something wrong. It just doesn't seem feasible that a craft could go that fast, not to mention the affect it would have on a human. I really wouldn't even want to make a guess. If my numbers are right then everything I learned in physics and quantum physics is all wrong and I should re-evaluate the effort that I put into my schooling and learning everything that I did."

Dylon just looked at him, then he looked at Kat. Kat just shrugged her shoulders. "Dylon, I've looked at them too and the numbers just don't make any sense."

Dylon took a deep breath before he started talking again. "Well, if that's the case, then I think we should launch the rocket with the craft first. Which means the very first launch of our program will look like a failure. The Lieutenant might have a hard time with this, not to mention the Peruvian officials that he has been sharing the details of our operations with."

Kat turned to Marcus with a look on her face that didn't need an explanation. He took her hand and spoke. "I know we need this day honey, but we really need to talk to Rosie and the Lieutenant about this information. I would hate to see her have to redo all their plans after receiving this news. Let's give it to them now so they can figure it in. We'll have plenty of time for us, just a little later than we planned."

She agreed and the three of them headed to the main house to get with Rosie to reorganize their schedules.

# Chapter 38

The week building up to the launch day, proved to be a little more work than anyone had anticipated. The information from *The Five* was the contributing factor for the flurry of activities. Rosie and the Lieutenant spent the bulk of their time restructuring guest lists and confirming who would be at which launch. The restructuring was based on the change in the launch order, once again due to the information received from the group, The Five.

Kat and Marcus went over the numbers from all of the data printouts that Dylon had compiled while building and testing the anti-gravitational device. They found that every equation they used to calculate the speed of the piece of equipment that powered the craft, gave them a set of numbers that were so staggering, that it was hard to comprehend. In fact, their best guess was that the craft could make it to Mars and back in three weeks, and that was based on numbers where the Earth's gravity had a profound effect on the results. They didn't even want to dare to calculate how fast the craft could go in space.

Kevin and Dylon spent their time making sure communications between the tower and the command

389

center were in good working order. When they were finished there they moved on to the rockets. They inspected every inch of them physically and when that task was complete they ran a thorough diagnostics scan.

They double-checked and even triple-checked every last program to make sure everything was going to go as planned. The only rocket that would appear to malfunction was now going to be the first rocket launched. It would be the one carrying the craft, but as far as the general public was concerned, it would be the rocket carrying the deep space probe.

As the days passed, everyone was feeling a little more anxious about the launches. There would be a total of four launches to start the Peruvian Space Program. Each launch would have just a handful of media personnel present by invitation only. The attendees were handpicked by Rosie, Kat, and the Lieutenant. Several government officials were also handpicked and invited to be present. The last country on the list was, of course, the U.S. government.

Rosie was not looking forward to dealing with them. Everybody else on the list would accept the fact, that the procedures being followed were normal protocol that had to be followed for security and safety concerns, except the U.S. officials. The normal protocol would be challenged and stretched until everything was molded the way they wanted it. A way that would give them what appeared to be the upper hand, but Rosie and Lieutenant Vasquez had already planned on that. They had a few cards up their sleeves to make sure things would go according to their procedures, not the U.S. government's.

## Launch Day

The countdown was getting near and Rosie and the Lieutenant were wrapping up their news conference. The tour of *the Estate* and the Rosier Aerospace Solutions complex went off without a hitch. The government officials from Brazil, Columbia, and Peru were very impressed. The media attendees were also pleased, but as the media often does, they were left wanting more questions answered.

There were only two occasions where a media crew had to be escorted back to the rest of the group with a firm explanation about the risks of espionage and sabotage. Not to mention how bad it would look if they were harmed in any way. That is, if they were to happen upon a character committing such an incredulous act.

By the time the countdown had reached thirty minutes, everyone had been escorted to the minimum safe distance. The media groups were all doing their own stories with the launch pad in the background, and the government officials had all gathered in the observation area. They were discussing the benefits that the deep space probes would present for their countries. The educational advancements and the career opportunities that would become available to them by having a space exploration complex on their continent.

The feeling in the air was a positive one and it showed in their faces as the countdown got closer to the launch time. Rosie couldn't help but feel bad for them, knowing that the rocket would appear to be a failure. The only thing that helped her keep her composure was her confidence in the plan. The plan which listed the steps that they would go through to insure the Peruvian government and the rest of the world that was watching, that failure was not an option and they would press on with the aggressive launching schedule.

As the countdown continued to get closer Rosie and the Lieutenant started opening the champagne. They filled the glasses and passed them around.

In the command center the excitement was at the same level. The champagne was being poured, but nobody wanted to pick up a glass until the launch actually happened. They didn't want to do anything to jinx it, so they anxiously waited.

When the countdown reached the final minute before lift-off, there was a flurry of activities from the media groups. The cameramen were all vying for the best position to record the rocket launching. The last crew getting set-up just in the nick of time as a thunderous noise came from the rocket. The exhaust billowed out to form an immense cloud as the rocket blasted off.

The officials in the observation room all raised their glasses and cheered as the rocket climbed into the atmosphere. Rosie stood there trying to play the part. The Lieutenant noticed and walked over to her. He slipped his arm around her and softly whispered in her ear. "This will work, we can do this."

Rosie knew he was talking about the plan of deception and returned his boost of support with a nod and a quick pat on the back. Then, they began to mingle and enjoy the celebration. Everyone was exchanging stories of their own dreams of a space program for the South American continent.

A couple of minutes later the phone rang. Rosie looked at the lieutenant and put on her best face, as she walked over to answer it. It was a very short conversation that ended with Rosie putting on a face

of dread and speaking these words. "I understand."
After hanging up the phone she walked over to
Lieutenant Vasquez, whispered something in his ear,
and quickly excused herself from the other guests.

Once Rosie left the room, the Lieutenant
explained to the others with great concern what had
happened. When the group heard the news that the
rocket appeared to be having some technical problems,
the room fell silent. The Lieutenant didn't have any
more details than that and suggested they retire to the
main house and wait while the others tried to remedy
the situation.

As soon as Rosie made it to the command center,
the call was made to usher the media groups and any
other stragglers to the main house. When every test on
the rocket was performed, then they would all be
briefed on the situation and the measures being taken
to reestablish contact with the rocket if they could.

When Kevin and Dylon were sure that every last
guest was on the way to the main house, they
proceeded to lock down the command center. The
only ones that remained were their group. When they
entered the control room, Marcus, Kat, and Rosie were
waiting for them. "We're all clear." Dylon said as he
walked over to the master computer where Marcus
was sitting.

Marcus promptly started typing in commands.

"The monitor's over there." He said and kind of half pointed in the direction where there were five monitors lining the walls. As everyone gathered in front of the monitors, Marcus called out. "Are we all ready?" Not waiting for a response from the others, he continued typing in commands. Then a small blip appeared on one of the monitors, followed by a cursor, awaiting the next command.

Marcus started talking while he was typing in the next set of commands. "If you will pay attention to the monitor on the right, it will be showing the view from the cameras on the craft. The monitor in the center is a view of the camera located inside the bay of the rocket. I've just sent the command to bring up both cameras."

With a few more keystrokes and a few minutes passing, both monitors flicked again, as if receiving a new source of information. A couple of seconds later, light started to stream through the seal that was the opening of the rocket stage.

The quiet excitement from the group was only apparent in their facial expressions and by the goose bumps which caused their bodies to tingle and their hair to stand on end. As the doors completely opened and the light filled the bay, the clamps that were holding the cargo stable slowly started to extend and gently push the payload out of its shell. Once fully extended, the clamps released their hold and the craft remained there, floating. The only sign of activity was the camera, panning over the craft and the view of the Earth.

Marcus typed in a few more commands and the camera stopped to focus on the retractable parts of the craft. This was the thing that worried him and Dylon the most. They were both very nervous about the decision to make that adjustment to the craft in order to get it to fit in the rocket stage. Dylon held his breath as he watched first one side and then the other extend to its full flying position. Everything seemed to be operating properly, but he would not know for sure until the diagnostics report was transmitted back to the command center.

Dylon felt once everything had been cleared through the diagnostics check, that he would forget everything he needed to remember, or at least the most important thing he needed to remember: Reese's birthday present, the one thing he promised him. A picture of the Moon, taken from the craft he had a hand in building, just slightly eclipsing the Earth. He quickly reminded Marcus to plot the course, to which he responded with a simple nod of the head.

Dylon then turned his focus back to the monitors and watched as the craft slowly came to life. There weren't that many lights on the craft, but Dylon knew where each and every one of them was located, and how bright they should be. As he watched each one come on in sequence, he gushed with as much pride as a father watching his child being born. Just the look on his face explained how much this actually meant to him.

With a smile on his face that stretched from ear to ear and eyes that were beginning to fill with tears of joy, anyone could see that this truly was a man watching his dream being born into creation. Kat walked over to Dylon and slipped her arm around her brother. "Are you going to be alright?"

He swallowed hard, trying the get past the lump in his throat and barely managed to get the single word out. "Yeah." He turned to Kat and gave her a big long hug. "Thank you, Elizabeth." He whispered in her ear.

Kat found herself quickly being consumed by Dylon's emotions and she almost started to cry. She forced herself to slow down the feeling though. Just enough to get out what she came over to tell him. "Marcus thought you might want to give the craft the first command for movement."

"Oh my God, I would love to." He said and tried to wipe his face a little, before heading over to the computer. On his way to the computer, Dylon first stopped at the table that had the champagne glasses poured. He picked up a glass and urged the others to do the same.

He held the glass up and started speaking. "Guys, I just wanted to say thank you for all your hard work. I could not have done this without such a dedicated group of people. You've given me your best and I can only hope that I will be able to repay you for it. I will be eternally grateful and forever in your debt." They all raised their glasses to the toast, and then Dylon walked over to the computer. He looked at the computer and then he looked at Marcus.

"All you have to do is hit the enter button. I've already typed in the commands," Marcus said and held up his glass again in cheers. Dylon did as Marcus told him and turned his attention to the monitor. The camera turned its focus on the Moon and then the craft slowly started creeping towards its target.

Dylon cocked his head to the side a little, trying to see if the craft was actually moving. Then he turned to Marcus with a question in his eyes. Marcus quickly picked up on it and started explaining. "Well Dylon, I figured we need time to run the diagnostics and we also need some time to explain what happened with our first rocket. With the craft moving this slow, it won't interfere with the diagnostics and it will give us plenty of time to lie our asses off and hope they buy it."

"Good thinking." Dylon said. He then looked

around the room, noticing the smiles that were plastered on everyone's faces, as a result of a successful first launch. Then he asked another question, directed at the group. "So how do we get ourselves in a somber enough mood to explain that the launch was a failure?"

Rosie was the first to respond. "That's easy just think of all the work that we'll be doing pretending to fix a problem that doesn't exist, just to make them believe us." With that said, everyone agreed and the smiles started disappearing. The group then gathered up a few things and left to join the others at the main house. They decided to let Marcus and Kat talk first, seeing how they had most of the computer experience and the plan was that the problem with the rocket would be blamed on a computer malfunction.

# Chapter 39

When the group made it back to the main house, the guests were enjoying an assortment of finger foods and drinks. The media personnel were the first to notice them standing there on the veranda. As the group was standing there, their guests started gathering around them. The chattering of the guest slowly died as they waited in anticipation of whatever news the group had to share.

Once everybody gathered in close enough to hear, Dylon started speaking. "Good evening ladies and gentlemen. Let me first start by saying that it has been a pleasure having you here with us. I had really hoped for better results today, but unfortunately, there have been some unforeseen difficulties. It's a little more technical than I can explain, so at this point, I am going to turn it over to our chief of propulsion and design operations, Marcus Williamson. Joining him is our chief computer program analyst, Elizabeth Rosier.

Marcus and Kat stepped forward when Dylon stepped slightly to the side. Marcus spoke about the fail safe program on the rocket. He explained how they would be able to set it on a crash course with Mars, if necessary. After he finished talking, he turned it over to Kat, and with a simple glance she began talking. The transition between the two was seamless.

"The computer is just not responding. It could be something as simple as a connection that came loose during launch, or as drastic as a micro-meteor piercing one of the computer boards. We have an extensive diagnostics program running as we speak. When it's finished, we should know exactly where the problem is and every possible route we could use to by-pass that area, if we can. This process usually takes about five hours. In the worst case scenario it could take up to eighteen hours." Kat paused momentarily to see if the guests were comprehending what she was saying.

The journalist from Peru asked the first questions. "So what affect will this have on the future of your program? Are you going to have to postpone or delay your launch schedule?"

"Well that all depends on what we find out from the diagnostics check. If it is a problem we can fix or bypass then we will, but if it isn't something we can fix. Well, we just really won't know until we get all of the details. As far as the launch schedule goes..." Kat glanced over to Marcus, who immediately picked up right where she left off. The two of them really complimented each other, and had the unique ability of really being in sync with each other's thoughts and feelings.

"As for right now the launch schedule will remain unchanged. Of course, this means we'll be working overtime running additional diagnostics checks on every operating system of each rocket. Then after the second launch, if we run into the same problem, we'll be able to decide more about the future of the program. As Elizabeth said it's really hard to discuss any definitive plans until we pinpoint where the problem lies."

With his last statement Marcus took the glass of wine that Kat was handing him and raised it in the air. "So if there aren't any more questions?" He paused just briefly to give everybody a chance to respond then he continued. "I would like to make a toast, to at least the first step in launching a space program for Peru. I would also like to add, that we will work even harder to make this a successful program for the country and for ourselves. May each of our future launches be more successful than the last." When Marcus finished, everybody raised their glasses to his toast and the group left the veranda to mingle with their guests.

\* \* \* \* \* \*

The next morning, before any of the guests awoke, Marcus, Kevin, and Dylon slipped out to check on the status and location of the craft. Each of the trio had their own reason for going. Marcus was anxious to see how the diagnostics check turned out, while Kevin was more interested in the location of the craft and if they would be able to start the test on the speed of the craft, where they would actually send the craft to Mars. Dylon was more interested in making sure the cameras were all in working order.

This of course, was something they were all interested in. Reese had requested a picture of the Moon partially eclipsing the Earth. That was the only reason they sent the craft towards the Moon. They initially denied Reese's request, but worked hard to fulfill the boy's wishes in time for his birthday.

As soon as Marcus brought up the cameras, they fully understood Reese's request. The view was breathtaking. The Sun had about three quarters of the Earth in daylight, but the Moon wasn't quite in position yet. Actually it wasn't even in the picture yet.

Marcus cursed under his breath. "Man, I was hoping I would be wrong. It looks like the Moon won't be in position for a few more hours, by that time we'll be in the middle of pretending to fix something. Probably have a few reporters on our heels too." He said and gave a disgusted look to Kevin and Dylon. "I can program it to take the pictures automatically, so we can view them later. I could actually have it set up to time lapse photo the entire process. If it is continuously dumping the pictures into the computer here we won't have to worry about a memory overload." This time when Marcus finished talking, he looked at Dylon, waiting for some kind of response.

When Dylon finally picked up on it he responded with a disappointed tone. "Yeah, go ahead. I was just kind of hoping to see it actually happen, but you're probably right. We're all going to have reporters following us around the majority of the day." With that said, the trio decided it was time to head back to the main house, before their visitors for the day woke up.

When the boys got back from their early morning obligations, they found that Kat and Rosie had already awoke and started preparing for their day. The girls looked up briefly when the boys came in. The brief glance was just long enough for the two of them to figure out the information they needed. They quickly turned their attention back to the journalist interview schedule they were working on. With everybody leaving today, there was a crunch to get some interview time in. These were for wrap-up questions that the journalists didn't get to ask last night.

Not too long after the boys got back, the guests started stirring. After giving the boys a copy of who they would be with for most of the day, Rosie placed the schedule near the breakfast area for each of the journalists to see. She and Kat would end up spending the rest of their time editing and preparing their own version of the footage from the previous launch for the next round of guests.

The day would press on until each one of the guests had finally left. There was a crew working on cleaning the launch pad and preparing it for the next launch, which was only four days away. As for the other crews working, it was all just a show for the visitors, part of the illusion that the first launch was turning out to be a failure.

The only thing that was keeping the boys pressing forward with the enthusiasm that they had, was the fact that when the day was done, the true objective of the all their hard work could actually begin. Plus, the fact that they would be able to give a soon to be eleven-year-old boy the birthday present of his life.

Rosie and Kat were in the process of putting together the welcome packets for the next round of visitors. The guests included the reporter from Peru, who had an exclusive on the progress of the entire operation, and government officials and media personnel from Japan, China, and Russia. When they saw the helicopter that carried the last of the visitors leaving, they quickly finished their tasks and headed out front.

Reese's parents had put on their best casual dress and were waiting with their son. They knew that Dylon and the rest of the group had a special gift for him and that they wanted to give it to him early for two reasons. The first reason being, that they would be too busy to actually participate in his birthday celebration. The second reason, was that they didn't want to take anything away from what his parents had planned for their child.

Rosie, Kat, Reese, and his parents all climbed into the cart that was in front of the house. They were headed for the command center where Dylon, Marcus, and Kevin would be waiting for them. Reese kept asking what they were doing and if Uncle Dylon was going to be there. When they pulled up in front of the command center, Kevin and Dylon were outside waiting for them. Marcus was on the inside getting the monitors turned on and setting up the computer to run the slide show of the pictures it had been taking all day.

He would have rather previewed them first, but time didn't permit it. He heard the gang coming down the hall. Reese was complaining about the blindfold they had put on him, to keep from ruining the surprise, but after they explained to him it was because of his early birthday present, he eased up a little. They guided him to the center of the room, facing the monitors. They all stepped back and told him he could remove the blindfold. Reese removed the blindfold and when he looked up at the monitor he was excited. "Wow Uncle Dylon, it's cool. Is that from our craft? Do you have more? Is there one of the Moon too?"

Uncle Dylon nodded his head and directed him to the computer where Marcus was standing. Reese hurried over to Marcus, who directed him to push the enter button to start the slide show. Just before Reese hit the key, a drive opened on the computer that contained a disc. "Just a second, bud." Marcus said as he retrieved the disc and put it in a case. "Okay, you can go ahead now." He said to Reese.

When he pressed the enter button, the show started running. The view of the Earth was beginning to come into full daylight now and you could see just the edge of the Moon starting to come into the picture. Reese got up from his seat and stepped towards the monitor to get a closer look as the pictures revealed themselves one by one.

The group was enjoying watching him. They got into a small discussion, about the boy and his enthusiasm for space. They discussed with his parents about their plans for his future education and the fact that whatever he wanted to get into his schooling would be taken care of. Their attention to the screen was distracted by their discussion. That is until they heard Reese yell out. "Uncle Dylon, what's that?"

Everybody turned their attention to the screen. They couldn't believe their eyes. There, on the dark side of the Moon, was something so unimaginable they had to look twice. "Pause it, stop it, do something, Marcus." Marcus was already in motion when Dylon had blurted out his command.

Everybody gathered in front of the monitor, mouths agape. "Marcus, is there any way we can zoom in on it?" Marcus was already working on that as well. "Check the monitor on the right, I'm sending the close up there." He said as he inserted a new disc in the drive. He entered the command to save the pictures to the new disc as they came up on the monitor.

"I wonder who it belongs to?" Rosie said as she stepped closer to check out the details. "Who knows?" Kevin said, "but whoever it belongs to, it hasn't happened overnight. That's a pretty big layout, they must have been working on it for years. It looks to be the size of a small city."

"Um....Dylon?" Marcus said, trying to get Dylon's attention. "Dylon, I think you should really take a look at this." Marcus said again, urging Dylon to come take a look at the message that was appearing on the computer screen in front of him. He looked up to see if it was appearing on the monitors, but it wasn't, just on the computer he was working from.

When Dylon made it to the computer where Marcus was sitting, the message was almost complete. He too, checked the monitors on the wall to see if the message was appearing on them, and found they weren't. He read the message as the others began to gather around.

*You should forget you've seen this. We can shut your operation down in a matter of a day, if not sooner. Ask Dylon, he should remember. We want you to succeed, just be careful where you step.*

## Five

After they read the message they all just looked at each other. Dylon quickly started talking to Reese's parents, urging them to convince Reese not to ever talk about the pictures. Kevin turned to Rosie and said. "Well, I guess we know who it belongs to now."

She nodded her head in agreement. Just then everything in the command center shut down except the computer in front of Marcus. The message on the screen started to disappear. All except for the words *You should forget you've seen this.* Then his computer shut down as well. Within a minute everything was restored. The group all looked at each other and it was Marcus who was the first to speak. "Now I'm not sure who to fear most, the U.S. government or The Five. What if they're one and the same? You know, like the Majestic Twelve."

"Who knows?" Dylon said. "I don't really think they are though, because they said they wanted us to succeed. If we succeed, the U.S. government wouldn't like that very much. They would lose a little bit of their control over things. I just think we need to be careful and we're never going back to see the dark side of the Moon, unless we're invited." As the others were talking, Rosie gathered up the discs. She looked at Dylon and let him know she could photoshop the picture Reese wanted. He in turn explained to Reese that Rosie was going to fix the pictures for him, without all of the lights on the dark side of the Moon which was something he could never speak about.

# Chapter 40

With the images of what they saw on the dark side of the Moon, still fresh in their minds, the group had concerns and doubts about performing the tasks for the next day. There was a little reluctance from everybody in actually getting going, until Rosie showed up. When she arrived she found everybody questioning what they wanted to do. 'Should they go back to the Moon? Should they trust the information from the mysterious group *The Five?*' These were just a few of the questions they were bouncing around.

After listening for a minute, she had all she could take, with the hem-hawing around and had to say something. "Children." She said, trying not to be too demeaning. "What exactly are we waiting for? Let's send this bird on its way." They all looked at her with a touch of disbelief in the words that were coming from her mouth.

"What?" She said in response to their appalled expressions.

"Well, aren't you the least bit interested in what's on the moon, Rosie?" Dylon said.

"Well, of course I am Dylon," she responded, "but they told us not to go. So with that in mind, let's get on with our original objective. Let's get a complex built on Mars, in my lifetime. Forgive me for being so abrasive about it, but come on, let's get the ball rolling."

"It doesn't bother you that *The Five* never told us about the base they have?" Dylon asked.

"Why should it Dylon?" She said. "Does it bother you that *we're* not telling anyone our true objective? There will be a time and place for what's on the dark side of the Moon, but right now, the time is to do what we all joined the group for. So let's do this so we can have a day of relaxation before the next round of guests start showing up. Don't tell me you wouldn't like to take a minute for yourself. We've all been working around the clock to get this accomplished, and to be quite honest with you I could use a day off."

Dylon looked around the room and everybody was slightly nodding their heads. When he looked back at Rosie, she started talking again. "You know, I never considered myself to be a space geek until you brought me into all of this. So don't give me that look, because this is all ultimately your fault."

Dylon was shocked, that is until he noticed that Rosie couldn't keep up the charade anymore, and started to crack a smile. They all started to laugh at the show Rosie just put on. They knew she was joking in the way she presented it, but everything she said had some truth to it. Marcus sat down at the computer and started typing in the I.P. address for one of the satellites orbiting Mars. He pointed out to everyone that there would be a message receiving device located in the observatory that would let them know when the craft arrived at its destination point. It was basically a small light that would start blinking when it received the signal.

He also reminded them of the projected two week travel time, but said it should be checked every day until then, seeing how they were unsure of their calculations of the actual speed of the craft. After he finished typing in the command he asked Dylon if he wanted to send it on its way. Dylon turned to Rosie. "Would you and Kevin like the honors of…" He paused briefly recalling Rosie's words. "How did you put it? Sending this bird on its way."

They both smiled. "I think that would be wonderful." Rosie said as she took Kevin's hand and headed to the computer. They both put their finger just above the enter button and Kevin said, "On the count of three." They all counted with them and when they hit the enter button, Dylon whispered a small blessing.

* * * * * *

A couple of days later, the next round of guests started arriving. The launch pad was cleared and the next rocket was being transported from the storage facility. The group had developed a routine and were slowly getting used to escorting the guests through the complex. The questions from the media were also developing into the same routine questions. 'What are the future plans for the company? Whose idea was it to start a private sector space program? Who's funding it? Are you experimenting with any new rockets or propulsion systems?'

As the day unfolded, the launch of the rocket carrying the satellite that would be orbiting Mars, among other things, was a success. The guests and the team were very pleased with the success that the day's events revealed. They were also pleased to find out what great hosts they had with the festivities of the evening. The Lieutenant and Rosie made quite a pair when it came to rubbing elbows with the high-ranking government officials from different countries.

The following day would be almost a repeat of the first visit. There would be a reporter following a different member of the team around the complex, getting in their last round of follow-up questions. While Rosie and Kat edited and prepared the footage of the launch for the welcome packets, for the next round of guests: Australia, the United Kingdom, and an additional member of parliament representing the rest of the European continents combined efforts for space exploration.

The team chalked up another successful visit as the last guest departed, but the pressure from the U.S. to cut in line was ever increasing.

Rosie stuck to her guns though, and refused to allow anything like that to happen. "With the amount of people you want to bring along with you," she said to the official on the other end of the phone. " You're just going to have to wait your turn. We are going to have to bring in extra security and everything has to be just the way you prefer. You know the other countries were more than accepting of the security measures and everything else we have in place. They didn't place a lot of demands on how they wanted things to proceed, you're the only ones that are doing that."

Rosie paused for a minute, while the person on the other end of the phone complained some more. "Well, I'm sorry if that's the way you feel. These are the procedures that need to be followed on our end, and we've bent almost every one of them to suit you and your demands. So, on that note.....should I count on seeing you, or should I go ahead and fill your spot with the next person in line?" She waited for an answer. "I thought so. Well, you have a nice day and we'll see you after the next launch."

The next couple of days were full of busy work, getting ready for the third round of visitors. The group had managed to catch one of the news stories about their company that the reporter from Peru had put together. She commented on the fact that even though the first launch was a failure, the second one went off without any problems and Peru now had a satellite heading for Mars.

After the news program had ended, Marcus remembered to go check on the indicator light for the craft. He asked Kat if she wanted to join him. Kat did not pick up on what day it was, and heard Marcus asking her again, this time in a different tone. "Oh, yeah honey." She responded. "I think I will go with you." As the two of them closed the door behind them, Kat asked Marcus. "Do you really think it's there already?"

"Well honey, you ran the figures with me. Do you think we made a mistake?" He said.

"No, I'm just not sure if we used the right formula to calculate it. I mean, four days seems like…well, it just doesn't sound right." She said as they drove off towards the observatory. It didn't take long for them to get there, and when they opend the door they were only a little disappointed to see that the indicator light wasn't flashing. They closed the door and gazed up at the night sky. Marcus reached down and took Kat's hand in his own. They walked around the observatory a little hand in hand. Kat noticed that Marcus would occasionally look up at the stars, and finally she asked him what he was looking for.

"I'm just looking at the stars. I just can't get over how many stars you can actually see down here. I've been down here almost a year and it still amazes me." He said as they continued their stroll. "You know what amazes me even more? The fact that something we built is up there flying around, sending back data to us, to let us know if *we* would actually survive in a similar craft. I was just really hoping our figures would be right. I was hoping to be the one to be able to say, 'hey, the time frame we gave you was an overestimated guess, because the numbers we came up with didn't sound right.' You know where I'm coming from, babe?" Kat nodded her head and responded.

"You wanna know what amazes me?" She said.

Marcus stopped and wrapped his arms around her waist. "Tell me."

"The fact that you waited, you just took everything for what it was. You didn't apply any unneeded pressure and waited, until I was finished with what I was trying to accomplish." She wrapped her arms around him, pulled him a little closer and softly whispered as she was leaning in for a kiss. "Thank you, very much, for waiting." They were

417

locked in their embrace for a good bit of time, realizing that as busy as they had been, they hadn't spent that much alone time together. The two of them decided to head back to the main house for a late night swim and maybe some time in the Jacuzzi.

As they were headed for the *Mule*, Marcus had to check the indicator light one more time. Kat just rolled her eyes and motioned him to go ahead. As he disappeared into the observatory, she got into the *Mule*. Marcus was in the observatory less than a minute, and he came back out jumping and shouting. "It's there, it's there." Kat perked up with excitement.

"Are you kidding me?"

Marcus jumped into the *Mule* and gunned it toward the main house. "No honey, I'm not kidding you. It's there, it's at Mars. We were right, I don't know how, but we were right. The data, we have to check all of the data to see if we can send a person in the craft. Oh my God, I can't believe it. It's actually there and we were right all along."

When they got back to the main house, Kat and Marcus discovered that everyone had already gone to bed. Kat turned to Marcus, took his hand and said. "Well, I guess we'll have to wait until tomorrow morning to tell them. So what do you say about that swim?" She winked at him and headed out the back door towards the pool. Marcus was beside himself. He was so excited about the craft being at Mars he could hardly contain it. On the other hand, he and Kat really hadn't spent a lot of time with each other since this whole launching schedule started. Finally he gave in to the latter, while trying to subdue his excitement for the first.

# Chapter 41

Kevin, Rosie, and Dylon were finished with breakfast and heading out the door when Marcus and Kat finally came dragging down the stairs. Dylon couldn't stop himself from giving the two of them a little ribbing. "So, did you guys ever see the light come on? It was awfully late when I went to bed and you guys were still out. You guys must have been up all night, just waiting for that little light to come on, huh?"

Marcus blushed a little, while Kat threatened to beat Dylon up again, like she used to do when they were kids. She took off down the stairs after him and he slammed the door behind him. When Kat opened the door, Dylon was already down the stairs. "Hey, space cadet." She called out after him. He stopped and cautiously turned around, half expecting her to throw something at him. "The light actually did come on and your little piece of crap UFO is just sitting out there, waiting for a command to bring it back. Wouldn't it be nice if you had the password to send that command?" Kat slammed the door shut behind her and locked it.

Rosie, Kevin, and Dylon all just looked at each other. Rosie cocked her head toward Dylon. "That didn't sound like she was lying." Kevin nodded his head in agreement with Rosie. Dylon just stood there in somewhat of a confused state. When he finally spoke he still wasn't sure what to think. "You know, I can usually read her pretty well. I don't think I've ever pissed her off enough to make fun of my work in that way."

When he turned to look at Kevin and Rosie, he realized they must have been thinking the same thing as he was, because they were already heading for the *Mule*. Dylon made a dash for it, good thing too, because he would have been left standing there. Kevin already had his foot on the gas pedal and was in motion when Dylon made it to the back of the vehicle. The three of them discussed what they were going to do to Kat if she was lying, as they sped off to the observatory.

Marcus and Kat grabbed a quick breakfast and headed out, but they were headed for the command center. They were pretty sure they would be able to get there before the others. After all they would have to go to the observatory first, just to make sure Kat wasn't lying to them.

As Marcus and Kat were headed toward the command center, she shared some stories of her and Dylon's childhood. They laughed almost all the way there as she told Marcus about all the times he pissed her off to the point where she would just lose it and he usually locked himself in his room until she cooled down.

When the others arrived, Kat and Marcus were sitting behind the main computer, finishing their breakfast. Dylon wasn't sure whether to be mad over them not telling him, or to hug them for a successful mission. He just paced back and forth, occasionally looking at them and making several failed attempts to say something about it.

Finally Marcus tried to help him out, in his own way. "Hey spazzoid, instead of pacing back and forth trying to figure out exactly how you're going to say whatever it is that you keep stumbling over, why don't you turn around and look at the monitors?"

When Dylon turned to look at the monitors, Marcus hit the enter button to bring up the pictures. The view that appeared on the screens was from the cameras that were mounted on the craft. There, in front of them, was an astonishing picture of the satellite they used as a directional beacon, orbiting Mars. Mars was in full daylight and, even though it is a barren planet, its beauty was more than any of them had ever imagined it would be. After gazing at the monitors for a moment, Dylon finally turned around to face Kat and Marcus, "But, I thought you said it wouldn't be there for at least two weeks?"

The two of them just smiled. "Well Dylon," Kat started speaking. "When we ran the numbers, they just didn't make sense. We used every method we could and still came up with the answer of a four day travel time to Mars. It was just so incredibly unbelievable, that we both agreed to tell you that it was going to take two weeks. Even then, you guys looked at us like we had lost our minds. I can only imagine what your response would have been if we had actually told you it was going to take a mere four days."

Dylon was almost in shock. "Yeah but that's like…Do you realize how fast the craft would have to be…."

Marcus cut into the middle of his conversation, just to help him out. "Yeah bud, it's approximately 375,000 miles per hour, give or take a few thousand."

Dylon just stood there with his mouth agape as Marcus continued. "Buddy, it's your craft and the anti-gravitational device you designed. We won't have any answers for you on why or how until we check out the data. So are you ready to go read some reports?"

Dylon turned and stared at the monitor as his mind tried to digest it all. "I just don't think we have enough time to read all of that information. The next launch is tomorrow and the guests…Well, the guests should be arriving in the next couple of hours." Dylon's head was reeling from trying to process all of the information flying around inside his brain.

"I've got to step outside for a minute." He said and made a quick exit through the door. Kevin, Rosie, and Marcus turned and looked at Kat, who responded. "He'll be fine, just give him an hour and he'll figure it all out." They didn't move, they just kept looking at her in a very disbelieving manner. "Trust me." She said. "He's my brother, I should know. He'll probably go to the display room and stare at his creation while he digests everything and figures out what to do next. If he doesn't do that he'll end up playing with Reese and those model UFO's."

The others shifted in their positions, after Kat's explanation of her brother's habits. Then they turned their focus on what to do next. Only after a small amount of debating, Marcus decided that they should bring the craft back. "After all, we have four days to figure out what to do." He said and started typing the I.P. address and the command to bring it in.

"Make that two days." Kat said, as she reminded him they would be busy two of those days with the next launch and the guests for that launch.

"You're too late babe, it's already on its way." Marcus said after he hit the enter button, sending the command to bring the craft to rendezvous with the second rocket, which was carrying the orbital satellite for Mars and two of the four Agri-pods for the Mars complex. The rocket for tomorrow's launch would be carrying a client's telecommunications satellite, the other two Agri-pods, and a few other items for the construction of the complex.

After doing everything that they could, Kat and Marcus decided to go take an inventory of everything that was going to Mars, just to make sure everything was in order. The two of them also had a few ideas they were playing with to increase water production from the Agri-pods. They had their own theory about how the water would act as a blanket and would not only help the planet to heat up a little quicker, but also help develop an atmosphere quicker. They were not at all impressed with the concept of putting a bunch of pollutant producing factories on Mars to create a greenhouse effect.

What they wanted to do was to produce a larger Agri-pod, actually a bunch of them, and line what appeared to be a coast line. A coast line of what could be an ocean.

Rosie and Kevin decided to go over the plans for the visit from the U.S. government. She wanted to know if he and Lieutenant Vasquez were comfortable with the amount of safety precautions they had in place. On their way to the airstrip to pick up the Lieutenant, Rosie told Kevin, "I just don't have a good feeling about their visit. If it were up to me, I would cancel it all together."

"Yeah, me too, but you and I both know all that would do is create even more speculation that we were doing something not completely above board. Like you've always said, Rosie, 'hide it in plain sight', or have you forgotten that?" Kevin said, giving her that 'you know what you need to do look.'

On their way to the airstrip, the Lieutenant's helicopter flew over. "It looks like we left just in time." Kevin said to Rosie, as he drove the *Mule* up on to the runway. When they made it, Rosie was happy to see Carlos was the one flying, with as busy as everybody had been they hadn't seen much of Carlos. She gave him a big hug and made some small talk before turning to the Lieutenant, who as usual, was overly flirtatious with his greetings.

"You really know how to make a gal feel good," Rosie said as she gave him a hug as well. "By the way, what does your wife think about all of this carrying on?"

"Oh, Ms. Rosie, she is my Queen and I always save the best for her." He said with a hearty tone in his voice.

"But of course you do." She said and winked. The three of them headed toward the main house to go over the plans for the dreaded visit.

The next round of visitors that would start

arriving pretty soon, had already been prepared for. The list included media and government officials from Europe, the U.K., and Australia, and of course the journalist from Peru, who was doing a continuing special of the entire operation.

\* \* \* \* \* \*

The guests for the launch of the third rocket proved to be the rowdiest of them all. They partied hard the night before and were up at the crack of dawn, bright-eyed and bushytailed, like nothing ever happened. This group was a little more laid back than the previous groups. Everyone at the estate agreed that these guests were the most fun of the three groups that had visited. On the other hand this group also posed some of the most difficult questions of the three groups.

This group was different from the last two groups that were mainly comprised of government officials and no scientists to speak of. Dylon felt at his best with this group. There was only one government official from each country, the rest of each group were scientists, eager to learn and take home what they discovered to share, develop, and grow. It really seemed that these guests genuinely wanted the group to succeed. A couple of them even offered the services

427

of a few of their own scientists and were more than willing to share the research they had performed on some of the experimental propulsion systems that were coming into play.

At the end of the day the launch was a success and the dinner afterwards even more so. Marcus was able to get some names of the scientists to contact for future information sharing of research results. Rosie and Marcus as well, offered an open invitation for future visits from this round of guests, after the aggressive launch schedule they set for themselves was complete and they could dedicate a little more time to research.

At the end of it all, as Kat and Marcus were going over the day, the only thing they were slightly disappointed with was that Dylon hadn't really made a decision on anything pertaining to the craft. As a matter of fact they hadn't seen a whole lot of him either, he only showed up for his appointed times to be there.

Then it really hit her, as she was sitting there thinking to herself. "He's been trying to figure this out all by himself. Instead of using the people he surrounded himself with, the people he depended on to help him with these problems." Kat turned to Marcus. "Babe, do you want to take a ride with me?"

"Sure, where are we going?" He asked.

"We're going to find that stubborn workaholic brother of mine, and then I'm going to give him a piece of my mind for being so stubborn."

# Chapter 42

When Marcus and Kat checked the observatory they didn't find Dylon, but they did find signs that he had been there. Just when they were getting ready to leave, they saw the headlights from another *Mule*, pulling around behind the observatory.

"That's got to be him." Kat said and she ran out the door, with Marcus not far behind her. By the time they reached the back of the observatory, they had just missed making it to the wall that was closing behind Dylon. "Well, at least I know where the entrance is now. Give me a day, and I'll be able to bypass the security code and put my own in." Kat said to Marcus.

"Oh, you mean like this." He said, as he walked over to the hidden panel and punched in a code. The wall started opening again and as the two of them headed inside, they noticed that the *Mule* had stopped about thirty yards in.

"I wonder why he stopped there." Kat said.

Marcus hunched over, started walking with a limp, and said. "Master, it must be the entrance to the secret lab." Then he quietly let out a ghoulish laugh. Kat punched him in the shoulder. "You are just completely deranged." As they got closer to where

Dylon parked, they heard noise coming from that area. It sounded like a movie playing, but they were still too far away to make it out completely.

When they got a little closer they noticed some light coming through a crack in the wall. They pushed on it to reveal a surprisingly large area that was divided into several different rooms. When the two of them stepped inside they were able to see a little more detail of the layout. The first of the rooms appeared to be the main work area. In the corner to the right was a large screen TV which was playing the movie *Stargate*. Then there was a computer storage area with at least thirty large computers in several different rows. To the right of the computer room was a smaller area that looked like hard copy storage, mainly filled quite a few filing cabinets and open shelves.

Kat gave a quick glance around but didn't notice Dylon anywhere and the movie playing combined with the sound of the computers running, it made it very hard to distinguish what sounds could be him.

Marcus had stepped away from Kat and was standing in front of one of the drafting tables. He noticed several drawings of more new transformable buildings. Nothing looked like anything that he had ever discussed with Dylon. These all seemed like new projects. Marcus began to wonder how extensive Dylon's plan for the Mars habitat was and started to feel a little overwhelmed by just the thought of it.

"Kat," Marcus whispered and motioned for her to take a look at what he found. "Has he talked to you about any of these things?" He asked as she looked over the drawings. As she glanced through the drawings she did notice what appeared to be a planet seeder and some type of transformable factory. "Yeah, but it was a long time ago. Hold on, this one... this is new." She moved the other drawings to reveal the partially covered one.

"What in the world?" Kat and Marcus both looked at the drawing. "It looks like some kind of gas converter, no, maybe an air filtration system." Marcus said as Kat moved some more of the mess to find the label Dylon usually put on his drawings.

The two of them heard some rustling behind them and Dylon's voice. Marcus turned around while Kat found the name of the drawing. When she turned around she saw Dylon walking towards them with what looked like a spreadsheet. Marcus poked Kat as they noticed he wasn't talking to anybody but himself. He was so involved in what he was working on that he didn't even notice them.

Kat decided to let their presence be known. "So when were you planning on telling us about the atmospheric converter, Dylon?"

"Oh shit." Dylon dropped the papers and fell over

the stool that he had just side stepped, as he jumped back from the voice he didn't know was there. Kat just snickered. She always got a kick out of surprising him when she knew he was way too involved with something.

Dylon got up and brushed himself off, then turned red when he realized that it wasn't just Kat standing there. He stuttered and mumbled and then finally asked, "What was the question again?"

Kat just laughed. "The question wasn't that important. I just wanted to let you know we were here, before you walked right through us." She said and knelt down to help him pick up the papers. "So have you figured it out yet?"

"Almost." Dylon said with anticipatory excitement in his voice. "I've just put in the last disc to upload the new data from the craft's gravitational field."

"You know D, instead of letting this consume you, you could have asked the rest of us for a little help." Kat said with a little concern in her voice.

"I know, but I just couldn't deal with the whole 375,000 miles per hour thing." Dylon said as they tried to neaten up the stack of papers. "I've struggled with it I just couldn't wrap my head around the concept of it. I mean really guys, 375,000 miles per hour? That's not even in the realm of comprehension.

Then I thought about the craft and the rockets. Obviously the craft has held up at that speed, but what about the rockets? The craft is made of a special metal compound, but the rockets, well they're made out of your standard high strength metal alloy. We haven't even thought of testing how it would hold up to the pressures of traveling at that speed. Hell, we didn't even have a clue that the craft would travel at that speed."

Kat and Marcus just stood there looking at Dylon, both of them trying to get a word in, but could not find an opportunity. Dylon continued talking while he paced. "So then it hit me, we're using an anti-gravitational device, and what does that device become when it's in an environment where there is no gravity? I'll tell you what it becomes, it becomes a gravitational device. If it's in outer space where its gravitational field is not affected by a planet's gravity, then it ceases to be anti-gravitational, so to speak. So then I had to figure out how big the field becomes, which I haven't yet. If it becomes big enough, though, it might actually envelope the rocket, or anything else it might be towing, and I won't have to worry so much about that item. Anything that falls inside that field will be protected, in theory. We'll know as soon as the last of the new data is uploaded and the computers do their calculations. Even then we still can only go on what we tell the computers. If we don't give them the right information then we won't get a right answer. So far I've only received two answers that have requested more data."

Kat looked at her brother, trying to figure if he had any idea what he was talking about or if he was just making it all up as he went along. "Ok, so what about the speed thing? How did you get past that and what is your logical explanation for it? Just so I know, so that when we get to that point where you want to reveal the crafts to the world, I might actually have a clue as to what you're talking about."

Dylon looked at her, knowing she thought he didn't have the slightest idea of what he was talking about. "Well, I haven't really gotten past the speed thing. I just changed my perspective of looking at it."

Kat and Marcus replied in unison. "huh?"

Dylon snickered a little. "Well it's like this, bear with me. The *Starship Enterprise*, travels in speeds measured in warps, right?" Kat and Marcus both rolled their eyes. "Yeah okay, for the sake of not arguing, I'll go along with this one," she said to her brother.

"Does anyone actually know how many miles per hour warp speed is? No, they don't, because it's irrelevant. You're traveling so fast that it would be ridiculous to break it down into miles per hour,"

Dylon said and paused to gauge their response.

"Well, what you're saying makes sense," Marcus said. "but who's going to be the one that tells the world that we've designed a craft that travels in warp speeds? We'll be needing it to escape, because we'll probably be laughed off of the planet."

Kat and Marcus both agreed, but still had questions. "So what information does this last disc of information contain? And how do you know that even if the rockets fall in the gravitational, that the alloy they're made of won't be affected?" She said with the tone she used when she was pointing out something that Dylon hadn't thought of. "And all of that aside, what in the hell are all of these computers doing down here? Really Dylon, I'm beginning to think that you're even weirder than I already knew."

"Damn sis, you're just full of questions now, aren't you?" Dylon said as he tried to keep track of all of them. "Well the computers I've collected over the years to keep track of the basic rules of physics and information that I can't seem to keep up with myself. The reason they're down here is that I wanted a safe place to store information. One that wasn't susceptible to the prying eyes of internet hackers and the viruses they carry with them. The more information I gathered, the more computers I needed. Eventually, I was able to connect them all together and come up with a program that basically turned them into the brains of the operation. Sorry, not trying to take anything away from you, but when I couldn't reach you, I relied on Hal."

Both of them laughed out loud and Kat responded. "Oh my God, Dylon. I can't believe you actually named the thing Hal. Did you not watch the movie?"

Marcus chimed in. "What are you talking about, Elizabeth? I think it's classic."

"Oh really? Well, when this thing turns on us, I'll ask you what you think about it then." She said.

Dylon snickered some more. "Anyway, the last disc contains the data that has been captured while the craft is slowing down, and that information is just as crucial as the travel speed and power, because it lets us know the reaction of the field as the craft is decreasing its power. When the craft is decreasing its power, the field size is most likely decreasing as well."

Kat and Marcus analyzed the information Dylon just gave them. After a moment of silence, Kat broke the ice. "So have you uploaded the content of metal alloys in the rockets?"

Dylon looked at her and thought about it. "Very good, sis," He replied "I don't think so, but I can get that information with a few keystrokes." Even though

Dylon had been kind of reclusive and overly involved in the research of the data pertaining to the craft over the past couple of days, he was happy that Kat and Marcus had searched him out.

Dylon had always been impressed with Kat's knowledge and capabilities. Sometimes he envied it, and thought if he didn't spend so much time daydreaming, he could probably be a little more like her. Then he always told himself, "If I was more like her, then who would come up with all of these crazy ideas? Besides, I like the time I spend in my daydreams."

The trio spent the better part of the early morning hours getting almost all of their questions answered by the computer. The few that didn't get answered would come down to a little more experimentation and a lot of blind faith.

# Chapter 43

Rosie and Kevin were sitting at the breakfast table for almost an hour before Dylon finally made an appearance. "Well good morning, stranger," Rosie said as Dylon was pouring himself some juice. "And will your sister and Marcus be joining us this morning?"

Dylon just shrugged his shoulders. "It was a pretty late night, but I'm sure they'll be getting up pretty soon. We came across a possible problem and I've been trying to upload all of the data from the craft when I found a little spare time. When I shared it with Kat and Marcus, they insisted on staying with me and running several scenarios of our options through the computer. There was still one last disc of data to upload thought, so we had to wait for that to finish."

Rosie's mind was already working on an alternate schedule for the day before her next question. "So how late were you guys up?"

Dylon reached for a piece of pound cake and answered. "Oh, I don't know, the last time I looked at the clock it was about three thirty."

Rosie's jaw dropped. "Good Lord, honey. Are you going to be able to make it through the day? I can shift some schedules around, you know."

"Thanks Rosie, just give me a couple of Dews and I'll be just fine. I'll probably crash early tonight, but I should be able to make it through the day." Dylon said as he was looking for more sugar-filled items on the breakfast table. He gathered up an assortment of Danishes and headed out the door to check on the last run of questions they asked the computer before they called it a night.

Another hour passed and Rosie and Kevin hadn't seen too much of anybody stirring. The two of them had walked out to the pool deck and were enjoying their morning coffee. Rosie glanced around at the pool and then over at the crew that was still cleaning up the mess from the night before, then she turned to Kevin. "Well, it looks like our guests also had a late night."

Kevin responded. "As long as they all had a good time, and from the looks of things, they did. I'll bet that schedule that you and Kat made barely gets used today."

Rosie just shook her head at the thoughts of it. "That would be fine with me. I could use an extra day to prepare for the dreaded round of visitors."

"Crap, is it time for them already? Can't we just skip over them?" Kevin said.

"Sure Kevin, they'll never even notice it," She said with a sarcastic tone, and started going over some of the things she could start working on. Sure enough, as the day pressed on, the guests one by one by-passed the follow-up interview schedule only to request a phone interview at a later date.

Kevin would end up spending most of his day shuttling the guests to meet their departing flights, while Rosie and Kat spent most of their time reviewing and restructuring the schedule for the upcoming round of guests. The visit from the United States would be the most trying on her. She knew who she was dealing with and knew to expect the unexpected. That's what was giving her such a hard time. "How do you plan for the unexpected, and why do they always have to be so difficult?" She muttered to herself.

Marcus and Dylon reviewed the work they had done the night before and even though the computer already gave them the answers, they both just felt a little more comfortable doing it themselves. After checking the gravitational field for about the fourth time, the two of them decided to go ahead with the scheduling of a meeting or a viewing, where they would attach to the rocket and send the first shipment to Mars. This rocket contained the orbital satellite for Mars and the first of the two Agri-pods, that would be part of the initial base.

As the day was winding down, the group started

heading to the command center. Dylon was the first to arrive, followed by Kat and Marcus. Kevin finished with the launch pad clean-up crew then he headed to meet the others. Rosie was still wrapped up in trying to make sure she had all her bases covered. When she realized what time it was she just threw her hands up and started talking out loud. "Oh screw it. Who am I kidding? I could have everything right, and they would still manage to mess it up somehow."

When Kevin and Rosie got to the command center, Marcus, Kat, and Dylon were checking out the view of the rocket with Earth in the background. At one point they were able to see both of the rockets that were in line waiting to be shuttled to Mars, but now the line of sight obscured the second rocket.

Kat, Dylon, and Marcus had decided the night before that when they sent the craft on its way they would set it to fly at an intermittent speed. During the day, when someone was able to monitor the craft they would boost the speed to almost the maximum power, but at night, when nobody would be monitoring the progress of the craft, they decided to let it travel at a much slower rate.

When Dylon finally noticed that Rosie and Kevin were there, he thought he would tease Rosie a little, like she had him that morning. He caught her eye and took a dramatic glance at his watch. "Rosie, so glad you could join us." He said with a grin.

"Yeah, whatever, Dylon. I'll tell you what, you can deal with the U.S. and I'll build your silly little UFO's. How does that sound to you? I'm sure I would have a lot fewer headaches if we did it that way," she said and laughed. Kevin reached to give Rosie a hug. "What's the matter, dear? Long day at the office?"

She gave Kevin a friendly jab. "Oh, I just want to get this particular visit over and done with. You know we could invite everyone in the world here and not have as many demands as we get from the U.S. I'm telling you, I'm over it." She said as she reached for the glass of champagne Dylon was passing around.

Marcus was sitting at the computer typing in the commands to begin the process of attaching the towing arm to the rocket. When Dylon made his way around to Marcus, he took the glass and then pressed the enter button to send the commands to the craft. He then stood and they all gathered in front of the monitors. A moment later, the towing apparatus started opening. It slowly but gracefully extended its arms and positioned them around the end of the rocket. Then it closed its grip until it had a nice firm hold.

There was a dual locking system on the towing arm. The first part of the apparatus was affixed with pads on the ends of the arms that could be used in a magnetic fashion or as suction cups, to secure the grip on the object being towed. The second part of the locking device would slide down the arms stretching them closed, securing the grip even more, before clamps locked that piece in place.

Once the towing arm had completed the maneuver, Kat was offered the opportunity to send the craft on its way, which she accepted. Afterwards, Rosie raised her glass with a quick toast and suggested that they take the rest of the day off to be refreshed for the next round of guests. She even made everybody promise not to talk about or do anything related to work. Of course she had to threaten to tie Dylon down to something if he didn't agree. Finally he nodded his head in agreement.

\* \* \* \* \* \*

As Kolminski stood there in the hallway waiting for someone to open up General Grant's office, a younger man entered the hall. He seemed kind of anxious, like he was in a hurry. Kolminski noticed the large envelope he was carrying. It was addressed to General Grant. "You seem like you're late for something. Is there anything I can help you with?" Kolminski asked the young man.

"Thanks, but I just have to give this to General

Grant." The man said as he stepped around Kolminski and reached to knock on the Generals door.

"The General is not in yet. Are you sure there isn't anything I can help you with?" Kolminski asked again.

"Oh man. Do you expect him any time soon?" The man asked Kolminski.

"Well, I expected him to be here already, so who knows when he'll get here." Kolminski noticed the envelope had the NASA symbol where the return address should be. "Would you like me to deliver that for you? I'm not going anywhere until I see him and you, well you seem like you really need to be somewhere."

"Sir, I do need to be somewhere else, but I have strict instructions to give this directly to General Grant." The man said and looked at his watch again.

Kolminski, being the character he was, had a way of shedding a different and perfectly logical light on things. He was very persuasive when after something he really wanted. "I perfectly understand strict instructions." Kolminski said and took a seat. "It seems like I've been waiting almost an hour now, but the General will make everything right like he has done several time in the past." Kolminski had only been waiting for ten minutes, but knew if the length of time was exaggerated the young man would make a decision he shouldn't have. "I'm sure he'll call whoever it is you're in a hurry to get to and straighten everything out for you. Unless, you just want to leave the package with me. Like I said before, I can't go anywhere until I speak with the General, but if you're in that big of a hurry I'm sure General Grant will understand not receiving the package."

The young man looked at the envelope, then at Kolminski. "Well, if you're going to be here anyway. I really am pressed for time." He thought hard before handing the envelope to Kolminski, but did and started to leave.

"Young man," Kolminski called out. The man stopped in his tracks, thinking he had just failed some sort of test. Kolminski continued. "Don't you think it would be a good idea if I could tell General Grant who this came from. You know, in case your supervisor calls to make sure it was delivered."

"Oh man, good thinking, thanks again, the name is Phillip Sturgill." The young man said and headed for the door. As soon as the man was out of sight, Kolminski glanced through the envelope. He read just enough to figure out the jist of the information contained inside. He removed the papers from the envelope, found an empty folder in the filing cabinet, and put the paper in the folder and in his briefcase.

It was another fifteen minutes before General

Grant arrived. He was surprised to see Kolminski waiting there for him. He gave him a funny look and then glanced at his watch. "Kolminski, I didn't think you were supposed to be here yet."

"You're right sir. I guess I've been so busy tracking down some last minute leads and confirming the information, that I completely misread our appointment time. I didn't realize it until I got here so instead of trying to fight traffic, I decided to just wait." Kolminski said.

"Last minute leads? What could you have possibly come up with, two days before our visit to *the estate*. Really, Kolminski, these people don't appear to be doing anything wrong at all. This whole investigation just seems to be a waste of our resources, especially for the first assignment of this new division." General Grant realized who he was talking to when his last words slipped out. "And that goes no further than between us, that is my own personal opinion which you should not have heard. Do I make myself clear, Kolminski."

"Absolutely, sir."

General Grant put his briefcase down and took a seat. "So what is this last minute information that you have gathered, Kolminski?"

"Well sir, it's not a lot, but apparently the Mars orbital satellites have been hacked into. There hasn't been anything obvious done to them, but nonetheless they've been hacked into." Kolminski stated.

"The Mars orbital satellites? And what does this have to do with?" General Grant said with complete confusion before Kolminski interrupted him.

"Sir, if you'll let me finish." Kolminski said and continued with his explanation. "They didn't notice it at first. It was so unexpected that nobody even caught it, so they barely even had time to track the source, but they did and were able to come up with....Well sir, they triangulated the source to *the estate*." Kolminski stopped, reached into his briefcase, and handed General Grant the information that was now in a plain unmarked folder.

General Grant flipped through the papers. "Do you mind if I keep these, so I can look over them." The General asked.

"Why should I mind sir? We're all on the same team right." Kolminski said and continued. "My contact is Phillip Sturgill, and there are also other contacts listed in there, but don't mention Phillip's name, I would hate to lose a good source of information."

The General looked at Kolminski with an expression that stated 'do you honestly think I'm that stupid?' but before he dismissed him, the General told Kolminski to bring his agent home. With the invite to *the estate*, there was really no need for the agent to remain.

As Kolminski walked out the front door of the building, he mentally gave himself a pat on the back for finding yet another tool of information to make things go the way he wanted them to. And quite possibly another step closer to getting the General's job.

When he made it back to the office, Kolminski sat down in front of his computer and started typing a message.

> *Agent Paschel,*
> *We will be arriving at the estate in two days at ten hundred hours. I'm sure there will be a build-up of forces happening in the next few days. Your prime directive is to infiltrate and be as close to Lieutenant Vasquez as possible, to hinder any strategic maneuvers that might occur. You are not to kill him. You are only there to make sure his forces think that he is still in control.*
>
> *I'm sure you can find a suitable location where he can be seen, but not heard. As I said before, his men need to think he is still in control. While you're taking care of that, we will be taking care of the inside.*

*Special note. General Grant will be present, but command of the operation has been assigned to me.*

*The General is a possible threat to the mission and in order to find the extent of who all is involved, he still needs to think he is also in charge.*

*Remember who got you this assignment and you will be fine. Our government is counting on you, and so am I.*

# Chapter 44

Dylon thought of his staff as family and didn't want to see anybody get hurt. This is what made the two days leading up to the visit a little more stressful than anyone expected. The group was trying to get the staff down to a bare minimum. They definitely didn't want the women and children there and with a lot of coaxing they were able to convince all but seven of the women to leave. These were the ones that absolutely refused to leave their husbands.

The Lieutenant was busy placing the six small units he was able to acquire in strategic locations around the perimeter of *the estate*. He didn't want it to look like they were ready to start a war, but he also didn't want the U.S. to think they were just sitting there not expecting trouble.

Rosie was at the point where her husband's training had kicked in. The others didn't know how to take her when she was in this mode. This was a side of her that they had never experienced. Everything that came out of her mouth sounded so serious, even if she was joking. They weren't really sure if they should laugh or ask how high she wanted them to jump.

This side of Rosie was definitely what Dylon and Kat had been looking for when they offered her a spot in the group. They just didn't realize how valuable she would become. She ran everybody through a quick personalized self-defense session. She blatantly pointed out their weaknesses and then taught them how to accept them in order to use them to their best benefit.

Rosie explained to each of them that if she didn't share with them what her husband taught her when he was alive, she would never be able to live with herself knowing she might have been able to do more to help.

After checking the distance of the craft and finding out that with the flight pattern speeding up and slowing down, it was only about a quarter of the way through its journey. Kevin and Marcus debated on whether or not the group should break off into pairs for the tour of the complex when the U.S. arrived.

Ultimately the decision would come down to Rosie and her schedules. When they presented her with their debate, she smiled. "I'm glad to know I'm not the only one worried about the U.S. coming to visit." She said and winked at them. "There are actually two different schedules set up. They are on my desk if you boys would like to review them and pass them around. I will let you know this though. Right now I don't have a definite idea which way it's going to go. It's a play it by ear plan and we won't know how it's going to go until the first card is played, which I suspect will be played by them. That, combined with a little women's intuition, all I can really tell you boys is that you're going to have to trust me."

The guys didn't argue and headed off to the main house to get the schedules.

\* \* \* \* \* \*

En route to *the estate*, the General was getting ready to review the mission objectives with the crew which consisted of Sergeant Mobley from the CIA, Lieutenant Steiger from the FBI, Mr. Kolminski, and Commander Campbell, whose title was Chief Assistant of the National Security Defense Review Board. All of the crew members also had a personal assistant, or at least that was their cover story.

Commander Campbell and the five personal assistants were all members of an elite undercover unit. Their assignment classifications usually required the highest security clearance possible, to review any of their missions. Even then, it was almost impossible to get any information. You had to know exactly the right words to use and the right questions to ask, otherwise you were only working off of a conspiracy theory and were usually made a mockery of for doing so.

The mission objective was to gather as much information as possible to ultimately shut down the operation. General Grant in his heart knew this did not need to happen, but his hands were tied by the bureaucracy that ran his country and his division. It was no longer 'Do the right thing because it's the right thing to do', but more of the mentality of 'Do whatever it takes to get it the way I think it should be.'

General Grant took a deep breath and tried to push his personal feelings to the back of his mind, before he started addressing the team. "Now when we first arrive, there is a meeting scheduled to discuss the ultimate objective of Rosier Aerospace Solutions.

There is a lot of ground to cover in this meeting, which should give you three hours tops to cover your assigned areas. The pilots will be staying with the plane to make sure your lapel pins are operating properly and recording everything you're seeing. The co-pilot is currently bringing them on line to make sure they are in fact operational."

"There is one particular area on your surveillance maps that we are interested in. It's not on our tour list of buildings, but there has been a lot of activity of some unidentified aircraft, near one of the older buildings. It appears to be an old hangar. Also, the thermal readings seem to have picked up areas that might be used for storage. Apparently, there are some areas underneath the grounds that create voids in the topographical charts, so we'll also need to be looking for any kind of hidden entrances." The General said.

One of the assistants slightly raised his hand to signify a question and with a brief glance from the General he proceeded. "Sir, if I'm understanding you correctly, you're asking us to look for a UFO?" He said with a question in his voice.

"Well, they're unidentified to us, so if that's what you want to call them, then so be it. The objective here is to see exactly what they are and whether or not they are equipped with any kind of advanced weaponry systems." The General paused briefly to read the response of his audience.

"The second item I mentioned was the possibility of underground storage facilities. What we're looking for here is any kind of weapons storage areas or weapons research and development labs. If we find evidence of such, we will be forced to report our findings immediately to the military base in Peru and they will begin operations to shut down this facility, until further investigations have been completed."

The General continued to review the details of the operation, making sure to put extra emphasis on the fact that this was strictly a fact finding mission. The main objective was still to see if there were any hostile intentions or a build-up of any weapons. "Keep in mind that intelligence shows there were some units deployed around the perimeter of *the estate* over the past few days. I wouldn't expect anything less. It appears to be only a precautionary measure on their part and I definitely wouldn't want to provoke any use of those forces."

\* \* \* \* \* \*

The day Rosie had been dreading from the beginning, had finally arrived. The amount of pressure she had been applying to everyone, made them very aware of the negative consequences that could come from the visit. It made them realize how important it was that they performed at their very best. Dylon and Kevin were waiting at the edge of the runway, as the designated greeters for the arriving guests.

The plane was coming in for a landing Marcus and Kat were working at what seemed like a frenzied pace, trying to make sure Rosie's last minute details for the meeting room were all in place. "I must say, the two of you look very professional today." Rosie said as they were making sure that every place setting had pencils, pads, and the most updated copy of all of the launches since they began their operation.

"I'm sure they're almost here Marcus, better go to meet them at the front door. Oh, and just to let you know, I'm pretty sure we'll be breaking off into pairs to give them their tour. Knowing them, they've got some kind of plan up their sleeves and I would rather not give them the upper hand. If we keep them separated they will have a harder time to pulling any funny business." Rosie said as he was leaving the meeting room.

Marcus gave Rosie a quick nod of acknowledgment and headed for the front door. Lieutenant Vasquez, who just came from the kitchen, met Marcus on the way to meet the incoming guests. "Are we ready for this, Marcus?" He said as they crossed into the foyer.

"According to Rosie no, but if I said no, could you make them go away?" Marcus smiled as he responded to the Lieutenant and matched his movements by reaching for the other handle of the double doors.

"Gentlemen, welcome. General Grant, what a nice surprise!" Lieutenant Vasquez said and extended his hand to give the General a firm handshake. "It's good to see such an old friend." The General returned his greetings and gave him a pat on the shoulder.

"Lieutenant, allow me to introduce you to my group." As the General was introducing the Lieutenant to the others, Marcus slipped around to let Dylon and Kevin know which schedule they were going to use.

"So who are all of these people, Dylon? I thought there were only supposed to be five." Marcus asked.

Kevin and Dylon both shrugged their shoulders. "Supposed to be personal assistants or something like that." Marcus headed back up the stairs to catch up with the group.

The Lieutenant had already led the guests to the meeting room. As each one of them entered, General Grant introduced them to Rosie, Marcus, and the Lieutenant....that is until he got to Kolminski, whom he knew already had a history with Rosie. Doing his best to maintain a workable atmosphere, he kept a close watch on Rosie and was ready to quickly divert her attention away.

Rosie's tone matched the look of disgust on her face when her eyes met Kolminski's. "You....I can't believe you actually had the nerve to show your face here."

"I assure you ma'am, it was all a simple misunderstanding." Kolminski said trying to smooth things over. The General stepped a little closer and with a polite push on Kolminki's, ushered him towards his seat.

"Come on, now Rosie," The General said and offered his hand to Rosie to assure her everything would be fine. "We've all got a little history behind us." He said trying his best to make light of the situation.

"That would be Ms. Patterson to you, Mr. Grant, and I can assure you that being dragged from my car and thrown into the back of this strange little man's limo is not what I would classify as a *simple misunderstanding*." Rosie said to the General, while Kolminski slinking his way to the vacant seat. When Rosie finished with the General, she turned to address Kolminski again. She quickly scanned the room and found him. Doing her very best to maintain her composure, she started. "As for you, little man. I had my fill of you with our first encounter, so you just better mind your P's and Q's because I'll be watching you."

Rosie turned back to the General and gave him a discerning look before continuing. "Now gentlemen, if you would be so kind to take a seat, I have a promotional video for you to view. Just a little something we put together, to let you know what our intentions are. You'll be the first to see it, but it will be released to the public after your visit. Any input will be more than welcome. It's only about ten or fifteen minutes long, then I'll be rejoining you with the founders and creators of Rosier Aerospace Solutions. They will get into a little more detail about our entire operation. Hopefully, they will be able to answer all of your questions and put your worries at ease." Rosie started the video and dimmed the lights on her way out of the room.

Rosie was furious, but she wasn't going to let them see that. Once she closed the door behind her, she huffed down the hall, cursing and muttering to herself. Just then Marcus came around the corner. "Rosie, we've got a big problem." Marcus said as he was approached her.

"No shit, Sherlock, that little weasel that tried to kidnap me actually works for them. He's in the room right now," She said, trying to get past the shock of it all.

"Yeah, well that's not all of it. They all brought their own assistants. So now we have five personal assistants standing outside with nobody to watch them." Marcus said with a slight uncertainty, about what to do now, in his voice.

"Those sneaky sons of bitches, fine. If they want to play games, then we can play too. Marcus, do they absolutely need you in this meeting?" Rosie asked, as she was already forming an alternate schedule.

"Well, not really, Kat knows most of what I know. And as far as the new propulsion mechanisms, other than the craft which they're not supposed to know about, we haven't even started researching them yet." Marcus said as he was practically running to keep up with Rosie.

"Alright then, for now, you're my personal assistant so keep up and don't question anything I say or do. You and Kevin are going to be on tour duty for the personal assistants, if that's what they actually are. Marcus, listen to me and listen good. You do not, under any circumstances, let a single one of them out of your sight, not one. As soon as we get outside, you get with Kevin and draw him closer to me, because I'm going to need your help." Rosie opened the doors, walked out, and started talking.

"Good morning P.A.'s, welcome to our facilities." She said in a loud voice. The guests all just kind of looked at each other and then at her like they didn't have a clue of what she was saying.

When Rosie started talking again she used an accusatory tone of voice. "That's what I thought. Gentlemen, if you're going to work undercover as personal assistants, it requires just a touch of homework on your part. P.A.'s…personal assistants. That would be you. Now why don't all of you gather in a little closer so I don't have to keep yelling."

Dylon leaned over to Kevin and whispered. "Damn, she's good. I mean, I suspected they were undercover, but I would never have called them on it."

Kevin just kind of snickered. "Yeah, you gotta love her for it though. Everything in plain sight, just the way she likes it."

Rosie gave everybody a moment to gather in a little closer. "That's good. I have some news I would like to share with you. You boys have been in our snipers' sights since you arrived. Now, to ensure the safety of everyone during this visit, not to mention the political relations between our countries, I will need some cooperation from you. Weapons, I need to see them, right here on the step in front of me. I can assure you that my men are not armed. You're more than welcome to search them if you like, but I'm afraid that you will find they have no weapons. So come on, let's see them, because I'm not going to put my men in harm's way so you can go on your little fact-finding missions. You can pick them up from the General after the meeting." The assistants looked at each other waiting for the other to make a move first, and Rosie's patience was growing thin.

"Men, I don't bluff and if you think that for one minute that the General will not back me, I can go get him. My husband served under him for years and you will also find that I don't play games either. So let's see those weapons so we can get on with this excruciating visit before I lose my temper." Rosie paused to let the men figure out what they were going to do. She waved Kevin and Dylon to her side.

"Dylon, will you go inside and get something to collect their weapons in? Kevin, you and Marcus will

be giving these gentlemen a tour of the complex."
Rosie was making sure to speak loud enough for the
others to hear, and slowly but surely, she could see
them removing their weapons as she continued to give
out instructions.

"Make sure you show them everything they need
to see, including the old hangar and the toys that are in
there. After all, a bird's-eye view of what they are
looking for simply does not do them justice." Dylon
had gathered up all of the weapons while Rosie was
giving Marcus and Kevin their instructions. When he
finished he returned to Rosie's side. When she looked
at the basket of weapons she returned her attention to
the assistants. "Now that wasn't so hard, was it?
Marcus and Kevin will be giving you a tour of the
complex, so you boys be sure to tell your guides
everything that you *need* to see. I really wouldn't want
to cause you any trouble with your superiors."

Rosie dismissively turned her attention from the
guests and faced Dylon. "So are you ready, then?"
Dylon nodded his head and the two disappeared
inside. Once inside Rosie ushered Dylon into the
kitchen. "Hurry, get me that pot, the one with the lid
on it." Dylon did as he was told and Rosie quickly
removed the clips from the guns. She grabbed a plastic
container and lid from the drawer and started
emptying the rounds from the clips into it.

"Put the guns in the pot and put it back on the shelf." She said as she was putting the empty clips into the basket. When she was finished she took a couple of deep breaths just to keep herself on an even keel.

They left the kitchen and were headed to the meeting room when Rosie started giving Dylon a pep talk. "Alright, let's do this. I know all of this is kind of unnerving, Dylon. Just keep in mind that this is nothing new. You've done this all before and these people are nobody special. We are *not* asking for permission to continue, we are simply selling a service, an endeavor." When they reached the door Lieutenant Vasquez and Kat were there waiting. Rosie turned to Dylon and straightened his tie. "Now before I introduce you all. I have one more thing to address and then I'll turn it over to you and excuse myself."

# Chapter 45

Rosie opened the door and entered the room. Dylon, Kat, and Lieutenant Vasquez followed her in and took their places in the front of the room. Rosie was in the center of the room holding the basket, with its contents concealed, close to her when she began talking.

"Gentlemen, I believe there may have been some minor miscommunication in regards to your visit to our complex today. Now, seeing how it's my job to oversee the scheduling and invitations, I will assume most of the responsibility of not being a little more clear about what is expected of you. Honestly, I don't know how I missed it. I guess I was just too busy making sure that we catered to all of your requests, that I completely overlooked it. If I had been paying more attention, I would have probably sent you a list of our procedures, instead of just a schedule of your activities for your time here at *the estate*. I really do have to apologize for assuming that you would show a little more respect by not insulting the intelligence of your hosts."

By the time Rosie had finished talking and making her way around the room, she had stopped in front of General Grant. She looked around the room and most of the guests had slightly hung their heads in shame. "General, I believe these belong to your, ahem, *personal assistants*. You can retrieve the rest of the pieces after your stay here is over."

She placed the basket of empty clips in front of the General and turned to the front of the room. "Now that we've covered some of the small concerns that I've been hoping I wouldn't have to address, I will turn it over to the founders of this operation. Gentlemen, Dylon and Elizabeth Rosier."

"Thank you, Rosie." Dylon stepped from behind the table at the front of the room. "Gentlemen, let me start by saying what a pleasure and honor it is to have you here with us today." Dylon, Kat, and Lieutenant Vasquez would talk for two hours explaining the ideas, the mechanics, and the security measures they were taking to insure the safety of not only the complex, but also the surrounding communities. They knew the products they would be working with would be catastrophic if they were to fall into the wrong hands and wanted the U.S. government to realize just how much they had prepared for that fact.

In addition to the two hours explaining the steps and procedures they were taking, there would also be another hour plus dedicated to a question and answer session. A small break for lunch was on the schedule and after that the group, personal assistants included, would head out to view the launching of the fourth rocket. This rocket contained the actual deep space probe, which as far as the guests and the rest of the world knew, was a replacement for the first one that suffered a critical malfunction.

* * * * * *

Kevin and Marcus spent their three hours giving the stiffs in suits the same tour everybody else would be taking after the launch. They tried everything they could to get their group to lighten up a little, but to no avail. Finally, when they asked them straightforward exactly what they were looking for, one of the guests kind of cracked a smile. "Do you have any UFO's?"

Kevin and Marcus laughed. "Yeah, but they're not actually UFO's. They are a newer version of the two experimental crafts from the sixties, I think. One is the American version and the other is the German version."

They headed to the hangar instead of the control tower. When they arrived, Marcus opened up the hangar doors and Kevin pulled into the building, right between the two crafts. The guests unloaded and gathered around the crafts. "Do they work?" One of them asked.

"Well, of course they work. They're a little loud

and blow a lot of dust around, but they work. Do you want to try them out?" Marcus asked.

The guests looked at each other before one of them answered. "We probably shouldn't. Do you have any plans or blueprints for them?"

Kevin responded to this question. "I'm sure there are plans for them somewhere, but that's a question you'll have to ask Dylon. He built both of them before we even arrived. A couple of years before we arrived as a matter of fact. By the way, shouldn't you already have plans for this one? After all, it's based off the model you've already built." Kevin said as he patted on the American version of the craft.

"If we did, that would be classified information that I couldn't share with civilians." One of the guests popped off, in response to Kevin's statement.

Kevin took offense to the way the man responded, and as far as he was concerned the tour was over. He looked at his watch before speaking again. "Wow, will you look at the time. If you guys want to finish up here we should probably head back to the main house. The lunch break should be starting pretty soon and I'm sure you have a lot of spy stuff to report to your bosses." Kevin said condescendingly, doing his best to try to offend them without causing too much friction.

Rosie spent the majority of her three hours of

time in her office, fussing and mumbling to herself as she reworked the schedule yet another time. She decided to break the group up a little seeing how there were five extra bodies with them. She would send the Lieutenant with the General and his P.A. to tour the buildings on the south quadrant of the complex. Marcus and Kat would take Commander Campbell, Sergeant Mobley, and their P.A.'s to the west quadrant. While Dylon and Kevin would take Lt. Steiger, Kolminski, and their P.A.'s to the east. All of this would start after the lunch break and the launch.

When she finished with the schedule, she went out to the pool deck where lunch was being set up. She wanted to make sure that there were plenty of alcoholic beverages and that they were one of the first things that the guests would see. Rosie was trying to give her crew the best opportunity she could. She figured if the guests actually did partake in consuming anything, then they wouldn't be completely up to par.

After checking every last detail, Rosie headed back inside. Just in time, too. She overheard Kevin mumbling on his way to the bathroom. "Condescending, ungrateful, mother…" She didn't hear the last of his words due to the bathroom door closing, but she knew what they were. A moment later Marcus opened the door with the guests behind him.

Rosie wanted to know the details, but was more

concerned in getting the guests out to the deck. "Oh good, you're just in time. Gentlemen if you will follow me, lunch is just about to be served." She led them to the deck and let them know it would be another twenty minutes or so. "We're just waiting for the others to finish their meeting. There are plenty of refreshments though, go ahead and help yourself. I have to make sure the boys head to the command center to check on the progress of the rocket for today's launch."

Rosie went back inside and caught up with Marcus. He discussed their tour with her as they headed for the kitchen. She gave him a copy of the schedule and who they would be partnered up with. Then she took the lunches she had bundled up for him and Kevin and placed them into a carrier.

About that time Kevin came into the kitchen. Rosie looked at him. "You don't even have to say a word, Kevin. I know all too well how difficult it can be dealing with these people. Now you boys take these and go do your business with the rocket and enjoy your lunch in peace. This will all be over soon and they will all go home." Kevin gave Rosie a wink and a big hug. "Thanks Rosie, you always know exactly what to say."

The boys grabbed their lunch and headed out the door. It was only a matter of minutes after they left that the door to the meeting room opened. Rosie watched the guests as they all came out and from their body/language and facial expressions, she felt they had a good meeting. This was confirmed when Dylon, who was the last to leave the room, glanced at her and gave her a quick thumbs up.

Rosie walked up to the General and guided them to the deck to meet up with the rest of their group. As each of them passed, they gave her a quick nod of respect, that is, until Kolminski got to her.

He started to say something, but she stopped him quick. "Before you even think about letting one word dribble over those twisted little lips of yours, let me bring up a saying my husband was very fond of. You can even ask the General and he will confirm it for you. The saying is 'let sleeping dogs lie'. I'm sure you are familiar with this saying." Rosie put her hand on his shoulder and guided him out the door. She glanced at the General. "I'll be with you momentarily, sir." Then she closed the door behind her.

Rosie pulled Kat, Dylon, and Lieutenant Vasquez into her office. "Kat, I'm going to need some help passing out these information packets for the tour after the launch. Oh, and here's a new schedule for you. You'll find out who you'll be paired up with and who is going to be in your tour party during lunch." Kat took the packets and looked at Rosie as if to ask, will that be all?

Rosie picked up on it right away and nodded to Kat, who left to pass the information to the guests. Rosie then turned her attention to Lieutenant Vasquez. "Lieutenant, you and the General have had a fairly good working relationship in the past, right?" The Lieutenant nodded his head.

"Good, you'll be with the General and his agent, or assistant, or whatever it is he feels more comfortable calling the guy. I'll need details, what they want, what their intentions are, and by all means I need to know if they have any intention of releasing us from this silly arrangement between his government and yours."

The Lieutenant smiled. "My dear lady, you know I would and will do anything I can for you, but that last one may be a little difficult. Ever since Kolminski has been in charge of the oversight of the treaty, I have not been able to get close enough to talk to General Grant. Not to worry though, Rosie, I will get as much information as I can." The Lieutenant nodded his head and left to join the others on the deck.

Dylon and Rosie were the only two left in the office now. She turned around and picked up a small box, about the size of a shoe box. "And what do you have there?" Dylon asked.

"Well, we're going to draw names to decide

which group is going to be with which tour guides. You and Kevin will be taking Kolminski and Lieutenant Steiger. You will both have to keep an eye on that little weasel."

Dylon let out a subtle laugh, "Oh, you mean twig boy?"

Rosie gave Dylon a sharp glance and spoke to him in the same tone. "Don't you be fooled by him. You and Kevin need to be extra alert and by all means, keep them in front of you."

Dylon took heed of her warning, but it posed another question. "So if you already know who is going with whom, then why draw names?"

"Perception and appearance, my dear boy, when I draw the names from the box, it appears that it's all a game of chance, but I've got it rigged. Everyone else will think that it was all just chance. Now before I draw the names you and Kat will need to go and give Marcus and Kevin a hand in preparing the rocket for launch. The Lieutenant and I will remain and explain how the rest of the afternoon should go. If we're lucky, they won't be able to find a way to screw it all up." Rosie smiled at Dylon and they headed out to join the others.

When Kat and Dylon finished their meals they gave Rosie a quick signal and a moment later she was in front of the group with the Lieutenant. "Good morning, or afternoon everyone. I would like to interrupt your meal for just a minute." Rosie waited until she had everyone's attention. "Now as you all know, we'll be launching the deep space probe that was donated to the Lieutenant's people, by the Rosier firm. Unfortunately when you're performing such incredible tasks, you need some incredible people to do these tasks. So, at this point, Kat…oh my goodness." Rosie turned a few shades of red before continuing. "Excuse me, Elizabeth and Dylon will have to be leaving us now to go help with that process. Before they go, though, I would just like to let them know that I decided to mix things up a little by drawing names for the tours after our launch today." Dylon and Kat both acted surprised, as they got up from their chairs to leave.

"Come on everybody let's give them a round of applause for doing such a wonderful job down here." Rosie said, trying to bring a little life to the overly serious crowd. The General was the first to start clapping as Dylon and Kat were leaving. The others slowly started joining in and when the two were no longer in sight, Rosie continued with the name drawing process.

After everyone was assigned to a tour group and finished with their meals, they all loaded up and headed to the command center for the launch. They made it to the command center when the countdown was at fifteen minutes. One by one the guests excused themselves for a quick restroom break. Apparently, the majority of them had consumed a little alcohol with their lunch, and the bumpy ride there didn't help matters much.

Kolminski found himself with the opportunity he was looking for. He waited until everyone else had made their quick trip to the restroom and when he was sure the time was right he took his turn. He made sure he was alone and then locked the door behind him. He pulled out his camera phone, took a picture of the map, and sent the photo to Paschel. Then he typed a quick message.

*General Grant will be in the south quadrant with Lieutenant Vasquez. Their first stop will most likely be the control tower for the airstrip. You can incapacitate the General and when the time is right, you can do whatever else needs to be done. Wait for my signal to do anything with the Lieutenant. General Grant will have an extra person with him, an agent. He is expendable. Everything else will fall into place, the Lieutenant and his entourage will end up taking the blame. Just make sure he doesn't signal any of his troops. Will wait one minute for confirmation of orders.*

# Chapter 46

The countdown was in its final minute when Kolminski finally rejoined the group. "Everything alright, Kolminski?" The General asked.

"Yes sir, it must be the food or the way it was prepared. Ethnic food always bothers me," Kolminski answered.

Some of the other guests had stepped outside to get a better view of the launch. With Rosie not taking her eyes off Kolminski, he thought he would feel a little more comfortable outside as well and excused himself to join the other guests outside.

Soon after Kolminski had stepped outside the rocket blew out a plume of smoke and steam that almost completely enveloped it. Then it slowly started lifting itself away from the immense cloud.

Everyone watched the rocket perform a perfect launch, but the only ones that showed any real excitement about it were the ones from the Rosier group. The General did manage to quietly congratulate Dylon on what appeared to be a legitimate space program. "The jury is still out on that, as far as anyone else is concerned." General Grant gave him a quick wink and broke away from the conversation to join his tour group.

The different groups left for their designated quadrant, to investigate for any activities that might be considered questionable or possibly threatening. Rosie quickly made her way back to the main house to do some last minute preparations. She was hoping that they would not be needed, but she didn't want to be caught with her pants down either.

As soon as she arrived she headed straight to the study to look for her purse and the weapon it contained. Upon finding it, she immediately headed to the kitchen to find a Ziploc baggie. After dropping the gun in the baggie she headed to the bathroom and removed the lid to the tank and dropped the gun inside. Rosie was hoping that she wouldn't need to use the weapon, but just couldn't shake the feeling that something bad was going to happen.

Rosie started speaking aloud. "Frank, if you're out there watching me, making sure I'm safe. Then all I can say is thank you. Thank you for teaching me everything you've taught me. If everything goes right, the only place I'll see you is in my dreams. If it doesn't, then I guess I'll see you soon. Love you, Frank."

\* \* \* \* \* \*

The two groups heading to the east and west

quadrants would take a little more time to get to their starting points. The Lieutenant's group though, was at their beginning point in no time at all. "I thought that we could start at the control tower. Just to give you an idea of our radar capabilities and to look at some of the newer security measures we're planning. We have some temporary units in place, but are anxious to acquire something more permanent, for the safety of everyone concerned."

The General nodded his head and they were at the control tower in a matter of minutes. The special agent who was posing as the General's personal assistant wanted to check all the floors before joining them in the control room at the top of the tower. The tower was only four stories tall, but for the small amount of traffic the airstrip had, it was just the right size.

The General and the Lieutenant headed on up to the control room. General Grant was impressed with the amount of sophisticated equipment the tower had. He was also pleased to find a chance to actually get to talk to Lieutenant Vasquez alone, without worrying about how his words were going to be interpreted or even worse, how they would be twisted.

As General Grant looked around the room at the equipment, in his mind he was going over everything he wanted to discuss with the Lieutenant. "Vasquez, I must say that you've hooked yourself up with what appears to be a very intelligent and capable group of youngsters. They're well-funded and very dedicated to their objectives. It's quite an impressive team. I'm just wondering about this plan to beat us to Mars. Don't you think that with all of the technology and years of experience the U.S. and NASA has behind them, that basically challenging us to a race to Mars is kind of bold for such a new, not to mention, young, company?"

The Lieutenant looked at the General. "Thank you very much, General Grant, but as far as a challenge is concerned, nobody mentioned challenging your country to a race. Why, there are countries all around the world, developing new technologies every day. A few of them are on the verge of some major breakthroughs, according to the rumors."

"I think it's a very good idea to get in on the ground floor of a budding new company. Especially one that has been nothing but forthright with the intentions of developing a new space program. Not to mention, their ambitious goals concerning the development of new technologies for space travel."

"Really Lieutenant, being able to beat us by ten or fifteen years? Do you honestly think that's possible?" The General asked, expecting Lieutenant Vasquez to back down a little.

Lieutenant Vasquez let out a hearty laugh. "Well, of course I do, General. Your country has already let it be known that you have no intention of doing anything in relation to Mars until at least 2050. Instead, you have decided to go back to the moon and develop a base there. I understand that this would be a huge stepping stone for the development of your space program and the exploration of other planets. Don't you think that if a private sector company wanted to pursue a base on Mars that everyone would benefit?"

General Grant nodded as his old friend Vasquez continued with excitement and passion about the subject.

"General, there has been so much that has happened with new advancements in technology. There's the robotics, the wireless capabilities, new and stronger materials being developed, and that doesn't even include all of the advancements in nanotechnology. I just think it would be a waste of time to put all of our energies into one venture. What happens if that one venture fails? Do you push everything back even further? I feel strongly, that if you have more than one party attempting to succeed in different areas of basically the same goal, that you will have a better chance at success." Vasquez looked at General Grant, who had been hanging on every word, and waited for a rebuttal.

The General only slightly nodded his head, as he thought about his response to a very convincing argument. How was he going to be able to tell Lieutenant Vasquez, the only reason his government was interested was the 'control factor'?

* * * * * *

The General's agent had searched through two floors so far. The first floor was nothing more than a large apartment. It appeared that it was used for pilots that might be staying the night before their next flight.

The second floor looked like it was the brains of the control tower. There were several small storage rooms, a large bathroom complete with showers and lockers, and a larger room where several large computer units set in a controlled environment. The agent assumed they were used for information storage and back up.

The surprise came when the agent made his way to the third floor. As he was entering the first room, he was knocked off balance with a right cross to the face. Apparently he had caught someone by surprise and their first instinct was to swing a punch. The two men scuffled on the floor until the agent was ultimately overtaken.

Try as he might, the agent could not release the

grip of the sleeper hold that his attacker had on him. The agent finally lost consciousness and as the attacker got up from his knees, the agent's body fell to the floor. The attacker wiped the blood from his lip as he stood over the agent's body. Then, with a quick movement of his foot, he crushed the agent's neck. He dragged the now lifeless body to a nearby closet and stuffed it inside, making sure he locked the door before he closed it.

He turned around to see how much of a mess the two of them had made while fighting. Then he listened to see if anyone else was coming. When he was satisfied that the coast was clear, he headed for the stairs.

With as much stealth as a cat hunting its prey, he crept up the stairs to the fourth floor. He put his ear to the door and listened to see if he could narrow down the location of the General and the Lieutenant. He felt confident that he could slip inside and make it to the shelter of the nearby restroom, without anyone noticing him, and did so with ease.

\* \* \* \* \* \*

The General had thought about the Lieutenant's words and was trying to build his own last plea without revealing the complete truth about why the

U.S. didn't want this plan to go forward. He did try and stumbled through until he just couldn't find a way around it.

"Lieutenant Vasquez, it's a privately operated space program. There are too many unknown variables to deal with, too many chances for valuable information to fall into the wrong hands. Are you really ready to put your country on the line, in the hopes that there will never be a security breach?"

The Lieutenant shook his head in disbelief of what he was hearing. The General knew he was failing miserably and knew he couldn't fool his old friend any longer.

"Lieutenant, as much as I hate to say this, it all comes down to control. Completely off the record I think you can do it, but for my president's sake and my country's sake, I have to say, I think you'll fail. My dear old friend, what I need you to do is show me a plan. Something that I can take back to them that will make them feel a little more comfortable about you and this private sector company launching a campaign to outperform any existing space program currently in place. Something that will make them feel comfortable enough to allow you to proceed with this process."

Lieutenant Vasquez was slightly taken by the General's words. "Allow us to continue," he thought to himself. Then he considered everything the General said, replaying all of his old friend's words in his mind and started to formulate a rebuttal, one that would put him back on the offensive rather than the defensive.

General Grant noticed the Lieutenant was taking a little more time to consider his words and took a moment to excuse himself. "While you gather your thoughts, old friend, I'm going to make a quick trip to the head."

\* \* \* \* \* \*

Paschel heard someone enter the restroom and quickly pulled his feet off the floor. When he was sure the General was preoccupied with the business he was in there for, Paschel slipped out of the stall. The General didn't notice he wasn't in the restroom alone. Paschel crept up behind him before he was even finished. Paschel pressed the gun against the back of the General's head and started talking. "No sudden moves and you'll walk out of here alive. Now, slowly put your hands on the wall in front of you."

The General did as he was told as Paschel pressed the gun even harder, just to get his point across. When his hands were firmly against the wall, Paschel  began patting down the General. In no time he found what he was looking for. He retrieved the gun and raised his own, bringing it down to meet the back of General Grant's head.

Paschel quickly gathered his duffel bag from the next stall. He placed the General's gun inside and grabbed a role of duct tape. It didn't take long to bind the General's hands and when he was finished he snapped open a vial of smelling salts.

The General slowly started to come around and Paschel helped him to his feet. Realizing his predicament, the General leaned against the counter surrounding the sink. "Oh no you don't, General. Come on, you'll have plenty of time to sit in just a minute." Paschel said as he grabbed him by the shirt collar and shoved him out the door.

Paschel put the gun against the General's head again. "One wrong move and it's over, understand?" The General nodded his head and they headed toward the control room.

The Lieutenant was looking out the window when he heard the door open. "General, I was beginning to think you got lost." The Lieutenant's words trailed off when he realized the General's condition.

He started to reach for his gun, but stopped when he noticed the man behind the General had a gun to the back of his head. "You catch on quick, Lieutenant." Paschel said. "Now if you don't mind, you can put it on the floor and kick it over this way."

Paschel gave the General a quick shove towards Lieutenant Vasquez and reached down to pick up the gun. He waved it at the chair, motioning the general to sit down. He reached in the bag and retrieved the duct tape and threw it to Vasquez. "Tape him up good. And make sure you do a good job or you'll end up looking like him."

The Lieutenant started to tape the General's ankles to the chair, but the entire time he was taping he was scanning the desk for anything that could be used as a cutting tool. Paschel was checking out the windows to see if anyone was near the tower. He went from window to window making sure everything was clear. The only person he noticed was someone messing around the helicopter.

Lieutenant Vasquez checked on the General's wounds as he was taping him. His eyes still scanning the desk for anything he could give to the General, without Paschel noticing it. Then he spotted something. It was a long shot, but worth a try. It was a small razor-type letter opener. Even though there was barely enough room for an envelope to slide into the slot, the Lieutenant figured it was better than nothing.

He slipped it into the General's hands and closed them tight over the opener. Lieutenant Vasquez then turned to Paschel and asked in an almost demanding tone. "So what exactly is it that you want?"

Paschel just looked at the Lieutenant, then he waved his gun, motioning for him to move closer to the window. "Right now all I need you to do is stay visible to your men, and don't try to signal them or anything stupid like that, or the General buys it."

Once Lieutenant Vasquez was where Paschel wanted him he held his hand up to let him know that was good enough. Paschel then eased back to the door to lock it, keeping his gun pointed at the General the entire time. After locking the door Paschel settled down in a position where he could keep both men in sight. He pulled out his Blackberry and quickly sent out a message.

The Lieutenant noticed that Paschel was preoccupied and took a quick glance out the window to see if there was anybody there. He noticed Carlos, loading the helicopter with supplies. He returned his attention to the control room and Paschel. He scanned the room, trying to figure out a way to signal Carlos, all the time keeping a close eye on Paschel.

# Chapter 47

Dylon and Kevin were keeping Kolminski and Steiger in front of them, just as Rosie suggested. Lieutenant Steiger seemed genuinely interested in gathering information for his country and had some very good questions concerning the operations of the estate and the need for so many buildings.

Dylon was happy to answer the questions and Kevin kept an eye on Kolminski, who was almost yawning as Dylon explained the process to Lieutenant Steiger.

"Well, Lieutenant, our parents and grandparents raised us with a strong sense of being self-sufficient. They would always say 'waste not, want not' and they tried to instill that into their businesses as well. A lot of the buildings in this quadrant of the estate are for that purpose. We process our own food supplies and the surplus is traded or donated to a lot of the nearby villages. You guys really got the short end of the stick on your draw of this quadrant to investigate. Most of the buildings here are pretty mundane."

Kolminski's phone gave off a quick chirping tone of an incoming message. Realizing that it was impossible to ignore, Kolminski tried to play it off. "Oh wow, finally a signal in this Godforsaken place."

He quickly pulled out his phone and read the message.

*"Package obtained and secured."*

Kolminski held up his phone to simulate trying to retain the connection by keeping the signal. "And there it goes. God, I'll be happy to get back to civilization." He shoved the phone into his pocket and huffed over to Dylon. "So, is there anything worth seeing at all in this quadrant?"

Dylon cocked his head a little to the side in response to Kolminski's sarcastic tone. "Well sir, not really. Unless you're into researching different procedures for packaging food products. There is the hydroponics research lab and a couple of structures that I've built to generate our own power supply. It powers the entire complex if you're interested in seeing that."

Lieutenant Steiger's eyes lit up with interest, but before he had a chance to say anything Kolminski continued. "I really don't understand this whole divide and conquer technique your team has devised. It all just makes me a little uncomfortable and I don't have a good feeling about it," Kolminski said accusingly.

"Divide and conquer?" Dylon looked at Kolminski with a puzzled expression. Kevin stepped up and started speaking before Dylon could continue.

"Excuse me, Mr. Kolminski, but we're just trying to cater to your agenda. Now maybe we misunderstood General Grant's requests, but I thought the tour was to give your people a complete understanding of the functions that were performed in every building on this complex, including the outer buildings of the estate."

Kevin paused and looked at both of them and before they got a chance to respond he continued. "Do you guys understand that your group is seeing more than any of the other guests from the other countries? The requests that you placed before us was a little more than we originally anticipated. Due to a limited amount of staff, merely for their safety I might add, the best way to fulfill your demands was to break you into smaller groups. I'm actually kind of insulted at what you're insinuating, Mr. Kolminski."

"Well I really don't care about that right now. All I'm trying to do is figure out what your intentions are. You do have to admit that it does seem a little strange to break up a much more formidable group than yourselves." Kolminski said with a matter-of-fact tone in his voice.

Kevin bounced right back with a rebuttal that left both Kolminski's and Steiger's mouths agape. "You're absolutely right, Kolminski. Your group has been split up for mainly that reason, but let me give you a little more insight to our reasoning. First, and foremost, to give you a complete tour of the complex, as I have already mentioned, in a timely manner. Second, to make sure that during the tour, everything that your government has all but demanded has been fulfilled. Third, and most importantly, the safety of my team. We do consider you a threat and you've already proven that you can't be trusted.

You arrive as our guests with a group of people that you claim to be personal assistants, but who are obviously nothing more than a highly trained tactical squad. So Mr. Kolminski, before you start throwing around insinuations about ill-intentions, maybe you should take a closer look at your own intentions and your lack of transparency." Kevin was getting a little agitated with them and unconsciously took a step back from them, revealing just how much he did not trust them.

There was a brief moment of silence as Dylon and Kevin eased over to the *Mule*. Kolminski was shuffling through his briefcase and Steiger was puzzled as to the next step. Kevin looked at the two of them. "Gentlemen, is there anything else you would like to see?"

Kolminski was still shuffling through his briefcase when he answered. "Not really, but there is one more thing I would like to ask you before we leave here." He finally found what he was looking for. "What can you tell me about this?" Kolminski pulled out the piece of paper and handed it to Dylon and Kevin.

It was a letter addressed to General Grant, and printed on the top of the paper was the NASA logo. They started to read it, but before they got to the subject of the letter Kolminski snatched it back and began explaining it. "What it basically says is that someone has been hacking into the satellites orbiting Mars. They missed the first one, but were able to triangulate the source of origin to your complex. To be quite honest about the whole thing, they didn't think anybody would be stupid enough to try it, and when it happened the second time, well naturally they called us."

Kevin and Dylon just looked at each other, praying that their accusers would take their actions as shock and disbelief that anyone on their team would do something like that.

Kolminski and Steiger tried to read their hosts' expressions then Kolminski continued. "So, I'm guessing that you don't have a clue as to what this is all about? Then, I'm sure you'll understand our mistrust of your intentions and your security measures."

Kevin didn't like the fact that Kolminski was putting him in a defensive position, and tried to turn it back around to get the upper hand. "Now hold on, how do we know this isn't something you just concocted? And why in the world would anybody want to hack into a Mars satellite? Especially somebody that was sending their own satellite there. Really, what would be the point?"

Kolminski found himself the opportunity to plant the seed of doubt. One he hoped would, not only make Kevin and Dylon ask questions, but also his partner Lieutenant Steiger. "Well what about Lieutenant Vasquez? How well do you really know him? If there was anybody that I would be questioning the motives of, it would be none other than a government official that could, at any time, take over your entire operation."

This was the last straw for Dylon, and the response he gave surprised even him. He had never stood up to an authority figure like this before. "What? You've really got some nerve. Lieutenant Vasquez has been a friend of the family since my father bought this place. For you to stand there and throw out such allegations so freely is really starting to piss me off. Wait a minute. On second thought, hasn't your General Grant been dealing with Lieutenant Vasquez from the beginning, when you guys pretty much forced his government to sign that stupid narcotics control and supervision treaty? I would think that if there was anything questionable about his character, that you guys would have already come across it. Unless of course, you're not as good as you profess to be. So as far as any wrong doing or ill-intentions, if you don't have sufficient proof of it I would prefer you completely drop these insinuations. We've been more than polite and open about everything we are doing and plan to do. Now if there are any more buildings that you wish to see on your list you need to say so. At this point I would really hate to waste any more of your time or mine. Ungrateful, disrespectful...." Dylon's final words kind of trailed off as he turned to get in the *Mule* and finish the tour.

Lieutenant Steiger was completely caught off guard by Kolminski's actions. "The fact that we were supposed to be collecting all the information we could on the workings of the estate and the complex must have fallen on deaf ears," he thought to himself. As Kevin walked over to join Dylon, Steiger turned to Kolminski and unloaded on him.

"What in the hell are you doing? As much as I agree with you about not having our group split up, I can't back you if I don't know where your head is. Besides, we are still supposed to be gathering as much intel as we can. Now how do you think we're going to accomplish that, if all you can do is piss off our guides? I'm telling you right now, Kolminski, don't pull that shit on me again." Lieutenant Steiger shook his head and turned around to see Kevin and Dylon both sitting there waiting.

Kolminski laughed a little and tried to play it all off. "That, that was nothing. Just trying to ruffle their feathers a little, you know, get them agitated to see if they're going to spill the beans about anything."

"Whatever, Mr. Bigman. I'm kind of beginning to think they're not doing anything wrong, but hey, it's apparently your game now. So have at it." Steiger held his hand out directing Kolminski to the *Mule*.

* * * * * *

Lieutenant Vasquez had looked for every option he could possibly use for a means of escape or for attracting Carlos' attention. He was almost to the point of giving up when he noticed a small panel to the right of the radar screen. He couldn't quite make out all of the words, but he did see one encouraging word, lights. He started edging closer, which ultimately put him closer to the General as well.

Paschel jumped to his feet and pointed the gun in his direction. "Just what exactly do you think you're doing, Lieutenant?" He started to walk a little closer, just to get his point across.

Vasquez looked Paschel square in the eyes before he started speaking. "I was just going to check on the

General. Make sure the swelling has stopped and make sure he's still a little coherent. You know, the sort of things you would do for an old friend," Lieutenant Vasquez said, then eased himself back against the control module directly in front of the radar screen.

Paschel walked past the Lieutenant to look out the window. "Don't waste your time he probably won't be in any shape to leave here when we do. And if you don't watch yourself you won't be leaving here, either.

The Lieutenant watched Paschel carefully and when he saw the opportunity he glanced down at the panel and found what he was looking for, runway lights. Now all he needed was for Paschel to return to the other side of the room and get preoccupied with something else.

General Grant had stirred during the conversation between Paschel and Vasquez. He noticed the Lieutenant's movements and could tell by his body language that Lieutenant Vasquez was desperately wanting Paschel to return to the other side of the room. He heard Paschel's comments and even though it might mean another swipe of the pistol to the cheek or head, General Grant wanted to try and help Lieutenant Vasquez out.

General Grant tried to move his chair, which got

Paschel's attention immediately. Paschel was in front of the General with his pistol raised, in just a few steps. "What in the hell are you trying to do?"

The General quickly blurted out the words before Paschel brought the gun down. "Water, could I please have some water?" He said in a hoarse and raspy voice.

It wasn't much of a diversion, but it was enough time for Lieutenant Vasquez to flip the runway lights on and off a few times. Then he offered to get some water for all of them. "I think there might be some water in that refrigerator. I could use a drink myself. I could get us all some if that's alright?"

Paschel waved the gun, motioning him to get the water. When the Lieutenant retrieved the water he glanced out the window and noticed Carlos looking up at the control tower as he walked across the runway. The Lieutenant quickly made his way back to the General, setting a bottle of water in front of Paschel as he passed by him.

When he handed General Grant the bottle of water he shook his head. "You'll have to hold it for me. There's something wrong with my arm." There really wasn't anything wrong with his arm. He just didn't want to reveal that he had already cut halfway through the tape around his wrists, nor did he want to drop the opener he was using for a cutting tool.

When the Lieutenant was finished, he sat the half-empty bottle beside the General, who thanked him for his help. It was only a moment later when Paschel jumped to his feet and cursed. "Shit, there's someone coming up the stairs. It looks like that simpleton who was loading the helicopter. Get rid of him now, or you're all dead." He ducked back out of sight and held his gun aimed at the General.

Carlos tried to open the door only to find it locked. He knocked and called out to the Lieutenant, who quickly opened the door. "Yes Paco, is there something you need?"

Carlos looked at the Lieutenant like he had bumped his head. "I was just checking to see if there was anything else you wanted me to load."

Once again Lieutenant Vasquez called Carlos by the wrong name. "No Paco, we'll be fine down here. Did you check with Senorita Rosie to make sure she has everything she needs to ship ready?"

Carlos nodded and answered. "No sir, I'll go see Senorita Rosa now, I mean Senorita Rosie." He turned and made his way down the stairs. Once he got outside he kind of skipped over to the *Mule*. When he was out of sight of anybody in the tower, he dropped the act. There was something going on and he wasn't sure what.

Carlos knew the only reason that Lieutenant

Vasquez would suggest he go see Rosie, was to let her know that something wasn't right. He pushed the buggy as hard as it would go. That is, until he noticed that one of the tour groups was already back. This meant he had to drop back into character and try to convince Rosie to give him a minute of time.

Carlos pulled the *Mule* up to the front of the house and gathered up some of the loose items out of the back of it. It didn't matter what it was, he just needed something to get Rosie's attention away from the others if she was busy. When he entered the foyer Rosie, Dylon, and Kevin were standing there. He wasn't sure what he just walked into, but Dylon and Kevin both looked like they just got a good reaming.

"Senorita Rosie, you show me where to put these?" Carlos said. Rosie looked at Dylon and Kevin and then looked at Carlos. She turned back to the two boys and spoke. "That little weasel just played you. He's up to something, I'm telling you. Just stay in here and let those two be for now." She then turned her attention to Carlos. "What is it you have there, honey?" Rosie said as she walked over to Carlos.

She started to look at the items he had and then just looked at him. "Well none of these things go inside." Carlos gave her a desperate look, but before he could speak Kolminski and Lieutenant Steiger came in from the pool deck. Carlos glanced over

Rosie's shoulder and then deep into Rosie's eyes. "You must show me, Rosie. I won't learn if you don't show me." Again he looked over Rosie's shoulder and back at Rosie, then he looked down at the floor. He was hoping that Rosie would understand that he didn't want to talk in front of Kolminski.

Rosie glanced over her shoulder and saw Kolminski standing there, then she turned back to Carlos. "That's alright dear, they make me uncomfortable too." She guided Carlos around the corner.

Kolminski heard Carlos pleading with Rosie and turned to Dylon. "So, having a little problem with the help?" He said and motioned his head in Carlos' direction.

Dylon just shook his head. "He had an accident that left him with the mentality of a child. Why don't you show a little compassion, dick."

When Rosie and Carlos made it around the corner and out of earshot of the others, Carlos grabbed Rosie's wrists and started spilling his little secret. "I am not the guy you think I am. I am a special agent for Lieutenant Vasquez. My whole character has been an act to make sure you guys were on the up and up. After we were satisfied you were, the Lieutenant decided to keep me around until after the visit with the U.S. was over, as a precautionary measure. Now, I think the Lieutenant and General Grant are in big trouble. They're in the control tower and when I went to check on them he was acting really strange. Not to mention the fact that he called me Paco, instead of Carlos. He sent me to make sure that you guys were safe and to warn you. These guys are getting ready to pull something and I need to get all of you to a safe location."

Rosie looked at him and couldn't believe what she was hearing. It wasn't really what she was hearing, but who she was hearing it from. She could usually tell a fake from a mile away, but this guy was good. She shook her head, just to bring herself back to the situation at hand. "I won't leave my crew and they aren't even all here yet. I've still got another group out there. Really there's nothing we can do right now without raising suspicion. I put a gun in the tank of the toilet. When the time is right we'll make a break for it. So for now, I suggest you bring the other Carlos back and wait until the time is right."

Carlos knew she was right. It was too risky to try to rescue half of the crew. He reached down into his boot and pulled out a pistol. He reached into the other one and pulled out another pistol and handed them to Rosie. She quickly turned and stuffed them behind some books on the shelf. When she turned back around, he had two more for her, one he pulled from behind his belt and the other from his shoulder holster. "At least somebody on our team came prepared," She thought to herself as she quickly stashed the other two guns.

She motioned her head to go back to join the others and picked up the things he entered the house with. As they rounded the corner she began talking like she was talking to a child. "I'm sorry honey, but this is the only thing that goes in the house. Besides, why are you worried about these little things? I know you couldn't have possibly finished everything on your list of chores to do today. Do you have your list?"

Carlos turned out his pockets and then hung his head like he was in trouble. "Don't worry I'm sure you'll find it back at the hangar where you were working earlier today. Why don't you run along now and see if you can find it?" Carlos turned and headed out the door and Rosie turned to look at Kolminski. "You are a grown man. Not only that, you are a representative of your country. More importantly, my country, and your behavior here today, well, it has been nothing less than disappointing. You have done nothing but tarnish your appointed position from the day I met you. Another remark about that man that just left and I will personally make sure you regret it."

# Chapter 48

Carlos left the main house and headed back to the helicopter. He had a secret stash of guns there and seeing how he just gave most of the ones he was carrying to Rosie, he felt a little naked. It didn't take long to get back to the hangar near the control tower.

Carlos wasn't sure if anybody in the tower was watching him or not, so he decided to load a few more boxes in the helicopter. He wanted it to look like he was still working, just in case.

After retrieving a few more weapons, a couple for himself and a couple for the Lieutenant and the General, he loaded some supplies for the control tower restrooms in the *Mule*. He cautiously glanced up at the control tower, but still couldn't see much of anything.

Finally, after fidgeting around with the supplies he had loaded, Carlos noticed someone in the window. He still couldn't tell who it was, but decided to slip a pistol in the box of supplies anyway. He hoped it was the Lieutenant, but couldn't tell. He buried the pistol with a few rolls of toilet paper.

It wasn't long before Paschel heard the sound of someone coming up the stairs again. "For not expecting any flights today, this building is curiously active." He snapped and glared at the Lieutenant.

"It's probably just Paco. He has many duties here. We try to keep him busy with small jobs that aren't crucial to the day to day operations of things. It makes him feel important. For the price he has paid to his country, I think it's the least we can do." The Lieutenant responded with a slight bitterness in his voice.

"Well, didn't you just tell him to leave no more than an hour ago? So what's he doing this time? I swear Lieutenant, if he comes in here I'll kill him. Mental or not, I don't care." Paschel said and stepped over to the side of the door, just out of sight.

"Oh relax, he's probably just restocking and cleaning the restrooms." Lieutenant Vasquez replied. Then he stepped a little closer to Paschel. "Tell me Paschel, how much are you getting for this little job you're doing?"

"What?" He blasted. "I'm not getting anything out of this. I'm just following orders."

"Sure you are." The Lieutenant stated with a hint of sarcasm.

Paschel waved his gun in the Lieutenant's direction. "You know, for somebody that's being held at gunpoint, you're kind of a smart ass. Do you always try to provoke your captors like this?"

Lieutenant Vasquez knew he was just pushing

buttons, but continued anyway. "I just find it interesting that you would be so eager to inflict so much pain on a commanding officer. The men in my service would have picked out a person of your character right away. You would not have made it to the position you're in right now. Even among common criminals there is a certain degree of respect and order."

Paschel let the Lieutenant talk, but slowly made his way around behind the General. He pulled the clip back on his gun. "Keep talking, Lieutenant, and we'll just go ahead and finish him off right now."

Lieutenant Vasquez slightly lowered his head and stopped talking. He was hoping that he had kept Paschel's attention diverted long enough for Carlos to finish what he was doing. With a quick glance out the window, Vasquez noticed that Carlos was heading off toward the main house.

\* \* \* \* \* \*

Back at the main house, Rosie was trying to get either Dylon or Kevin away from their guests long enough to clue them in on what was going on with the Lieutenant's tour group. It seemed like everything she tried one of the guests had to tag along. She didn't want to be blatantly rude to a member of the U.S.

government, but they were really beginning to work her nerves.

When she had finally had enough, she turned to Dylon, whose shadow was Kolminski, and said. "Dylon, I'm going to the office. When you get a minute to spare, I would like to talk to you alone. I have a couple of ideas for scheduling the classes that have requested tours of the complex. You know we now have several Universities in Peru that are interested in seeing our operation and I just want to make sure we are not double booking ourselves."

Kolminski objected. "I really don't think it would be a good idea to have a bunch of students traipsing around up here. I really hope that you plan on prescreening them with some sort of extensive background check."

That was the last thing Rosie needed to hear. It was the final button that needed to be pushed. She turned her attention away from Dylon, who kind of melted into the wall after seeing the look in her eyes. The focus of her energy was now on Kolminski. She had all she cared to take from him and he was getting ready to find out.

"Excuse me? Correct me if I'm wrong, Mr. Kolminski, but the last time I checked, YOU are a guest here and this operation isn't under any government control. And if by some odd chance that it were I do believe the first government in line would fall into the hands of Lieutenant Vasquez's command. Now if there is nothing else you want to add, I do have work to do. And no, you don't need to know every little detail of any future tours or visits from other students, governments, or possible investors." She thought she was finished and turned to go to her office.

Kolminski didn't stop. Instead, he found another opportunity to plant one more seed of doubt to sway Lieutenant Steiger's indecisiveness. "Speaking of Lieutenant Vasquez, have you talked to him lately? I've tried several times to reach our General and haven't had any success."

Rosie paused momentarily and then continued into her office. She picked up the hand held and cued up the Lieutenant. She really wasn't expecting an answer, but she still wasn't sure who was behind what Carlos had told her earlier. If it was who she was suspecting, she had to make it look like she was unaware of what was really going on.

She waited a minute before turning and closing the door. She placed the radio on the desk and looked out the window, trying to figure what to do next. Then she noticed two more vehicles approaching the house. She knew one of the *Mules* would be Kat and her tour group. She hoped the other one would be Carlos.

Rosie opened the office door and saw Kolminski waiting there where she left him. She didn't even acknowledge him. Instead she headed to the foyer to guide the returning group to the pool deck. Once the group had made it outside to get some refreshments, Rosie turned and almost knocked Kolminski over. He had followed her every step, waiting to get an answer about the General. "So, I'm guessing you didn't get a response on the radio?"

Rosie glanced at Dylon and he came over to join her. Then she responded to Kolminski. "Don't play dumb. It doesn't suit you well. I'll give them thirty more minutes and if we don't hear from them by then, well I guess we'll have to go look for them. Now if you'll excuse us I'm going to get a bite to eat before it's all gone." Rosie knew she had to buy herself some time to find out from Carlos what the plan was. She only told Kolminski, whom she suspected was behind the missing members, thirty minutes to shut him up. She took Dylon by the arm and he escorted her to the deck.

When the two of them made it out the door and Rosie felt comfortable enough with the distance between them and Kolminski she whispered into Dylon's ear. "Find Carlos and tell him that *you know*. Find out what he needs without blowing his cover." She removed her arm from his and started to mingle with the other guests. She was curious to see how their tour of the complex went.

Dylon didn't say anything in response to Rosie's request, but an odd look came over his face. Several thoughts ran through his mind, but the one that stuck out the most was his question about who was really running this operation.

Dylon did as he was told and made his way around the pool deck. He scanned the grounds to see if he could see any movement. It was only a moment later when he noticed Carlos messing around with the filtration system for the pool. He made his way a little closer to Carlos and when they caught each other's eye, they both knew.

Carlos closed up the filter and grabbed a skimming net. He headed right past Dylon towards the far end of the pool. Dylon turned and watched for a minute then slowly made his way towards Carlos. When he was close enough for Carlos to hear him, he made a quick scan of the others to see if anybody was watching them.

When he felt confident that the others were preoccupied he started talking. "My instructions from Rosie are to tell you I know, and to see what you need."

There was a brief pause before Carlos responded. "I need a distraction near the control tower. An unidentified agent has the Lieutenant and the General held at gunpoint in the tower. He's not ours and he didn't arrive with the others. I don't know whose side he is on. The distraction needs to be a big one. Not your typical hand grenade at a pile of oil drums. I really need this agent's attention drawn for a good amount of time."

Dylon nodded his head, but was almost dumbfounded. The man he had known to be a simpleton was talking in a manner he wasn't accustomed to hearing. Not only that, but he was asking for assistance in what sounded like a pretty dangerous operation.

When Dylon finally answered Carlos, he stumbled and stuttered all the way through it. "Well, I might… I mean I have something that might work. I don't know if it would be good enough. It would have to be me….and getting out of here is going to be…Well, next to impossible."

Carlos moved around the pool a little with the skimmer pole and Dylon followed. Carlos looked Dylon up and down, as if to size him up, then he spoke. "They've been up there for a while now. Whatever you do needs to happen soon. You have to find a way. Rosie will help you to make sure it happens. I'll be waiting." Dylon looked across the pool to find Rosie and Carlos stepped away to put away the net. Before Dylon could turn his attention back to Carlos, he had disappeared.

When Rosie had finished mingling with the guests she continued to make her way around the pool to get with Dylon. When she approached him she whispered. "Walk with me." Before Dylon even got a chance to say anything or ask how long she knew about Carlos, Rosie continued. "So what does he need and how much time do we have?"

Dylon brushed aside the questions he had and answered Rosie. "Well, he said whatever we do needs to happen soon I kind of got the feeling that he's still not sure who's behind it all. And what we need, would be a distraction. A big distraction that would do more than just startle someone. The only thing I can think of requires my presence." Dylon paused for a moment, waiting for a response. Rosie didn't say anything, but you could tell her mind was working.

They kept walking and when they were just inside the door, Rosie turned to Dylon. She looked straight into his eyes, as if she were trying to read his mind. It made him kind of nervous and he started to look away, then Rosie spoke. "I have a pretty good idea about what you're planning and I really don't want to know. Just be careful. Now if you're going to help any of us, you need to disappear and quick." Rosie turned to go back and join the others, but Dylon grabbed her arm to stop her.

"Rosie, do you remember the disc?" he asked.

"Of course I remember the disc. Don't be silly, nothing is going to happen. Now hurry up, before anyone sees you leaving," she said and started to turn away again. Once again, Dylon stopped her from leaving. "The password Rosie, I need to hear you say it. I need to know someone remembered the password." Dylon pleaded.

"This is just silly, Dylon. I know what the password is, but I'm not repeating it. You're going to go and do what you need to and when you're finished I'll see you right back here. Now let go and get out of here, so I can keep everybody busy." Rosie pulled away and headed out the door to mingle some more.

Just then Kolminski, Steiger, and Sergeant Mobley broke out into a heated discussion. They hadn't realized how loud they had gotten until they felt the stares of everyone present. Rosie quickly turned to check on Dylon and just caught a glimpse of him dodging around the corner of the house. She turned her attention back to the guests and the commotion they were creating. She noticed Commander Campbell was standing away from the rest of his group, just watching.

Rosie slipped up beside him. "So who's winning?" she asked the commander, trying to get a feel for his take on the whole situation. He glanced at his group and then back at Rosie. "Well, by my score card your group, but my score card doesn't count. We're missing a leader and somebody is more anxious about taking on that role, than they are in finding out where the leader is. Have you heard from your Lieutenant Vasquez yet?"

Rosie just shook her head. "You know, there is a room where all of this can be discussed in private. I would like to sit in if that's alright. Unless of course, you need to figure out who's in charge first."

The Commander had been keeping an eye on Rosie since they got there and he figured out he wasn't dealing with your ordinary civilian. No, he could sense a touch of training in her, somebody that knew a little more about how the government worked than most. "I think we'll take you up on that room and maybe we can knock a few heads together. Then after that we can bring both of our groups together to find out what to do next."

Rosie nodded her head and made her way inside to ready the room they started in that morning. Marcus, Kat, and Kevin had decided to ease away from the group when Kolminski first started getting loud. It seemed that nobody in the group was all that thrilled about taking orders from him. That's when Commander Campbell made his way over to the group and strongly suggested they finish their meeting inside.

* * * * * *

Dylon had slipped around the side of the house and hopped into one of the spare *Mules*. After the commotion had started at the poolside it didn't take him long to get out of sight of the main house unnoticed. By the time Rosie convinced the guests to use the conference room, Dylon was already pulling up to the back of the observatory.

He had the entrance opened and subsequently closed behind him quicker than he had ever done before. Inside the tunnel he had to turn on his lights. Soon after entering the tunnel he stopped at his safe room. He ran inside and found the only computer there that was connected to the rest of the estate.

He quickly brought up the *Vision Scope* program and readjusted the focus starting point for all of the cameras. The beginning point was set for the control tower. From that point, anything that had an odd flying pattern would automatically be recorded. Then he ran back out of the room and headed for the storage facility under the old hangar.

\* \* \* \* \* \*

When Rosie was finished catering to the U.S. government's needs and they were all settled in the room, she quickly made her way to the pool deck. Kat, Kevin, and Marcus were anxiously waiting to see what was happening.

Rosie hurried over to her crew and started explaining what was going on. "Listen closely, because we don't have a lot of time. The Lieutenant's tour party is missing. Well actually, they're being held captive and it appears that, from the argument we just overheard, the little weasel is next in line for command. If that happens, it will not bode well for us.

Next, apparently the Lieutenant has had his own operative hanging out keeping an eye on things. This turned out to be a good move on his part, because that's who's going to save his ass."

Kat was listening closely, but she noticed that the Lieutenant wasn't the only one missing. "Excuse me Rosie, but where is Dylon? I mean, shouldn't he be here for this too?"

Rosie kind of sighed a little. She knew that question was coming, but she was hoping it would be later. "Well, that's the next thing. I'm not sure what's going to happen when they come out of there. So if anybody asks, he probably went to run some reports on the launch. It's something that one of us usually does."

Most everybody accepted that answer, except Kat. "So where is he, Rosie?"

"Honey, he went to help Carlos with something. I don't know what, I didn't ask. If we tell them that we don't know where he is though, it just won't look good." Rosie was hoping that her answer would ease Kat's worries. She was pretty sure it would, seeing how nobody except Dylon and herself knew that Carlos was the Lieutenant's operative.

\* \* \* \* \* \*

Not long after the meeting started, two of the 'personal assistants' slipped out. They made their way through the foyer and eavesdropped in on the conversation Rosie was having with her group.

Unbeknownst to Rosie and the others, they were able to get just enough information to head out on a mission to figure out what was going on themselves, and hopefully to save face as well. Their orders were quite simple. "Find out who's behind whatever is going on and report directly to me, only to me. The only people I want to hear what you have to report, is

you, me, and God." These were the words the
Commander spoke to them earlier in the evening
before the argument broke out.

* * * * * *

Carlos was already in position when he noticed
someone leaving the main house. All he could do was
hope it was Dylon, but when the vehicle headed off
toward the observatory, he wasn't so sure. Twenty
minutes later, he noticed another vehicle leaving the
main house. He thought for sure that this was Dylon,
because it was headed in his direction.

As the vehicle got closer, Carlos grew more
concerned. It was making no effort to conceal its
arrival. He lifted his scope, just to make sure it was in
fact Dylon. "I didn't think the boy was that stupid,
those special agents are surely going to get someone
killed." Carlos said as he quickly put his scope away
and started to look for a different place to hide.
"Maybe I can find a different way in." he thought to
himself as he slipped around the corner of the tower.

# Chapter 49

Behind the building, Carlos found a ladder that ran to the top of the tower. There were several small panels at varying heights near the ladder. They appeared to be access panels, but to what Carlos didn't know. He began to climb the ladder and tried to open the first one he came to. Unfortunately, it was locked. As he continued to climb he hoped he would have better luck with the others.

\* \* \* \* \* \*

Paschel was standing near the window fidgeting with his phone, when he caught a glimpse of movement out of the corner of his eye. He turned and studied the source of the movement and noticed the *Mule* heading straight for the control tower. Then he turned to Lieutenant Vasquez. "If that half-wit comes in this building again I'm going to kill him. Then, orders or not, I'm going to kill you too."

Vasquez picked up the pair of binoculars near him and looked out the window. Vasquez saw not one, but two passengers. At this point, he grinned, because he knew it was not his man. Paschel, just realizing that

Vasquez had a pair of binoculars, snatched them from him.

As Paschel peered through the binoculars, he realized the two men in the *Mule* were part of Kolminski's group. Vasquez could see the life just kind of drain out of him. "Well, that no good, double-crossing, son of a bitch." Paschel reached for his gun and turned to the General.

He aimed at the center of his chest and pulled the trigger. "Sorry General, but nobody has any use for you anymore."

It happened so quick, Lieutenant Vasquez didn't have a chance to react. When he did make a move to stop Paschel, it was thwarted by a blow to the head with the binoculars. Paschel knelt down beside the unconscious Lieutenant. As he wiped his gun clean he began speaking. "On the other hand, Lieutenant, you are going to be the fall guy." Paschel put the gun in the Lieutenant's limp hand and fired another round. "Nothing like a little gunshot residue to seal the case." Paschel said and stood up to make his way out of the building before the agents showed up.

He only made it to the third floor when he noticed the lights of the *Mule* shining in the door on the bottom floor. Paschel tried to get the best vantage point to ambush the two agents that would be entering the building any minute. He figured if he could at least take out one of them, then he would have better odds of getting out, before the rest of the party showed up.

* * * * * *

Carlos almost lost his grip when he heard the shot. He hurried up the next few rungs of the ladder and tried the hatch to see if it would open. It slid open pretty easily and he maneuvered inside. As soon as he was inside though, another shot was fired and the echo it made was almost deafening. Carlos laid flat on the floor and listened for any other movement from the next room.

The only sounds he heard were those of someone scurrying down the stairs and then stopping. When he felt that it was safe to start moving again he pulled out a small flashlight and scoped out the room he was in. It looked like an electrical storage room. He scanned the room to find another way in or out and all he could find was an unused return vent, just another victim of the recent upgrades.

He crept over to the vent and knelt down. He peered through to see if there was anybody in the other room. Carlos noticed one man on the floor. It was the General, but there were too many obstructions to see anything more than that. He had to get in there. He was pretty sure he would be able to get in before anybody came back in the room.

* * * * * *

The agents also heard the gunshots. They radioed the Commander and reported the incident. They didn't wait for a response. They turned down their radios and got into position. In a matter of minutes one of the agents kicked the door open and the other one took a quick peak inside. When he thought the coast was clear he lunged through the door and hid behind a steel beam upright.

The second agent wasn't so lucky. As soon as he made it through the door, Paschel fired off a couple of rounds. The first one pierced the agent in the neck and the second grazed his ankle as he fell to the floor. The first agent returned fire, but he knew they didn't accomplish anything. He did a quick scan of the area around him. He was hoping to find something he could use to create a distraction, something that would give him enough time to get into a better position.

Then he spotted a fire extinguisher. He grabbed it and tossed it up to the first floor landing and ducked back, right before Paschel fired off a couple of more rounds.

* * * * * *

The Commander was getting everybody loaded up and paired off. His group and the Rosier's group were getting ready to head to the control tower where the gunshots were reported only a few minutes ago. Commander Campbell was checking all the members when he noticed one was missing. He turned to see Kolminski at the top of the stairs, talking on a cell phone.

The Commander sent the others ahead knowing they would not go full throttle until he caught up with them. He was furious with Kolminski and called out to him. "Hey dickhead, now do you see why you're not the one in charge? I've got men in the line of fire and you're chatting on the phone. Where in the hell is your head at, man?"

Kolminski looked at the Commander with a condescending sneer on his face. "For your information, Commander Campbell, I just called in the two Harriers that have been standing by just in case something like this happened. ETA is approximately two minutes. This will all be over soon and when it is, I'm sure you'll find that the Rosiers had this planned all along."

Commander Campbell all but lost it. "Well a lot of fucking good that is going to do us. What do you think is going to happen? Do you think your Harriers will be able to take out a lone gunman with heat seeking missiles? Really man, I honestly can't figure out how in the fuck you got the position you're in. I suggest you get your ass in gear and get down there with the others for a little hand to hand, before I give you a few lessons of my own."

Kolminski was pissed that somebody actually had the nerve to talk to him like that. He was smart enough to know though, that this is one time he needed to follow orders and handle the problem later.

\* \* \* \* \* \*

The agent peered around the corner to try and get a bearing on where Paschel was. He needed to get back outside where his odds of living were a lot better. He couldn't really see where Paschel was but he could see the fire extinguisher. That was all he really needed to see. He lifted his gun and took aim. One shot is all that it took. The extinguisher exploded, releasing a cloud of fire retardant chemicals. It was just enough cover to allow him to duck back out the door.

Once he made it out the door, he ducked behind the *Mule* and reloaded. He then grabbed the radio. "I could use a little help down here. I'm down one and have exited the building for a better vantage point."

Lieutenant Steiger responded. "We're on our way Jones, hang tight."

The two remaining agents split away from Lieutenant Steiger and headed towards the north side of the control tower. They were hoping to come in behind the action and catch Paschel in the crossfire. The Commander and Kolminski caught up with the group only moments later. He directed everyone to follow him to the runway between the hangar and the control tower.

Kolminski started dropping back little by little, until he was at the back of the group. He slowed his speed until he was just barely in sight of the Rosier's group.

Coming in from the north side of the tower, the agents radioed to Jones. "You still with us, Jones?" There was no response. They picked up their speed and as they were coming over the hill another *Mule* rammed into theirs. One of the agents was knocked out of the vehicle, which subsequently flipped on top of him. The other agent was able to hold onto the steering wheel and remain mostly in the vehicle. Paschels vehicle was also thrown onto its side partially covering his leg.

The agent and Paschel were both knocked a little

senseless from the collision and it took a minute for them to clear their heads.


\* \* \* \* \* \*


As Carlos started to squeeze through the vent, he noticed the Lieutenant was starting to stir.
"Lieutenant, are you alright sir?" Carlos said as he finished climbing through and got to his feet. He hurried over to check on his leader. He helped the Lieutenant, who was rubbing the spot on his head where Paschel had struck him, to his feet.

He looked over at the General and shook his head. "We need to check on the General, Carlos." As the two of them made their way to the General, he also started to stir. The Lieutenant hurried his pace. "Old friend, I thought for sure you were finished." General Grant pulled his hands apart as he had finished cutting through the tape, right before Paschel had shot him.

Carlos knelt down beside him and finished cutting the rest of the tape that had him bound to the chair. "Do you think you can stand, sir?" he said as he removed the last piece of tape. The General nodded his head and the three of them moved over to the vent. Carlos tried to hurry their pace for fear of Paschel coming back. When they were all inside the room

Carlos explained that they would have to climb down the ladder.

After a few groans of discomfort the three of them were slowly moving down the ladder. Carlos was out first to help steady the General, followed by the Lieutenant who also tried to help steady the General on their way down.

Once down the ladder, they worked their way to the opposite end of the building, away from the shooting. As they came around the corner they were taken by surprise. The General was in awe of the object he was seeing in flight for the first time. The Lieutenant and Carlos just looked at each other as they watched the General take everything in.

Dylon cussed and mumbled to himself over his nervousness. He too, had heard the beginning of the gunfight and in his haste, had messed up just about every maneuver he attempted, including bringing it out of the hangar.

\* \* \* \* \* \*

Paschel had managed to come to his senses a little quicker than Hanks, the last remaining agent. He gathered up his weapon and the Blackberry and started to make a run for it. Hanks pulled himself up against the *Mule* and took aim. He fired off a shot that caught

Paschel in the lower leg and he tumbled over a couple of times before rolling onto his back. He sat up and returned fire at Hanks, who was now walking towards him. Hanks emptied his gun and Paschel fell back.

When Hanks made it to Paschel to confirm that he was dead, he noticed the Blackberry. He removed it from Paschel's hand as he checked him for a pulse.

\* \* \* \* \* \*

The Commander and the others were approaching the runway and noticed the craft that was hovering at the same height as the tower itself. Kat saw the craft and knew instantly where she would find her brother. "Lieutenant Vasquez, do you think he's alright?" she asked Marcus.

Commander Campbell radioed for his men, but the only response he received was from Hanks. "Hanks, I see three men at the other end of the tower. Go check and see who it is. And by all means go behind the building, I don't know if this thing is putting off any radiation or not." Marcus called out to the Commander. "You don't have to worry about radiation, but I would worry about where he lands it." Then, with Kat hanging on tightly, he sped off behind the tower to catch up with Hanks.

\* \* \* \* \* \*

Rosie and Kevin had hung back a little, just to try and keep Kolminski in their sights as they approached the runway. By the time Commander Campbell, Marcus and Kat were arriving at the runway, Kevin and Rosie were about seventy five yards behind them. Kevin noticed Kolminski veering off to the left, heading towards the hangar.

When they were sure that Kolminski probably felt safe that nobody had seen him, they turned around and eased up to the hangar as well. Kevin stopped at the corner of the hangar and got out of the *Mule*. He asked Rosie to wait while he checked to make sure it was clear to follow. Kevin peeked around the corner just in time to see Kolminski go inside.

Commander Campbell started looking around and noticed with a quick head count he was missing a few people. Before he could really take a good check on the group, he heard something off in the distance. It was a familiar sound and as he recognized it, he quickly scanned the group again. "Shit, Kolminski!" he blurted.

Before he could even get turned around the Harriers came into view. "Search the grounds, men. We're looking for Kolminski. He can't be too far. I want those birds called off and he has the only phone line to them."

The group all split up to search the surrounding buildings. They hadn't moved more than a few feet before the Harriers buzzed by them. As soon as the pilots saw the craft, they broke off in opposite directions and the craft shot straight up in the air about fifteen thousand feet.

The flight leader immediately got on the radio. "Kolminski, what in the hell was that? I thought you said we were giving support to ground crews."

"It's a prototype for an advanced weaponry drone. Take it out." Kolminski commanded.

The pilot questioned the orders. "But sir, I thought procedure on crafts like this was to confiscate them for research? We could force it to land."

Kolminski's voice came back over the radio. "With the maneuver I just saw, I seriously doubt you could. Besides, I'm standing here looking at a fleet of at least seven. Who knows how many more they have hidden? So just follow your orders and take it out." Kolminski's eyes kind of glazed over with excitement, as he looked down through the opening in the floor.

Dylon cursed as he worked the two joysticks that controlled the craft. "I really wasn't expecting a dog fight. What in the hell am I going to do now?" He hovered there for a minute, trying to collect his thoughts and figure out his next move. As he watched the monitors, he noticed the planes getting closer and figured he was running out of options.

He came to the conclusion that the best thing to do would be to just land the craft. But this option also came just a little too late. As he checked the monitors again, he saw that the jets had fired two missiles.

He wasn't the only one to notice it. Kat and Marcus also saw the missiles launch from the jets. Kat urged Marcus to pick up the pace, all the while hoping that the craft was just another remote control craft. Her questions wouldn't be answered until they made it to Carlos. When they finally made it to the three men at the other end of the tower, Kat's heart sank to her feet.

"Carlos, where's my brother?" she asked in a panic. Carlos just looked up at the craft, confirming Kat's worst fears. "Get me to the Commander, Marcus." she blurted. Marcus pushed the throttle as far as it could go, and the two sped off in the direction where they left the Commander and the others.

When they made it to the Commander's *Mule*, Kat jumped off the ATV before Marcus could even stop. She was in the Commander's face before he realized it. "Stop it! That's my brother up there. Call your men off he's not doing anything wrong! Why are you just standing there? Do something!" Kat yelled as she was beginning to thrash out at him.

Marcus came up behind her, after he got the ATV stopped, and tried to get her to calm down a little. He noticed the Commander was trying to say something, but couldn't get a word in. He finally directed his attention to Marcus and began talking. "It's Kolminski, we have to find Kolminski to call off the jets. He has the only phone to contact the pilots."

Marcus nodded his head and tried to urge Kat to get back on the ATV. He turned back to Commander Campbell. "Have you checked the old hangar? I'll bet that's where he's at." Then, they heard a single gunshot coming from that direction.

* * * * * *

Dylon finally fell back into the groove of flying the craft. The evasive maneuvers he was performing were pretty impressive. Still, the missiles were gaining on him and the jets were hanging back just far enough to be safe. Dylon noticed while checking his gauges and instrument panel, that all the fancy flying was taking a serious drain on his battery supply.

"I have to get rid of these things," Dylon said as the missiles closed in. He took the craft straight up. He knew the Harriers wouldn't be able to keep up at that speed. The missiles, on the other hand, only lost a little distance on Dylon. He was okay with this because his whole plan included the missiles. He ducked behind a cloud and slowed just enough for the missiles to close the gap. He had positioned himself between the jets with the sun behind him. He could see them, but they could not see him.

He lined up his craft with one of the jets and when he felt the time was right he increased his speed. The missiles were right on his tail. The pilot knew he couldn't outmaneuver the craft, so he decided to try and outrun it. Dylon just stayed on his tail, but the missiles were still gaining and he began to get a little nervous.

Dylon picked up his speed a little, talking aloud the entire time. "Just eject buddy, that's all you have to do. Nobody wants to see you get hurt, so just eject." The pilot noticed the craft closing in and kept watching as he slowly reached down for the eject lever. His attention was broken when he heard a voice come across his radio. "Eject Hawk, I'm closing in. From my line of sight you're not going to make it if you don't." The pilot ejected and Dylon breathed a sigh of relief. "Thank God."

Dylon edged his throttle up a couple of notches and blew by the Harrier. He barely skimmed the top of it, but passed it like it was sitting still. The rockets slammed into the back of the jet.

Everybody on the ground stopped momentarily and looked at the explosion. Kat just buried her head into Marcus's back. "It's alright, babe, he's still flying." Marcus noticed the pilot's chute open and breathed a sigh of relief. Then he turned to catch up with the others, who were all in a hurry to get to the front of the hangar.

In the skies above the hangar, Dylon brought the craft around and buzzed by the other jet in the hopes of getting him to back off. As he blew by, he saw two more missiles being fired. He cursed himself for not designing the craft with firing capabilities. Then he noticed on his radar screen that the two blips from the missiles had now turned into four. "Damn, man." he said aloud this time, as he once again found himself trying to evade the missiles.

Dylon noticed the Harrier had maneuvered itself around to the far end of the hangar. The pilot guessed that Dylon wouldn't lead the missiles near anything that might put someone in harm's way. And he was right. Once again, Dylon took the craft straight up. He knew the missiles couldn't make a ninety degree turn. He hoped it would buy him just enough time to do some quick calculations. He glanced at his power supply again. He was now down to a third of the power he started with and knew the craft would soon go into safe mode and shut down.

It was a safety feature he now wished he didn't have. There was only one option remaining to escape the missiles this time. As he went over the calculations, he hoped he had enough power supply to pull it off. Not to mention the fact that he wasn't even sure if it would work. He checked the monitors and the distance of the missiles. Then he put his hands on both joysticks.

# Chapter 50

When Kat and Marcus had made it around to the front of the hangar, Rosie was standing there keeping the Commander from going any further. She was trying desperately to explain to him that Kolminski had Kevin held at gunpoint. When Hanks, the only special agent still alive, pulled up he was also trying to get Commander Campbell's attention. All he had to do was hand over Paschel's Blackberry to the Commander.

When Rosie saw that she had momentarily lost her spot in line, she immediately updated Kat and Marcus of the situation. By the time she had finished, the Commander was waiting to talk to her to come up with a plan of action. He and Rosie stepped aside for a minute. Five minutes later, they rejoined the group. Rosie ushered her group around and explained exactly what they needed to do.

Sergeant Mobley took General Grant and Lieutenant Vasquez and headed back to the main house to help them tend to their wounds. Carlos stayed back, in case his help was needed.

After both groups had gone over the plans with everybody and they were all on the same page, Rosie questioned the Commander. "Do you really think Kolminski is going to buy all this?"

He looked at Rosie and nodded to Hanks, who immediately tossed him a pair of handcuffs. "Well Rosie, if you think you can somehow signal your guy without Kolminski picking up on it, then I think it will work. And just to make sure you all get away safely, I'm giving you the keys to the cuffs. As soon as you are out of sight take those cuffs off and get away from the hangar."

Rosie thought for a minute and then suggested something else. "Commander Campbell, if I can't get a signal to Kevin, it might help if one of your men were holding me at gunpoint. The gun doesn't have to be loaded, but Kolminski won't know that."

The Commander agreed and passed the order along. Before he knew it Rosie had already taken a couple of steps towards the hangar door. "Hold on a minute, Rosie." He took a couple of quick steps to catch up with her before he spoke again. "You really want this to be over with don't you?"

Rosie gave him a sharp look before responding. "Commander, all I want to do is make sure my crew is safe. And right now I have two in harm's way. So are we going to do this or not?"

Commander Campbell lowered his head a little and responded. "I fully understand, Ma'am." He waved his arm in a big circle to get everyone to pick up the pace.

When they made it to the hangar door, Commander Campbell called out to Kolminski as he swung the door open. "Kolminski, you were right. They're all up to no good. I don't know what it is they're trying to hide, but they killed the General."

Kolminski turned to see Rosie, Kat, and Marcus. They were all being detained by some of his group. The Commander pulled his gun out and tossed the only pair of handcuffs he had to Kolminski. "Here you go bud, I'll let you have the honors of cuffing this one. Hanks, why don't you come get this traitor and put him with the rest of them, while Kolminski and I have a little talk."

"Yes sir." Hanks said and left Rosie's side to retrieve Kevin and put him with the others. Hanks hurried over and took Kevin by the arm. When he was sure they were out of earshot he whispered to Kevin. "Sorry we had to do it this way Mr. Felderson, but it was for your own safety."

Kevin gave Hanks a sideways glance. Then he looked at the hangar door where the others were. He was just close enough to see Rosie sneak a wink in, and then he knew. When they made it to the hangar door all of them were guided away. The Commander and Kolminski watched them all leave, before he turned to address Kolminski.

"Kolminski, I want to tell you what a fine job you've done down here. And this," The Commander said as he gazed down at the crafts in the lower storage area. "well, this is what we've been looking for all along." By this time Commander Campbell had maneuvered himself around to put Kolminski between him and the hangar door.

Kolminski beamed with the satisfaction of finally being recognized for his true potential. The Commander glanced over Kolminski's shoulder to make sure that everybody was gone. He reached into his pocket to find the Blackberry Hanks retrieved from Paschel. "Of course, I would like to be able to thank your liaison as well, but unfortunately he didn't make it."

Kolminski tilted his head a little. "I'm not sure I know what you're talking about sir."

"Oh, I think you do, Kolminski." the Commander said as he pulled out the Blackberry and opened up the messages. "But what I really need you to do first is call off the remaining pilot."

Just then, they heard the Harrier skimming over the hangar. It seemed so close that they both ducked for fear that it would be coming through the roof any second. Kolminski found the opportunity he was looking for and tried to snatch the Blackberry out of the Commander's hand. The Commander jerked his hand back and swung around, knocking Kolminski's gun loose with his other hand. The gun chimed as it fell down the flight of stairs leading to the lower storage area. Two shots fired off as it bounced down, causing both men to duck. This ultimately gave Kominski the opportunity to disarm the Commander. A scuffle for the remaining weapon ensued.

As Rosie and the others were running away from the hangar they saw the Harrier swing around to the other end. Their focus was now on Dylon's safety and his attempt to outrun the missiles. The only thing they could do is watch and pray. With the Harrier hovering at the other end of the hangar, everyone assumed that Commander Campbell was successful in getting Kolminski to call off the jet.

Kevin and Marcus were the only ones that thought about the power supply, but didn't dare mention it. Neither of them wanted to be the one to say that Dylon didn't have much hope of getting out of this alive. So they just watched and their anxiety increased with each maneuver he made.

The last set of maneuvers puzzled them all. He shot down and waited until the missiles were almost upon him and then shot straight up about fifteen thousand feet. He shifted slightly to the side, which forced the missiles to take a wider turn to come back around to meet their target.

Dylon hovered while he checked all of his settings. He readjusted his pitch slightly, to keep him from shooting off into space. He gave himself just enough of an angle to slowly drop towards the earth. "God I hope this works." He said as he checked the monitors and the radar to see where the missiles were.

He pushed the power supply level to maximum and flipped open the cover for the button to change the power output. He checked the screens again and nervously put his hand on the throttle control. The rockets were closing in on him and if he didn't do everything at just the right moment, he wouldn't make out alive. "Focus." he said to himself, trying not to think about the what-ifs.

Kat screamed out loud. "Do something Dylon!" Then she turned to Kevin and Marcus. "What is he doing? What is he waiting for? Oh God, don't just sit there Dylon. Do something." She brought her hands to her face and watched as the missiles got closer. Her hands started shaking as the craft just hovered there. It was almost as if he was waiting for them to get closer. She couldn't stand not knowing what her brother was thinking. Not knowing what his next move was going to be.

"Oh God, please let this work." Dylon said aloud as he watched the missiles get even closer. His finger trembled as it hovered over the power output button. He checked the power supply again it was now down to only a quarter remaining. He let out a sigh of anguish and muttered again. "Please God." The missiles were less than a hundred feet away now and closing fast. In his last moments he pushed the throttle all the way forward. He wrapped his hand around the controls and readied himself to press both buttons at the same time, the power output and the speed control.

Kat fell to the ground as the four missiles made impact and exploded in a massive fireball. "Noooo! Oh my God. Noooo!" Marcus put his arms around Kat as she began to fall to the ground. Kevin closed his eyes and dropped to his knees. Rosie's heart sank to her stomach. It was as if every ounce of life had drained out of all of them when they watched the horrific explosion.

Kat lifted her head from Marcus' chest. "Why? Why didn't he do something? Why did he just sit there and let them destroy him? I don't understand." Marcus pulled her close again and she continued to cry. He didn't say why, but knew that the craft had probably ran out of power. He knew that Dylon probably couldn't have done anything.

Kat squirmed and struggled from Marcus' embrace. "No. This is not the way it was supposed to happen." Marcus tried to pull her back to him, but she jerked away and started walking off. "No, this isn't right. It's not right at all." She walked away from the group shaking her head, refusing to accept what just happened.

The further away from the group she got, the angrier she became. She couldn't help thinking about who was responsible for all of this. Kat looked straight ahead as she wiped the tears from her face. She was getting closer to the hangar and with each step her anger grew to an uncontrollable rage. She reached down into the bottom pocket of her cargo pants and retrieved the small pistol she had stashed there.

Marcus knew she had the gun and when he saw her reaching for it he told the others. Immediately they began running toward her to stop her. It was hopeless though, because Kat couldn't hear anything. All she was focused on was taking care of the man that killed her brother. The only real family she had left.

When she entered the hangar, she stopped and focused on her target. The only person she saw was Kolminski. She didn't see Commander Campbell, nor did she see the gun that Kolminski was holding on him. She also didn't see that the Commander was bloodied up from the fight the two of them had just finished. All she could see was Kolminski and was ready to finish what she came in there for. She raised her gun and took aim.

Marcus feared for Kat's life and broke away from the group. He was running faster than he had ever run in his life. When he rounded the corner of the hangar door, he screamed out and lunged towards her. His scream finally broke through her rage and broke her concentration, but it was too late.

Kolminski also heard the scream and pulled his attention and his gun away from Commander Campbell, who was on his knees in front of him. As Kolminski turned to face and take aim at Kat, she pulled the trigger. Both guns fired almost simultaneously.

As Marcus and Kat fell to the floor, Kolminski's bullet grazed Marcus' thigh. Kolminski wasn't so lucky. Kat's bullet hit him in the shoulder, knocking him slightly off balance. At about the same time, Commander Campbell had raised up from his position on the floor and attempted to disarm Kolminski.

His actions only proved to worsen Kolminski's situation. As he reached for the gun, Kolminski jerked away. He continued falling backwards and over the edge down into the lower storage area. His fall took an almost identical path as the Commander's gun did earlier, bouncing several times down the stairs, before lying motionless at the bottom.

* * * * * *

Hanks and Commander Campbell spent the rest of the evening checking to see how many casualties they actually sustained. The Commander thought they were finished and was ready to head back to the main house, then Hanks reminded him about Kolminski. "I'm sure he's dead. Honestly, do you think you could survive a fall like that? Didn't you see him lying at the bottom there, all twisted and mangled like a pretzel?"

Hanks almost laughed out loud at the Commander's comments before responding. "In any case sir, we still have to move the body."

"Unfortunately. Too bad we can't just leave the little maggot there to rot." Commander Campbell said. "Well, let's get it done and over with. He's the last one."

Hanks pulled the *Mule* around to collect the last of their losses. When they got inside the hangar, Hanks headed down stairs. He wanted to see what kind of mess they had to clean up. Commander Campbell was retrieving a body bag when he heard Hanks yell out. "Sir, we've got a live one!"

"You've got to be shitting me." Commander Campbell said to himself. "Check him again, Hanks. We don't need to pull help away from the others on a false alarm."

"He's trying to move, sir." Hanks called out.

"Oh jeez, just shoot him." The Commander mumbled, before actually calling out to Hanks. "Make him remain still, I'll bring a stretcher." Before he headed down with the stretcher he made a quick call. "General Grant, it's Commander Campbell. I've got some bad news. It's Kolminski sir, he's still alive." There was a long pause at the other end of the phone. Commander Campbell actually thought the call was dropped. Then he heard the General start speaking.

"Stay your position, Commander. Carlos will ready the helicopter and meet up with you to transport Kolminski to the nearest military base possible. The Lieutenant and I will contact the M.P.'s and debrief them of the situation. I'm sure he'll get the treatment he needs, in a better equipped facility." The General hung up the phone and apprised Carlos of the situation.

Commander Campbell headed down the stairs with the stretcher. It was a struggle to get Kolminski on the stretcher. There were so many mangled broken bones they had to move. After a lot of screaming from Kolminski, the two of them managed to get him up the stairs.

Carlos's timing couldn't have been better. He was pulling into the hangar when they were taking their last steps up the stairs. He pulled right over to them and they placed the stretcher right on the back.

Hanks crawled in to steady the stretcher as they moved Kolminski to the helicopter. As they started to leave, the Commander made some hand gestures, signaling Hanks to head to the main house when he was finished.

As Kat was bringing another round of Betadine, bandages, and water to help everyone tending to their wounds, she heard a text tone on her phone. And hers wasn't the only one she heard. Everyone in the Rosiers' group had received a text message. They all paused and looked at each other with a touch of dread in their eyes. Rosie reached for her phone and read the newly received message.

> *You should turn the TV on. Any news*
> *channel will do. The General should watch also.*
> *Everything will work out fine, you'll see.*

## The Five

Rosie's throat knotted a little when the thoughts of what this group called The Five could be up to now ran through her mind. She slowly walked over to the TV and turned it on. She flipped through the channels until she came to *BBC World News.*

*Earlier today, at an undisclosed location somewhere on the South American Continent, a tragic accident occurred during the test flight of an experimental craft that was developed by the Rosier Foundation. Several people, Rosier staff members and visitors among them, were killed during this accident by falling debris, when the remote-operated craft went out of control and had to be destroyed. The test flight was overseen by a General Grant of the United States government and also by a Lieutenant Vasquez of the Peruvian government.*

*This is the first time ever in the history of any space exploration program, that a Government has allowed a private sector company to explore and experiment with any unproven technologies regarding space exploration.*

*Senator Emerson, who is a co-founder of the newly created division, headed by General Grant, was kind enough to give us an exclusive off-air interview, earlier today. He explained that if it hadn't been for his Government conducting a continuous surveillance of this particular location, for over fifteen years, the project would*

547

*not have been allowed. In his words, quote, "This fledgling company has proven themselves, more than once, to be just as concerned with the outcome and security of any discoveries they might make," unquote.*

*He also stated that both Governments, directly involved with the oversight of operations, have toured the complex and felt confident about the lengths the company has taken to keep the research guarded from falling into the 'wrong hands'. The accident, in their eyes, was just an unfortunate hazard of dealing with unknown and unproven technologies. But in order to advance beyond our current technology, some sacrifices will ultimately have to be made.*

*Representatives and scientists, from countries around the world, who have visited the complex have also expressed the same opinion. To quote one of them, who wished to remain nameless, "If any 'private sector' company should be allowed to openly experiment with new space travel technologies, then this is the company that has definitely proven themselves to be up for the challenge."*

*So good luck to the Rosier Foundation and their new endeavors. What an excellent opportunity for scientists around the world to be able to finally present and test their aspirations, without the limitations that some agencies may put on them. Wow, this really has to be a boost for the future of any space programs. What do you think Jane?*

By the time news report was over, Rosie had made herself and the General a drink. She turned off the TV and walked over to the General, who was just sitting there with his mouth open. "Does this mean you're going to leave us alone now?" She asked as she handed him his drink.

The General was a little dumbfounded by the news report, that hadn't even gone through a declassification process yet. What surprised him even more was the fact that Senator Emerson so readily divulged the information. He began to wonder himself, "Who was really in charge?"

When General Grant didn't respond right away, Rosie went ahead and answered her own question, for him. "Well General, it looks like you don't have a choice in the matter. Apparently the same people that have been pulling our strings, are now pulling yours. Let me give you a small idea of who you're dealing with. The group is called The Five. Get used to them, because just when you think you've got them figured out, they change the game plan."

# Epilogue

It had only been a couple of days since the U.S. government had left the estate, and soon the workers would be arriving. Kat was not looking forward to this, for with the arrival of the workers also came little Reese. She didn't have any idea how she was going to be able to keep it together let alone, explain to him why he wouldn't be able to see his Uncle Dylon anymore.

Marcus, Kevin, and Rosie were able to help Kat keep her composure through most of the questions to fill in the holes of the report needed for the U.S. government. The holes left by the worldwide news brief that 'The Five' had released. Ultimately everyone agreed that according to the follow-up news releases, the initial report was widely believed as being accurate and was also accepted with more enthusiasm than even they anticipated.

In addition to the excitement revolving around the news brief, came some unexpected and unexplainable benefits. The President of the United States called General Grant to personally congratulate him on a successful mission and to inform him of the abolishment of the treaty and the surveillance of the estate and complex. In the end, when all of the congratulatory remarks were finished and almost all of the ties cut, General Grant and his men had left and the Rosiers' group was left behind to finish their tasks in peace.

This was Kat's next set of hurdles. The tasks they started, Reese, and of course there was the video. The video that everybody was ready to watch. Everybody except Kat she had been putting it off and rightfully so. She knew when she watched the video she would actually be accepting that her brother was gone. It was a step she wasn't ready for.

Kat just stood there looking out the window at all the things her brother had dreamed of, and then built. She thought about the things he would present to her. Always telling her, "I know you can make it work better. I know that you can make this ten times easier than I have." She smiled at the memory before thinking. "That's what I'll miss the most, rebuilding his stupid little toys and projects." She turned away from the window, wiped a tear from her cheek, and headed into Rosie's office, where everyone was waiting.

Rosie noticed Kat entering the room with a look of dread on her face. Rosie asked her, "Are you sure you're ready for this, kiddo?"

Kat shook her head no, but her answer was

almost a yes. "It's something that needs to be done, so we can all figure out where to go from here."

Rosie solemnly lowered her head in response to Kat's answer. She walked over to the computer and cued up the video to the spot where it asked for the password. She typed in the words 'Novus Orsa', and the disc continued.

When Kat heard Dylon's voice she instantly brought her hand to her face, a reaction she developed to help herself try to keep her composure. The video diary continued to play and everyone got lost in Dylon's words. They all dearly missed the young man and the outlook he had on life itself. To him, everything was just a simple problem of perspective.

*"Well. Obviously, something went wrong somewhere. That's the only reason you would be watching the rest of this video. What can I say? We tried. Thanks, guys, for the A-plus effort. You can all go home now." He paused for a long moment before he continued talking. "Seriously, guys. I know that might be what you're feeling like right about now. Deep down though, I know that's not what you want to do.*

*"When I asked each of you to take part in building 'my dream', that was a lot to ask. Then*

*you actually said yes, and gave my dream your all. Well, let me just say I was flabbergasted. So I watched you, all of you, for the past year. I watched how excited each of you became, when your part of this dream building team fell into place and did what it was designed to do. That's when I realized it. When I saw your eyes light up with excitement, it hit me. This isn't just my dream.*

*"You all could have easily told me no, but you didn't. So if you want to quit, and walk away from 'my dream', then by all means, do it. Before you do, though, do me a favor and take a good hard look at your own dreams and what you want to accomplish if you continue. I know you can do this without me. Please, don't let this dream die. I think you'll find that if you do, a piece of me that's inside each of you, will die too."*

*Dylon reached up the turn off the recorder, but stopped and sat back down to continue his video diary. "By the way guys, the password, 'Novus Orsa'. It's Latin for New Beginning or New Start. So what do you say? Would you like to be part of a New Beginning?"*

# From the Author:

Once again I would like to give a special thanks to my three friends and proof-readers. The constant demands on receiving the next chapter made writing the book even more of a challenge. This is a good thing.

However, there is a special 'Thank You' story, I would like to share with all of you. I was standing in the office one day, explaining to Barbara my ideas about the Agri-pod that I was actually trying to build. The problems I was having with trying to figure out how to make it work. This led into my passions, as well as my frustrations, about the current space programs.

She got so wrapped up into my passion about this topic. She made a suggestion, which I kind of blew off at the time, only because I was into talking about my hopes and dreams. That suggestion though, turned into a seed. It was planted at just the right time. Whether I consider myself an Author or not, the seed not only grew, but flourished into an idea to set myself up to write a trilogy.

So I would like to say once again. Thank you to my little gardening friend. Thank you so very much,

Barbara Spiwak. What a wonderful gift to give to a friend. Several small little words have opened my eyes to a whole new world of possibilities. I will never be able to thank you enough.

I would also like to thank my many readers for the success of this book. Without you, I would just have a handful of papers that would probably end up in the closet collecting dust.

# Novus Orsa
## The Dream Awakens

# A novel by
# Grant Payne

# www.authorgrantpayne.com

Reese really missed his Uncle Dylon, but he was also still a kid and really missed playing. Especially with a big brother figure like Uncle Dylon was. He had already asked Kat, who only scolded him for calling her by that name. "I don't know how many times I've told you young man, my name is Elizabeth. You need to start calling me by that name before I have your parents talk to you about it."

Reese quietly mocked her as he left the room to find Marcus. He met him as he was going down the stairs and eagerly held out the remote for the craft. Before Reese even got to ask him Marcus started talking. "I'll tell you what little guy. You go make sure the batteries are all charged up. Then I'll come find you. I need to talk to Elizabeth first."

A huge smile came across Reese's face and he ran off to the observatory to make sure he had all the batteries charged that he could. He waited and waited some more. When he realized that nobody was coming he fussed and mumbled. "Fine, I didn't want to play with you stupid grown-ups anyway." He walked around the observatory and as he came to the door where he and Dylon would spend a lot of time, he decided to go in.

The hours they had spent checking the Vision Scope program would have probably bored most children Reese's age. Reese enjoyed it though. Dylon had taught him a lot about checking the program and he had gotten pretty good at it. When he entered the room he noticed the light was flashing. He walked over to the light and noticed that the day of capture was the day of the accident.

Reese stared at the light and the time indicator for a minute. Debating on whether or not he should check the program.

He slowly made his way over to the computer and sat down. Every step he made in opening the program to view the activities of that day seemed to take forever. As he went through the video he slowed it down to advance in ten frames increments. That's when he found it. He actually backed it up and slowed it down to one frame per shot to confirm what he saw.

When he got to the frame he needed he sent it to the printer and anxiously waited for the printer to spit it out. He watched as it printed and could see clearly. There was a fireball from the explosion in the upper right hand corner of the print. The lower left corner of the print though, showed a completely different view. There, as plain as day, was the craft, escaping the explosion.

\* \* \* \* \* \*

With the loss of her brother, Kat was having a difficult time. Then with new information, that Reese found while playing on the computer, there was a small glimmer of hope. When the first search party returned empty handed, that hope started to fade. Then, when she found out that what looked like a crash site had been found, but also had been wiped clean of everything. Well, that just pushed her into a deeper depression than before.

On top of everything else, she was late. She knew this was something Marcus wanted, but could not force herself to be excited about it. For Kat, this was just one more decision that had to be made. A decision that fell into Pandora's box, along with all of the others. What changes would be placed before them, with what should have been an easy decision. Everybody else had already decided to continue with the space program they started. So why was she having such a hard time making up her mind?

Once again, Kat found herself tired of thinking and decided to retire to her bedroom. Like so many days before, she was in bed in the middle of the afternoon. Kevin, Marcus, and Rosie were left tending to the program by themselves. "It's only been six weeks, Marcus. Put yourself in her shoes, she's lost everything she had, everyone that has ever meant anything to her." Rosie said.

"Well thanks a lot. That makes me feel really good." Marcus said with somewhat of a hurt tone to his voice.

Rosie simply turned to Kevin and asked him a question: "Tell me Kevin, have you ever shared your story? The one about the young woman you helped? I think it would do us all some good if you shared that story with this young man. It might actually give him a better frame of mind in dealing with the woman he supposedly loves."

Kevin nodded his head in agreement and Rosie continued talking. "I'm going to find Carlos and see when his next trip to the village is. If I remember correctly it's today. I hope I haven't missed him." She turned and left the hangar leaving the two men to finish their work.

* * * * * *

The man that was normally adorned with various medals of achievement was in a very plain civilian outfit. One that made it easy for him to blend into the crowd without being noticed. He checked several times to see if he was being followed as he made his way down the street. He fell in behind a group that appeared to be heading to one of the many bars scattered in the downtown district.

When he saw where he was he faded away from the crowd he was following and slipped into the alley virtually unnoticed. There was only one light in the alley that barely lit the door it was hung above. It was a perfect deterrent for unwanted visitors. The man strode past the door, like he had many times before. He headed to the last door in the alley.

As he was approaching the door, it opened slightly. Just enough to let him know they were expecting him and entrance was being granted. In the many years the man had been visiting this place, he had only been denied access once. He tried to remember if he ever got an answer about why he was denied access that night, but couldn't recall the memory.

There wasn't anyone in the foyer when he closed the door behind him. He shuddered just a little when he heard the automatic locks clicking. He counted as they clicked, just a little thing he did to ease the unsettling feeling that it gave him. When the eighth one clicked, the inner door of the foyer opened up revealing a long hallway. Again there was very little lighting.

The hall was lined with doors, all of them being

closed except for the room they would be meeting in. He made his way down the hall and entered the room. The meeting would be very brief. Over the years, the man had worked his way up in the group enough, to at least be granted answers to several of his questions, in return of course for a favor of their own.

The meetings were always kind of an odd occurrence. Names were never used, not even aliases. The questions would be asked and answered accordingly. If a question wasn't answered it was considered information you didn't need. There were no reasons given, the question was basically treated as if it were not even asked.

Interviewer:
"We read the report you filed and were very impressed." the interviewer said as the man took his seat.

Man:
"I would hope so, I watched your report four times to make sure I didn't miss anything. By the way, how in the Hell did you pull that one off?"
Interviewer:
"You sir, of all people, should know how gullible civilians are, especially when they're gathering their information from their beloved media. It wouldn't

surprise me that if in the next decade they pull another Orson Wells trick, just to see if they still have what it takes."

Man:

"Right, understood. So what happens to their space program? Are they going to be allowed to continue?"

Interviewer:

"Well of course they are. Are you sure you watched the report four times? The program should do just fine, with a little friendly guidance from time to time."

Man:

"What about the craft and the young man, Dylon? I heard some rumors that.....well that he might be still alive."

The interviewer opened his briefcase and pulled out a large envelope. He slid it across the table to the man. "This is what we need. It may take some time for you to gather all that is on the list. We'll be in touch when we decide on a deadline. At this time it is not considered to be a high priority. Nevertheless, don't dilly dally. All that could change in a moment's notice. Were there anymore questions you needed to ask us?"

Man:
    "I think you answered everything I needed to know. Actually, there is one more question. What if I get this finished before you contact me?"

Interviewer:
    "We'll know."

*You have just read a preview of the next book.*
*Novus Orsa: The Dream Awakens*